ME ABOUT YOU

HANNAH HAMRICK

AUTHOR'S NOTE

Hi, friend!

Let me be the first to welcome you to Lakeland University! Thank you for picking up Me About You, the first book in the Lakeland Bears series. I'm so happy you are here.

The idea for Sutton and Cooper, along with their crazy bunch of friends, actually came to me while I was editing Summertime Friends (my debut novel). Between bursts of writer's block and fatigue, I'd jot down chapter ideas or accidentally spend far too many hours writing about a MMC who is down bad for his (ex) childhood best friend who sees him as nothing more than her rival.

When trying to decide what to write next, it was them pushing to the front and asking for their story to be told...specifically Jaxon Greene (you'll understand later).

Jumping into a new sub-genre, one that's popular and is dense with incredible authors and books, is nerve-racking. I can't shy away from admitting how nervous, but also so freaking excited, I am to step into this space. As a long-time sports romance reader, these stories have been my happy place, and I always knew I'd eventually land here.

Writing Me About You and plotting the remaining books—

which, if you were to ask me about, I'd probably spill because they're tropes I'm dying to write and characters I can't wait to expand—carried me through a transitional part of my life. These characters became my friends, my family, and I hope they can become yours.

I love as a reader and author to get a peek behind the curtain. So if you read this, here's me drawing back the curtains. Or if you skimmed it, this next paragraph is the most important.

I wanted to mention that while this is a hockey romance, I have altered a few details for readability and timeline purposes. It is standard for women's ice hockey in the NCAA to host their tournaments before the men's tournament. However, you will see that they are after the men's. This is due to where books two and three are going.

If you have any questions, want to chat more, or unhinged thoughts, my DMs are always open (@authorhannahhamrick).

Enough of my yapping, happy reading!

Xo, Han

CONTENT WARNINGS

ME ABOUT YOU is a romantic comedy full of banter, laughs, a down bad MMC, and a side of angst, but I also wanted to make readers aware of a few content warnings:

- Explicit language
- Explicit sexual content
- Alcohol consumption
- MMC that experiences anxiety and burnout (on-page anxiety attack)
- Serious hockey injury (off-page)
- Mentions of infertility (neither MCs and off-page)
- References to adoption

As always take care of your heart and mind. If you have any questions about any thing listed above, please do not hesitate to reach out on IG (@authorhannahhamrick).

ME ABOUT YOU PLAYLIST

Angeleyes - ABBA
Sorry I'm here For Someone Else - Benson Boone
Fireworks - Hazlitt
The Alcott (feat. Taylor Swift) - The National
Into Your Arms (feat. Ava Ma) - Witt Lowry
Kiss Me - King Henry, Sasha Alex Sloan
Higher Ground (Reprise) - ODESZA, Naomi Wild
Clara Bow - Taylor Swift
bittersweet - Madison Beer
On the Way Down - Ryan Cabrera
Crush - Ethel Cain
Chasing A Feeling - LEON
Happier - Ed Sheeran
undressed - somber
I'm Alive - Celine Dion
Anything - Griff
I Knew It, I Know You - Gracie Abrams
Beggin For Thread - BANKS
Sue Me - Audrey Hobert
Bruise - BETWEEN FRIENDS
Mess It Up - Gracie Abrams

Revolving Door - Tate McRae
Ruin The Friendship - Taylor Swift
Backwards - Jonas Brothers
Nice To Each Other - Olivia Dean
imgonnagetyouback - Taylor Swift

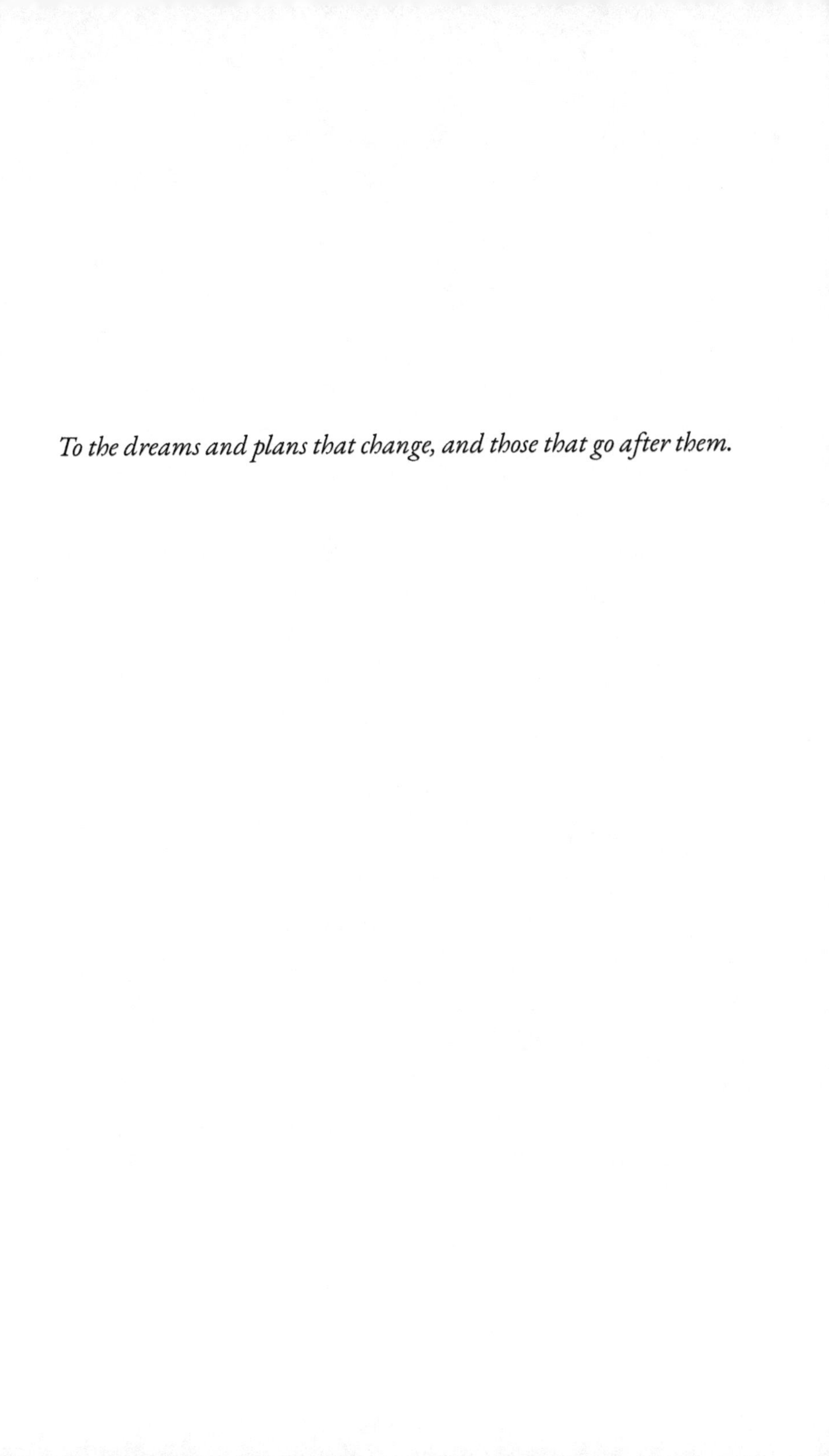

To the dreams and plans that change, and those that go after them.

ONE

COOPER

"IT'S incredible how much you two look alike. Twenty-five years older...or younger"—the reporter laughs at their unamusing and overused joke—"and you'd be twins. Add in the helmets and names on the back of your jerseys, no one would be able to tell you apart on the ice."

Dad smiles. Even *that* is an uncanny resemblance—the same slightly heavier bottom lip and dimple carved into our right cheek.

Add Ryn Carmichael's unsurpassed skills on the ice to the 'Renaissance sculpted' smile, and it's no wonder he's one of the greats. A walking billboard for aspiring hockey players.

"He's far more handsome," Dad responds, bumping his shoulder into mine. "Better player, too."

"I think that's yet to be seen," another reporter cackles out with hint of sarcasm, but still a punch to the gut. "On the hunt, though. Cooper, you're halfway through the season and halfway to one of your father's most coveted NCAA records." Dad's name is tied to five major records, all have been surpassed in the past decade except for 'Most Goals Scored in a Single Season'. "Do you think you'll be able to reach *this one* before the end of the season?"

This one.

As if breaking records is the only way to define my success. The idea has my jaw tensing, teeth grinding, but you'd never know. Pasted on my face is the golden Carmichael smile everyone is expecting.

I take a big inhale through my nose before exhaling. Slowly. Giving myself a minute to not snap. To refrain from screaming out that I don't care about breaking his records. I don't want to be him, I want to be me.

"Reach it?" I tilt my head. Let a corner of my mouth rise higher than the other to form a teasing, cocky smirk, playing into their hand the way I've trained myself to do. "I'm going to beat it. Finally put this old legend to shame. It's about time someone breaks the record."

In the distance, behind the cameras, Mom is rolling her eyes.

She didn't have to come, but insisted. Her phone hasn't left her grasp even though a production intern keeps telling her to put it away. Jordan, my little sister, and I made a bet during a break in filming how many photos and videos she'll take. I bet over one-hundred.

Dad was invited to do a docu-special on ESPN for retired athletes and their kids actively playing college sports. Apparently, we are all 'Future Legends' as the series is titled.

Everyone except for me.

Jordan is sitting in a chair to our left. Dad and I are on a loveseat, which is way too small for us. Knees bumping anytime we move. I'm not sure they accounted for our broad shoulders and thick thighs. Large screens behind us are filled with pictures of our family from over the years—I count the seconds it takes for the pictures to switch, vying for a distraction. It's thirty-two.

Dad's been retired from the league for a decade. He was drafted out of college by Minnesota where he spent thirteen years before retiring. I was starting middle school, but Jordan and I were already deep into playing hockey. Our older sister, Molly, was in every production our school and community put on. He easily had a few more years in him, but we are his greatest achievement, and he didn't want to miss any of it.

At least my sister's achievements aren't weighed against his career. They're lucky, especially Jordan.

She hasn't received a single question from the reporters asking about breaking records, picking apart her shots, or comparing her to Dad.

You are a spitting image of your father. Shorter, but wow, the Carmichael genes.

You didn't want to wear the same number as your dad? Were you afraid you couldn't fill in the big jersey?

Didn't your father have double-digit offers?

Staying in college to pursue mathematics instead of starting your contract with Carolina. Interesting decision. What did your dad think about that?

It started when I was deciding on college, and Dad's alma mater didn't recruit me. No one even asked me if I wanted to go to Ohio State University...I didn't.

That minor fact about me was brought up twice already in the interview because at least my sister received an offer.

"Why are you watching this again?" Jaxon picks up the remote from the arm of the couch, pausing the recording. "Isn't this your third or fourth time now?"

Jaxon Greene, my ultimate hat trick: best friend, roommate, and teammate. We were assigned roommates our freshman year. Sharing the smallest dorm room on campus—I'm talking we could hold hands from our twin beds—does something to you, bonds you in ways you probably shouldn't be bonded.

"You've got a famous dad? And share in his hockey genetics?" he tacks on. I turn my head, glowering. "That's so cool. Why haven't you ever mentioned that? No one in the house knew."

"I—" I shut my mouth.

It doesn't matter that I know he's being sarcastic. Jaxon is the team clown. Loud and never takes anything serious. He's easy going, doesn't succumb to stress or pressure; he wouldn't understand. I'm not sure any of my roommates would. All they see are the opportunities it has provided me—which I am grateful for, I never want that to get misconstrued.

I hate the added pressure that comes with it. Maybe someone stronger would thrive in the added limelight. Maybe someone braver would use it to their advantage. Maybe someone steadier wouldn't be burning out because of it.

I'm not someone.

But no one would know.

I wish Jaxon pausing the recording could pause the nagging in my head.

"Soooooo." Our other roommate, Chase Jones, walks into the living room, clapping his hands together. "I know it's my turn to drive, but I have zero gas."

"You never have any gas," Jaxon rebukes.

"There's no point. I can walk to class, and if I need to go anywhere, usually one of you is going somewhere."

"I'll drive." I snatch the remote dangling from Jaxon's fingers and power off the TV.

It takes me thirty seconds to get off the couch, my body imprinted into the cushions from where I've been rotting all morning. I came in here after making a protein shake, planning to get ahead on semester reading or watching highlights from last night's NHL games I fell asleep during. Instead, I ended up on my phone.

I think I finally understand why it's called doom scrolling.

One forty-five-second clip and I'm mindlessly digging the TV remote out from between the cushions and pulling up the episode, fast forwarding to segments on our family.

Since the episode aired earlier during winter break, this has happened a handful of times. And I end up in the same spot, same head space.

Over the back of the couch is my sweatshirt. I tug it on, the aglet smacking me in the face as I hustle up the stairs, three at a time, to my room to grab my shoes and bag.

Downstairs, the front door is open. The frame filled with my roommates waiting for me to fish my keys off the kitchen table.

Walking over to them, I know I'm nowhere near ready to be out on the ice, already skating on a thin layer in my mind.

"Dawson." Dawson Karlsson, teammate and the house chef, turns around. "Think fast." I toss my keys at him, and he catches them, only fumbling once. Thank goodness he's not our goalie.

"Are you not coming with us?" he asks, running a hand through his shaggy brick red-brown hair.

"I'm going to walk."

"You good?"

Jaxon is throwing his and Chase's bags in the trunk while Chase uses a snow brush to remove the dusting that accumulated this morning on my windshield.

"Shotgun!" Jaxon yells, but Dawson and I ignore him.

"Ten thousand steps a day resolution isn't going to hit itself," I joke.

Dawson eyes me wearily. Then nods. "If you're late, I'm not doing extra down-and-backs because of you."

The engine roars to life. As soon as they're out of the driveway, I tug on a winter coat and a Lakeland beanie, the navy-blue bear logo stitched into the gray fabric, before starting my venture to the rink.

It's not a far walk. Maybe twenty minutes. Practice is in an hour, so I have time, especially since campus is practically a ghost town. We're technically still on winter break, and most students haven't returned. Winter sports teams and students doing J-term are the only people here. Even the juniors and seniors who are in off-campus housing are avoiding this central part of campus, now a winter wonderland.

I'm crossing the lawn when I spot a mess of red curls bouncing along a shoveled path.

I don't know if I should be excited to see her. Probably not. At least I should pretend not to, but it's the best part of my day.

Sutton Davis is heading my way for once, not purposely

avoiding me or pivoting to take the long way to wherever her destination is.

That's when I see her hazel eyes narrow on me. The late morning sun striking them just right, making the green overtake the browns and blues. They remind me of the perfect summer day out on the lake.

People wear their hearts on their sleeves. Sutton wears hers in her eyes.

They've always given her away, ever since we were six.

Where they used to look at me with admiration—us against the world—now, they look at me with disgust. Distrust. Abhorrence.

And it doesn't make me want her any less.

She speeds up. So I speed up, just to annoy her. Just to be close to her.

"Hey, Dave." A cheeky grin covers the corners of my mouth as the nickname rolls off my tongue. The name started as a joke. Coaches always called her Davis, and I wanted to be different. I give her a once over. "Tan's holding out."

She stares up at me. Chin tilted, but not by much at five nine. Sutton may be tall compared to most girls, but I still have four inches on her.

"Can't say the same about yours."

"Is that your way of telling me you missed me the last bit of vacation?" Our families traveled together for Christmas, like they do every year, but I had to leave early for hockey.

She starts to throw me a bone. "You're right, I did—"

I can feel my brown eyes go wide, and if I could see myself, the irises probably sparkle with hope. When was the last time she admitted anything remotely like this to me? When was the last time she *wanted* my presence?

It eats at me.

It's another weight on my shoulders. Another notch on the pressure gauge. Another reminder that I'm not the person people want me to be.

"—n't," she finishes.

My shoulders sag, settling at the bottom of that lake her eyes are still the color of.

I bite my tongue. Shove the version of Sutton and me that I wish we could be back into the box I keep in the corner of my mind. Right next to the overflowing box I keep everyone's comments and comparisons about me.

The door doesn't close. The hinges are cracking. It makes mornings like today harder to manage.

"One day you'll realize, and admit, you love me."

"I'd rather eat nails."

"Whatever you say, Dave." I reach out and adjust her purple earmuff. "Going for Ariel today?"

Her jaw twitches, eye dropping to the Kelly-green Lycra hugging and showing off her muscular legs.

"And you are? Flotsam or Jetsam?" Why does her asking me which annoying eel I am make me want to smile?

"They are identical and inherently neither is cooler than the other, but if I had to pick—"

"I don't actually care."

Jetsam. That's who I'd pick.

Sutton attempts to step around me, but I move with her. Sliding to the left, then right. "Move Carmichael."

"You didn't tell me you were cleared to run."

"Must have forgotten that we tell each other things. My bad." She pauses. Steps around me, using my momentary slip in focus, and starts running again. "Oh, wait," she calls out behind her. Then waves goodbye with her middle finger.

Sutton's pace isn't fast, and she still favors her left leg, but seeing her running again is a tendril of happiness I cling to. I pull on it like it's a rope dropped into the hole I've dug myself into, and start to climb out.

My eyes are attached to her like a magnet as she grows smaller in the distance. A mess of auburn curls and childhood dreams in a sea of snow.

TWO

SUTTON

"WAS THAT COOPER?" Meave, my older, adoptive sister, asks around my labored, burning breaths.

Each inhale is as if a shard of ice is puncturing my lungs. That's what I get for running in the cold. Today, if you'd believe me, is a warm Wisconsin winter day with a high of thirty degrees.

"Unfortunately," I groan, elongating my stride to skip a patch of ice.

"Tell him I said hi!"

Lakeland University might be frozen over, but hell has most certainly not. Thus, me going out of my way to speak to Cooper Carmichael will not be happening.

"No," I respond impassively because she knows better.

"Are you ever going to forgive him?" Meave must have me on speakerphone. Through my headphones, I can hear the clattering of her paintbrushes and splashing water as she rinses them.

"Why would I do that?"

"Because you two were best friends once."

"You and Elliot are my best friends. I don't need him."

I stop at a red light, bounce on the balls of my feet, waiting for the signal to turn green. Each time my left heel taps the sidewalk, there's a lingering strain of pain in my knee. Which wouldn't be there if it weren't for him.

"Plus, why should I forgive him when he's never apologized—"

"That's not how forgiveness works, Sutton," Meave cuts me off, but I keep going.

"—*and* enjoys reminding me how much better he thinks he is than me. Cooper Carmichael is nepotism's finest, conceited, arrogant, and—" The first boy to break my heart. Ridiculously attractive. Has a dimple in his right cheek that deepens when he really smiles, not the fake one he's been wearing since we started college, which makes me question why I hate him. I hate that he's monopolizing this call with my sister. "Why are we talking about him? This is not why you called."

"Have you heard from your advisor yet?"

Today has been marked on my calendar—the one hanging on my apartment fridge, digitally on my phone, and shared with Meave and my roommate, Elliot—since November.

Today is the second anniversary of deciding to hang up my skates after I never recovered from the terrible triad. Better known as tearing your ACL, meniscus, and medial collateral ligament. The blade of the player that collided with me, cutting open my thigh, was the cherry on top. I had to have two reconstructive surgeries and twenty stitches in my left leg during my junior season in high school.

Doctors were convinced I'd be able to play again. And I tried. Throwing myself into every PT session and workout. Spending endless time on the ice my senior year with my dad. But I was never able to get it back.

That was the second-worst part of all this. Watching my childhood dream go up in flames. Becoming a professional female athlete was already a long shot. Opportunities limited, especially for women's hockey, but I was determined to do it.

The worst part was that it was his fault. If he hadn't shattered our friendship, I wouldn't have been left weak and vulnerable right before a game that needed my entire focus. I'm not letting seeing him—I can't let it—this morning ruin today too.

Today should be the final stitch in reconstructing a new dream for myself.

Today I'm supposed to find out if my independent study request is approved.

Lakeland has a stellar psychology department, one of the country's best student health centers, and resources. Top rated in every category. But it wasn't till I had officially changed my major that I learned they don't have a sports psychology major *or* minor.

I thought about transferring, paperwork filled out and one click away from submission to three schools, when my new advisor, Dr. Manning said, *Let's build one.* We pieced together courses I would need to take, collaborating with some of her colleagues and friends from other Universities. Adding classes such as kinesiology and exercise physiology to my required courses.

"Not yet," I confess, optimism wavering.

I'm not confident I'll hear back. The day is already halfway through, and with how close we are to the semester starting, I can't imagine the department would approve it now. We submitted the request before Thanksgiving break.

It was always a long shot.

Maybe I should have transferred.

"The day is still young," Meave reminds me, always visualizing the cup half full.

Her optimism bleeds into me. It always has. My childhood is dotted with Meave's positivity and belief in me. The day our parents met me—the day she convinced them we were a package deal and she wouldn't be their daughter if it meant leaving me. Skating for the first time. Running for class president. Selecting a college to play for after I didn't get recruited to the one I wanted.

"I've gotta run, Sutt, but I'll have my phone on me," she says on a deep exhale, a clattering sounds in the background. "Call when you find out?"

"I will. I love you, Meave."

"I love you the most."

Our call disconnects, and my phone automatically picks back up on the podcast I was listening to. I tap an earbud, turning down the volume so I can pay attention to my surroundings. There's only half a mile left to my apartment.

I turn the corner and notice a black SUV slowing down, gradually getting closer to the curb. My pace picks up, but the car matches.

When a tinted window starts to roll down, I move my hand to my running belt. Trying to be stealthy, I unzip it, tapping in my passcode and pulling up my contacts. Campus safety is one touch away.

I almost fall over from relief when I spot sandy blonde hair.

"Jesus Christ, Elliot."

Elliot Jones, my now soon-to-be ex-best friend and roommate, whistles, then starts singing "Track Star".

We've lived together since our freshman year. There were an odd number of freshman hockey and soccer players, and we volunteered to live together. Ironically, neither of us play anymore.

"I was about to call security on you," I sing back, terribly matching the tune of the song.

"Oh, come on, Sutton. Chill out. There are zero serial killers at Lakeland."

"But there are men."

She snorts. "That's true." Her ride keeps pace with me as I check both directions and cross the street to the next block. "Where are you running?"

"Home."

"Want a ride?"

"We live right there." I point to the entrance of our campus-owned apartment complex. The brick sign is covered with snow.

"But what about all of the serial killers?"

Elliot doesn't let up. Doesn't drive faster either. The car rides the curb, and she talks the entire time, recounting her winter break back home.

That's how the rest of the afternoon goes once I take a hot shower to defrost my limbs. We lie on the couch, sit on the counter sharing a bag of grapes, then reorganize her closet when that idea shoots across her mind. Any silence between us is like an intermission, before one of us dives right back into our winter breaks and the latest gossip.

It's not like we didn't already know everything, but there's something special about a friend you can recount the same story to again and again and they never get bored. Break was boring enough without Elliot. Our apartment has been quiet this past week without her and her bubbly, no filter, convincing personality.

A quick bribe of promising to clean my bathroom for a month was all it took to get me to go out with her tonight. I think she knew if I didn't occupy myself, I would have sat on our couch, going between refreshing the emails on my phone to staring at my computer until I heard from my advisor.

However, Elliot failed to tell me that our girls' night also included our motley crew of hockey boys. We beat them to the bar, finding a table close to the live music. I've always loved that The Tipsy Bear hires performers from school. Lakeland is just big enough that it's easy to get lost in the student population, but it's places like this that make it small.

One by one, they all walk in.

Chase Jones.

Jaxon Greene.

Dawson Karlsson.

Surprising us both, Beckett St. James. He's a rarity to see out.

Luckily, Cooper is nowhere to be found. Which might be the second surprise of the night, because these are his roommates and best friends. Wherever they go, he's usually somewhere close by.

I'd like to say they were my friends first, maybe Dawson and Chase, but Beckett and Jaxon are his. Elliot is mine, and that is something I will take to my grave, even if he likes to bicker with me about that.

I know I shouldn't be keeping score, it's not healthy, but I am. When it comes to him, I'm always keeping score.

"No Cooper?" Elliot asks for me.

The guys shrug as if it were a rehearsed dance.

"Wasn't home when we all left," Chase responds, taking a seat to Elliot's left. He plants a kiss on her temple. "You smell nice."

"Wonders what hair washing day does for a girl."

Elliot flips her long blonde hair over her shoulder. Chase smiles at her before taking a strand of her hair and twirling it around his finger. They're close—probably the closest either of us are with the boys. They met during orientation because they have the same last name, and the rest of us were a game of dominoes. One at a time, they adopted us into what is now our sometimes dysfunctional friend group.

"I'll text him," Elliot adds. "Chase, go take that empty seat next to Sutton"—she points at the empty chair to my right—"and Jaxon lean in. Kiss her cheeks, I'll send him a picture."

They comply, shuffling around the high top. Elliot takes a photo with a shit-eating grin on her face.

"That's enough," I tell them, cautiously pushing at their shoulders. "I'm not trying to make him mad."

Unlike Cooper, who does everything intentionally to get under my skin—such as choosing to go to the same University as me—I don't go out of my way to annoy him. There's nothing I can have that he can't also have or do.

"Only jealous?" Jaxon asks with a bite, as if he knows something I don't. He grabs a beer from the bucket in the center of the table, the neck of it hanging loosely in his hands. As he takes a sip, he flicks his brows up at me, awaiting a response.

"*Me*?" I point to myself in a laugh. "Make Cooper jealous? Maybe in my third life, and if I were the freshly frozen pond out back of his house."

Only Dawson gives me a pity laugh. Chase smiles tightly and

returns to his seat next to Elliot. Beckett is a statue as always. Jaxon slides over a chair with a dramatic sigh, pulling out his phone to show Dawson his latest viral dancing video.

"No one wants to sit next to me?" I'm only slightly kidding. "I don't bite."

"Yeah, but I do, baby." Cooper slides into the chair next to me. Swings his arm around the back of mine and tugs it closer to him.

My spine goes rigid, shoulders cementing themselves to the wooden chair. But the lower half of my body decides it doesn't hate Cooper at this moment.

A warm, spicy desire pools in my core when his mouth is a ghost against my cheek, then inches its way to my ear. There's a hot breath tickling the sensitive skin. I think he's going to whisper something in my ear, but he doesn't. No, the boy nips at my earlobe.

I shove him away. "I hate you."

Cooper smiles boyishly at me. "Keep telling yourself that." He winks, and adds, "And me. It turns me on."

I catch it from my peripherals. I don't dare turn my head to look at him. Cooper's always been able to read me. Uses my eyes against me.

He'd see what that wink did to me. He'd know my throat is tight and I'm trying to discreetly clear it. He'd know my internal temperature is reaching its boiling point. He'd know I'm thinking about him doing it again.

"That's my cue to go," I announce to the group. Everyone is pretending not to watch us interacting.

They've done a good job balancing our dynamic. Egging it on, like taking a picture and sending it to him, or soothing it over when they know we're pushing it too far.

"Nooooo," Elliot groans. "I don't want to be the only girl tonight."

"You won't be. This one"—I thumb point at Cooper—"will have at least three to join you soon."

Cooper doesn't say anything at first. His face falls though, but only momentarily. He pushes a water cup away from him.

"I'll behave tonight. Maybe only two." I look at him. His brown eyes are locked on me. "Or *one*."

"In your dreams, *baby*."

"Oh, *I know*. See you in them every night."

Across the table, there are a series of snickers. When I flick a glance at Chase and Elliot, they both immediately grab their drinks, taking sips like nothing is going on.

I whip my head back toward Cooper.

He takes off his hat. Runs a hand through the damp brunette strands. Flips the hat in his hand around, pushes it back on. Backwards. His number stitched in silver above the adjustable strap.

"How was your run?" he asks.

Dawson shoots up. "Did you reach three miles? I was tracking your Strava account over break and saw that you were up to two and a half."

I nod with pride. I dive into telling him about what my PT is saying about my progress and how taking Elliot's cycling classes have helped build back muscle in my legs.

Cooper runs his tongue over his teeth, silent during all of this.

An hour later, the large wooden table is littered with empty plates. I'm finishing my second Diet Coke of the night, watching my tipsy roommate flirt with a local. The Tipsy Bear is on the outskirts of campus, right before the road that takes you into downtown Bensen. Most people who live in Bensen avoid this place, but there are always a few brave souls.

"Sutton," Jaxon sing-songs loudly to get my attention. "Come play pool with us."

I debate going over there. Dr. Manning still hasn't called or emailed me, and it's not like a game of pool is going to stop her. I refresh my student email one more time before slipping my phone into the back pocket of my black denim overalls.

I grab a water and head over to the guys. There's a small ledge that Beck is leaning on. I set my drink next to his, and when I ask how he's doing, all I get in response is a noncommittal shoulder shrug. But that's Beck for fine.

Elliot finally peels herself away to rejoin our group. I trade the water in my hand for her vodka soda.

"No *friend* tonight?" I comment.

"Only you snuggle bug."

She rests her head on my shoulder and lets out a yawn that mine chases after. I'm about to ask her if she wants to get out of here when my phone buzzes. Elliot groans when I pull it out, trying to swat it away. I put my arm in the air, phone out of reach. My fingers frantically swipe and type in my passcode.

I slip around her, scurrying away from the pool table to the bathroom hallway.

An email from Dr. Manning is staring back at me.

Maybe I shouldn't have checked my email. Ignorance is bliss, right?

They accepted my independent study with one stipulation: I have to do a case study with a student-athlete. And just my luck, they've already chosen one.

THREE

COOPER

"CARMICHAEL!" Coach Mathieson yells from across the ice. He pushes his glasses up the bridge of his nose before planting his hands on his hips.

Staring at him, even from the other side of the rink, I get why the girls on campus fawn over him. Coach is in his early forties and—I have no shame admitting it—hot. Light brown skin, a tight jawline that's always sporting a well-taken care of beard, broad muscular shoulders, and I quote *'biceps for days.'* Plus, a smile that is as ruthless as it is bright.

There's a big question mark around why he never played professionally. Coach was drafted to play for Toronto, but never made it to training camp. A year later, he was hired by Lakeland as a GA, then assistant, before taking over as head coach seven years ago.

I've always wanted to play for him. I've always wanted to be a Lakeland Bear.

When I was being recruited, it was blatantly obvious when a coach wanted me for the name stitched into the back of my jersey. The attention and money they thought would come to their program if a Carmichael played for them was at the center of the way they interacted with me.

It took Dad one visit centering on him to suggest that Mom take me on the rest. He deflected questions the best he could without coming off as an asshole—he has a reputation to hold up too. It never change his involvement at home though. He sifted through my film, putting together highlight reels or offering to make calls.

But I didn't want *that* help. Didn't need him to do anything on my behalf.

I love my dad. He's my idol, but I didn't want, or asked, to be compared to him. I didn't want to be tied to him as a player. Much to my chagrin, I am.

All I wanted was a school to want me for me. Want *me* how I want *this* for myself—or at least how I thought I wanted this.

It's not Dad's fault. He's not asking or telling teams, media, or random people in the grocery store to treat me this way. He's never asked or expected me to be more than I am.

I've hidden it, never wanting him to know that my chest would get tight periodically. Sometimes my head would spin out like a spinning top, and my shoulders felt heavy because of him.

Coach Mathieson was different, though. He never cared about the name on my back. He cared—cares about me. His tone and motives have never changed. Coach saw a boy who loved the sport and wanted to carve out a legacy and path for himself.

I knew it the moment he called out my mistakes in my film. Followed it up by asking if I brought my skates, and then taking me out on the ice to fix them.

He's like this with everyone on and off the ice.

I skate over to him. Chest heaving and out of breath. There's a slight twinge of pain in my back that stings with each pass of my skate over the scratched-up ice.

I need an ice bath and an hour with a massage gun.

"Off the ice. They need to get it Zambonied. Girls have a game tonight."

I nod, my exhaustion is internal too.

Coach sighs, mumbles under his breath about taking away my key to the arena if I keep pushing myself too hard.

"See me in my office after you shower."

I knock on his door thirty minutes later.

"Hey." I shut the door behind me. "Is that for next week?" He's standing at a whiteboard writing names and drawing lines between Xs and Os.

"I'm thinking of moving Scott"—a sophomore who was out with an injury at the start of the season—"to Jones' pairing. Thoughts?"

"We need speed getting back to the net. Adams has been getting beat at least seventy-five percent of the time. Chase has been trying to pick up the slack, but it ends up leaving the backside open. Scott is one of the fastest defensemen we have. Have you timed him?" I scan the board a second time. "Do you want me to—"

"Add another thing to your plate?" He turns to me, features set sternly. "You don't need to do it all, Carmichael."

Even before being voted captain, I'd say yes to anything Coach or another teammate asked. But as captain? I don't feel like I have a choice. If the team needs something, or someone, I take care of it. Doesn't stop the guilt that races parallel to the need of taking care of my responsibilities.

"But I'm the captain," I still say.

"And I'm the coach. I have assistants who are paid to help. Anyways, Jaxon is faster than you."

"He is not," I scoff.

Coach lets out what I think is a laugh—I at least get him to crack a semi-smile.

"Sit." He gestures to a large leather armchair in front of his desk. There are two of them, but he doesn't take the other. With how cozy his office is, you'd think he lives here.

He leans against his desk, arms crossed in front of his chest. Biceps straining against the team-issued green and navy quarter zip.

"Have you thought about moving Horváthski back to defense? He used to play in high school."

"Good thought, and yes, I have. He's needed on second line, though." Coach takes a deep breath. Unfolds his arms, gripping the desk next to his legs. "I didn't ask you in here to talk lines and plays."

"Look, about earlier. I know you said I can only be on the ice for an hour after practice. But—" I almost confess everything to him.

"This isn't about your ice time—well, actually, it could be. I didn't want you to work with Scott because I've already added something to your plate this semester. Do you know who Dr. Manning is?"

The name sounds familiar, but nothing rings a bell. I shake my head no.

"She's a psychology professor here who reached out to all of the coaches looking for a student athlete for an independent study, and I volunteered you."

"Why?"

He ignores my question. "You are expected to do this, Cooper. Full participation. No bullshit, no loopholes."

"Am I off the team if I don't?" I clinch my jaw, fear squeezes my heart.

"Do I look like I want to lose the Frozen Four this year?" I don't either. "I've already forwarded you the details. Due to the length of the project, you'll be starting prior to the semester beginning."

"When?"

"Tomorrow."

———

THE NEXT MORNING, I rinse my plate and put it in the dishwasher before telling my roommates goodbye.

"Where are you going?" Jaxon says around a bite of soft

scrambled eggs. I love my best friend. He's truly a genius, probably the smartest out of all my roommates, except when it comes to street smarts...and table manners.

A piece of egg falls out of his mouth, hits the table, before he picks it back up and shovels it into his mouth along with another bite.

"Out. Maybe on a run."

"I'll come with. Let me finish and go change."

"Oh. Uh. That's okay." I half smile. Tight, the kindest fake smile possible. "Remember the last time you ran after eating? You coined it Mt. Pukevious."

"That was like two years ago." He leans back, fork raised in one hand, the other rubbing his stomach. "Made of steel now."

"It was four months ago."

Jax rolls his eyes at me. "Fine," he blows out. "But how long will you be? I need to go to the bookstore and pick up a few things before classes start next week."

I don't know how long today will be. Coach's information was minimal, basically nothing but a time and a place to meet this morning.

"What time does the campus bookstore close?" I ask.

"Seven."

"I can take you," Beck offers, walking into the kitchen. His onyx hair in disarray, and rubbing at his cerulean eyes.

Jaxon rattles on about somewhere else he needs to go, and I use the distraction as an opportunity to sneak away.

I googled Dr. Manning last night after finding her on the school's web directory. Coach failed to mention she has an extra twelve letters next to her name, was a sports psychologist for an NBA team, and now teaches because she thinks it would be *fun to influence today's youth.*

If my nerves weren't already enough, I'd be slightly intimidated by whoever this mini-me in the making is.

Parking out front of the student library, I glance around. There are three other cars in the parking lot. The designated meeting location was a coffee shop on the second floor. It's in the farthest wing of the library, past the silent working spaces.

Rounding the corner, I...

Absolutely not.

Her back is to me, but I'd recognize those deep auburn curls anywhere.

The ringlets shift against her lower back. Half of them pulled back into a loose bun with a pencil holding the hair together.

On the chair next to her is a floral patchwork jacket she got for Christmas from my mom. I was with Mom when she found the vintage piece and almost burst into tears, exclaiming it was the perfect gift and only needed a little bit of TLC.

I approach her the same way you'd approach a wild animal—who am I kidding, I'd never approach a wild animal. Our family dog is friendly and Jordan used to try to bring home any injured animal she found outside, but I was still the kid at the back of the group during animal demonstrations at the zoo. Would pretend to touch the snake and encourage my classmates to be the ones to feed a baby animal. My approach is slow, not wanting to startle her. The galloping of my heart fast enough for the both of us.

Does she know I'm the student? Or was she only told a meeting location also?

I've done a lot of idiotic, borderline pathetic things intentionally to stay in Sutton's orbit. Is this my karma?

Her focus doesn't waver from whatever she's working on. Sutton's computer is to her right, a notebook to her left. She's tapping a pen to a beat against her color-coordinated notes.

Inhaling, I give myself a moment to compose myself.

I fail.

The same weird waves of uncertainty and doubt crash over me.

I should have pushed Coach for more details.

Sutton drops her pen. It rolls off the table. She turns and bends down to reach it at the same time I drop to my haunches to pick it up.

Hazel eyes flare wide, parallel to mine.

My gaze flicks to her throat and her slow swallow.

"Th-thanks," she stutters, taking the pen from my hand. Sutton straightens, back stiff.

I stand and walk around the table to the chair opposite her. My hands curl around the top.

"What are you doing here?" she bites out. "You need to leave. I'm supposed to be meeting someone."

"I know." My eyes bounce to her notebook, to her, back to the notebook—picking out a few bullet points on stress and sports—and then back to her. "I'm the someone."

"What?" So she didn't know it was me. "I'm meeting a student-athlete who's supposedly struggling with—" Sutton stops speaking. Picks her chin up, and recognition registers all over her. "You?"

"Me." I nod.

Sutton bursts out laughing, clapping a hand over her mouth.

"Yeah, right. Come on, Cooper. This isn't funny."

"You're the one laughing, Dave."

Her eye twitches at the nickname.

"You just can't let me have one thing, can you? Is this supposed to be a joke?"

"I didn't know it was your project."

"I find that hard to believe. You always do this." The whites of her eyes show. "You're telling me you, mister golden boy, captain of the hockey team, is supposedly struggling with stress and anxiety?"

My eyelids flutter.

I pull off my beanie in an attempt to cool off.

This means Coach knows, must have mentioned it in his response.

"Yeah." My voice is unsteady. "Surprise."

I can't tell if Sutton believes me. Her facial features are stoic. Jaw slowly dropping open, and it sort of feels like I'm the animal on display at the zoo.

Before she has a chance to respond, I take off.

I'll tell Coach I can't do this. Ask one of my roommates if they can work with her. Find another team captain.

I don't know, but it can't be me.

It already hurts that the girl I love hates me.

Now she knows my biggest secret, too.

FOUR

SUTTON

COOPER LEAVES WITHIN A BLINK.

I turn over my shoulder and watch as he storms down the stairs.

I should go after him, but I'm glued to the chair. There is a battle going on within me. The devil on one shoulder is convincing me this is payback for what he did in high school. That finally I have the ammo to do exactly what he did to me. On the other shoulder, the angel is reminding me that he used to be my friend, that our families are close, and I could help him.

My case study...

Still frozen to my seat, I pull my phone out of my backpack and dial Dr. Manning.

"Sutton?"

"Hi. Morning, Dr. Manning. I'm sorry to be calling you this early. I hope I'm not interrupting any—" There is an echo of child laughter from her end, and I realize I am interrupting. Of course I am, her niece is visiting. "Never mind."

"Aren't you supposed to be in your first session right now?" she asks, ignoring me, and stopping my thumb from hitting end.

"About that. Is there another student available?"

"Is there a problem with Mr. Carmichael?"

Yes? No? Maybe? Everything is a problem when it comes to Cooper.

One of the reasons I look up to Dr. Manning is her no bull-shit mentality. Meaning she isn't going to accept my half a decade's worth of dislike and rivalry as a valid excuse.

Still...I try.

"We don't see eye-to-eye. We have a pa—"

Dr. Manning hmms. "I see."

"Not like that. We've never been romantic before."

"Okay," she says leerily. "Whatever is going on between the two of you, put it aside. This industry requires you to be unbiased. And there is no other option. This is a requirement from the department chair, Sutton. You have a choice: work with him or we drop the independent study."

I sigh, a long, drawn-out huff. "Fine."

"Is that all?"

"Yeah. I'll see you next week."

The line clicks at the sound of a squeal in background.

I groan, slouching forward till my forehead hits the table in front of me.

My worst nightmare is coming true.

I need Cooper Carmichael.

Checking my watch, I've wasted twenty minutes of the time I allotted. I'll figure it out, but in the meantime, I need to clear my head, and I now have an hour back in my day.

Any spots in your next class?

ELLIOT

What are we sweating out?

I'm about to tell her, but I stop at the fresh memory of Cooper's knuckles going white, gripping the chair when he admitted he is struggling, as if it was the first time he's allowed the truth to emerge.

I've been there. After my injury and during recovery, realizing I'll never play again.

I respond with a half truth.

Had some free time pop up.

ELLIOT

Bike 15

———

"LAST TWO MINUTES! Lower your resistance to thirty-five from forty. We will be in the saddle, but when the beat drops"— Elliot smiles, sending a devious brow raise across the room— "turn that resistance back up! Minimum forty-five."

Her cycling classes are the best. She's been teaching on campus for the past two years.

The rec center drops classes on Sunday for the following week. If you don't log in precisely at two, you won't even make it on the waitlist for her cycling or mat Pilates classes. And even then, students show up in the hopes that someone no-shows.

I adjust the red knob, pulling back my resistance. My legs are killing me as I try to keep up with the eighty-to-one-hundred cadence she calls out. Even though I've graduated from cycling to running in physical therapy, my left knee still throbs occasionally —the pulse syncing with the beat of the song.

Elliot is already calling out another cue. "In ten, we are out of the saddle. Resistance minimum forty-five and maintain cadence. Ready? Three. Two. One."

A Justin Bieber remix carries us through the last minute of work before our cooldown.

The song changes, and everyone sits back down, toweling off and grabbing their water bottles. Elliot leads us through five minutes of stretching before high-fiving the group at the door.

I unclip my shoes, then hang around till everyone is gone.

This was her final class of the morning, and I promised her when I showed up, I'd help her clean before we went to lunch at the coffee shop in town.

She bounces over to me, straight hair tied up in a high pony with her emotional support scrunchie. "What'd you think?" Elliot asks.

"I don't think I'll be able to move tomorrow." I offer her a half smile, half grimace. "That was your best one yet, Elle."

Her cheeks are tipped pink. Unlike the rest of us, whose cheeks are tomato red from the intensity of cycling for forty-five minutes, Elliot looks like she could hit the red carpet. I swear she's glistening instead of sweating. Her self-tanned skin is highlighted by the periwinkle set she's wearing.

"Thanks." She bites her lip. "Wanna know something? You can't tell anyone."

Did I miss the memo that today is National Secret Day?

"Yeah, of course." I give her a weak smile, bracing for my second secret bomb of the day. Elliot never keeps anything from me. I give myself one second...then another to question our friendship before I mentally slap myself.

I follow her to the cabinet in the corner of the room to grab a rag and disinfectant spray. We start wiping down the bikes and weights.

"I submitted an audition tape for a new virtual cycling studio. It's a stationary bike that people can buy and then take classes whenever they want. I'd record different rides—time, music, intensity."

"What! Why didn't you tell me sooner?"

"Because let's be real, they aren't going to accept a college junior. They probably received applications from instructors who have been doing this for more than two years."

"So? Does *not* mean they are better than you. When are you supposed to find out about next steps?"

She shrugs. "I'm not sure. Application window closes in two weeks."

"No keeping it a secret when you find out." I tug at the end of her pony.

"Fineeee. It was on a whim, though, so I don't expect anything, and I would have told you once I heard back. I didn't want to get my hopes up."

I know a little something about that.

"Is this the revelation about what you want to do postgrad?"

Elliot has had seven majors since we started college. She came into Lakeland undecided. After your first semester, you are required to declare a major, which she did until Elliot decided to play leapfrog from one major to the next.

"Yeah. I've always loved fitness but never saw it as a potential career."

"People make a career out of everything. If you love it, you should go for it."

Elliot smiles warmly, nodding. She drops our towels in a laundry basket before grabbing a mop. I dust the cubbies in the corner, putting the few abandoned water bottles in the lost and found.

"Ugh," she groans. "Don't they know I have the patience of a racehorse?"

We finish cleaning while Elliot tells me more about the company and daydreams about opening a studio someday. By the time she's handing me my coat, she's decided to go back to a business major and schedule a meeting with her advisor.

I tug on my floral beanie, taking my curls out of the braid I had thrown them into. All of my baby hairs are either glued to my skin by sweat or trying to make a break for it.

We're walking out of the studio and down the hallway toward the exit, passing one of the three weight rooms. We both fall prey to letting our eyes roam over the guys working out. Simultaneously, our heads rotate to the left. I swear I see Elliot's tongue peak out of her mouth, wetting her lips.

I know it's a double standard, but come on, it's a large glass window, and a majority of them opted not to wear shirts. It'd be the number one exhibit if colleges were a zoo. Men in their natural habitat. Flexing in the mirror to see who has the biggest biceps. Pretending they did one hundred chest presses when they only did eight.

My eyes catch on one guy: Zach Brighton.

I've had an on-and-off crush on him for the better part of my college years.

Zach is a pitcher on the baseball team. He's tall with thick muscles stretching both his shirt and shorts. He flips up the hem of his shirt to swipe at his brow, flashing a tattoo that stretches up from the waistband of his shorts and wraps around his ribcage.

He's not as defined or sculpted as our guy friends. More broad. Large and a little softer, but you can see how strong he still is.

Zach drops his shirt, talking to one of his teammates. Dirty blond brows pinch together, his green eyes magnetizing beneath them.

Someone squeezes my bicep, my head jerking in their direction.

It's just Elliot. I was so enthralled with him for a minute that I forgot where I was.

"Zach is smiling at you!"

"What? No, he wasn't," I immediately combat.

She turns my body, and she's right. "Explain that."

An already enormous smile grows when our eyes catch. Signaling something to the group he's working out with, he sprints through the entrance.

I keep walking, dragging Elliot with me. Her steps slow purposely.

"Sutton?" My name echoes behind us, bouncing through the other voices in the hallway.

"Keep walking," I whisper to her, only to take a step forward and trip. Elliot is stopped dead in her tracks, my body ricocheting, momentum taking me down.

Shoes screech on the floor as Zach whirls in front of me,

catching me with one arm around my waist. He helps me get my bearings, steadying me back on two feet. Over his shoulder, I spy Elliot biting her lip, stifling whatever witty comment she wants to say.

"Clumsy?"

Are voices supposed to be hot?

I stare blankly at him. Words to formulate a response swirl in my head but get lost somewhere on their way to my tongue.

Answer him, Sutton. Anything. One word. Yes or no. It's not that hard.

"Y-yes. N-no."

Oh my gosh. This cannot be happening.

My cheeks burn with embarrassment.

I smack a hand over my face. This is not how I imagined our first conversation going. I've pictured it in my head countless times. Working it one way, then reworking it another. Each time I'm confident and easy going, entirely myself, and he falls head over heels for me.

I'm not shy or stunned. I'm not inexperienced or afraid to say the wrong thing. I'm not the little girl who watched everyone else get chosen to go on dates with potential families. I'm not on the sidelines of my life; I'm the main character.

Why is picturing something so much easier than living it?

"I'll catch you either way," he says, ignoring the way I'm also clumsy with words. "We've never formally met. I'm Zach."

"I know." Okay, so maybe I shouldn't be myself. My feet jitter. Shifting side to side, my toes curling on the soles. "I'm Sutton Davis."

"I know." He hands me my water bottle. Our fingers brush, and I try not to appear too utterly freaked out. Zach blushes, and for a second, I think he might be as nervous as me. He shifts on his feet. "I've wanted to ask for your number for a while, but—"

"We have plans," I blurt out awkwardly. "Elliot and I," I modify my statement.

Elliot frowns, eyes falling shut as she shakes her head. She's been giving me tips for talking to the opposite sex, but I've apparently forgotten every single one.

I dated a guy in high school briefly. Then someone else most of freshman year, but haven't since.

My roommate steps in as my lifesaver—literally and figuratively. "We are going to lunch. I'd offer for you to join, but I think you are needed back in there." She points to the weight room where we are collecting a small crowd who pretend not to be watching us. "But she'd love to grab coffee sometime. Do you have your phone?"

"I don't drink coffee," I whisper to Elliot.

"Shut up," she whispers back.

Zach shakes his head no.

Elliot reaches into my coat pocket, fingers like chopsticks, and pulls mine out. She types in my passcode and opens a new contact —note to self: change passcode. Flipping my phone around, she passes it to Zach. He hands it back, and she returns it to my pocket.

"Thanks, Zach. Tell Tyler to text me." She winks, then drags me down the hallway.

Twisting backward, I find Zach still standing there, a smile on his face. I lift my hand, tight and in front of my chest, waving bye to him. He returns the gesture before miming a phone to his ear, then pointing at himself and mouthing *Call me.*

FIVE

COOPER

TWO DAYS AFTER EVADING SUTTON, Elliot walks in through the front door of our house. Jaxon and Chase trail behind her, bickering about which Batman is better.

"You can't possibly be picking Bale over Keaton."

"West is a classic we haven't considered." That's Chase.

"No, no, no. Out of the running. I'm putting a red sock in your laundry if you don't tell me right now how you are picking Bale," Jaxon threatens.

"Could you even find a red sock?" Chase taunts back.

"You know I'm colorblind, you dick."

They land on either side of me on our sectional and pick up the other two wireless controllers on the console table. Mindlessly, I restart our racing game to add them in, listening to their debate move to Catwoman.

I don't know where Elliot disappears to, but I can hear her voice. "You two are insane. The obvious choice is Pattinson."

Our house is two floors with a basement. Spacious and recently renovated. The finished basement is used solely for parties. Thrifted couches line the perimeter, and Jaxon built a make-shift bar in a corner last summer.

The main area is spacious. All of the expected rooms: living, dining that we actually use for nightly dinners and studying, kitchen, and a laundry room that is exploding with dirty clothes from whoever is up on the schedule. We have to keep that door shut, even with a diffuser it always smells like someone's sweaty gear.

Dawson's room is on the main floor in a converted den. Beck, Chase, Jax, and I live upstairs. I'm in the primary, and before anyone asks, I did pull the captain card. Not to be a dick, but there was no way I was sharing a bathroom for another year with Jaxon. After freshman year, I had paid my dues—luckily, Beck is a clean freak and makes him clean it on Fridays before he's allowed to go out.

Beck's dad bought the house. He won't talk about why it frustrates him when you ask about it, but his eyes become blue-tipped daggers, and he walks away, slamming his bedroom door behind him.

I love our house. The proximity to campus and the rink. The way we've allowed it to be a revolving door to our teammates and friends. It's never quiet, never empty.

It's a distraction.

Elliot reappears, a bowl of fruit and water nestled in one arm.

"This was at our apartment." She drops a beanie into my lap.

I look down at it. Run the material between my fingers.

When I walked away from Sutton in the library, I didn't bother to pick up my hat. I readjusted the backpack hanging off one shoulder, spinning on my heels, and bolting. I didn't care about anything else, except getting away at that moment.

I felt it when my grip tightened on the chair. A lightning bolt through my body, constricting my heart and suffocating me.

I glance down at the black hat and am struck again.

You're around people, Carmichael, you can't do this here, one version of me coaches. *They can't see you like this, what would they think?*

I pass the controller to Elliot. "Here. You play. Bottom right screen with the blue turtle shell."

She takes it from me, an inquisitive set to her face as she watches me leave. Jaxon and Chase are too focused on the race to comment on me getting up, the couch breathing with my removed weight.

The jingle of someone crossing the finish line follows me up the stairs and drifts under my door as I close it behind me and lock it.

My room is dark, only lit by the desk lamp. A yellow haze casts a shadow of me pacing back and forth on the wall.

Did Sutton tell her?

Why didn't Sutton bring this back? Does she hate me that much?

Is Elliot going to tell my friends? Or who else?

I tug my phone out of my Levi's. Swipe it open and go to Sutton's text thread, her contact still the nickname I gave her in middle school, and reread her last message.

DAVE

Cooper, don't make me beg. I don't have another option.

That was two days ago. I haven't responded till now.

Did you tell Elliot?

Her response is immediate. Surprisingly. She's not the best texter—at least in our group text, she never responds, but that could be because of me. I try not to read too much into it, even *before* she was never the best texter, always preferred passing notes or talking on the phone.

DAVE

Huh?

She gave me back the hat I wore to our first session.

DAVE

I'd hardly call that a 'session' when you stormed off in the first two minutes.

Did you tell her?

DAVE

Seriously? I'd never cross that line and put my future career in jeopardy.

Answer the question. Yes or no?

DAVE

Carmichael...

She's your best friend. You two tell each other everything.

DAVE

Not everything.

So you didn't tell her?

DAVE

Why would I tell her?

I don't know, Dave. Call it payback.

DAVE

There it is. I'm not as low as you. I'd never ruin a friendship.

Is this you admitting we were friends?

There's a lapse in her response.

I stop burning a path into the area rug in my room. Inhaling deeply, a looseness in my lungs that hasn't been there lately.

I want her to say yes. Remember those days like I do. Not that they ever leave me. What should haunt me in my dreams are instead a life jacket thrown to me when I feel like I'm drowning in my brain. Her smile is the top buckle. The way she'd grab my hand and interlock our fingers during a scary movie is the middle buckle. And the bottom buckle is the secrets we've kept for each other, the pieces of her she's only ever given to me, and the ones I've given her.

The thing about life jackets is that when you tighten them, you have to be mindful of the excess strap. If not, you can get caught in it, hurting yourself in the process.

My phone buzzes.

DAVE

I didn't tell her.

I'd never do that to you.

Never?

I find it hard to believe, but I try to convince myself otherwise. Give her the benefit of the doubt, as I always do to a fault. I'm immune from anything else.

This could simply be her practicing patient-doctor confidentiality.

Or maybe she means it.

This is Sutton, I force myself to remember.

Between her words, I see the fragments of her promise. Despite what I did to her—for her—Sutton still cares about me.

When you grow up with someone the way we did, they become a part of you, and you grow with them. Sutton is an organ that my body needs. Placed somewhere between my heart and lungs, they adapted her into their functions.

If you were to do a CT scan, you'd see a piece of her there. The one I can't let go of, even though I know she wants me to.

I think our history is that of a fairytale. We are just caught somewhere in the middle, the conflict between the main characters, but you know they'll get their happily ever after.

Sutton's parents are high school sweethearts, and my mom was always their third wheel. Their friendship stretched from coast-to-coast and through college, where my mom met my dad. It was serendipitous that our dads were drafted to the same team out of college.

Sutton's parents are my second family. Her mom would stay the night when our dads were on away game stretches before they adopted the girls.

Her parents moved three doors down when they were going through the adoption process. Something about manifesting by purchasing a five-bedroom house with a pool, that simply had to be filled with kids running around.

It was a crystal blue day, not a cloud in the January sky, when they brought Sutton and Meave home. Mom had hung a huge banner across their porch.

They had told us they were adopting one little girl. Meave popped out of the car door first before turning around and extending a hand to another little girl.

I'd never seen that color of red hair before, or that many curls. Her hair was in pigtails on the top of her head. Shorter than it is now, but always everywhere.

I didn't understand the word beautiful when I was six, but that's what I thought when I said to my sisters, *Wow, she's pretty.*

My sisters, Jordan and Molly, teased me for weeks after about having a thing for redheads. One time at Disney, we were at a princess character breakfast, and Ariel was the only character I'd take a photo with. Bright maroon cheeks and a toothless smile that I'll never be able to live down.

Maybe it is redheads, but I think it's only Sutton. Always has been.

Sutton behaves as if her purpose in life is to make me not want her. She doesn't realize, though, that my entire existence is wanting her.

I was always the only boy among the four girls. She never made me feel left out. We were the ones to skate together. I carried her on my back when she fell off her scooter and busted open her knees.

We were inseparable till high school when she became *friends* with Izzy. That friendship ended with me taking the blame for an Izzy-sized mistake, and my friendship with Sutton snapping like a thin thread.

I've been working ever since to sew it back together.

Just like I've been trying and failing to sew myself back together.

I fling open my door. Sneakers haphazardly on my feet, one of them untied, and run down the stairs.

"Do you know where Sutton is?" I ask Elliot.

"Should be at the..." She looks down at her phone. "Never mind, she's at the grocery store."

———

I FIND HER IN PRODUCE, meticulously examining apples. No bruises, firm enough that it'll crunch when you bite into it. Slightly yellow, especially if they are Honeycrisps.

"Heard that one's poisonous," I say, walking up next to her, plucking one from the pile and twisting it in my hand.

"Go away, Carmichael."

I don't. She pushes her cart to a refrigerated section of fruit.

I pick up a package of berries, check the bottom, and then place them in her cart.

"I'm sorry," I say.

"For what?" She continues shopping, not minding me trailing behind her or the items I'm dropping into her cart. She has a long, lined piece of paper listing all of her groceries in categories. Little boxes next to them that she checks off as she adds them to her cart.

I take the pen tucked behind her ear, reach around her to check off berries.

"Assuming you'd tell Elliot."

"There isn't anything to tell her." Really? "Besides being volunteered, I don't know anything about—"

"You laughed," I interject, the truth falling out of me. "That's why I left."

Sutton stops and turns to face me, one elbow resting on the handle of the cart. "I shouldn't have laughed." And then she apologizes, genuinely. Sutton is the kindest person I know, but to me, there's an edge, like a dog with a spiked collar daring me to get close. "I asked Dr. Manning again about getting a new student."

She continues shopping, turning down the aisle with bread and cereal.

"Will that put you behind?"

"Yes," she says bluntly. "I'm already behind everyone else who attends schools with the major." She rambles on under her breath, and I move to the front of the cart.

Her attention is focused somewhere between oatmeal and her thoughts. The front of the cart rams into my abdomen. I let out a tight groan, coughing to clear my throat and suck in a ragged breath.

"Then I'll do it."

"Don't worry about it. Move, *please*."

"No. Not till you agree to let me be your partner on this."

"I'm not a pity project, Cooper."

"That's not what this is. I don't think of you that way."

"Right." She rolls her eyes and tries to move the cart around me. I take a step to the left, blocking her path.

Sutton sighs, eyelids fluttering against her freckled cheeks. Constellations across both of them. You can't count them, there are too many, but the left has more than the right.

"I'm not doing this with you," she says.

You don't want to do anything with me is what I want to say, but instead I ask, "What will it take for you to let me help you?"

"Nothing. If you wanted to help, you would have responded to my texts." She has a point.

I let go of the cart. Drag my hands over my face and through my hair. I hate myself for hurting her, over and over. The more I try to stay in her atmosphere, the further away I feel.

How do I keep fucking up with her?

I'd do anything for her. She could tell me to get on my knees and beg, or stand in the middle of campus dressed like a fool and sing a Hannah Montana song. I'd give up hockey for her if she asked. I'd do anything she wants.

"Leave me alone, please."

Anything but that.

There must be something sticky on the floor because my feet don't move. I'm stuck watching her examine ingredients in boxes of cereal for one, then two minutes. Mustering up enough courage to walk away, I pass by her and silently scream out an apology for everything.

I'm about to turn for the exit when there's a death grip on my bicep. In my rush out the door, I forgot a coat. A T-shirt is not ideal for a Midwest winter.

Her hand is warm, hot enough that it's burning into my skin.

Sutton's breathing picks up, and I can feel it dance across the skin on the back of my neck when she whispers, "Does he see us?" The tip of her chin rests on my shoulder.

"Who?" I look around the checkout. "Zach?"

"Yes. Now shh."

"He can't hear you, he isn't—never mind, he's walking our way," I warn.

"Stay in front of me. Tell him I'm not here."

"Why?"

Before she can answer, Zach is standing in front of us. "Hey, Carmichael."

"Zach. What's up, man? Did you have a good break?" I clap his outstretched hand, giving him one of those bro hugs. Stepping away from Sutton, revealing her behind me.

"Yeah, it was good. Saw my parents in Tampa. What about you?"

"Quick. Only got a five-day break this year."

"That's right. I saw your double-win last weekend against the Firehawks. Shutout both times? St. James is on fire right now."

"The entire team is, man. When do you start spring training games?"

"In a month. I'm ready, I think this is our year." Zach's hope isn't far-fetched. A freshman came in pitching almost one hundred as a lefty. "Are you with Sutton?"

"Oh-uh-um...no," I stutter around the sentence. Around the entire question. I get he's asking me where she is physically, in the grocery store, but my mind immediately jumps to being together *like that.*

He stares at me, confused.

"Hi," her sweetly smooth voice responds. Sutton's head peaks through under my armpit.

I adjust my arm around her so that she's standing next to me.

"Hey." Zach grins, bigger than I've ever seen him smile. There's an essence of nerves, but they don't outweigh his confidence. "You haven't called me yet."

"I-I-I've been busy." She picks at a curl. The strand bounces with the movement. "Prepping for classes, searching for a summer internship..." Sutton starts to ramble on, and I subtly tap her upper arm to get her to stop.

"Any that you are excited for?"

"Dr. Manning's abnormal psychology class."

"Me too. I didn't realize you were taking that."

Sutton nods, and her face blooms red. She swallows slowly, tugging at the strand of hair more. "We've been in the same classes since freshman year," she admits slowly.

Zach runs his tongue along his front teeth, and if I were him, I'd too would be embarrassed for not noticing her earlier. "Can I walk you to class on Monday? You live in the campus apartments?"

"Oh. Well...Elliot and I usually..."

I jump in, jealousy itching up my spine, but I'm also trying to sort through why she's embarrassed right now. "She's walking with me. Old traditions of starting the school year together." I snake my arm around her tensing shoulders.

"Didn't realize you two were close."

"Sutton"—her shoulders roll back, a rigidity overtakes her. Shit, I never call her Sutton—"likes to pretend we aren't." That's not completely a lie.

Zach sways, clutching his basket tighter.

"I guess I'll see you around. In class or something." He gives her a once-over and walks away. I don't like it.

As soon as Zach is down an aisle, Sutton moves my arm off her.

"Never do that again." She jabs a finger into my chest.

Do what? Defend her? Put my arm around her? Say we are close?

Probably option D: all of the above.

I hate how much this hurts, knowing that she doesn't want me.

Sutton drops her finger. My hand jolts forward with the smallest movement, and it takes a conscious thought to stop. To not grab hold of her and never let go.

Her hands move to her face, covering the entirety of it. Pale blue nails with small, darker blue dots look fresh.

"Ugh," she groans, then talks to herself. Soft enough I can't make out what she's saying. Sutton groans again, dragging her hands over her face.

I add up the equation. "You like Zach?"

Her eyes flutter. Her hands pressed against her mouth and maroon cheeks.

"You didn't see or hear anything." I open my mouth to talk, but she continues, "Or do you want to tell everyone about this, too?"

"No." I pause, exhale, and restart. "Dave, I came here to apologize to you. I'll do the project. I don't want to screw this up for you."

Sutton takes a long inhale, shutting her eyes and reopening them. "You don't get it, do you? Doing this for me isn't going to get us anywhere. The only way this could work is if you want this for yourself."

I blink and she's moving into a checkout aisle, I know she doesn't have half of the items she needs. Once again, I'm frozen in place. This time, because her words are shackles on my feet.

I think about it. Think about how it felt when Coach told me not to help, and I felt relieved even for a second, not to have to give away a minute of my day. I think about the pieces of me being pulled at, that I freely give, because if not, then who am I? Every time an article comes out comparing me to my dad and I feel the pressure to be more than I am.

How long am I going to let this go on before I let it consume me? Before there is nothing left but a shell of who I am? Before my love for the game runs out?

SIX

COOPER

THE PUCK WHIRLS behind the goal, unlike my thoughts of Sutton, I can't pass them off to a teammate. I can't restart the drill from the top.

Since classes started earlier this week, I've waited for her on the lawn, outside the psych building, and in the lobby of her apartment building. Trying to find a way to convince her to let me do this project with her. Sutton is right. I need to do this for me, but she's also wrong. I can and want to do this for the both of us.

A couple of scouts are at practice today for two seniors hoping to be free agents. Skating back to the other offensive players to switch drills, I overhear them mumbling about me. My head swivels over them at the first drop of my name, but Coach puts a steadying hand on my shoulder. *Pay attention, ignore them.*

Ignoring them is easy. Ignoring the corner of my brain that their presence and words scratch? Decapitating.

I speed off the ice when practice is called. My safe place, my haven, is the one place I don't want to be right now.

My teammates can't see me spiral out.

My ribcage feels like a prison. Each beat of my heart or thought that floats by is like being slammed into the boards.

No one follows me into the locker room.

Swiftly, my skates are unlaced and I'm changed. I bypass a shower, grabbing my bag, and heading out.

Jaxon's voice echoes in the hallway to the lobby of the hockey arena "Cooper," he calls out again. It's muffled by my speed, the distance, the low buzz between my head.

The fresh air outside hits me like a tidal wave. I suck it in. Try to fill the space in my lungs. Gasp, again.

I smack a hand to my chest. Pause for a moment when I catch a glimpse of her car.

Sutton looks out the driver's window, our gazes locking.

My next breath is easier, smoother.

She parks, but I'm in my car now.

The time between getting into my Jeep and Jaxon opening my bedroom door without knocking is a blur. His phone is pressed to his ear as he jumps on my bed next to me.

"Is this new?" he asks, pulling the phone back and picking up my comforter.

"You ask that every time you come in here."

He shrugs his forgetfulness off. "Do you want to go over to Elliot and Sutton's tonight?"

"Stop inviting people over," I can hear Elliot gripe through the phone.

Jax rests his phone on his exposed thigh—the guy runs warm, never wearing pants even when it drops below freezing—tapping speakerphone. "I'm only inviting Cooper!"

"Which means the whole lot of you will also tag along."

"Beckett doesn't hang out with us anymore. Cooper barely does either." He turns my way and pins me with sad puppy dog eyes. Deep in his forest eyes though is the lingering question of why.

The past few months have been the heaviest I've felt. Painting a smile on my face and showing up how they've needed me is more draining, and I find myself turning to silence and being alone more and more. I'm careful about disappearing, but apparently not careful enough if he's noticing.

Have they all noticed?

Beckett has a valid excuse for not hanging around with us. He's from around Bensen, and goes home to help out his sick mom with his little sister.

A door across the hall cracks open, and our six-five goalie leans in my doorway shirtless. His chest is covered in black tattoos. There's a spot on his right arm covered in Saniderm, fresh ink that he's definitely not supposed to have gotten during season underneath.

"I can hang tonight," he says casually.

"See!" Elliot exclaims. There's whispering in the background.

Jaxon points at Beck. "Now that's definitely new. What is it?"

"I'm going to pick up my sister from basketball practice. Text me the plans."

"You should go shirtless for the moms! Isn't someone supposed to bring snacks each week? You could be the snack," he jokes while Beck stares at him emotionless before pushing off the doorframe and closing his door.

"If you come over, you have to bring pizza," Elliot finally says.

"Done. Cooper will pick it up."

I smack his arm. Give him a look for volunteering me, and push a hand through my hair.

Elliot must have put her phone on speakerphone too because we can hear their conversation clearly. "Yeah, pizza is good," Sutton says, barely audible. It'd be easy to miss but my ears have a frequency reserved for her.

"What kind do you want?" Elliot asks Sutton.

"Oh, it's okay. I'll eat cheese or pepperoni. Whatever he gets is fine."

"You sure?"

"It's pizza."

"Okay, get whatever, Coop," Elliot tells us.

"See you in an hour?" Jaxon asks.

"Perfect. Byeeeeee."

Jaxon hangs up and turns over on my bed. He rests his head

on a closed fist, elbow digging into the bed. "You okay, man? You stormed out of practice. I was calling for you, and then when we got home, you were asleep."

"I think I ate something weird," I lie. I hate lying to him—to any of my roommates, but they wouldn't understand, and what would they think about me?

Ungrateful. Selfish. Spoiled. Or worse...maybe they'd agree.

His face brightens, then falls with horror. "Did you eat one of the green containers? I had one for breakfast and thought it smelled funky. Was good with hot sauce on it, but we should tell Dawson."

"Yeah, that was probably it."

"Feeling up for tonight? I can grab the pizza."

"I'll get it."

"Sweet. Request me and I'll split it with you."

I nod, but I won't request money from him.

YOU'RE PUCKING AWESOME

LOML JAXON

Chill @ E+S's tonight?

DAWSON

Out with Jake. Cool if he crashes?

LOML JAXON

Grab wine and beer on your way over (:

BECKY

We have an early morning tomorrow

LOML JAXON

What does that have to do with beer?

CHASE

baby b is boring. doesn't want to be hungover

DAWSON

Who is Baby B? I thought he was made up.

BECKY

Fuck off.

Becky has left the group text
Chase has added Becky to the group chat

CHASE

something lite please baby

Sutton will want savyb

LOML JAXON

I swear I'm naming my future daughter
Savannah Beth and calling her Savy B

BECKY

Since I can't leave the group chat, I'm
moving out

They keep giving Beck shit. He's the quiet one—sort of a grump. Communicates in eye rolls and grunts, so even getting thirteen words out of him is impressive. Dark black hair, trimmed close to his head. His broad shoulders and thigh-sized biceps are covered in tattoos. It's cute in the mornings, though. He comes down the stairs, silent like a mouse, into the kitchen to make an Americano, wearing his glasses.

Ignoring them, I dial the only pizza place near campus as I start my car. Antonio's is a family-owned restaurant that has been in town since 1960. They deliver a well-crafted East Coast style pizza, but their Detroit style is better. I order two extra-larges of each type with an array of toppings. Plus, an order of dry-rubbed wings.

Who knows when my roommates ate last. Not like that matters anyway—they probably ate after practice, and are still empty pits.

———

"YEAH, you've told me five times. Now, don't be an ass. The pizza is getting cold."

Elliot is threatening to not let me in because I'm late. I guess threatening cold pizza is her limit. The door clicks to unlock and the light flashes green. Using one hand, balancing the pizza in the other, I finagle the door open. Rinse and repeat when I reach Sutton and Elliot's door.

Pretty proud of myself for not dropping the pizza. Almost did getting out of the elevator, my Birkenstock clogs catching on the metal gap.

"Beer in the fridge," Dawson calls from the couch as I set them on the counter. Separating them into smaller piles.

I grab two beers—one for me and one in case anyone needs another.

Everyone is in the living room. Jaxon, Elliot, Sutton, and Beckett are on the couch. Chase is lounging on the couch in front of Elliot, twiddling with something on the coffee table.

"What happened to the couch?"

Where the campus-issued, blue-gray, patent leather couch used to be is an oatmeal-colored, linen, J-shaped couch. Plush and appears far cozier than what they used to have. I don't even bother taking the open spot next to Sutton, even though it's gotta be more comfortable than the floor spot I head to.

"Too angular," Sutton says while Elliot chirps, "Uncomfortable. We—I convinced the building manager to take it to storage when I found this on Facebook Marketplace. The guy let me have it for a hundred bucks. A steal!"

"A steal, or did you flirt?"

"Does it matter?"

Before I can sit down, Sutton stands, and I follow her back to the kitchen. In the cabinet next to the microwave, she pulls out plates.

Back to me, Sutton quietly mentions, "You're off the hook. I found someone else to work with."

"I told you I would do it."

"Well now you don't have to."

I shake my head, trying to not let my disappointment show.

I flip open a box of pizza, taking the top plate and slide two slices onto it, and open a ranch cup. Sutton is staring at me when I face her and offer her the plate.

"That's not cheese or pepperoni."

It's not. It's her favorite. She hates admitting that she likes pineapple on pizza. When I ordered the extra pizza, I debated asking for a bag of M&Ms too. Write out I'm sorry on it, then she'll know how deeply I mean it.

"Right, it's pepperoni and pineapple with hot honey."

"No one else likes pineapple."

"But you do." I don't hate it, it's not my favorite flavor combo, but I know no one else will eat it. I'll pick off the pineapples once they become unbearable.

"You didn't need to do that." She takes the plate, then mumbles, "You don't need to do anything for me." Her words don't match the tenderness in her voice.

"You know, a thank you would suffice."

Big hazel eyes peer up at me. There's a softness in the rivers of green that branch out across her iris. Flecks of gold that draw me closer to her, I can feel my body shift in her direction for a better look, a need to count each one.

A moment passes between us, as if we are peering through a looking glass at the friendship we once had. I blink and it evaporates.

We're interrupted.

The guys crowd their small kitchen, breaking into the other boxes of pizza and wings. They layer and stack their plates exactly as I expected. I slide the box of pizza I got for Sutton away from their greedy and grabby hands.

Chase makes a plate for Elliot, adding the crust he tore off his slices to her plate. I watch as he walks over to her. She's sitting next to Sutton, laughing about who knows what.

Even through her loud laugh, I hear Sutton's. Whatever

remnants of anxiety from earlier today vanish at the sound, relieving the tightness in my chest, and I swear she's better than the ashwagandha tea I stomach at night.

"We were playing 'put a finger down' before you got here," Jaxon says with a mouthful of food. He swallows and wipes his mouth with a napkin. "We should restart. Sutton was the only one with five left anyway."

Sutton tosses him a fake smile, tilting her head with a slight shake back and forth, a hint of annoyance in the curl of her lip that she masks with playfulness in her bright eyes.

Everyone puts up five fingers. I use my other hand to devour my slices, forgetting to pluck off the tropical fruit. The back of my neck, the skin that is exposed underneath my hat prickles, and I turn enough to see from my peripheral that Sutton is watching me intently. When she catches my gaze, she quickly looks away, cheeks tinted.

I go first.

"Put a finger down if you've been to Europe."

Everyone else drops a finger. Sutton goes next.

"Umm..." She searches for a statement. Picks up her wine glass and takes a few sips, then blushes. "Put a finger down if you've had sex in public."

"Does a car count?" Dawson asks.

"Oh." Around the room, everyone drops a finger unanimously. Sutton drops her hands to her lap, masked by the coffee table. "This is awkward."

"Why?" Elliot asks casually, nonchalantly.

"I assumed there had to be someone else that hadn't—"

"You and Nathan never—" Jaxon starts about her freshman year boyfriend.

"No. We, uh, yeah, we did stuff. We just never—"

"I knew I couldn't stand him. That twatwaffle should have spent less time with his head in a textbook, and more time between his girlfriend's legs."

"Jaxon!" Elliot warns, bonking him upside the back of his head.

"Ow," he lets out, at the same time, I bark out, "Don't talk about her like that."

"Sorry!" His hands fly up in front of him. "Just reminding everyone how much he sucks."

"Apologize to Sutton," Elliot demands with a snap and point.

"I'm okay, Elliot," she pipes up, slipping her game hand out from under the table, her thumb folded down. But I notice the half moons up and down her pointer finger. It's a nervous tick she's had since we were kids. There's a scar on her left palm from pushing into the flesh so hard that it bled. It's barely noticeable, most probably don't even see it, given how faint the crescent is. I've always thought of Sutton as the sun—personality, her attire, everything really—and myself as the moon. Especially lately. You can't have one without the other. The moon doesn't shine without the sun.

Sutton clears her throat, and I quickly rip my gaze away from her when I realize I've been staring. "You go, Chase," she follows up with.

He immediately goes, catching the rise of my brow and silent plea for him to get us out of the conversation. "Put a finger down if you've hooked up with someone in this group."

You'd think we'd all know each other by now. Three years of friendship between all seven of us, plus my sister and her roommate, Xanie. They were easy additions when they started at Lakeland, both on the women's hockey team.

But the response to Chase's turn is a reminder that there is always something you don't know about a person...or that we all keep secrets.

It's as if the music being streamed on the television glitches and the AC turns off with how quiet and palpable the tension in the room becomes.

Eyes bounce from one person to the next. Lingering a

millisecond longer on me and Sutton as if something has happened between us.

I wish I were putting a finger down.

Sutton laughs sardonically, head tipping back, exposing her throat, untamable curls falling down her back. It's my least favorite of her laughs—not that I have them ranked or anything.

"One day," I joke. My voice, the playful tone I've mastered.

Jordan eyes me from the kitchen where she's pulling the cheese off a slice of pizza. If I knew she was coming, I'd have gotten a dairy-free one for her.

Distracted with my own patheticness, I blink and miss how subtly Elliot *and* Jaxon drop a finger down. No one missed it. There's a concert of surprised responses floating around the living room.

"You and Elliot?"

"What the heck? When?"

"No way."

"Seriously?"

"Really? You and Elliot?"

"Alright. Come on now, don't say my name like I'm not the best he's ever had," Elliot says, pulling her hair back and starting a braid when Chase takes over, weaving the three strands.

All heads turn to Jaxon who is wearing the cockiest shitting eating grin.

"Tell me I'm wrong," she taunts.

"You are." He takes a sip of his beer. "I'm"—Jaxon points the neck of the bottle in his direction—"the best you've ever had."

"Honestly, I don't even remember it." Elliot levels him with a look; eyes narrowed, cat-like, and lips pursed together with the smallest hint of an uptick on the left, her dimple digging into her cheek.

"Come on," he groans. "Remember when you ro—"

"Ha. See." Elliot thrusts a waggling finger in his direction, cutting him off from whatever juicy detail he was about to reminisce on.

"Whatever."

"Can we go back to the question of when did this happen?" Dawson asks, mouth slightly agape. "And why is this the first we've ever heard of it?"

"I don't tell you about everyone I've slept with," Jaxon lies knowingly.

"Last semester for like a month," Elliot admits.

"A month?" Dawson's mouth falls all the way open.

They both nod. Elliot casually responds, "It was supposed to be a one-time thing. We were both a little drunk off one too many tequila shots. I got ditched at a party, and Jaxon walked me home."

"I had to carry her, she couldn't walk in her heels any longer."

"He's forgetting to add the part where I didn't want him to carry me, and I tried to jab said heels into his ass." Elliot huffs, rolling her eyes at herself. "But when he held the door to our apartment open for me, I thought it was the sweetest thing and kissed him."

"Apparently, you did a lot more than kiss him," Chase says, his shoulders wear his regret in asking.

"Did you know about this?" Dawson turns to Sutton.

Her hands are up in front of her. "I plead the fifth."

Jordan and Xanie sitting down pulls the conversation away from Elliot and Jaxon.

"No cheese?" Jaxon asks, picking it off her plate. "That's pretty boring, little Carmichael."

She glowers at him. "Sorry my dietary restrictions are boring. How about I eat the cheese, and then you have to deal with the consequences."

"You know I'll take care of you anytime. Just say the word."

Jordan ignores him, and we return to the game.

Dawson takes his turn next, and we play for another half hour. Whenever someone loses, we reset and keep going. No one repeats a statement, but Sutton wins every time. She never loses more than a finger or two.

Quietly, she excuses herself from the group. No one else notices, busy watching whatever game is on and complaining about classes.

My eyes trail her as she places her plate in the sink, rinsing it first, and disappears down a hallway.

I follow her lead, I stand up and take my plate to the kitchen. In their cabinets, I find a mug to start a cup of tea. While the water is boiling, I wash the plates in the sink from tonight.

Sutton hasn't returned.

A door closes, or opens, then there's another almost unnoticeable closure.

I pad down the hallway toward her bedroom. My hand burns from the hot porcelain, and when I turn to knock, hot tea splashes over the side.

"I'll be right out," she sniffles.

Is she crying?

There's a skip in my heartbeat, a hollowing out of my stomach. It's like there's a faucet in my brain and someone turned the handle just enough that it drips. Each drip forms a puddle of panic that settles in my stomach.

"Dave, it's me."

"Go away, Cooper." Does she have those three words queued up or something?

I knock again. Sutton cracks the door open.

"What do you want?" Her facial features match the sharpness in her voice. Sutton spins around, walking away from the door she left open. The crack is big enough that I can see in. She sits in the middle of her bed, pulling her knees up to her chest, and rests her forehead on top of them.

She changed. She's not in her dusty pink sweater with cherries all over it and vintage denim overalls over top. They are traded for green pajama bottoms tucked into white ruffled socks with dogs on them and an oversized shirt.

On my next exhale, I push open the rest of the door with the back of my shoulder. Sutton doesn't pick her head up.

The mattress dips underneath my weight, causing her body to lean toward me. I scoot in next to her, careful to not spill the tea on myself or her purple comforter.

"Here." I offer her the tea, turning the handle in her direction, so she doesn't burn her hand.

She looks at me, then bounces to the mug.

"Are you okay?" I ask.

We must be in the twilight zone because she answers. Truthfully.

"No." She takes a sip, and I hope I remember how she takes it correctly. "Honey and lemon with a splash of milk?"

"Yeah."

Sutton raises the mug to her lips, the rim fitting between them. She breathes in deeply and out through her nose. "Sometimes I make this just for the smell. I don't even drink it, just sit here and breathe. It reminds me of Mom."

"I didn't know that," I admit.

"Now you do." She rests the mug on her knees. "I think about her and Dad a lot."

"Is that why you're crying? You left your phone in the living room. I can go get it and we can video them."

"Yes." I shift to get up. "No, not that. Yes, they are why I'm crying." She shakes her head and curls fall forward, hiding her away. Mindlessly, I reach out and push them behind her ear so I can see her, read her eyes. "Partly.

"I get jealous of their love. That they found each other so young and make it all look so easy. Tonight reminded me how I've never had anything like that and probably won't."

"You've dated, what? Two guys."

"That flopped miserably. Mom had one boyfriend. Dad." Hazel eyes roll at me, and I can't help but crack a smile. "Now, I can't even talk to a boy."

"You talk to all of us."

"That's because I don't have a crush on you goons. When I was dumped for the second time, I thought of myself as..." Sutton trails off, letting all the air out of her lungs. Then takes a large whiff of the steam rolling off the tea. "It's like that stole something, and I can't figure out how to get it back. It's been way over a year, and I'm fumbling over my words and emotions, not to mention my own two feet. My crush talks to me, and what do I do?" She lets out a groan. "Embarrass myself. Zach probably regrets giving me his number now."

"I can help you," I blurt before my better judgment can catch up to my heart that's slipping from her back pocket.

When it does catch up, it's screaming at me. A flashing jumbotron that reads *What are you thinking?*

Sutton chokes on her sip of tea. The mug on the verge of tumbling from its delicate position. "Help me?"

"We're friends."

"We aren't."

"We're friends," I repeat with more confidence, and since she's being truthful, I lie down a few of my cards even though I know it might hurt and say, "You are the most confident person I know. You deserve the love you want, and if you need help getting it, then I'll help."

"And how would you do that?"

Once again, this wasn't well thought out. I shrug. "Think of me as your dating tutor."

That earns me a laugh, number three on the list of favorites.

Why would I want to help her fall for someone else?

Insanity?

Stupidity?

A desperate need to make up for my mistake? The part of me that is okay with never having her if it means she's happy?

"What do you get out of this? If I agree."

"You take me back as your student athlete in your case study."

"That's you helping me twice, and I don't want to owe you Carmichael."

"Is it?" I smile. Softly, almost too nervously. "You were right. I need to help myself." I let my guard completely down. Reveal how bad of a place I'm in. "I don't know what's wrong with me, but it's getting worse. I'm having issues skating and getting out of bed. Any mention of the future is a boulder on my already thin ice. If I don't take care of this, get help, then I don't know—"

"Cooper," she whispers my name. Pain wells in her hazels.

"Don't pity me, Dave. Agree to this. We can help each other."

"Okay."

"Okay."

"Now, leave." She shoves at my shoulder. I stand, but not before tugging on a curl like I used to do as a kid. "I don't need anyone to think any monkey business is going on back here. This deal between us doesn't change anything. I still hate you."

"We'll see about that," I toss over my shoulder, walking out of her bedroom and returning to our friends. "Tomorrow."

SEVEN

SUTTON

HE'S LATE.

I knew this was some sort of joke to Cooper. Yet, for whatever reason, I decided to believe him. Give him a wide-open shot at redemption. I took away every defenseman and goalie in his way, and he still missed.

I never should have let my life fall into the palm of his hands. My heart used to be there, but I retrieved it years ago, only after he shattered it. There are a few bruises on it, a few indentations from where his fingers held it tightly.

I wonder what those fingers would feel like on my body. Where he'd leave bruises if he...*focus, Sutton*.

Cooper Carmichael has always been attractive. Even as a kid when he hadn't grown into his body. His limbs long and gangly, muscles pre-developed and softer. Or when he decided he had to have frosted tips, the bleached blond quickly fading to a rusty orange.

He was my first crush, which I chalk up now to being because of how nice he was to me. Besides Meave, no one asked me to play or wanted to be my friend. Being Cooper's friend was like being picked first for recess kickball every single second.

In middle school it crossed my mind what it might be like to hold his hand.

In high school it crossed my mind what it might be like to kiss him.

In college, apparently, I think about what it would be like to do a whole lot more with him. This isn't the first time it's crossed my mind or my dreams.

Because behind my dislike of him, every way that he makes me furious, how he hurt me, or ruined my future, there's still the six-year-old girl stretching out her hand to the boy with sparkling brown eyes and a friendly smile.

Too bad time machines don't exist.

I reach for the notebooks I laid out, strewn across the table with sticky notes and highlighted notes circled three times. I pack up my belongings. Shove them into my tote bag and stand from the wooden table in the library study room we had agreed to meet in.

I tap on my phone to check our texts. Yup, says two. It's now half an hour past that.

Instead of walking home, I take a left out of the building with a gut feeling. Pass between more brick academic buildings and the conservatory before I need to cross the street.

My foot taps mindlessly as I wait for the light to change. I click the button to cross the street again.

"*Wait!*" it shouts out to me. The robotic voice boils my blood. A taunt. A reminder.

I've been waiting. Years worth of waiting, and instead of apologizing, he dug a deeper grave. Chasing me around like a pawn on a chess board. Chased me here.

I was so excited about my signing day. I was the first female hockey player from our high school to be recruited to play Division I. I knew Cooper was being recruited, even someone living under a rock would know. He's the best.

Mom and Dad hadn't told me which school he chose. Probably because I was lucky enough that Lakeland even wanted me still. My scholarship and place on the team contingent on my recovery after colliding with another player in a game last season —I should have seen her coming, been smarter about maneuvering around her or passing off the puck, but I was distracted. All I could focus on was what Cooper did, our fight earlier that day.

A silent growl works its way through me as I think back.

I fixed my hair three times. Re-rolled the sleeves of my shirt to the perfect cuff. Made sure none of the patches Meave helped me iron on a pair of overalls were loose..

Walking into the auditorium where my high school hosted signings, my assigned table was set for two. I sat down, confused. Five minutes later Cooper walked in through the same door, a Lakeland hockey sweatshirt on and his brown hair tucked into a backwards hat.

"You did this on purpose," I whisper-growled when he sat down to my right.

Cooper leaned into me, turning his head so that only I could hear him. "The school had everything I wanted."

"A spot for a short hockey player?"

Cooper laughed. There was a melancholy to it that now that I think about it, isn't there anymore. *"Exactly," he said.*

"You can't just let me go, can you?"

"No, I can't."

"You don't know me. I don't know you. As soon as we get there, you get that?"

"Whatever you say, Dave."

"Stop calling me that."

"What should I call you then?" He paused, inched closer. "Mine?"

I burst out laughing. Snorted and slapped a hand over my mouth. "No."

Memories of us—good, bad, my favorites, come and go as if they are waves on a beach. Calm one minute, violent the next. If I'm not careful I can get pulled into a riptide of them.

I stomp across the street on a mission, when I'm outside the rink I see Cooper's car.

I suppose sometimes you can trust your gut.

Someone from the coaching team is leaving.

"Wait! I need in the rink." I rush forward, my knee stings at the sudden sprint and lingering memory. They hold the door open for me. I give them a smile and say, "Thank you so much! I forgot my student ID and am meeting one of the players for a project. We're running behind."

They give me a thumbs up when I notice their headphones in and phone open on a call.

"Sorry," I mumble with an apologetic shoulder shrug.

Taking in a slow inhale of chilled air, the smell of stale popcorn from a game days ago and chemicals from the coolant, my lungs fill with longing.

It happens anytime I think about lacing up a pair of skates again, braiding back my hair and slipping on my helmet, or the roar of a crowd. The burning desire to be the best, to win. I haven't skated since reinjuring my knee and making the decision to stop playing. There's always a part of me, the same one that wonders about my birth parents, about what my life would be like if I was still playing.

And I would be if it weren't for the boy I find skating, pushing a puck through a series of orange cones.

"No surprise finding you here." My tone harsh, unaware to its implications.

He cuts, skating over to me and stopping abruptly. A shower of ice trimmings hit me.

"Hey." Cooper smiles brightly.

"Don't 'hey' me. I waited thirty minutes for you."

His face falls with realization. Chest heaving as he slips off a glove, dropping it to the ice. He twists a wrist to look at the time. Something rattles in his sleeve, another bracelet of sorts, but I can't see it through his sweatshirt sleeve.

"Fuck," he curses under his breath.

I sigh, shaking my head. "Unbelievable. No, you are believable. Predictable. This was a mistake, again. Fool me twice, shame on me."

"Okay, okay, okay. I'm sorry." He throws his hands out.

"Your apologies mean nothing to me. There's never any action behind them." I stand tall, shoulders back and gaze into his brown eyes.

There was one time when I was nine that I thought they were the most beautiful eyes in the world. Wanted to look at them for the rest of my life. What a foolish girl I was, overrun with preteen hormones. Easily swayed into an unrealistic fantasy.

Cooper peers down at me.

He's taller in his skates. I quickly give him a once-over when I realize he is still in his pads from practice. Practice jersey removed, he's wearing a team issued sweatshirt. Our school logo in the center of the navy fabric with Bears Hockey sandwiching it.

"Didn't practice end almost two hours ago?"

Cooper lifts a hand, squeezing the back of his neck. He takes a slow inhale.

"Why do you need two more hours of practice?" I ask, my tone becoming solid.

"I have to be good enough," he chokes out.

"For what?"

My brain is trying to figure out if it's supposed to be in friend or psychologist mode.

"I have to be better than him," Cooper modifies his statement. It still means the same thing.

"Him? As in your dad?"

His Adam's apple bobs. The skin taut over each swallow. "Yes."

"Does he tell you that?" Cooper shakes his head no. "Does Coach tell you that?" He shakes his head again, but it's more disjointed. "Who?"

"Does it matter who? If not them, someone will. There's no

room for error out here." He swings a hand back, gesturing to the ice. "No room to not be perfect. We're already halfway through the season and I'm nowhere near being on track to hitting his stats for junior year." He keeps going, rambles increasing in speed, decreasing in volume.

"That's okay."

"It's not, Dave. It's not okay." He starts stuttering over the same word. And then it happens.

He's spiraling. And quickly.

One moment his body is upright, the next he's slumped against the boards.

"Cooper," I shout, terrified. Pushing through the door to the ice, I move in front of him and drop to my haunches, leveling myself to his eyesight. "Cooper," I say again, calmer despite the panic raging through me. "Are you okay? Let me call one of your roommates or Coach."

"N-n-no." He's sweating. A lot. He was already sweaty when he skated over to me, unbuckling his helmet and removing it. Brown hair flattened. This new layer is glistening across his brow, between waves stuck to his olive undertone skin. "I don't want them to see me like this. I never wanted you to see me like this."

Leaning into his space, I want to make sure he can hear me. If his panic attack, which this clearly is, is anything like the ones I've experienced, then his ears are ringing and sound is muffled as if he's underwater.

"I always see you, Cooper Carmichael. Even when you don't want me to. Even when I don't want me to."

His eyes pinch shut. Lines creasing at the corners.

"Sutton. Why am I like this? Why does this happen?"

Cooper starts to shake his right hand, trying to free it from his glove. I reach out but pause. "Can I help you?" I ask gently, seeking his permission.

"Please." The break in his voice is cutting me wide open. If anyone was around, they'd see the hurt he's caused, sure, but they'd also see how my ribcage grew around the pieces of him I've kept. All the years of friendship and growing up together we did. They'd see how parts of me are only holding on by strings he used to sew me together.

I undo his glove. Slip it off his hand and set it on the ice. Immediately he palms his chest, right over his heart.

"Slow down," he tries to tell it.

"We should get you off the ice," I advise. "You need to—"

"I can't move," he cuts in. "Can you sit? Can you stay with me?"

Exhaling, I sit down next to him.

Great choice in outfits this morning. The floral skirt I'm wearing bunches around my waist, exposing my thick thighs that thankfully I decided to cover with tights. Unfortunately, they do nothing to stop the cold seeping in through them, chilling my skin.

It's not warm enough yet for me to be shaving frequently. Short, light-auburn hairs stick through the black tights.

But none of that matters. I whisk the thoughts away and focus on Cooper.

How long has this been going on? Does he get them often? Do they happen whenever he's on the ice by himself?

That question terrifies me. I open my mouth to ask, but from the corner of my eyes I see him taking staggered breaths, eyes still sealed shut.

I try not to imagine him out here alone or going through any of this alone. He said he didn't want anyone to see or even know he's the student I'm working with.

After quitting—I like to say I retired—I was ashamed of myself. Ashamed of how my body was failing me, how my mind was failing me and allowing negative thoughts to become my beliefs about myself. I hid away until my family—mainly Meave— encouraged me to go to therapy.

Meave had been volunteering with kids, mainly those with autism or down syndrome and using art as a form of therapy. She told me therapy can come in all shapes and sizes and there's nothing to be ashamed of from seeking it out.

"You're already in therapy to heal your knee. Why avoid healing here?" she asked, tapping my temple.

I asked her to come with me to my first appointment. Meave held my hand as I recounted what happened. Squeezed it when I explained how I had been feeling since. It was nice to not be alone in what I was going through.

I watch Cooper and I don't want him to be alone in this.

There's a breath of relief that fills me when I remember he confessed that he wants this for himself, that this isn't him helping me but the other way around. It might not be the complete therapy he needs, but maybe this is his way of asking to not be alone.

I reach out my hand to him. "Here."

There's a moment of disbelief. I see it crash over him and the fight he's internally battling. Eyes fluttering open, wider each time till brown eyes rimmed in red look deep into mine.

He grips my hand like it's a floatation device, like I could save him.

Then interlaces his fingers with mine.

I don't scoot closer to him. Giving him space and waiting for his direction with this. But I do place our hands in my lap, rub my thumb over his knuckles.

"Breathe," I coach. "In and out." I repeat this several times. "Breathe. In and out." Watching as his breathing slows, and he starts to come down from the rollercoaster that panic attacks can be.

I readjust my legs, uncrossing and recrossing them.

"Don't leave me," he mumbles. "Not yet."

"I won't."

His hair is long enough that a loose strand is stuck to the center of his forehead. I lift my hand, gently pushing it back, and run my hand down his face.

Cooper stops me, cupping my hand. Holding it against his face.

"I hate this. I hate all of it. You'll he-help me, please."

"I'll help you, Coop."

EIGHT

COOPER

THE BELL above the door to The Mean Bean, everyone's favorite coffee shop in downtown Bensen, chimes as I open it. There's a group of three girls balancing to-go cups, books, and their phones in their hands not paying attention. I keep the door open for them, assuming they'd run into it otherwise.

It's busy, no surprise. Most of the tables are taken, couples sitting in each other's laps on the mismatched couches. I scan the place, searching for deep auburn curls.

My gaze sweeps over people I recognize, and some I should but don't. I flash my golden smile at them either way, increasing it when two girls studying in the large bay window wave at me—I went out to dinner and hooked up with the brunette once freshman year.

I check in the back and amongst the hidden nooks for Sutton, ensuring my smile stays plastered to my face. I'm the confident, golden hockey captain they expect me to be. By the time I conclude she isn't here yet, I'm exhausted.

Making a final sweep of the place, I find a wooden table near the back with a chipped checkerboard painted on it. Slightly secluded, tucked partially behind a large bookshelf that has books and games you can borrow.

I drop my backpack into one of the chairs and tuck my hockey duffle behind the table. We agreed to meet this morning between my morning skate and classes. I walked here after practice, preferring to park at the rink. Made it in record time.

Did I think I'd beat here her? No.

Is there a part of me that's delighted, and possibly wants to brag, that I beat her? Absolutely.

I could use the spare minutes. My upper-level math classes are kicking my ass. We've barely made a dent into the semester, and I'm already reminded why most athletes choose to go the route of communications, or something not as time consuming or daunting.

But college has always been important to me. Not just playing, my education, too—even more so when Sutton's plans were flipped upside down because of her injury.

I thought she'd recover. If anyone has the grit and ambition to come back from multiple complex tears and a blade to the upper thigh, it's her. The amount of emotion she pours into everything she does is contagious. Admirable. Even when it's hating me.

And she did recover...or so everyone thought.

Sutton already blamed me for what happened in high school. Claimed that if we hadn't gotten into a fight before her game—not like the bickering matches we get into now. A friendship-ending, relationship-altering fight—she wouldn't have played distracted.

Almost two years later, wearing number twenty, she skated out onto the ice for her debut as a Lakeland Bear. I was in the stands with the rest of the men's team and watched with a strange combination of wonderment and fear. I almost broke one of the plastic charms of my bracelet, white knuckled as she received a pass.

Maybe we could be friends again.

Maybe she'll overcompensate, favor her right leg.

Maybe she'll score. Show everyone the damn good player she is.

Maybe...maybe this is...

Sutton was hooked by a defenseman, then tripped. All the air in the arena went stale. My lungs were as dry as the Sahara. She stood up, and at first glance, appeared fine. Skated back to the bench. Seated, she took her helmet off, and that's when I saw it. Sucking in air, tight jaw, and every other blink, there was horror in her eyes.

A week later, Elliot asked me to bring something by their dorm. I don't remember what, the memory confiscated by Sutton opening the door, phone pressed to her ear. Hazel eyes rimmed in red, and the collar of her green striped shirt damp. She snatched whatever was in my hand, slamming the door closed. Through thick walls and thick doors, I heard her conversation with her sister. I knocked again. She didn't answer. Slumping onto the floor, I sat there, devastated, as she told Meave her doctor suggested she stop playing.

I fell backward, Sutton almost trampling me when her door finally opened again.

Sutton groaned, staring down at me. "You didn't need to wait around to gloat. Hockey's yours."

It never has been just mine. Never will be, but I don't think she realizes that.

I fiddle with the plastic skate charm on the bracelet tucked underneath my long sleeve. Turning it over and over as I make my way back to the counter to order.

Five minutes till our scheduled meeting time, I second guess myself. I shouldn't have ordered her a drink. What if she doesn't drink chai tea anymore? What if she drinks black coffee or doesn't do any caffeine at all?

I push up on the table and almost tip our drinks over. My hands grip the edge of the table to stabilize it. I can feel eyes on me, and when I turn around, several are staring at me—at my slightly panicked state. I force a weak, closed-mouth smile.

Get it together Carmichael.

Sutton likes sweet treats. Always has. Sutton has never been able to say no to candy at the movie theater or a milkshake from the drive-thru. But it has to be chocolate, she refuses anything else.

I scan the case of baked goods, because if she doesn't want the coffee this will make up for it. Right?

My stomach growls.

Okay, sue me. I have a sweet tooth too. Girls aren't the only ones who can do a hot walk to grab coffee and a sweet treat—that was Jaxon and I's Friday afternoons over the summer and fall.

The blueberry scone is calling my name. I order one of those and a chocolate birthday cake donut. Now I'm the one awkwardly balancing an armful of items to our table, trying not to drop the goods.

"You're early," she greets, brows scrunched in surprise, fifteen minutes later.

I cough and drag my attention away from the cluster of blueberries on top of my scone to her. "Came straight here after practice."

"Sorry I'm late." She's a minute late.

"You have nothing to apologize for. Honestly, if you didn't show up, I wouldn't have been surprised." I let out a singular ha.

"I told you we're doing this." Sutton shrugs her canvas tote bag off her shoulder, letting it hang off the side of her chair. She doesn't respond as she pulls out her laptop, a folder, and two pens.

"I'm sorry." I nudge the thrifted mug toward her. "About the other day," I clarify, but not entirely. The apology isn't for missing our session, but for my panic attack. I didn't mean to have one, or make her stay with me during it.

She held my hand, talking to me, brushing my hair and sweat away till it passed. Didn't question, or judge, me when I admitted to hating the feeling even though I could tell she wanted to. Sutton helped me stand up and skate to the door for the locker room. Told me she'd wait till I showered and changed to drive me home.

"Please don't apologize about that." I open my mouth to speak, but Sutton shakes her head. "It's nothing to be ashamed of."

I temporarily change the subject, stalling us from diving into the storm that is my head right now. "You still drink dirty chai lattes with oat milk, right?"

She takes it, gently. Her fingers curl around the handle. Bright purple nails with a metallic finish stand out against the faded pastels.

"Sorry if it's cold. I ordered when I got here," I add in, a foreign, nervous anticipation taking over my tone.

Sutton brings the cup to her mouth. Takes a sip, then another. She sets it back down in front of her, and I'm holding my breath. Foam clings to the corner of her mouth. The tip of her tongue sneaks out, licking it away.

"You remember?"

"Never forget." I have to swallow discreetly, my words staccato, then remind myself not to be jealous of foam.

Something flashes through her eyes.

She opens her mouth to say something, licks her lips, again. Then shuts it, turning to grab the folder and rifles through it.

"We should get started. I only have an hour."

Sutton hands me a stapled packet. She walks me through the overview of what we will be doing. Explains that each of our 'sessions' together will look different. Some will be evaluations, some might be working through an activity. She wants to go at my pace and mold this to work for me, which I appreciate. I ask a few questions, she answers; everything is going smoothly.

"I don't want people knowing that we are working together," I work up the courage to tell her.

"Yeah, caught that vibe when you ran out on me. Why? Am I some sort of dirty secret?"

I swallow. "Not you..."

"Part of my job is confidentiality. It's none of my business to tell anyone about what you are going through. I'm only subjected to tell someone if you ever want to hurt yourself." There's a tremor in her hand and she looks at me in my eyes. "You aren't thinking that, right?"

"No. I promise."

"Okay." Our gazes hold and we inhale in sync. Sutton reaches out for the donut at the same time I do and our fingertips graze. "My paper and the evaluation will all be anonymous. Okay?"

"Thank you."

She flips around a paper that looks like a test. "This is our pre-evaluation. This will help me gauge where we are at now. You'll do it at the start of each month to track progress."

I skim the questions. "Are you going to ask me *how does that make you feel*?" I joke. Sort of.

"No. Not necessarily."

"But you will?"

"Take the evaluation."

We fall into a foreign yet comfortable silence. I read and answer a question, circle the number correlated, and peek up at Sutton between each one.

She's either scribbling onto a paper or chewing on the end of her pen. The cap mutilated with teeth marks. Her mom does the same thing.

"Done." I slide the paper over to her side of the table.

"And how did that make you feel?" Sutton jokes, bright eyes peering up through her lashes. A hint of a curl upward to her glossy lips, probably cherry flavored.

My shoulders shake with a laugh, and she matches it with her own.

Truthfully, I don't know how I feel about this. Eager? Nervous? Ansty? Hopeful?

"I need to get to class, but I'll look over this and then we can coordinate a time to meet next. You are away this weekend for games, right?"

"Yeah."

"Then next week?"

"Sure. Can I walk you to class?"

She shakes her head, curls catch on the strap of her tote. "I think I can manage."

A few paces away, everyone sees me chase after her. "And what about tonight for *your* first lesson?"

"Oh. Yeah, sure. I kind of forgot about that."

"No you didn't. I'll pick you up, I have an idea."

NINE

SUTTON

IF COOPER WASN'T ALREADY the bane of my existence, it would be dating.

Truthfully, I don't understand how to date.

It's not rocket science, but why does it feel impossible to master? It shouldn't be this complicated.

I thought being with someone would be natural. And before anyone wants to throw unsolicited advice, yes, I know relationships take work. And yes, I understand I'm in college and have years ahead of me, but it shouldn't be this strenuous of an effort for attention...or affection.

It should be neck kisses, hands in my hair, and aimless drives. Counting freckles, memorizing your coffee order, and bumping elbows when you brush your teeth. Nothing and everything simultaneously.

Maybe I'm wrong. Maybe I'm searching or expecting too much. Probably so, if my track record proves anything. Maybe it's the love that I grew up around, so I know it exists. Maybe it just doesn't exist for me. Maybe it's boys because let's be real, it's not like they make it any easier.

But apparently Cooper can.

My stomach flips as if it's a coin. One side embossed with nerves, the other an anticipation sort of excitement like you're going up the first hill of a rollercoaster.

When I agreed to this, I was wearing blinders. I didn't think this through and now all of those thoughts and questions compound on me.

You want a relationship, not hook ups. How exactly do you teach someone to date? How is he going to teach me to date?

Cooper doesn't date. I mean he does date, as in goes on a singular date. Probably a way to wine and dine a girl before sleeping with them. I've never seen or heard of him dating.

Not that I care what he does...

I don't.

"Are you sure about this?" Elliot asks quietly, leaning into me.

I roped her into coming with me tonight. She loves the idea that Cooper is helping me become more confident with dating. "Definitely can't miss this," she said while slipping into a pair of skintight jeans.

He's walking ahead of us. A dark pair of jeans hugging his legs, a gray Henley with the sleeves pushed up, and a backwards Bears hat.

"Nope. But I'm going to do it anyway. I mean, what's the worst thing that could happen?"

"I like that attitude." She loops an arm around my shoulders.

We find the rest of our friends standing on the far side of The Tipsy Bear. I knew they'd be here; Cooper mentioned they would be in the car. It is packed, and I'm starting to second-guess myself. When Cooper asked about speed dating, I didn't expect this.

The entire back half of the bar is roped off. Against the wall is one large booth. A series of two-person tables are sandwiched between chairs. The booth side is filled with some recognizable faces, but a handful I don't know.

"These seats are taken," I hear Jaxon's voice carry across the place.

A couple moves to the next table.

"Yeah, those too. This whole section is, but I can help you find a table somewhere else." He leaves his post, guiding them to a cluster of tables by the air hockey table.

Cooper says hey to everyone while Elliot and I settle up behind them. Two hands curl around my shoulders, squeezing twice. I glance up and see Jaxon has returned.

"You excited?" He's beaming, energy bouncing off him.

"Not anymore."

"Ah, come on, Soot." Jaxon calls me Soot because my hair reminds him of a fire. "This is going to be great."

Seeing more people pour into the space, I whirl to face Cooper. "Remind me again why you thought this was a good idea?"

"Your pre-eval had me thinking. You need one too. I need to know what I'm working with."

"And my terrible encounter at the grocery store wasn't enough?"

"No. Here, you'll be able to date multiple guys in the span of—"

"I know what speed dating is," I growl, annoyance tickling up my spine.

"I've already assumed we are going to need to work on being comfortable with small talk."

"These are my friends." I gesture to the people in a half circle around us. "I'm comfortable with them."

"But you don't know them." He mimics my awkward hand wave, pointing to frat boys and other guys from Lakeland. He must read my face because he follows up with, "Yes, Dave. Small talk. You are, and I say this kindly, terrible at it. Especially with people you don't know."

It's not that I don't like small talk in general. Sure, with the male population, it makes me more nervous, and I end up forgetting how to form sentences or how to pronounce basic words, or in the worst cases, start rambling off unnecessary facts. I prefer deeper conversations with meaning.

You can tell me your favorite color, but I also want to know why.

I love getting to know people, remembering tidbits about them, and making them feel seen. The stretch of years in the foster home, all I craved was someone to see me. No one deserves to be invisible.

"Fine." I blow out a hot breath. "Let's get this over with."

———

THE FIRST FEW rounds are easy. Chase, Dawson, and Jaxon all hyping me up. My fourth speed date is Beck.

"How'd you get roped into this?"

His jaw twitches. "Cooper owes me a night of babysitting."

I ask him another question, but he doesn't answer. Sips on his beer and broods. We sit there in silence for the next three minutes.

He flexes his hand against the glass when his phone buzzes, but Beckett doesn't reach for it. There's another notification, and this one, I swear, has a rare smile peeking through. Maybe if I close one eye and squint the other, I'd see a true Beckett St. James smile.

"You can answer that," I encourage.

His light blue eyes snatch on mine. That sliver must have been a figment of my imagination with how tightly his lips are pressed together.

"Or not," I quickly modify my answer. "Is that a new tattoo?" He pushes up the sleeves of his sweater, and on his forearm is a large drawing. It looks like a child drew it.

Beckett is covered in tattoos. I've seen a few, mainly on his arms and the one on his thigh, but apparently his entire torso and back are covered too.

"Madeline drew it." That's his little sister.

"That's sweet. Does she want to be an artist? Next time Meave comes to town, she could—"

I'm interrupted by a loud commotion and laughing coming from the other end of the line of tables. I glance over to find Elliot with her head thrown back, laughing with a student I don't recognize. Maybe he's a freshman?

The buzzer goes off. Another hockey player sits across from me—he must be how Cooper found out about this. Apparently, two of them were talking about signing up at practice.

He's cute. Really cute. Softer features, his face isn't cut like glass as most of the team. Buzzed blond hair and dark forest green eyes. There's a smattering of freckles on his left cheek and a birthmark next to his right eye.

"I'm Seb Horváthski," he introduces himself with a heavy Swedish accent.

I stare at him. All the comfort I had with my friends evaporates. I wouldn't call this intimidation, but suddenly I don't know what to say...or even my name.

A strong hand cups my shoulder. Then I feel him kneel beside me, his next exhale tickling the shell of my ear. "This is where you tell him your name," Cooper whispers, voice dipped in honey. Sweet and coaxing, worming it's way through me.

"I'm Sutton."

Seb smiles. It's crooked and charming.

Cooper is back in my ear, giving me pointers and coaching me through the seven minutes. Our conversation is clunky and awkward, but I don't think Seb cares.

Three more rounds go this way before Cooper pulls me away from the group. We find a table in the adjacent corner.

Crossing my arms in front of me on the table, I bury my head between them. A groan slips out of me. "Ughh."

The chair across from me is pulled out and turned around so that the back is pressed against the table. Cooper slides into the seat, resting his crossed arms along the top.

"So—"

"So that was terrible."

"You had your moments."

I perk up, barely able to glower at him through my lashes. "And by moments, you mean when you had to remind me of my name or when someone asked me my favorite color and I told them how white is technically not a color, or went on a rant about how rude it is for people to believe that Cleopatra was Egyptian. She wasn't, by the way; she was of Macedonian Greek descent."

He snickers, tongue running along the bottom of his teeth. "God, you're something else." Cooper doesn't say it negatively, but more...amusing, affectionate.

"You're going to fix me, right?" I ask into my arms, head buried again.

A hand snakes between my elbows, tapping my chin. I move it up, barely. Cooper takes my chin in his hand, encouraging me to sit up straighter. Taller. His touch transferring confidence into me.

We are interrupted before he can answer.

"That was so much fun! I got four numbers and have a date tomorrow night," Elliot says, diving into the booth next to me. Cooper drops my chin, and I lean back into the seat just in time for an arm to be thrown over my shoulders.

At least someone got something good out of this.

Tonight cemented what I already knew: I am completely out of my league with Zach. How am I supposed to have full-fledged conversations with him when I can barely even talk to guys who I'm not interested in?

You'd think as someone who is studying the brain, I'd be better at understanding my own. Put these guys in a class or make them my lab partner, and I'd be perfectly fine. Conversation would flow naturally—I'd even initiate it, then never want to stop, finding every detail about them.

I like people. I like talking.

I like to think of myself as an extrovert. Bubbly, outgoing, and overall a confident person.

But put me in a romantic type of scenario, and I become a deer in headlights. A baby deer in general. Barely able to stand on my own, wobbling with each step I attempt.

Why am I like this? I ask myself, tuning out the conversation happening around me. I can feel my heart sigh.

My parents are high school sweethearts. They never split. Not during college or Dad's first few years in the league while Mom was finishing up school. They've overcome everything life has thrown at them—unexpected loss, cross-country moves, infertility.

Never once has their love wavered.

Having a front row seat to it was one of my favorite parts of my childhood.

I don't remember my real parents, and I'll never know if they loved each other, or the dynamic of their relationship.

But what I do know, what I do have, is my parents' love. Mrs. and Mr. Carmichael's, too.

They make it seem easy. Sure, I know they probably fight— I've heard disagreements, watched them make mistakes, they aren't immune to that. What they do so well is choosing each other every day.

Dad once told Meave and me that love is as much an action as it is a feeling.

Meave at least had found someone long term.

So why is it so hard for me? What am I doing wrong?

I guess that's what I'm looking for. Someone to choose me every day.

My back falls deeper into the booth behind me, listening to Elliot talk. I'm straddled between my thoughts and the present moment. And if I had a third leg, it would be in the past.

Dawson and Jaxon join us at the table.

Taking the final sip of my drink, I push the glass covered in condensation to the center of the table, excusing myself to the bathroom.

Cooper's leaning across from the women's restroom when I

exit into the dark hallway. No one else is back here; both bathroom locks say vacant.

I take a small step forward, into the only space between us after he pushed off the wall, only to stumble backward into the door. Cooper catches my head in the cradle of his hand before it hits the door.

Ensuring I'm steady, he pulls his hand away, taking hold of my chin again. The touch more urgent than it was earlier at the table.

A desperation in his flaring pupils. Moonlight pours in from the window in the exit door to the left of me. Paints him golden.

"There is nothing to fix about you because nothing is broken. Just because you aren't good at this"—he waves his free hand around—"doesn't mean there's something wrong with you. *Please*, don't think there's something wrong with you." The way he says please is as if he's begging. I try to fight staring at him, but his touch and words are a lasso around me. I fail to look anywhere other than in his eyes. "Can you do that for me?"

Clunky and tight, I nod.

"No, Dave. I'm a words kind of guy. I need to hear you."

"I'll try." Yes would have been a lie. So would no.

Those two words must be enough; his mouth softens. "Good girl." And those two words have they non-existent gap between my thighs closing in. Hopefully, he doesn't sense the way my legs press together. I'll add this to list of reasons to hate him.

"Plus, this is practice. All that matters is game time."

"Practice," I say, annoyed, and definitely not with any ounce of appreciation. Butterflies in my stomach try to escape at the loose smile painted on him, but I keep the net over them tight.

"Repeat it back to me. What did we just learn?" He's still holding my chin, his face closer to mine. The buzzing around us irrelevant, we are completely isolated in a bubble.

"Practice makes perfect."

"And?" His hold, his stare, they burn into me. Tug at something that's been long forgotten...on purpose.

"I'm not broken." Cooper doesn't realize how badly I needed that reminder. "There's nothing wrong with me."

"And you're wanted." His thumb swipes up my cheek, pushing a loose curl behind my ear. Eyes drop to my mouth, and for a minute, I think he might do something stupid like kiss me. Stupidly, I'd probably let him. For practice...of course.

Cooper finds my eyes again. He stares at me for a beat. I blink and he's heading out the back door. I want to chase after him. Say it back. Tell him that he isn't broken either.

TEN

SUTTON

I SHOVE an arm into my sweater, exchanging my bag from one shoulder to the other, to pull the extra layer of warmth over my head. Days have passed since the speed dating, and finally it's the training rink chills my body. There's been an underlying warmth consuming me, a fire stoked by my brain failing me and replaying Cooper in the bathroom hallway.

It's been easy to ignore him, it's one of my best skills, except being paired up for my independent study. Which is the only reason I'm at his practice.

The Pond is Lakeland's training rink for the ice hockey and figure skating teams. It's located in the same building as the main arena, on the far side of the entrance and main concourse. Team locker rooms are between the two with hallways and entrances that lead to each.

I climb the metal bleachers opposite the players' bench. There are only seven rows, but I select a seat in the top row where the lights are dimmer. Hopefully Cooper or anyone from the team doesn't notice me.

Their practices are closed. Exceptions are made for scouts from the NHL, and today me. I stopped by Coach Mathieson's office on Monday, asking him about practice and game schedules, evaluating any rules Lakeland enforces about overtraining and student-athlete balance. At his openness, and rather heightened interest in my study, I threw out the ability to sit in on a practice or two. He granted me access to anything I wanted.

I tug a beanie down over my ears a little further, slip the pen out from behind my ear. Call me old school, but I love taking notes by hand. My laptop is tucked in my tote bag just in case of hand cramps or smudges—perks of being left-handed—or if I need the gloves I last minute stuffed in my bag.

A shiver rakes through me, and I swear I can see my breathe.

Memories surround me, a blanket to the cold. It's been two years since I've set foot in this building—at least before the other week. But it's been even longer since I've watched him play live.

Cooper's talented. Raw and natural, you can tell it's in his DNA.

There's always been late nights and extra hours spent on his game because he loved it. Practicing in the street in rollerblades when it was warm, and out on the pond in his backyard as soon as it was safe enough to skate on.

Nothing changed when I started playing, except instead of me sitting on the sidelines watching him, I was out there skating with him. We wanted to be the best. We wanted each other to be the best.

The player I'm watching on the ice isn't him though. Of course he's still one of the best out there, anyone could see that. But knowing Cooper how I know him, much to my chagrin, you can see the tiny hesitations in a face off, the faintest pinch in his shoulder blades, the frustration in himself if he's beat in a drill.

They finish practice after focusing on defensive power plays.

I have one note written on my page. Circled, underlined, and highlighted.

Does Cooper love hockey still?

That's my biggest question at the end of the two-hour practice. Thirty minutes in and I was questioning my belief in what, or who, he was playing for.

"Great practice, everyone. Hit the showers," Coach Mathieson's voice carries. "We have morning skate tomorrow followed by film review. Then be back at the arena at four ready to go. Greene, don't forget to show up in a suit or everyone is skating seven extra down and back next practice."

The freshman next to Jaxon nods frantically, completely terrified of his coach.

Coach Mathieson can be scary. His exterior is more German shepherd, but the inside is like a golden retriever. He's tough when he needs to be, but compassionate and a total softy most of the time. His heart is too big. These players, even the women's team, are his family.

He used to attend our practices when he could. Makes the guys attend our games if they weren't playing at the same time.

Cooper skates over to the bench first once they are dismissed, opening the door for everyone to file off the ice, knuckle-bumping their gloves as they head in. He rolls his shoulders back, inhales sharply, and as his first teammate reaches him, a forced smile is slapped on his face.

Once the area clears, I creep down the bleachers slowly.

I walk around the boards, dragging a finger over the lip. New paint, navy to match our school's colors.

There's a harsh, grating noise that has me turning over a shoulder. Cooper pops out of the entryway, unbuckling his helmet and setting it on the bench next to where he sits down.

Slowly he exhales a dragged-out breath, eyes shutting.

He repeats this a few more times before pulling up his practice jersey to wipe sweat and a lock of hair off his forehead. His brown hair is dark with sweat and wavy because it's overgrown.

"You could use a shower." I cross my arms in front of my chest. "You're stinking up the arena."

He doesn't laugh at my joke.

I open the side door leading into the team bench. Straddling the silver bench, I sit close enough to him that my shoe bumps his extended skate.

"What are you doing here?" he asks, eyes still closed, head tilted back.

"Coach said I could come."

He looks forward, eyes opening, and chews on his cheek.

"Do you miss it?" he asks, looking out over the scratched-up ice. Cooper drags in a lung full of air.

"Every single day," I say softly. "It was the biggest part of my life for a long time. I didn't know who I was going to be without it."

I stare at him, my resolve getting the better of me, crashing down. Spending time with Cooper lately has me questioning why I've been so mad at him all this time. The further I remove myself from the grudge I'm holding, I realize it seems petty and stupid.

But then I blink, and I can hear their laughs, the names I was called, how lonely I felt after he betrayed me. My game that night and crashing into the boards, being told I've done the impossible tearing my ACL, MCL, and meniscus.

"You figured it out though." He says it more like a question.

"Took some time...and therapy." I add that because I want him to know I had to ask for help too.

He takes a glove off, pausing before taking the other.

"Do you love it?" I ask him after another beat of silence.

This drags his attention from the ice to me.

The skylights in the roof let in enough sunlight that it helps offset the bright white of the overhead lights. A ray is hitting his brown eyes just right. They're bright and broken. Sparkling, but it's like the last few seconds of a sparkler before they burn out.

I scoot closer to him, still awaiting an answer.

"Yes," he whispers as if he doesn't want anyone to know the truth. He checks over his shoulders to make sure we are alone. "But not like I used to."

I stay quiet, seeing that there's more to this, hoping that it gives him the space to elaborate and get this off his chest.

"Playing's lost its magic touch. Going out there every day, I'm not playing for me which I hate. But if I do, it feels wrong, like I'm failing my dream or the player people expect me to be."

"And who's that?"

Cooper pulls at the Velcro on his glove, tongue running along his bottom teeth. "My dad. Perfect. Who even knows." He throws his head back. "Ask a different person on a different day and they'll tell you who I am."

"Who do you want to be?" His laugh is humorless, as if I'm joking but I'm not. I use his words from the other night with a slight modification. "There's nothing wrong with the player that you want to be."

Cooper stares at me. Deep brown eyes muddy, a fight in them to believe what I'm saying.

"When's the last time you skated for yourself?" I ask.

"Winter break freshman year of college."

He doesn't need to recall that afternoon, but it plays in my brain like a movie—it was one of the last times I played. It was shortly after that I tweaked my knee again and needed another surgery. Jordan and I were outside on the pond in their backyard messing around. She had just committed to Lakeland University. Cooper and our dads came outside, joining us on the ice. We played three-vs-two till our older sisters and moms came home from last-minute Christmas shopping.

They joined us. The nine of us switching on and off the ice, sipping on homemade hot chocolate till the sun set, painting the sky in an electric ombre. Pinks and oranges with a dark, moody purple.

It was easy that day, just like it is now, to forget about everything. Reverting to our old friendship. Bickering like an old married couple, and gifting smiles like it was a Christmas miracle.

"You didn't win," I remind him, "I blocked the shot."

Cooper shakes his head, mouth fighting a smile. "It hit the inside of the post and bounced out *after* hitting your stick."

"It did not."

"Whatever helps you sleep at night, Dave."

"What changed after that?" I bring us back to the present, carefully dancing on thin ice.

"After my game winning assist in the Frozen Four and receiving the Tim Taylor Award, people took more notice to me. I wasn't just Ryn Carmichael's son who had inherited his hockey genes. I became *'is Ryn Carmichael's son going to be better than him?'* and *'can Cooper Carmichael fill his father's skates?'* or *'Carmichael is fast, but is that good enough to land him a spot on a team or will his last name carry him again?'*"

I remember the goal. I remember when the reports and videos went viral. He'd already received attention when being recruited in high school, but this was different.

"Have you talked to your dad about this?"

"He'd be ashamed, or try to step in and say something. What am I then? The boy who needed his dad to handle his business for him? I'm handling it."

"And look where that's getting you." I scoot closer to him, leaving a sliver of safe and comfortable space between us. "The stress you are putting on yourself is causing your panic attacks."

"How do I stop stressing?" he asks me as if I have all the answers. To that specific question, I wish I did.

Hearing him speak about our first love cuts me deeper than it should. It was taken away from me unexpectedly, but he'll lose it all on his own. If he continues at this rate, Cooper will burn himself out.

"I don't have all the answers," I tell him truthfully and cautiously, "but I'm going to help you. Case study or not."

"That sounds awfully like something a friend would do."

"Don't push it." I tilt my head, brow arched playfully. "I'm doing this for our mutual love of the sport."

Or because deep down he is my friend. Shoved away in the back of the closet that you stick junk in, tell yourself you are going to organize but never get around to, and somehow ten years later it has accumulated enough stuff that if you open the door it'll cause an avalanche. That's where our friendship is. I didn't throw it away, only put it in a place I'd hopefully forget about it.

Except Cooper never let me forget about it, or him.

"For starters, I don't think you need extra ice time. Your schedule is already jam packed with classes for your major—and everything else you said yes to." Like me, my case study, and being my dating coach. "The extra what? One…"

He makes a thumbs up, motioning it upward for me to increase the number. *Is he serious? He can't be.*

"Two." Cooper doesn't do it again. "Three?"

"Depends on the day."

"When has that ever been healthy?" I scold him. "Maybe an hour, but Cooper, you have to cut back. Your body needs rest."

"Okay. Yeah, okay. I'll try. Coach is meeting me in thirty minutes to work on a few skills with me. I was going to skate around till then, maybe run some drills, but…" He pauses and his eyes dip to the ground, then back to me. "Would you want to skate with me till then?"

I gulp, tug at the top of my sweater. My PT hasn't cleared me to skate again yet, but I want to. Especially right now. The pull to get back on the ice has never been stronger. I feel stronger. Running, cycling, and staying consistent with the stretches and workouts she's given me has helped.

"No." His face immediately falls, and for the second time today Cooper Carmichael cuts me a little bit deeper. "I haven't been cleared yet," I quickly add, like it's helpful.

"Right, your knee."

I fiddle with a curl, tugging on the end and wrapping it around my finger. Swallow heavily. Cooper fidgets, jaw flexes, and if I didn't know better, he's wearing his remorse.

I spot Coach returning. "I'll see you Thursday. Seven, my place."

"It's a date."

"Not even close."

ELEVEN
SUTTON

I SWEAR I blink and it's Thursday. But that's college for you... sort of. College is this weird matrix where days are quick but the years go by within a flash of a camera. Pictures taped and pinned around my room are the only reminders of the memories collected over the past two and a half years. But these days are also long. Sunlight stretching and bleeding into the night, hourless and boundless, somehow letting me accomplish my to-do list and more.

Eighteen credit hours, my independent study on top of it. Classes in the mornings. Labs and case studies littering my evenings, appointments with my PT and therapist squeezed in between the cracks. Moments spent lying on the couch studying or procrastinating with Elliot, a rom-com or dramatic reality TV show lightly echoing in the background. Weekends or random intrusions from our friends, because the proximity of a college campus is unmatched, people that start as strangers quickly become your family.

Sometimes I don't ever want college to end. Lucky for me—I send up a wish to the universe, manifesting or whatever people call it—I'll get four to six more.

I think people take it for granted. The opportunity to attend. The chance to be on your own for the first time, even if it's disguised behind roommates and your parents sending you money for beer in a weekly card. The unknown destination and adventure to discover yourself.

Since I was first asked what I wanted to be when I grew up, I've thought about college. That picture became detailed when asked what school I wanted to play hockey for. It was almost as if I could reach out and grab it. And I almost did.

Everything had been falling into place...for the most part. I hadn't gotten an offer from my dream school, but my second choice—Lakeland University—was right there eager for me.

Freshman year checked one box after another. A roommate that became my best friend. A friend group that feels like a family, albeit Cooper. A major and coursework that is challenging but doable. A month in and already having a boyfriend I was head over heels for. And hockey. I might not have been starting as I hoped or my coach had anticipated, but all signs were pointing to a strong recovery and future.

But playing scared and favoring your good knee is easy for your opponents to spot. One trip, what wouldn't have been a bad for another player, forces your hand in deciding to retire your skates.

Things started to unravel again. It felt as if high school was repeating itself. My ex dumped me. The next day Elliot and I got into a massive fight—luckily it only lasted for a week and not years.

On top of that, my major felt pointless, and I was back to the questions that started it all: what do I want to be when I grow up? Who is Sutton Davis?

In the moment, those first two years, it was easy to be upset. I wanted to do everything in my power to reverse time, but now, retrospectively, that wasn't the college experience I was meant for.

This one...I can't pinpoint why, but it feels right.

After my last class, I opted to study in the library. Spent the entire two hours researching stress in correlation to athletes and burnout. I ended up printing off three articles for Cooper before heading back to my apartment to meet him.

Elliot texted me on my way home, asking to check our mail. The key to our mailbox doesn't work when I turn it. Staring at the black lockboxes with silver numbers, I laugh at myself. Lost in thought, I'm trying to unlock box number sixteen—my old hockey number—rather than our apartment number.

Two steps to the left, our mailbox is tucked into the corner. Unlocking the door, I tug out our stack of mail, smiling at the corner of a bright blue envelope sticking out. A key on a chain drops from the middle of the stack.

I guess neither of us have checked the mail in a few days.

The fallen key is for one of the package mailboxes. I locate the box, 3B, and pull out an unexpectedly heavy, medium-sized box.

Closing the mailboxes, I start to head upstairs. Cooper should be here soon...or now.

Over my shoulder, I hear him being buzzed in through the lobby doors by one of our neighbors. A senior education major who must have the sun embedded in her skin with the glow she continuously has. Her hair is the color of golden rays and eyes the color of the gulf.

I actively tune out their conversation, but it's hard to ignore her body language. The manicured hand she places on his bicep, how she bites on her bottom lip after giggling. When she walks past me, the cherry red tint to her cheeks is obviously not make up. There's a different pep to her step, almost a glide as if she's on cloud nine from one minor interaction with Cooper.

A dull ache starts with each heartbeat, and an urge to throw up works through me.

Am I...am I jealous of her? No. Impossible. I can't be. I don't get jealous, and I definitely don't get jealous over him.

"You can't help yourself, can you?" I bite out, reclasping the reigns of my emotions.

Cooper shrugs, walking over to me. "It doesn't take much to be a nice person."

"Flirt," I correct.

"That wasn't flirting."

I scoff, "Yeah, right."

He takes a step closer to me, presses his lips into a line, pushing them out slightly and I wonder how they'd feel pushed onto mine. *Get it together, Davis.*

"Trust me. You of all people, Dave, should know what my flirting looks like."

Is Cooper saying he flirts with me? If being a dick is flirting, then I may need to find a new dating tutor.

His gaze locks on mine, a deep depth of brown pulling me into them like a violent current.

There it is.

The chasm that separates us. The reminder that I'm standing on one side of a bridge waiting for him to waive the white flag, missing a part of me.

The hole that he used to fill isn't this flattened surface. It's jagged and when I try to patch it up, or fill it with someone else, I cut myself and I'm thrown right back to the reason why we are like this.

"She lives in the apartment directly below me." He looks confused, then stifles a laugh. "For later."

I turn to the stairs, heading for my apartment, my steps forceful, loud. He's right behind me, the extra step putting us at equal height.

"You're jealous." Cooper's smug voice is in my ear.

"Am not." My cheeks heat.

"You don't need to be. I have no plans to stop flirting with you." With that, Cooper sprints in front of me, taking the stairs three at a time.

"I win," he tells me when I reach the landing of my floor a second after him.

I brush past him, body feeling like it was electrocuted, turning the key and going into my apartment. His groan from where I purposely grind my shoulder into him is satisfying.

I drop the mail on the counter.

"Elliot. Package."

She bounces down the hallway, hair freshly washed and thrown up into a twisted towel, oversized shirt, and a green clay face mask cracking on her skin.

"Oh. Hi, Cooper. This is a pleasant surprise."

His brown eyes bounce from her to me. I give him a subtle shake of the head, silently telling him I still haven't told her. When I shrug my shoulders, I hope he understands I'm telling him it's up to him.

"I'm the student athlete working with Sutton." Cooper looks like he's holding his breath. Is he expecting Elliot to laugh? Question him? I've never seen him this nervous before.

"Cool." She shrugs it off casually, not asking any further questions. "Well, I'm going to my room. Let me know if you want to catch up on *Survivor* later."

"Yeah, I'll grab you after he leaves." Elliot flips through the mail before excusing herself, taking the package with her. I flatten my palms on the counter and take a deep inhale, now that it's just Cooper and me. "Do you want something to drink?"

"Water, but I can get it."

He does. Reaching into the correct cabinet on his first try, lifting a glass with cherries etched into it, and pulling the filtered pitcher out of the fridge. It's too comfortable for my liking.

Cooper pulls out a barstool and sits down, resting his elbows on the counter, his backpack in the chair next to him.

Refocused on the mail, I pull out the envelope that had me excited in the first place. It's my favorite piece of mail every week. Has been since I started college, he's never missed a week.

On the front in terrible handwriting is my name and address. The same little drawing of a lion on skates is in the right-hand corner.

The first time I ever went to the zoo was my seventh birthday.

Dad told me I had hair like a lion. I went as one for Halloween that year in a homemade costume to match Meave's tiger. Jordan was a black panther, Molly a cheetah, and Cooper was a jaguar, but all I wanted for my birthday was to see one in person.

Our zoo had lion cubs that year, and he arranged a special meet and greet with them. That same year I started to learn how to skate. Dad always joked about me being a lion on skates.

I know it's silly and honestly, kind of stupid, but that year was a pivotal year in my life, and it stuck.

I flip the card around, opening it without giving myself a paper cut. I read his card as a smile blooms on my face. Tucked inside is a folded twenty. For gas, or beer, or whatever. I pocket the money before putting the card back in the envelope and pinning it to the fridge with a magnet. After I'm done with Cooper, I'll add it to the box in my room.

"Is that from your dad?" he asks when I turn back around.

"How'd you know?"

"My dad writes me one too."

"Really?"

He laughs out a, "Yeah. Think they sit around and write us letters together?"

I can picture it. Our parents already spent a lot of time together, but now that they are empty nesters, it's probably obscene.

"While our moms drink wine and gossip? Probably." I walk to the living room, grabbing my laptop and the folder for tonight from the couch. This morning, I typed up questions to go through. I pull out the third barstool, two down from him. "I don't know why he sends me money. I told him to stop, but he refuses. Dad still fills Mom's tank up every Sunday like he did when we were growing up. He started doing it for Meave and me when we turned sixteen. I've convinced myself he still feels obligated to do that now."

I hate that Cooper is so comfortable in my place, but what I hate more is how I'm getting more comfortable in his presence.

The walls I erected, the ones meant to push him out, are being chipped away.

"He wants to take care of you. He's setting an example of how any guy should treat you."

"I've never thought of it like that." I purse my lips, think about all the other ways Dad has set the bar high. When I think about my parents and their relationship, it's always as a unit, not individually.

"That's what we'll work on tonight. After whatever you have planned, so you have what? An hour or so to think about what you are looking for in a boyfriend and how you want them to treat you."

"Okay." I open my folder and sift through the documents, finding the one I need. "Wait, your dad sends you a twenty too?"

"Learned from the best, I guess." He turns his chair and body to face me. "So, what's this?"

I start to explain to him everything I researched. The shifted and new plan for our study—I can't think of it as only mine anymore. We both have a lot riding on this. Cooper, maybe more.

Excited, tangents turn to word vomiting. Minutes pass by before I need to take a sip of water. I'm not positive that he understood a word I just spewed, but when I curiously peer over the lip of my glass at him he's staring at me with a vintage Cooper Carmichael smile. Eyes starry and attention engrossed as if he's hanging on to every word I say.

I set my glass down. "What?" I ask incredulously.

"Keep going." He smiles bigger, and flips the page to more of my notes.

———

MEAVE HAS her phone propped up against a plastic cup facing her. She's on her art stool, one leg balanced on the top, tucked into her butt. The other bouncing up and down.

Her chestnut brown hair is tied up into a messy bun with two paint brushes pinning it together. Baby hairs and loose strands stick out everywhere.

The biggest show of her career is coming up. Some fancy schmancy studio in the Chicago hired her as an art studio assistant when she graduated from Savannah College of Art and Design. They're starting a new up-and-coming series; and Meave is the first to be spotlighted.

She's been working on these newer pieces since October. Honestly, she's more together than I had anticipated when she answered my video call two hours ago.

"I still can't believe you applied to be on a dating show."

"That's what you don't believe? I can't believe they are wanting to do a casting interview." She laughs, dipping her brush in the water. Meave picks up a new, thinner brush. "When my friends and I all agreed to submit applications, I was the *last* one they thought would make it on. I didn't take the ninety second video seriously. I filmed it after a bottle of wine. When we get off the phone, remind me, and I'll send it to you."

I change my position on my bed. Unfolding my legs and rolling over to lie on my stomach.

"If they ask you to be on it, are you going to do it?"

Meave shrugs, dropping her head one way, then the other.

"Seriously?" I exhale. "Mom and Dad—"

"Would laugh. It's not like I'd fall in love with anyone, or that I'm ready to. Plus..." She pauses.

Besides wanting to check in on her show, I called my sister because three weeks ago she broke up with her long-term boyfriend. They'd been doing long distance since high school, and when she moved to Chicago after college she realized they weren't the same people they were at sixteen. Their break up was 'mutual', but Meave still cried for seventy-two hours straight, held up in the second bedroom of her industrial loft apartment that she uses as a studio.

Can't wait to see the art that came out of those days.

The tip of her tongue sneaks out the corner of her mouth. It's always done this when she's concentrating—homework, art, painting her nails, it never mattered. Meave leans into her easel, nose about to touch the canvas.

"If I did go on the show, it'd be for the wrong, I mean selfish, reasons. I'd gain all the followers just to yap about my art. They'd be highly disappointed to find out that I am in fact an old woman trapped in a twenty-four-year-olds body."

"You are not an old woman."

"Sure," she says humorously. "The two cats, an enthusiasm for needlepoint, carrying hard candies in my thrifted purse, playing Mahjong, volunteering at the community garden, and a bedtime that is occasionally before the sun sets. Nope, not an old woman."

"I think you're interesting." She does have a mature palette. I snort quietly. She gives me a placating smile. "But you are okay? You are doing better?"

"You sound like Mom." She turns to face the camera. "Yes, Sutton, I'm okay. Leland and I had lunch the other day. We are going to be friends."

"*Friends.*"

She swirls the paint brush in front of her, accidentally painting a lavender streak across the lens. "You have zero room to talk."

"Uh. How?"

"Cooper is helping you find a boyfriend."

Meave wipes the paint off with the sleeve of the flannel tied around her waist.

"That isn't the same. We never dated, and we aren't friends."

"Dating. Being infatuated with each other from the ages of six to sixteen. Tomato, to-mah-toe."

"Literally no, Meave."

She blows out a very older sister breath. "Whatever. How is your tutoring going?"

"Good." I think.

My sister picks up her phone, bringing it closer to her face as if she's trying to examine me through the screen. "Sutton Davis, are you blushing?"

I touch my cheeks. Warm and tingling like a bag of Pop Rocks.

Yes. "No. Sunburnt from a run this morning."

"It rained."

"Stop stalking me."

"Never. I'm your older sister and I have the right to do whatever I want."

"You aren't my sister. Kidding," I say when she drops her blue eyes, all cat-like. "Cooper is actually picking me up tonight for our next lesson."

My phone pings.

COOPER

I'll be there in twenty.

Is that enough time?

Should be.

"I've gotta go Meave. I need to get dressed, and I have zero clue what I'm going to wear," I groan and flash the camera down at my body—warm and wrapped in a fluffy robe.

"Wait. You'll never guess who I saw when I was home last weekend."

"Who?" I rummage through hangers, my I-hate-everything-in-my-closet mood not helping.

"Izzy and Dylan sharing a hot chocolate. And I mean *sharing*."

"Drinking out of the same mug would be rather impressive." The sarcasm leaks through the phone.

"He *kissed* whipped cream off her."

I pull out a polka-dot sweater dress and switch my phone to the other ear. "Thank you for letting me know."

"Seriously?"

"Meave, I've really gotta go. Cooper's on his way."

"Text me after, or I'm calling Cooper," she says in a rush as I hang up.

I take a slow inhale. My high school best friend and my ex-boyfriend dating, or whatever they're doing, isn't what bugs me. Probably should, but it's the reminder of more people who make dating and love seem easy.

TWELVE

COOPER

AFTER SPEED DATING—BESIDES being stuck in a loop of replaying how I almost kissed her, our lips mistakingly close, eyes pleading and speaking everything we (me) haven't been able to say —I decided maybe a practice date would be better. A way to ease her into light conversation, becoming comfortable with small touches. Sutton hated the idea at first, but finally came around to it.

This is not a real date.

This is not a real date.

Repeating the mantra does little to convince me. It might not be a real date to Sutton, but it is to me. I'm above average at faking it. But this, I can't.

Elliot lets me in. "She's in her room."

I snag a glass of water, exactly as I did on Thursday, then head down the hallway to her room.

"Elliot, can you come tell me if this outfit is okay?" Sutton's voice floats from her bedroom, a nervous tick to it that makes my heart skip a beat. Is she as nervous for this as me?

This is not a real date, I forcefully tell myself again.

She's staring at her reflection in a floor-length mirror when I peak in. "Better than okay," I tell her, leaning against the door frame.

Eyes meet mine through the mirror, mouth pursed in a tight smile. She's refusing to blush. The fight is in the way her hazels shift. It lasts one, two seconds. Freckled hands run down the front of the skirt, jaw clinching for a split second, and it's obvious that she's uncomfortable.

"It's all Elliot's," she tells me. "I wanted to dress like all the other girls."

The skirt is a color she'd wear, but far shorter and tighter. A ribbed, white, high neck tank is basic, but that's not a word I'd ever use to describe Sutton's style. I like the oversized leather jacket.

Does she look good? Yes, always.

Could I stare at her long, muscular legs all night? Imagine them wrapped around my waist? Without a second thought.

But she isn't confident in her outfit which speaks volume.

I find confidence beautiful. Wearing what you want. Expressing yourself.

When she's in her denim overalls over colorful T-shirts and sweaters, or skirts with thrifted graphic tees, completely herself, that's when...that's when I really can't look away. Her aura is bright, and she commands all eyes on her.

On the bed is an assortment of clothes that I assume, recognizing some, are Elliot's. Nothing of hers is in sight.

"You don't need to dress like everyone else."

"But that's what guys want." She sighs.

I push off the door frame and walk toward her. "Who told you that?"

"I watch it happen."

"But no one has explicitly said you need to dress this way to be wanted?"

"No," she mutters.

Sutton's back brushes my chest as I step into her. I squat

down, putting our heads side-by-side in the mirror. We stare at each other for a beat

"My style is weird. *Whimsical*," she says the word as if it's been used as an insult before. "Girly. Different."

"It's not weird. Truthfully, Dave, most guys won't remember what you wear." Sutton was wearing denim shorts with a strawberry print and a white T-shirt the first time we met. Her Velcro shoes lit up, and she was wearing white socks with a frill, as she still does today. "But if what you wear determines your beauty or if he wants you, then he's the wrong guy for you."

She sucks in a sharp inhale. "But what if I want to look beautiful?"

"You already are." There's my first slip up of the night. Quickly, I cover it up with a question. "Does this outfit make you *feel* beautiful?"

"No." She gulps.

"You should be wearing something that you feel beautiful in. I *promise* it translates to everyone around you."

"Okay." Sutton chews on the inside of her cheek. "But—"

"Let me show you." I stand up and head into her closet.

In my hands as I walk back out is a black slip dress with 3-D, multi-colored butterflies all over it.

Sutton spins to face me, still fidgeting with the hem of the mini skirt. "You should wear this," I suggest.

Sutton takes the hanger from me, holding it in front of her body in the mirror.

"I love this dress."

"I'd love to take it off of you." There's a second slip up. My filter must be on break because I didn't even think twice before saying it.

"Do you think about doing that?"

This isn't a real date.

But this...this can be good. I can admit the truth and deem it a lesson.

"Yes."

"How often?" Neither one of us skips a beat. Eyes beating into each other through the mirror.

"More often than I should."

Her eyes narrow as she says, "You should stop doing that."

"I've tried." Damn, I sound desperate. "Get changed, Dave, we don't want to be late."

———

SUTTON REACHES for the duck on my dash. Runs the tips of her fingers over it delicately, and I flick my gaze to her face. Catch a reminiscent smile before turning my eyes back to the road.

She's been quiet after asking a million questions about what we are doing tonight, and my only response was *you'll see*.

My grip is tight on the steering wheel as I pull my Jeep into the parking lot and cut the ignition. Sprinting around my car, my palm slips on the handle. I'm nervous.

"The community center?" she questions, climbing out of the car, bypassing my extended hand for help.

If I was a betting man, I'd have bet Sutton was expecting me to take her to a romantic dinner. I suppose in a way, I am, but instead of sitting down to eat, we're making our dinner.

I mumble out an inaudible answer.

"What was that?"

"You'll see," I clearly enunciate.

We head to the entrance, the large poster that caught my attention the other day is still hanging up in a window.

Sutton hesitates, reading the bold letters.

If there's one thing to know about Sutton, it's that she loves rom-coms. There isn't one she hasn't seen at least a hundred times or can't recite. Her favorite being *The Princess Diaries*.

The community center in downtown Bensen hosts an assortment of classes and events. Conveniently, tonight is a themed rom-com cooking class; and they're showing none other than *The Princess Diaries*. When I was running through downtown, the flyer wrangled my attention, dragging me inside to reserve us two spots—which I had to beg for and promise tickets to our upcoming sold-out game against Yale.

"And you suggested I wear this for a cooking class?" She gestures at her dress. The socks and Mary Jane heels are the perfect 'Sutton' touch.

"You should absolutely be wearing this dress." I give her a one-sided, cheeky smirk. "You look beautiful."

Glossy lips curl inward. "You don't look half bad yourself." Sutton proceeds to check me out, not shy to the way her head shifts to look at my butt.

I run a hand through my hair, remind myself again that this isn't a date *and* that Sutton doesn't like me like that.

———

INSIDE, they hand us each a white apron. We help each other tie them off in the back and make our way to our stations in the industrial kitchen. A large projector screen set up in the front, the movie's title screen already queued up.

The instructor is walking around, making sure everyone has everything they need for us to get started shortly. She explains how tonight will work, prompting us on our first step in making the dough, and we're off while the movie starts.

Sutton is spooning the pizza sauce onto the rolled-out dough. Using the back of the metal spoon to spread it in circles. Her elbow bumps into me, and she instantly apologizes, "Sorry."

"Lesson number four hundred five." I'm making up numbers. "If you want the guy to know you are interested in him, touch him. Playfully, like that little bump. Or find a reason to pick something off his shirt, maybe his hair."

"Seriously?"

"Yeah."

She tries it, but instead of touching my hair, Sutton swipes red sauce across my cheek. "Oops."

I stick my finger into the excess, lathering it up with sauce. I swipe it across her cheek. "Only fair."

I pick up a napkin to clean my face, but she stops me. "Let me," Sutton offers.

She takes the napkin and cleans my cheek, her other hand cupping my sauce-free cheek. I still so close to her. I count her freckles, see if there are any new ones.

"How was that?" she asks, dropping the napkin into the trash.

"Good." I blink several times. "Yeah, that was smooth."

Truthfully, I'm flying by the seat of my pants with this date because believe it or not, there isn't a guide on how to take your childhood rival—her inaccurate term for me that I overheard her call me to Elliot once. I've always enjoyed, thrived even, being competitive with her, especially after our friendship imploded. She might see me as her rival because of it, but she could never be mine—that you secretly have a crush on, on a fake date to teach her how to date. No internet searches help either.

I've been on dates before, so I'm not completely clueless how to behave, but those always ended up as a means to someone's bed.

There's no discussion on toppings after we add cheese. We both know there's only one option; and it's as if the instructor knew as well.

I start to reach for the bowl of M&Ms. Sutton has the same idea, our fingers brush.

"Sorry," we both say in unison. We reach again, fingers brushing a second time but instead of pulling our hands back like we did the first time, they linger there. A blush prickles my cheeks, mirroring Sutton's.

I run my pinky up hers and her breath hitches. "You should add them."

"Oh. No, that's okay." Her tone changes. "Actually...you should," she tells me suspiciously. "I'd love to see what you'd put on the pizza."

Our connection is lost, Sutton crosses her arms, leaning her left hip into the counter, diligently keeping a watchful eye.

I start with a heart. One by one, placing the chocolates in no particular order to outline the shape.

When I finish the bottom point, I peer over at her to capture her thoughts. She's glowering at me, but there is a hint of a sparkle in her eyes as to what I'm about to put on the inside.

I move the pizza out of sight, putting my back to her. "It's a surprise."

Sutton lets out a huff. "I hate surprises."

"I know," I taunt.

Carefully, I place the candy onto the pizza. The key to making it look good is first let your pizza cool and to not press the pieces too far into the cheese. A subtle touch, not a press.

It takes me longer than I thought to write it out, but perfect timing because Michael is getting his *I'm sorry* pizza from Mia.

"Ready?" I spin out of the way. "Ta da." In the middle of the heart is *S + C*. "You know, for you and me."

"I get it," she bites back. I can't tell if she's stifling a smile or laugh. "Couldn't spell?"

"Nah. I'm hungry. I call dibs on eating the S."

"Fine. I guess I'll eat the C."

"You can taste me any day, Dave." She bursts out laughing, and I'm right there with her. "That was not what I meant."

We devour our pizza, cutting it into four large slices, forcing us to fold them like tacos to eat, while the movie finishes.

"Guess what," Sutton says, dabbing the corner of her mouth with a napkin.

"You're finally ready to admit you broke your grandma's antique vase."

"Never. Izzy is dating Dylan."

I almost choke on my crust. Coughing, I pretend to be shocked. Surprised at this unfortunately not new information. Honestly shocked they're still together. "Are you okay with that?"

"I think so. That was years ago, and I never see either of them anymore." At her response I drop the topic and start cleaning our cooking space.

The bubble we were in the previous three hours pops as soon as I cut the ignition. Heat fiddles out, the cold air outside cools the space between us. Sutton bids me a good night, declining my offer to walk her to the door.

I stick around, watching till she's inside and vanishes up the stairs.

THIRTEEN

COOPER

SUTTON ASKED me to meet her at the rink. It's been a week since our what felt real but was only a practice date, and I've barely seen her. We met once last week for a session, but because of a game we had to reschedule our second one.

We got destroyed in that game, asses handed to us, and social media had a field day. I don't know what they are trying to get out of tagging me in negative videos and tweets. I'd tell them to say it to my face, but they have. Either way it worked. Mission accomplished.

During our post-game interview, several reporters threw passive aggressive questions my way. Coach had to step in, but I was in my head the entire bus ride home. Slumped against the windows, headphones in, and jacket hood pulled tight over my head. Day after looked the same. Shutting myself off from the world, including Sutton. I cancelled on her, again, but I'm hoping to make up for it today. Coach gave us the day off after a grueling practice last night.

The walk from my car to the entrance of the arena is brutal. Temperatures dropped this morning, even dipping into negatives with the windchill.

Our arena is an angular building, modern in comparison to

the rest of campus. Large glass windows and clean steel instead of brick covered in ivy. Banners of Tatum, a senior defenseman, Beckett, and myself are in three rectangular windows to the left of the doors. To the right are three players from the women's team.

Sutton's outside, one hand is stuffed into a long puffer jacket, ankles crossed with a tote bag from her collection leaning against her shins, an old Bears Women's Hockey gear bag slung over her shoulders. Her free hand grips a hockey stick.

As I get closer, I spy soft pink lips ticked up at the corners, kissable and mischievous, and chin tilted up at my larger than life body.

"I can get you a signed copy if you'd like. I'm sure there's a life-size poster around here somewhere you could tape above your bed."

"Perfect. I've been looking for a new dartboard."

"I thought I was done with the whole 'overtraining.'" I air quote overtraining. My tone half joking, half serious.

"You are." Vibrant hazel eyes level me with a stern look. "This is different."

I scoop up her tote and offer to take her duffle as we head inside. Sutton admits to having scheduled an appointment with her physical therapist to get cleared to skate again when I stare for too long at her lacing up her skates. I guess my roommates took her skating over the weekend. While jealousy combs through me, I'm happy that she's found a family here. People she can trust.

I want her to trust me again.

Even though our friendship is on the mend, there are still stitches needing sewn, conversations we need to have.

Sutton makes me pinky promise to not laugh at her on the ice. "It's been two years." I hate the painful reminder, hate the way her jaw tenses and eyes go heavy as she says it, knowing full well she associates me with her injury. It's why I can't be upset she asked my friends to be the ones to skate with her initially. Of all the people I'm letting down, letting her down hurts the worst. Hearing what reporters have to say about hockey seems like nothing when I think of Sutton. "It'll be like watching a baby giraffe walk for the first time."

Spoiler alert: it's not.

The Pond's ice is smooth except for the grooves she's creating. I'm leaning against the boards when she confidently stops in front of me, a cheek-splitting, mind-altering grin on her face.

"Knee good?" I check in with her.

"For now." She's has a brace over her leggings. "Odds one of those keys goes to the equipment closet?"

"Why? No one's here. You don't need privacy to kiss me."

"If there's any kissing happening, it's you kissing the ice when I pummel your ass into it. We're playing MOOSE." A welcomed lightness takes over me hearing the name of the game we used to play as kids. It's your standard HORSE rules, but we changed the name. Moose felt more appropriate for the ice.

Mood lighter, mind quieter. "It's on, Dave."

I come back out of the locker room with my hockey stick and a bucket of pucks.

Everyone probably expects me to let her go first, but that's not how we do it. It's not what Sutton would want either. We're in the center of the ice, sticks tucked away, our hands free except for the gloves we're wearing.

"Rock. Paper. Scissors."

"You are supposed to say shoot." I suffocate her rock with my paper. Sutton huffs, rolling her eyes. "Redo."

"Best two out of three," I banter back.

"No."

"Yes."

"No. Reset. We go on shoot."

"Rock. Paper. Scissors," I repeat, pausing for dramatic effect. "Shoooooooot." Now I'm just enjoying her annoyment and the shade of crimson her cheeks and ears are turning.

"Ha." She pretend cuts my paper. "I win."

Right, she wins and not because I saw two fingers shift

slightly in her fist and knew she'd throw scissors. Thus my tossing paper. Sutton skates off to her first shot position.

"Let's make this beneficial to both of us. When you miss, you answer a question."

"I'm not missing." Lips pressed all sassy. "*And* how does that benefit me?" she laughs out, passing the puck to herself. Left, then right.

"You have to trust me."

Her shoulders look like they have a shoelace going through them, pulling them taut. Chin tilted slightly up in refusal to look at me.

I skate over to her. Push a lock of hair behind her ear. It's minimal, but there is a twitch in her posture. "Can you do that?"

She takes a measured breath. "Fine."

Sutton makes her first shot, taking it easy on herself. I follow it up with a goal.

I skate to the left side, farther out from where she positioned herself, and shoot. I make it.

"What d—"

"I didn't miss," she cuts in, then shoots her puck into the back of the net. "See."

We go back and forth till finally she misses with a huff. There's minor annoyance on her features when she spins to face me. "Alright, ask your question," she says sarcastically.

"Why did you and your ex break up?" There's a laundry list of things I want to ask her. Things I want to know about more intimately instead of from a sideline view.

"Off limits," she fires back hastily.

"Make the shot if you don't wanna answer." My brows raise, tone and attitude a mirror to hers. "What happened?"

He wasn't you, I hope she says, but that's a foolish thought. For her I'd be a fool, I think.

None of the guys know. It's the one thing even Elliot has been tight-lipped about. Which is probably because none of us liked him, and we always made it apparent.

"He wasn't the one," Sutton says simply. "Your shot again."

I earn an M after another three rounds. Sutton earns her next letter on the following shot.

The question I want to ask her isn't the one that comes out of my mouth. Hooked on her last answer, curiosity has been skating circles in my mind. Who is the one? What does he have that I don't? Am I never going to be good enough to be like my dad *and* the person she wants?

Winded, the heavy rise and fall of my chest masks the thumping of my heart against my ribcage. Grip tight on my stick, it might slip if I don't fight to keep my hand steady.

"Define the one. What characteristics are you searching for?" To add to the pain, or throw her off my scent, I add, "What is it about Zach that you are attracted to?"

"That's two questions." Sutton rubs at her knee. "Don't judge me, but I want someone fun. I want to laugh so hard my mouth hurts from smiling. Intentional and observant. Someone that knows me well; they notice the unspoken and unseen. I want him to love me to his fullest—eventually, doesn't have to be right away. A deep, all-consuming love that lives in the life we build with each other. Quiet, loud, and everything in between. I want our love to be tangible." Her brows push together. "What about you?"

How do I describe her?

If you were to look up my type in the Cooper Carmichael dictionary, it would be a picture of Sutton Elizabeth Davis. Probably my favorite picture of her taped in there. The dictionary a disguised scrapbook of memories.

She's my type. My only type—there's a reason I've never hooked up with a redhead or another female hockey player. It's why I swore off relationships. They'd never be her, and that's unfair to them.

"Smoking hot. Smart. Strong." Easier, safer words. "Like me."

She huffs in disgust. "You are such a playboy. Tell me." Sutton skates into position for her next shot. "When did you last get your helmet sized?"

"Start of the season, why?"

"I think your ego is getting too big, it's killing brain cells."

"Haven't you heard? Bigger the ego, bigger theeeeeee..." I drag out the word, skating in her direction. I whip around her, beady hazel eyes tracking me, mouth pursed but cheeks pink. "Get your mind out of the gutter, Davis. Bigger the heart."

She digs her elbow into my gut.

I don't skate away, forcing her to take her shot with me hovering behind her. She smells good. Fruity. Cherries? Or a berry of sort. Maybe both.

Sutton misses. Rolling her eyes at me, she skates behind me. "Only fair."

"Yeah, only fair." I wind up, every muscle in my body is relaxed for a beat, rippling with momentum and precision. The space between the toe and heel connecting with the puck. It soars to the back of the net, and I bite my bottom lip to refrain from gloating.

I can hear the smoke exhaling from her nose.

I snicker to myself before asking my next question. "What qualities do you admire about yourself?"

"That has nothing to do with dating."

"It does. I think you are intelligent—your mind is creative yet analytical, a sponge. You are relentlessly compassionate to others. Helpful and patient. Your hair has a wild spirit that I think is an external expression of who you are inside. Meave might be the wild child, but you are in your own captivating and magnetic way."

"Cooper—" Her tone is a warning.

"Make me stop. Tell me." I stare down at her.

Sutton scrunches her nose, thinking. "I admire...I admire my drive. When I know what I want, I go after it. Even though I'm not confident in dating, I'd like to say I'm a confident person." I nod, encouraging her. "My style." She pauses, and I know there's more in there she's not saying. "Oh. My flexibility."

I cough.

"Now who's mind is in the gutter, Carmichael. I'm adaptable." Her gaze falls to her knee. "Forced or not." Shoulders roll back, standing tall, the skates giving her extra inches. "Do you want more?"

"Up to you."

"Hmm...one more. I like my hair, too."

We keep going until Sutton earns M-O-O-S-E first, but only by one letter. Together we skate back to our bags. She sits down, unlacing her skates and putting the guard back on. I take a drink of my water, spraying it into my mouth. My upper body warms and when I dip my eyes, I catch her staring at my throat, pupils flaring at each swallow and bob of my Adam's apple.

"One more question." She shakes her head, in the way that pulls you from a daze. "Why skating tonight?"

Sutton answers with a question. "Did you have fun?"

"A lot."

"There you go." Her expression is soft but mixed with the sharpness that comes when she knows she's right about something.

I think I get it.

Not once did I think about hockey, the game and gravity of it. Only for that short blimp did I fall to the stress, otherwise I was light. Relinquished.

Out there on the ice was the old—fuck, that word hurts because it's not old. The guy who loves hockey is in me still, I know it. I felt it tonight.

"Thank you, Sutton," I say to her outside the arena.

She smiles tightly. "Good night, Cooper."

FOURTEEN

COOPER

DAVE

Hi

Hi

DAVE

Where are you?

My bed. Where are you?

DAVE

Not there…

attached a video

I CLICK PLAY. Her face fills my screen before the phone tumbles to the ground.

Are you drinking?

DAVE

Definitely not

Maybe a little

I'm typing when her next message pops up, beating me to it.

DAVE

Okay...moderately

Your spelling is impressive

DAVE

I'm impressive

You are

Is Sutton Davis drunk?

DAVE

Who is that?

Thought I was Dave

You hate when I call you that

DAVE

That's not true

Okay, Dave

DAVE

Okay, Coop

I'm hungry

Want me to pick you up?

Sutton shares her location with me—indefinitely—but I know what party she's at. We won a hard earned game tonight and my roommates wanted to celebrate. I had a beer with them here, reaching for a second in the fridge when they left, but it's sitting next to me undrank. I have an exam tomorrow and a study packet from tonight's review I missed ready for download.

I climb out of bed and slip on a pair of sweats and grab my second favorite sweatshirt. It's cold out, and I doubt from the video she sent me that what she's wearing is very warm and is most certainly out of Elliot's closet.

Ten minutes later, I'm opening the door to the basketball

house. It takes me almost another ten to locate her. People stop to chat or offer me a beer. I'm pulled in a million directions before heading to the basement.

To the left of the stairs, I find Chase and Beckett on a couch facing the table Sutton is dancing on. The leather skirt she's in is short. Long, muscular legs stretch for days from this angle and the added height from the knee-high, heeled boots she's in. The entire outfit is black, which I'm not used to seeing her in. Everything Sutton wears is bright and colorful—even the only pair of black jeans she owns have some sort of flair to them.

Sutton's hips move freely to the music with Elliot and another girl with dark hair. She's familiar but I can't pinpoint how.

"Hey, Cap," Chase says. "Thought you weren't coming."

"I'm not. Picking up Sutton."

"Oh?" Chase replies, intrigued.

I nod my head at the dark-haired girl. "Who is that?" Her baggy sweatpants and fitted crop top make her stand out. No one else is dressed as casually.

Except Beck, who pulls the beer away from his mouth. His icy blue eyes and chipped electric blue nails—courtesy of his little sister—are bright even in the dim lighting.

"Iris," he bites.

"Do you know her?"

"No. But there is a rumor going around that she is a backup dancer," Chase chimes in excitedly. "Part of those insane world tours and is in music videos. She's been taking online classes but is back this year."

I peer at Beckett to see if he knows her. He grunts and gets off the couch. "I'm getting another beer." Standing in front of me, he slips off a bracelet and hands it to me. "Madeline made this for you. Wear it."

The elastic stretches to the size of my wrist. She must have used her brother's wrist to fit mine. Beck disappears before I can show it off to him, quiet for his large stature.

I silently laugh, pushing the friendship bracelet under my sleeve. Then return my search for—

"Cooper!" Sutton squeals. Across her face is a smile that's reminiscent of the same one she gave me when I asked her to be my friend over a decade ago. Bright and stretching from ear to ear as if the freckles on her cheeks are pulling at the sides of her mouth.

I allow my gaze to roam over all of her. I'm normally careful, but not tonight. Not when she's doing the same. My hair is a mess, and I'm pretty confident there is a stain on my sweats, but none of that matters when she stares at me like I'm the only one that exists. My shoulders relax, releasing any tension.

"Hey, Dave."

"Are we getting nuggets?" she yells over the music.

"Whatever you want." I try to hide my amusement at the sparkle in her eyes and the slight sway in her body. "You done dancing on the table?" Sutton nods. "Need help?"

"Mhmmm." She hums, stretching her arms out to me.

Against my better judgement, I bypass them, gripping her waist and picking her up, then setting her down on the ground. She waves goodbye to everyone, even says hello to people she definitely doesn't know.

As soon as we are in my car, she takes off her boots and moans. "I hated these, but I promised Elliot I'd wear them. Did you like them?"

Did I like the way they were molded to her calves or stopped at the knee, exposing the skin on her thighs, places I've imagined my hands being?

"Of course." I reach behind my seat and snag the sweatshirt I brought with me. "Here. Put this on so you aren't cold."

She takes the sweatshirt but places it in her lap. "You didn't say please." Sutton tilts her head in my direction, smoldering.

"*Please.*"

A sleeve hits the roof as she stretches her arms, slipping each one uncoordinatedly into the sweatshirt, and then pulling it over her head.

Sutton buckles in and takes the water I also brought with me, drinking the entire thing on our drive.

"What do you want?" I ask as we drive up to the menu.

Sutton unbuckles herself and leans over me to order.

"A ten-piece nugget. Large fry." She pauses. "Oh! And a chocolate shake. Please," she tacks on.

Her face spins. Right in front of me. She smells good, even with the faintest hint of tequila—she's a lightweight. Probably had two drinks tops, I bet.

"Are you not going to get anything?"

Wasn't planning on it, but she convinces me with one flick of her eyelids and a pout.

"I'll do the same."

———

SUTTON OPENS the top of her milkshake and dips a fry in. Her moan bounces off the walls of my Jeep. Strikes me in the chest. Flickers up my spine, finding a spot in my brain to lodge itself into.

I'll be hearing that in my dreams tonight...if I can even sleep.

Haven't been able to sleep lately—barely finding time. My mind energized despite the exhaustion weighing down my body, but tonight I'll be up for other reasons.

"I love French fries." She moans again.

"I don't think I've ever seen you eat one before."

"Don't be ridiculous, Cooper," she says in the tone of Miranda Priestly in *The Devil Wears Prada*. Rom-coms, I told ya. "They're my favorite food."

"No, they aren't. Your favorite food is a pizza."

"That's a meal," she retorts, dipping two fries in this time.

"Kiwi."

"I had a good one this morning," Sutton exclaims, a smile

trickling from her. "Did you know they are good for your digestive system? I have to eat them now because you know what they say. Hot girls have stomach issues." She giggles at herself. "But, I love fries too."

"That's true." I smile lightly.

"Spaghetti." Sutton bites her bottom lip after blurting out my favorite meal. My head falls, eyes watching her fingers twiddle with the red and white straw. "At least it used to be. I guess I don't know anymore."

"Maybe if you spent less time hating me, you would," I say, realizing when her face falls it came out sharper than I meant.

"I don't...I don't hate you."

"You've been drinking." I make up the excuse for her admittance.

"Does that matter?"

Now I feel guilty, because no, it doesn't. I've been so messed up lately that even getting this attention from her helps ease the pressure building inside of me. It turns down the dial of the pressure cooker I've become. Invisible steam creeps out of me.

She doesn't know she does that for me.

She doesn't know that when I'm around her, even in the same room or house, not even talking with her, she makes me feel more alive than I have in years. Sutton allows me to be me—the guy who was out on the ice last week, the one I focused on being this week in my games—not the person others have concocted me to be.

"No," I finally respond.

"Plus, drunk words, sober thoughts. Right?" Sutton steals a nugget from my container, already having inhaled all of hers.

"Anything else you wanna get off your chest then?" I egg on.

She purses her lips as if she's thinking, curls spilling over her shoulders and fanning across my cloth seats. Sutton rolls her head, pressing the side into the head rest. "Nope."

I offer her my final nugget, withholding the fries, and ask, "Where should we go now?"

"I don't know," Sutton says into the bag, digging for a napkin. Wiping her hands off when she finds one. "Where do you want to go?"

Anywhere you are. That's what I want to say, but I bite my tongue.

"I can take you home," I offer.

Please say no. Please say no. Please say no.

"I'm not ready to go home." She pops up straight. "Maybe we just drive?"

We drive around for another twenty minutes. To nowhere, really. Laps around campus.

Finally, I start to head toward her apartment complex. I stop a few blocks away, pull my car over, and cut the engine.

Sutton unbuckles her seat belt and turns to face me. She pulls her legs up onto the seat and manages to sit crisscross, accidentally flashing me her underwear. I swallow harshly. Her milkshake is in one hand, the other is playing with the straw again.

I mimic her. Unbuckle and turn to face her, but only pull up my right leg to bend beneath me.

She looks like she wants to say something.

"What's rolling around in your beautiful mind?" I ask.

She rolls her eyes at me. One corner of her mouth ticks up. "Beautiful?"

"Yeah, beautiful. Big and organized and calculated and stuffed with information. Maybe too much, but still beautiful."

"Your brain is beautiful, too. Even the dark parts. You just have to learn to find the beauty in them." Sutton's arm stretches forward and rubs a thumb over my temple.

"I'm trying." She pulls back, but I catch her wrist. My thumb brushing over her racing pulse point. "I've got a good teacher."

She huffs, loudly. Then lets out a singular laugh. "Yeah, well, I don't."

"You don't?"

"No! He's never asked me once to practice kissing."

"That's a damn shame. Maybe it's because he doesn't want to see you kissing other people."

"Maybe he should be the practice dummy then."

"*Sutton...*"

"*Cooper,*" she mimics.

"You've been drinking—"

"And I could still recite the entire periodic table or list all NHL MVPs from the past decade."

That makes me laugh. I almost choke because I was inhaling when she cut me off.

"Prove it," I dare.

Sutton groans dramatically, head falling into the headrest, and the smirk on her lips is tempting me. She rattles off the elements—in order—till she gets to osmium, that's when I stop her.

"Okay."

"Okay, what?"

"You are only mildly, just a teensy bit, intoxicated." One corner of my mouth creeps up the side of my face. Muscles as loose as my tone.

"And smart."

"And smart."

"Don't forget you told me I'm beautiful." I won't. Ever.

"You are only mildly, just a teensy bit, intoxicated, smart, *and* beautiful. Better?"

"Much." Sutton settles back into her seat, she shifts, dropping one of her knees down. Then the other. "So you gonna kiss me?"

"Do you want me to?"

"*You* want to." Want is too little a word for this. Need. Might die if I don't. Desperately crave. Poisoned, and this is lifesaving.

"For practice?" I hope she doesn't catch the instability in my tone. My brain is playing a three-way game of tug-o-war.

"Practice." She hunches a shoulder as if she too is using the word as a scapegoat.

Motioning her to me, I curl two fingers in my direction. "Come here," I beckon, dipping the words in honey and demand.

Sutton scoots closer to the center console. Leans forward, propping her elbow up on it. I watch her. How slow she swallows. How her eyes are heavy, loaded with desire and impatience.

I exchange the hand under her chin for my pointer finger. Push it up so we are level, and drag her closer. I start to close the gap, tugging on the final threads of my sanity.

There's no going back for me after this.

Our mouths are the closest they've ever been. I can see the specks of emerald green in her hazel eyes. There are new freckles on her left cheek.

Dangerously slow, I rub the thumb of my free hand over the patch of them. I cup her cheek, but my hand is too large against her face. My fingertips graze and sink into the roots of auburn hair.

Sutton lets out a warm exhale.

Stop delaying. Kiss her. My mind screams at me, but I want to relish in this moment for a second longer. Make sure my brain is clear. I don't want to miss a thing. I want to be present.

"Cooper," she pleads, "please."

I plant my lips on hers, take her bottom lip between mine, in a singular kiss. A test to see how badly she wants this, too.

Intrusive thoughts slice through me. Seconding guessing that this is nothing more than a joke to her. That I'm a joke to her now that she knows what I've hidden away.

But it isn't. She wants this, maybe even me. Sutton doesn't let me pull back, instead kisses me.

What have I been missing out on?

Her mouth is pliable, moving with mine. Flexing and conforming to each push and pull. It's as if we're puzzle pieces that fit. I swallow the throaty moan that comes out of her when my tongue dips into her mouth. My own feral one chasing after it.

I need her closer. Sutton must need the same, she climbs over the console, lips never leaving mine.

I can't lie. This isn't my first car make out session—or hook up. No other girl has ever gracefully maneuvered herself into my lap as Sutton has. I usually end up with an elbow to the face or gut, and a knee to the balls. One time, I even landed myself a black eye.

Not tonight.

I undo her ponytail holder with one hand, slip it onto my wrist. Use the other to pull the lever to recline my seat back. Her hair becomes blackout curtains, cascading around us in a sea of red and curls and cherries.

When have I not been blacked out by her? Senses overwhelmed by her?

My left hand, free, finds her waist. I hold onto her. Let my fingertips graze the bare skin between her waistband and the bottom of her shirt.

When I pull her against me, she lets out a breathy whine.

Sutton moves her kisses from my mouth to my jawline. Onto my neck. She bites down on the curve, and I hiss.

"Sorry," she says, slightly frantic and embarrassed.

"Don't be. I liked it." I move her mouth back to my neck. "Do it again."

She does. Sucks on the skin after, before kissing it and finding her way back to my mouth. I capture her swollen lips, dragging the bottom one with my teeth.

"Vampire fetish?"

A husky and needy chuckle comes out of me. I pull her against me again.

"I believe it was you who made us stop our family road trip because she *had to have* the newest book."

"And wasn't it you whom I found in the middle of the night with a flashlight under the blanket reading *my* book?" Sutton's question broken and between kisses.

"Whatever you say, Team Jacob."

Her mouth falls open, and I imagine everything I want to do with it.

I kiss her again. More explorative than the first. Her tongue sinks into my mouth.

When we break apart, this time, I know this kiss is over.

It takes Sutton a minute to form a sentence, breath fogging up the glass. Her chest quickly rises and falls. "What did you think? Any tips?" She swallows quickly as if the questions are soured milk.

At least they've soured me. That kiss...it ruined all other kisses. I don't want anyone else knowing how she kisses, or to feel the clinging and possessiveness of her lips on their skin. She tasted sweet tonight, I bet she always does, and it's a decadent treat that I want reserved for me.

"I don't know. Might need another." I lean in to her, but she swats at my shoulder, turning her head to let my mouth meet her cheek.

"Seriously." She giggles.

I shake my head no.

"Come on, Coop."

Maybe I should give her a bad tip? Tell her something that'll make her a bad kisser. Suggest not to use her hands to touch and explore. No pulling at their hair, or kissing down their neck, leaving trails of herself everywhere.

"Kiss anyone like that and they're a goner."

"Okay, okay." She eyes me wearily. "I should go." She climbs back over the console, almost knocking over the remnants of her milkshake. "Thanks for this." Sutton opens the door, taking her trash.

Left on the floor of the passenger seat is her leather boots.

I open my door to get out, grabbing them quickly.

"Dave, wait." She turns to face me. "Your boots."

"Oh, yeah. Thanks." Sutton outstretches a hand for them. "Elliot would probably kill me in my sleep if I lost these."

"Here." I kneel in front of her, requesting a foot with my open palm.

Taking the left shoe, I put her foot in them gently. My hold on the sole, then ankle. I zip up the boot, my other hand smoothing up her calf.

I'm focused on the closing leather, making sure not to pinch her skin, but sneak a quick peek up at her. She's staring down at me raptly. Before repeating this on the other leg, I squeeze the top of her calf which causes a sharp inhale from her. Then move to the next leg.

"Thanks for the ride," she says when I stand back up.

"I can drive you the rest of the way."

"No, I'm fine. I...I uh..." I can tell Sutton's flustered, her skin flush. "Need to clear my head. The air will help."

"Text me when you get home?"

She leaves without a response, but my phone buzzes as I pull into my driveway.

DAVE
I'm home.

Good.

DAVE
Thanks for practicing…

Anytime

DAVE
You're pretty good at it too

Best kiss ever?

DAVE
LOL

If I say yes, will it go to your head?

Nah. Might just make me wanna kiss you again.

Good night, Sutton

DAVE
Good night, Cooper

FIFTEEN

SUTTON

THE TWO HOURS I'm supposed to be spending with Dr. Manning this morning is useless.

It's like that game, Six Degrees of Kevin Bacon. Somehow, everything keeps going back to Cooper. Being around him isn't easier either.

I'm plagued by our kiss. The faint, ghost-like feeling of his lips on mine that feel too real and have my fingers dusting over my mouth. Vivid, lucid dreams when I'm sleeping, and mind-consuming fantasies when I'm awake.

Are kisses supposed to be *that* good? Is good even the right word to describe it? Would foot-popping be better?

Dr. Manning dismisses me, clearly sensing I'm distracted. I pack up my stuff mindlessly, and say goodbye, at least I think I do.

"Sutton, wait up." I stop, my loafers skidding to a halt in the hallway outside of Dr. Manning's office.

"Hi." He relaxes, pushing a hand through his blond hair, letting it linger on the back of his nape. His hair is freshly cut, the sides almost buzzed, revealing the tips of his ears that are turning pink. It's strange feeling like I make a boy flustered...or want to chase after me.

"Zach." I return his friendly smile. "How are you?"

"Better now." The dry-fit long sleeve he's wearing stretches across his broad chest when he inhales. "You're a hard person to track down. Did you know that?"

I give me head a quick shake. "Well, you found me now."

"Can I walk you to your next class? It's next to mine...I believe." The pink on his ears morphs to red and spreads to his cheeks. It's cute. Really cute.

"Tracking or stalking?"

Zach laughs and butterflies spring to life from their cocoons inside me. "How's your independent study going?"

My ears and shoulders perk up. "I didn't know you knew about that..." I trial off. Once again Cooper and that stupid kiss infiltrate my thoughts. "Um. It's keeping me busy with research and the paper portion, plus my case study is a bit more..." Personally challenging? Unraveling me instead of his intrusive thoughts and anxiety?

"I get it." Zach laughs nervously, and I hope he doesn't get it. "Did you lose your phone?" he asks as we head through a bustling lobby and outside.

As expected, Zach holds the door for me. Then takes my bag as I pull out a beanie and scarf to twist around my neck.

"I'm sorry, I've been meaning to text you." My apology is sincere. There's a Post-it in my planner with an unchecked box that says *text Zach.*

"We can resolve that. Do you have your phone now?" I nod. He opens his hand palm up in a simple request.

I dig my hand into the center pocket of my overalls, dropping my phone into his palm. Zach taps the screen, turning it around to get my passcode. I have to slip my glove off to enter it. My phone unlocks, and he pulls up his contact.

"The baseball is a nice add. Thought you might have forgotten that other sports exist outside of hockey."

I see what he's asking between the words. He's not talking about the sport, but Cooper. Zach doesn't have a reason to ask or worry about him. I want to ask why he's beating around the bush, but I don't.

There are answers there, I don't think I want to hear or face. Not yet. Maybe not ever.

Cooper and I work this way.

What way is that? My heart taunts. She's got a sarcastic little voice. Thinks she's smarter than she really is—look at the mess she led us into before.

"I like emojis. Look at my contacts. Everyone has something that's associated with them."

Zach's phone rings with a notification, the text he sent himself from me, before he rambles off contact names and the emojis next to them.

"Mom and a flower?"

"She owns a flower shop."

"Meave and a paint brush?"

"My sister is an artist."

"Do I even want to know why Jaxon is a trident?"

"Probably not. I'm also pretty sure he updated that himself."

"Would I be able to update mine after a date? I have a baseball clinic I'm volunteering with this weekend, and we finish up pre-season two-a-days next week, but—"

"I'm free next weekend," I interrupt, or unattractively blurt out, with an eagerness I'm going to tell myself is confidence.

"Friday?"

"It's a date." I have to suppress my excitement.

"I'll text you our plans." He wiggles his phone, giving me a wink.

Zach returns my phone, and I immediately add our date to my calendar, and send a quick text to Elliot that contains one too many exclamation points. We finish walking to class making simple small talk before we split to go to our respective classrooms.

I'm a robot heading to my unassigned but self-assigned seat.

I'm going on a date with Zach.

And while we were talking, I didn't fumble over my words once! I was cool. He made a joke, I kinda made a joke back. He didn't think my contacts were weird. I didn't think about kissing Cooper once.

Because it meant nothing. Absolutely nothing. It was practice.

And I'm going on a date with Zach.

This is great. This is what's supposed to be happening.

So why am I running my fingers over my lips?

Maybe I'll kiss Zach on our *date*.

That's one way to stop thinking about kissing Cooper. Because I'm not. I can't be thinking about him like that. I'm not thinking about him, or his hand gripping my hair with the right amount of intensity that it blissfully hurt, or the sounds he let out when I bit his lip.

I'm not—my thoughts are cut off by a smoothie cup being placed in front of me.

"Elliot said you left in a daze this morning, and this was still in the blender." I turn to find Cooper casually leaning onto the row of desks in the lecture hall. Elbow bracing his weight. "Thought you might be hungry."

My stomach growls. Loudly.

Cooper sweeps his hand, pushing the cup toward me.

"Drink up. We've got more dating practice tonight and I don't need my star student malnourished."

I take a drink from the orange straw, and about choke.

Did he say practice?

My eyes whip to his, then his mouth.

"Not kissing," he jokes. "But good to know you're thinking about it."

"I. Am. Not." I make sure to enunciate each word.

"Why not? I am."

Okay, so maybe I am, but it meant nothing, and I'm going on a date with Zach, and I need to be thinking about that. And I hate Cooper.

"Zach asked me out on a date," I say as if it's a blade or insult I can wield. Recentering the both of us with the purpose of this whole arrangement. "I said yes."

"Oh. Cool. That's cool." Cooper goes tense. Jaw twitching and an unreadable expression takes over his eyes.

My professor announces the start of class, and before I get a chance to say anything else to Cooper, he disappears.

SIXTEEN

COOPER

SUTTON SHIFTED BACK into her usual demeanor after she told me about Zach asking her out. Across the room glares and sharp quips, but now they feel forced.

Tried to text her about it, but she's left every single text unanswered except for one. Replying to give me an adjusted session time and place for today.

I tuck myself into a study booth in the library an hour before I'm supposed to meet Sutton. This isn't my favorite library—mine is on the east side of campus and is much smaller—but this is hers. The booth is up against a brick wall with a large window that overlooks campus. Today, it's gross out. Gray and cold. Snow is melting which means it's turning black from being trampled and over shoveled.

I finished my test early and came here instead of heading home. I love my roommates, trust me, I do, but it's very rare for the place to be remotely quiet. Someone is always doing something—cooking, playing video games, watching television, someone. Studying is impossible there. I can barely get through two math equations before my mind wanders to them or somewhere else. With back-to-back games coming up, I want to get ahead on my homework.

Plus, I knew if I went home, I'd end up shutting everyone out. Today's been a bad day, but I'm trying to be better.

Time ticks by, and I expect Sutton to be here by now. She's never late, but once it's fifteen after four, I get concerned.

After another ten minutes, there's an unease that takes root in my stomach. I call her twice and it goes directly to voicemail. I snatch my keys off the table and get to her place as quickly as possible.

I slam on the steering wheel when I get caught behind a mail truck. There's no room to go around them; the left side of the street is lined with parallel-parked cars, campus parking passes hanging from the rearview mirrors.

Their blinker turns on, flashing in the same direction I need to go. The last time I was scared like this was when my dad called about Sutton getting hurt. I couldn't get to the hospital quickly enough.

Except this time, when I show up, I'm not letting her shoo me away. Mom was angry with Dad for calling me, but he explained how I deserved to know because no matter what, Sutton is family.

Sutton being family has been my scapegoat. Whenever she gets mad at me, rolls her eyes, and even insults me, I tell myself that she's family. It's my Trojan horse.

Because even a crumb of Sutton is better than nothing.

Maintaining my position in Sutton's life hasn't been easy. There is a minefield between us, and I risk it every day to stay close to her. I've held tight to this belief that maybe one day we'll at least get back to how we once were.

I shift my backpack to my other shoulder, push up the sleeve of my sweatshirt. Immediately, I pull it back down, covering the colorful bracelet on my wrist.

I knock on their door after sneaking in the main door behind another student.

After the fourth time, there's finally movement from the other side of the door. The lock unlatches, and at an unhurried pace, the apartment door peels open.

"Hello?" the redheaded, sleeping zombie on the other side of the threshold croaks.

She's in an oversized sweatshirt and pink fuzzy socks. A stain stretches across the pocket. Half, more like a third, of her curls are in a bun lopsided on the left side of her head. The remainder of her hair is either matted to her forehead or sticking out in unconventional ways.

"What are you doing here?" Sutton bites out, displeased and confused.

"We're supposed to be meeting."

"That's not till tomorrow."

"Dave, it is tomorrow. It's almost five."

Sutton looks appalled. Horrified expression to match her horror movie appearance. "Oh my god. I slept for twenty hours. I missed everything today." She turns around, walking gingerly into her apartment, leaving me in the doorway.

I trail behind her, taking the open door as an invitation to come in.

"Are you feeling okay?"

"Obviously not." Good to know that even sick, appearing to be on her deathbed, and having had twenty hours of sleep, she's still partially herself. "People should rethink the phrase there are no dumb questions."

Sutton opens the cabinet with their cups, grabbing a glass. All her movements are sluggish. In front of the sink, she wobbles. Sets the glass down, one hand curled tightly around it, the other bracing the counter for support with a lethargic shake of her head.

My feet cover the distance in four large steps. I stretch my hand flat across her lower back to steady her.

"Here. Let me." I take the glass from her, filling it with water. "You should sit. Can you walk to the couch?"

"Yes, Cooper," she deadpans, but I see the fight in her eyes. The lowering of her resolve when she tries to take a step and immediately uses the counter again as a crutch. Hazel eyes that lean more green today, fissures of amber crackling through them, tip up to the ceiling, then straight forward. On me, but not exactly. Sutton stares at the wall behind me and, on an exasperated inhale, says, "No."

I stifle a smile. Have to restrain myself from pulling out my phone and documenting the moment. It might not have been her explicitly asking for my help, but between the two letters, I know she is.

I debate carrying her bridal style, but I don't want to push my luck. Fireman style is absolutely out of the discussion.

"Come on." I lift an arm over my shoulder, let her weight lean into me. I brace an arm around her waist.

Depositing her on the couch, she lets me prop her up. Back against one side, legs out in front of her, and tucked into a blanket. I hand her the glass of water and encourage her to finish the entire thing, even when she gags after the first sip.

Her skin is dull, cheeks incandescent, the color of her hair. Even with how much sleep she's gotten, there are dark circles under her eyes. Sutton breathes lightly.

Kneeling beside her, I press the back of my hand to her forehead. She's feverish.

"Do you have a thermometer? I think you have a fever."

She nods. "Bathroom closet." I stand up and start heading down the hallway. "Can you get me some more water?"

A few minutes later, I'm back. She sips on the water, placing it down for me to take her temperature.

"Open," I say, kneeling beside her with the thermometer hovering by her mouth. Sutton doesn't fight me, opens her mouth, lifting her tongue. "Good girl."

I place it under her tongue, and she closes her mouth.

Cheeks pink as she tracks my every move.

We wait for the thermometer to buzz. The seconds pass by achingly slow. It's not like we are waiting on big test results or anything life or death, but the air seems to grow thicker, the walls closing in on us.

When she breathes, I find myself breathing with her.

And maybe it's because I've thought about this. Taking care of her. Growing old with her. All of the sickness and in health stuff you hear about in wedding vows.

A singular curl falls across her face, tipped in my direction on the pillow. I push it off her face, dampened with sweat, capturing it on my pointer finger. Twirling it, the strand gently wraps around my finger, like she has me wrapped around hers. If only she would realize it. Sutton blinks, and I think for a millisecond that maybe she does. That the past few days have been a facade.

A beeping sound cuts through the space between us. I drop the curl. She presses up, moving into more of a sitting position.

We both reach for the thermometer. I refrain, letting her remove it and read her temp. Ninety-nine point eight. Right under the threshold.

"I think it's food poisoning," she says before I can ask. "Whatever I had in the dining hall last—two nights ago—must have been bad."

I snort a laugh. "Which one did you go to?"

"Cub Club."

"And you didn't remember how sick we all got our first semester on campus from there?"

"Apparently not, because I had the Mexicali Caesar wrap, too."

"Oh, Dave." My joking tone cracks a smile on her turned down mouth. "There's no thinking. You have food poisoning for sure." She huffs. "When's the last time you ate?"

"Some time yesterday, I guess. Maybe breakfast. Or lunch?" Sutton pauses. "Lunch, but I couldn't keep it down. I haven't been able to keep anything down in"—she counts on her fingers—"thirty hours. Probably more."

At the same time, I joke, "Yeah, I can tell."

Her brows perk up, then fall with realization. She sniffs her sweatshirt, then pulls a chunk of hair in front of her nose. Sutton covers her mouth, pretending, maybe not, to gag.

"I smell disgusting." Her nose scrunches.

"I think there's throw up stuck in your hair here." I gesture to other side of her head. "Let me go start you a bath."

"That's unnecessary. I can do it."

"I know, but I want to." Energy levels aside, I know she can do it. There's no doubt in her independence and ability to take care of herself. But I meant what I said, I want to.

"Cooper." It's a hesitant warning, a quiet plea not to push us. The box we've drawn around us is bending; we're pushing at its seams.

I shake my head. I don't care. "Please, Dave. Let me take care of you."

"You just want to see me naked."

"True." My chest laughs. "But baby, I wouldn't need a bath to get you naked. If I wanted you naked, I'd already have your clothes off." I lean forward. "Trust me." Holding her chin, tone softer, I repeat myself, "I want to take care of you. Puke and all."

———

SUTTON FINALLY RELENTS after three long exhales. I carry her to her bathroom, after she once again tries to walk and looks like she is in a game of pinball in her hallway.

She sits on the counter while I start the bath. I work in silence, the only sound coming from the water falling from the faucet. Dipping my hand in the water, I turn the handle to the left, cutting off the water.

Lukewarm, because anything else won't help her fever.

I shut the door behind me. Not quick enough. Not slow enough either.

As soon as I tell her the bath is ready, she starts slipping off her sweatshirt. That's when I bolt.

I wasn't lying when I said this wasn't a ploy to get her naked. Sure, yeah, I wasn't going into tonight thinking I'd get to see the sporty bralette she was wearing. The way the spandex fabric stretches across her breasts, the dusty pink color light enough that you can see her brown nipples. Or how when she breathes, her abs go taut, freckles kissing her skin like I wish I could.

Tonight, I thought would be like all the others. We'd meet on whatever she had planned this week. Watch or listen to a podcast, head to the rink to skate, or find an alternative form of movement.

Maybe I'd convince her to eat dinner with me, or watch this new show streaming online that I found and thought she'd like.

We'd run through whatever theoretical questions she assumes Zach would ask her on a first date because I know she probably has flash cards or some study material for it. As much as I hate the looming date, I still want her happy and confident.

I was lying when I said if I wanted her naked, I'd have her naked. I think I've wanted her naked since I was fourteen and realized what sex was. In those seven years, this is the closest I've ever been.

I tug the door closed and head to the kitchen.

I'm leaning against the counter, waiting for my mom to text me back.

Finally, she does.

MOM

link attached

Here is the recipe! I always prefer blending a cup or two of the vegetables with some broth, then adding it back into the pot while the noodles cook. It makes the soup creamier and more hearty.

Are you sick, honey?

No. Sutton's had food poisoning for the past 48 hours.

Needs some nutrients.

MOM

Electrolytes will be good too. Does she have any?

How my mom knows I'm here, I don't know. Motherly intuition, I suppose.

I check around the kitchen and don't find any sports drinks or hydration packets. Before texting my mom back, I order a grocery delivery.

> I got some.

MOM

Okay, that's perfect, honey. Keep me updated on how she feels. I'll let her mom know, she's been trying to get a hold of her.

> Slept all day.

MOM

You take such good care of her. I love you.

> I love you, too.

The soup is on low when Sutton pads into the open concept living room-kitchen. They don't have a dining room, only a bar with four counter-height stools.

She's toweling off her hair. Scrunching up her curls repetitively. A bottle of product is balanced underneath her armpit as she walks in.

"Oh." Sutton drapes her towel over the back of a chair. "I didn't know you were still here."

"I made—"

"Is that your mom's chicken soup?" Color starts to return to her.

I nod and a wave of relaxation comes over her. Turning my back to her, I ladle two servings into the bowls I set out.

This soup was a staple for my childhood. Whenever one of my sisters or I were sick, she'd make this soup. We thought it was magic; whatever she put in it instantly healed us. That was definitely a placebo effect, but the soup did help. Filled with protein, broth, and other nutrients to help replenish our systems.

We'd rock-paper-scissors to choose who would play sick if we went without the soup for some time. I don't think we ever fooled Mom—whoever it was still had to go to school—but she played along, making a pot. Even Dad would get in on the game.

Mom would be proud of the results. Everything in the bowl is perfection, down to a tee, smells and tastes like mom's.

Sutton is sitting at one of the barstools, eagerly waiting. Her stomach releases another growl, loud enough to wake her neighbors downstairs.

Steam wafts from the top of the bowl. Pink lips pursed in the smallest O, Sutton blows on each spoonful before eating.

After finishing her first bowl, she eats a second. Without becoming nauseous after three bites. I'd call that success.

Magic chicken soup: 53

Sickness: 0

Before cleaning up the leftovers—I doubled the batch, thank goodness—I snap a picture and send it in our family group chat.

Sutton collects our dishes, rinses and adds them to the dishwasher.

I pull the sports drinks I purchased out of the fridge, setting them on the counter. She picks up the blue one, taking it to the couch.

"Do you want to watch a movie?" she mumbles.

The heel of my right foot is sticking out of my shoe. I was in the middle of putting them on to leave when she asked.

I don't allow myself to chew on her offer, I heel-toe my Birkenstocks off and walk over to the couch. Lying on the chaise, Sutton's feet reach my thighs.

Sutton scrolls through two streaming sites before landing on her pick. She presses play on *A Cinderella Story,* and I know it's because she had the biggest crush on Chad Michael Murray as a kid. I get it. I mean, look at the dude, when the drought ends and he's cupping Hilary's cheek to kiss her.

We quote the entire thing, sounding a lot like a duet audiobook. After we finish this rom-com, we let auto-play queue up the next one.

No conversation passes between us. Only us regurgitating our favorite lines, laughter, and a few tears till Sutton starts to doze off.

Eyelashes flutter gently against her cheeks. They're the darkest shade of red, almost brown. Long and curl upward naturally.

She's fighting sleep but eventually waves the white flag. Her mouth falls open to release the cutest little snore I've ever heard.

Sutton sleeps through the rest of the movie. I don't try to leave when it ends, letting her head rest on my shoulder. A third starts, and finally after this one ends I carry her to bed and leave.

SEVENTEEN

SUTTON

ZACH PULLS out my chair for me. I loosely smile up at him, murmur an appreciation caught off by his height. It's intimidating tonight. This isn't a new revelation, but for whatever reason, tonight he's too tall. Two inches to be exact.

Casted carefully down on me are vibrant green eyes that remind me of a freshly mowed grass, or new leaves blooming on trees in the spring. He cleans up well. This is the first time I've seen him in anything other than sweats or cargos. Dark denim stretches across thighs, hugging the curve of his butt perfectly—sue a girl for looking and calculating if a coin could bounce off of it. The tan sweater he's in matches his golden hair with messes of caramel through it.

I don't know why Elliot says blond boys aren't attractive.

"Thanks," I say as he hands me the menu. Our knees clash under the table. "Sorry." I adjust mine, scooting back in the chair to sit straighter. "I've never been here. Have you?"

Without scanning the restaurant, I surmise that it's packed. Voices ricochet off the walls, blending with music that could be turned down. Waiting thirty minutes for a table is also a dead give-away. The coastal American restaurant opened before winter break. An awarded chef in Chicago, originally from Bensen, wanted to open a place in his hometown.

I may have read their bio on their website...and looked at photos on their social media before Zach picked me up. Dishes appear to be inspired by the West Coast while heavily influenced by the Midwest. They homemade pasta and parmesan fries are calling my name.

"Twice, actually."

At first, this wasn't my ideal first date. Honestly, ever. The movies or some sort of activity are more my pace. Something that can harvest time I'd otherwise have to spend talking. That was before Cooper, though.

While I was sick, a snow shower blew through, bringing a bitter chill with it. Anything outside was out of the question, even walking through downtown that still has wintery Christmas lights strung between lamp poles and wrapped like spaghetti in the leafless trees.

Dinner is great.

A date with Zach is great.

Finally feeling like myself again after being taken out for half a week with food poisoning is great.

I woke up in my bed the morning after Cooper took care of me. Dazed and groggy. I don't remember ever going to my room. I've rewound the night, but all my memory recalls is laughing at him quoting whatever movie incorrectly. We watched two, maybe three, I don't know, I lost track.

Cooper must've carried me to bed before leaving. In the kitchen, there was a note attached to a box of electrolyte packets telling me to drink these and take it easy. Underneath the teal box was a filled-out packet of what we were supposed to do during our session. His writing is chicken scratch, but I scanned through it to the last page, finding a smiley face and a boat.

I laughed freely, scratching at the lingering headache I had, and something warm wrestled deep inside me. Old feelings reawakening from the hibernation I forced them into. They stretch, clawing at the bars of their entrapment. God help me, they better not want out, or escape on their ambition.

He called me later that day, but I was on the phone with my parents. Cooper didn't leave a voicemail, didn't text either. I sent him one, though. A simple thank you.

I ate the soup again for dinner. Elliot couldn't help from indulging in a bowl, reminding me of us as kids when we used to mastermind being sick to get Mrs. Carmichael to make this soup.

By the next morning, I had bounced back.

I almost cancelled tonight, slightly apprehensive about eating food that was not cooked in my apartment. One minor complaint to Elliot, she stole my phone and called me out on my bullshit. Lovingly reiterating how long I've been waiting and wanting this before dragging me into the bathroom to help me with my hair.

"On other dates?" I hate the question immediately.

A buzz of worry that I've already ruined tonight climbs up my spine, each vertebrae a rung. That buzz plummets, crashing out.

If I slip under the table, will he notice? Or when the waiter comes by, I can ditch? There's got be a back exit, probably through the kitchen.

My teeth grind together behind my tight-lipped smile. Isn't that rule number one on a date? Don't bring up exes or past dates?

"If my mom counts, then yeah," Zach plays it off.

"Does your family live in Bensen?"

He shakes his head, hands fiddling with the laminated menu. "I wish. My family is in Tampa. Mom travels abroad for work most of the year. When she's in the States, though, she always spends a weekend here."

"What does she do?"

"Designs wedding dresses."

"Your mom is the real-life Elizabeth James." I gape. I force myself to take a drink of water so I don't pathetically end up salivating like a dog waiting for a treat. "Did you travel with her as a kid?"

"She is blonde." I don't miss or ignore the fact that he understood my reference. "No. She was a stay-at-home mom after she had my brother. We rarely bought clothes because she would make everything from scratch. Not that you'd ever know the difference. When I was in high school, Dad submitted her designs to a company. He went part-time with his job. Said it was time for her to chase her dreams."

I don't even know his dad except this one measly, outrageously romantic fact, and I admire him, want to send my compliments to the son he's raised.

"Does he regret that now?"

"Not one bit." Zach pushes up the sleeves of his sweater, and my gaze catches on a forearm when he refills my water.

"Your dad reminds me of mine," I admit.

After retiring from the league, my dad works in my mom's flower shop. He's shit at putting together a bouquet, absolutely no eye for what pairs well together. It always ends up with my mom redoing the order, but those seemingly ugly bouquets decorate our house.

He'd do anything for my mom.

Their love is tangible. I swear I can reach out and feel it. Put it on like a coat or dump it into a bath and bathe in it. They grew up with each other. Their hearts grew around each other.

Is that why mine feels like something is missing...

"Except mine is the opposite of athletic." He relaxes, comfortable and casually, into his seat. It helps ease the remaining tension within me.

Leaning an elbow on the table, I rest my chin in my hand. "Impossible. You're the starting pitcher for the Lakeland Bears," I say, doing by best impression of an announcer at a sporting event. It makes his boyish smile grow.

"Truly, though. My parents do not have an athletic bone in their bodies. Amazingly, I'm a D1 baseball player, and my brother is a D1 swimmer. They both tried to practice with us growing up, but quickly learned that coaches are there for a reason. No one knows where we got it from." He flips over the menu, not reading a single wine or cocktail listed. "Are you close with your parents?"

"Mhm," I hum. "And my sister."

"You said she's an artist." I like that he remembered. "What kind of art?"

"Meave will work with any kind of medium she can get her hands on, but her favorite is painting and pottery." I could gush forever about Meave. "She got really into functional pottery during her last year at SCAD. Made Elliot and I a complete dining set, serving platters, and even a butter shaped—" I am gushing. And rambling. Like he cares. "Sorry. I didn't mean to ramble." I grab for the closest curl to play with.

"Don't be. It's cute. Do you have any pictures of her art?"

A million. I slip my phone out of my bag. Opening the album I have them saved into, turning the phone for both of us to see. He listens the entire time I gab about each one, zooming in on details, asking questions periodically.

"She always wanted to be an artist," I answer his latest question, tucking my phone away.

"What about you? Always knew you wanted to be a sports psychologist."

"No." I shake my head, nose scrunches up. "Injury."

Zach nods with what I'm assuming is understanding, but I can tell he wants to know more. And I bet he would have asked, or waited till I shared, if it weren't for the waiter stopping by to take our orders.

I debate texting Cooper when Zach excuses himself to the bathroom. Let him know that if this date were graded, I'd at least be trending toward a B plus. The girl I was only a month ago is nowhere to be found. The one stumbling over her tongue, and feet, isn't the one sitting across from Zach.

Relaxing into the chair, we maintain a casual conversation.

Easily. He explains the various pitches, demonstrating how he holds the baseball with a balled-up napkin and when to use each.

I attempt and fake pitch him a two-seam. His head falls back with a contagious laugh.

"My hand-eye coordination is rusty," I joke, relinquishing a laugh myself.

"Maybe next date I can teach you."

I chew on the inside of my cheek. Maybe I should bump that grade up to an A.

There's a loud raucous that tears my attention away from Zach. Across the restaurant, in the bar area, far more casual than where we are sitting, I spy Chase, Dawson, and Jaxon. The latter is picking up a tipped-over stool. There are four water cups, four beers, and four plates, but only three of them.

Dawson catches me staring at them and waves hesitantly. Chase follows suit. Cautious as if he doesn't want to get caught. I wave back, the motion contained.

"Point me in the direction of the bathroom," I ask Zach, and he points to the left. I scoot back and excuse myself. "I'll be right back."

I did have to go to the bathroom, but I also needed a minute to get my confusion out. Did Cooper send them here to spy on me? Are they supposed to report back? Give him new ammo to use against me?

Post splashing water, and recomposing myself, I push open the door to the bathroom and almost hit Chase in the face.

"Hey, Sutton." His tone doesn't match his apprehensive body language.

"Um, hi. Didn't know you were coming here tonight."

"Surprisingly, they have the best wings on campus. Beats The Tipsy Bear every time."

"I'll have to try them sometime." Chase starts to walk away. I elongate a step and clasp his shoulder. "Everything okay back at the table?"

"Yeah." The word is clipped.

"Oooo-kay."

"How's the date going?"

"You can tell your friend it's amazing. Asked me on a second date already." The attitude I reserve for Cooper is very rarely dished out to anyone else. I'll apologize to Chase later. I brush past him, shoulder knocking, not waiting for a response.

EIGHTEEN

COOPER

ELLIOT'S BOLDNESS and lack of filter can be annoying. Like does she really think I could forget about the date when it is stapled to the interior of my eyelids so that every time I blink, I'm reminded that Sutton's going out with another person that isn't me? As if she doesn't see that I care about Sutton?

I know this was the whole point of me helping her, but it doesn't stop me from wishing that maybe she'd have decided not to go. See my feelings for her.

My phone bounces off my mattress and onto the floor. The brick slips out of my hand far more often than it should.

I run my hands along my jaw and neck. Massage the taut skin that needs shaving, tense with frustration, and overwhelming fear that I'm losing her even more than I already have.

You never had her my brain screams at me. I want to shake it, tell it it's wrong, that at one point she was just within a fingers grasp.

This is ridiculous. *You are ridiculous.*

I should never have told Sutton I'd help her. What was I thinking?

I take a deep drag of air, trying to expand my tightening chest, refusing to answer the rhetorical question.

Luckily—maybe, I don't know anymore—I have to leave for practice in thirty minutes. As if being on the ice is going to do anything but drag me down a different tunnel of agony.

ESPN's been hot this week. Longer segments dedicated to NCAA hockey as the tournament peaks over the horizon. Deep dives into team and individual player states. Comparing conferences and light-hearted bets being made about who will win it all. I watched some but had to stop when I got tagged in another comment from someone who hides behind their phone, believing they know more about a specific play than Coach, I turn off that feature on social media. That's progress, I tell myself.

We had two days off this week. Neither of which I went to the ice or stuck around the weight room, which I would have done before this semester. Ignoring my phone on the ground, I change and head to the arena.

———

JAXON TOSSES his practice jersey into the laundry bin in the center of the locker room. Slumping onto the bench next to me, he reaches behind himself into his locker to grab his phone.

"Kappas are throwing a party tonight. You in?"

I shake my head no, lacking the care to remotely sound interested. Usually I can, but not tonight.

My stomach somersaults, but not in a good way. I'm a can of soda, shaken up at the thought of going to a party, flirting and interacting with people I don't want to be around.

Disappointment is all over Jaxon's face. I hate it, but it doesn't change anything.

Bending over, I unlace my skates.

"You haven't been out with us once this semester, what's up, dude?" he asks as he continues to take off his gear.

"Too busy doodling Sutton's name in a heart," Beck quips, though his features are stone.

"Not true." Okay, maybe, but it only happened once in fourth grade. I swear. And I had perfected my Superman S.

She isn't the only reason I haven't been out this semester. Is my free time being taken up by her case study or coaching her on dating? Yes. Is the remainder of the minutes I'm awake—who am I kidding, even the minutes spent sleeping—consumed by her? Also yes. Call me pathetic, but being consumed by her is far better than the ugly monster living and roaring in the dark corner of my brain. Remembering that tonight is her date is probably why I woke up being swarmed by a dark cloud.

I'm mentally on empty, and there isn't a gas station anywhere near where I've stranded myself. That I'm to blame for. One can only pretend for so long before it catches up to you.

Slowly, I'm making my way back. I can sense it.

"Will you at least come grab a bite with us?" My best friend levels me with a look. His green eyes speak everything he isn't.

Can you see through me?

I want to ask him. Maybe even beg him to. I want to tell him the truth. I want to be the friend he deserves, the guy he met freshman year when we were assigned as roommates.

"Sure." I give him a weakening smile.

There's joy on his face. The way he throws an arm around me, dragging me into him part side hug, part noogie. The laughter that rattles in his chest begins to fill my tank.

Jaxon was insistent on trying the new wing flavors at this restaurant downtown. It's been open for several months, but I've yet to go. Cool atmosphere, and the beer is cheap.

We order an assortment of appetizers. Dawson is off tonight from his role as Captain Nutrition Plan. Reluctantly, but not really. He reads over the menu and then advises which dishes would be most suitable.

"Just shut it for a night," Jax groans.

"You had two bowls of rocky road last night," Dawson chirps back.

"And? Watch me do it again tonight."

I reach forward, dipping pita into one of the three dip cauldrons. The chip starts to crack under the weight of my scoop.

"You're telling me you'd rather have ketchup shooting out of your pointer finger than hot sauce?" Jaxon posed the ridiculous question and I guess didn't like Chase's answer.

Chase's response is muffled as if I'm suddenly underwater.

I feel her before I see her.

My attention is torn away from the conversation. Over Dawson's shoulder—he's sitting across from me. So while his mouth moves to give his answer, I hear nothing. My attention barely focused on him, but her—she's walking in.

Zach has a hand on the door, holding it open for her. His other hand is on her lower back. I read her lips, *Thank you,* before he leads her to the hostess stand. Then again, hand still on her lower back, to their table.

In my line of sight.

Someone upstairs must want me to see the results of my labor, or dangling the future I want in front of my face.

He pulls out her seat. Hands her a menu. Checks all the boxes of being a perfect gentleman. And by her reactions, I surmise she's enjoying every second of it.

However, I am not.

I must be staring.

The rest of the table turns their heads or leans to gaze around a supporting beam.

"Is that Sutton with Zach?" Chase questions.

"Why is she with him? Did you know about this?" Jaxon asks.

"Yeah." I take a swig of my light beer. Then another.

It dawns on Jaxon. Demeanor brightens as he says, "Our speed dating practice worked? Hell yeah."

They pester me with questions, wanting more information

about our other lessons. I tell them about most of them, leaving out the part about our kiss.

"I still can't believe you've never snogged her," Jaxon says around a bite. He's been watching a British dating show and keeps dropping their slang.

"We did."

Dawson spits out his beer. "You kissed?"

So much for leaving out the kiss.

"Do not tell her I told you," I say sternly.

"I knew you had a hickey the other week." Jaxon sets down his fork. "Now, I'm confused. You two kissed and have been hanging out, but she's here with Zach?"

"We aren't hanging out," I growl. The frustration behind it is directed more at me than them. Maybe even slightly at her. "Can we forget that she's here?"

Chase changes the subject. "Did you see the game last night between Toronto and Florida?"

Between songs, the entire place fills with laughter. Her laughter.

Under the table, my hand involuntarily flexes. Fingers splayed out against the air.

I haven't stopped watching Sutton and Zach. He leans forward with a napkin, wiping something off her face. Then must say something funny because she's laughing.

Again.

Full body. Her shoulders bunch up and down. Her head tilts back, and her smile encompasses her entire face.

I hate watching how he looks at her, like he knows where every single one of her freckles are. The constellations on each cheek, or the one on the inside of her left knee. Does he know about the patch on her lower back, underneath where his hand sat earlier, that she jokes is her tramp stamp?

I hate that he gets to push a strand of her hair behind her ear. There's no nerves. No hesitation in her as he does it. I hate how easy it is for him to be around her, pull these moves that he prob-ably pulls on every girl, and watch her fall for it.

Who am I kidding? His reputation on campus is squeaky clean. He's the true golden boy.

It's a strange feeling. A nothingness that is filled with reality. This is my reality. This is what I agreed to.

"I have to get out of here." Out of this chair. Out of this bar. Out of my head.

I get up from the table, not realizing the amount of power and intensity I let out. My hands grind into the grain of the wood as the chair beneath me clatters to the floor. I take a step backward and trip over the bottom rung.

Hitting the ground, I think I'm hitting the bottom of my well. Emotionally, mentally, and physically.

Everything is adding up around me, and I can't do it. I can't handle it.

Dawson lends me a hand. Chase and Jaxon are cleaning up their spicy margaritas dripping over the edge of the table. An ice cube hits my head and slides down my nose like a ski jump.

"Do you want me to go with you?" I don't know who asks, sounds meld together.

Three of my best friends stare at me. Their expressions range. Dawson and Chase like they don't recognize the disheveled and unwinding person in front of them.

But Jax...Jax is stoic, his typical class clown disposition gone. He gives me a nod, finishes his beer, and pulls out two twenties from my wallet.

"I've got him," he tells the others.

Throwing an arm around me, we walk out of the bar.

"Home or—"

"Do you think Beck still has a bottle of whiskey?"

"The one in the back of his closet that he hides in the bottom drawer of his dresser? Yeah, he has it."

We leave his car in the lot. Walk the twenty-five minutes home in silence.

Two hours later, the bottle is empty.

———

MY DOOR CREAKS OPEN. The hallway light blinding. I squint and let out an intoxicated growl. Rub my knuckles into my temple.

"Cooper Carmichael." Maybe the growl came out of her. The glow from my bathroom backlights her. A halo around her body. She's so pretty. Maybe I could give her a trophy off my shelf and tell her it's for the prettiest girl in the world. Even infuriated she's pretty. "Did you seriously send your friends to spy on my date?"

"Do you think you could be mad a little quieter?" I groan and she releases a witchy cackle good enough for Halloween. "I was there. We were getting dinner."

She creeps across my room to my bed, crawling on it, till she's sitting in the middle. Legs tucked underneath her. Arms crossed, eyes glowering at me.

"How was your date?"

"If you were there then you should know." She lowers her volume. "Were you sleeping sitting up?"

"What do you want, Dave?" It comes off more aggressive, more hurt, than I mean it.

She starts to scurry off my bed, mumbling words I can't make out. I reach out for her. My center of gravity is nowhere to be found; I miss her arm, catching her ankle instead.

Her skin is smooth. Warm. Silky.

"Don't go."

"Give me one good reason."

"Is this a new dress?"

Sutton's eyes drop down her body. Roaming like mine. "Uh, yeah."

"And y-you-your hair? Is that new?"

"No." I think she smiles, I can't exactly tell. "These are the curls I was born with."

"But you wore it differently."

"Elliot did it."

"It's nice. You look nice." I cough, which makes the pounding in my head intensify. The room tilts, but what's new? My whole life has been tilted off axis because of her. "Beautiful. Did he tell you that?"

"He did," she says slowly, or maybe that's me processing tonight. Or the alcohol. Whatever.

"Did you kiss him?"

"No."

"Did you want to?"

"*Cooper*," she warns.

"I'm sorry," I apologize several times. "You're happy." I don't ask because deep down I know she is. And who am I to take that away from her?

"Yeah. He—"

I cut her off. Because what I am is desperate. Desperate for her. Desperate to cling to the only person who anchors me. "Do you think we could ever be happy? Could I ever make you smile like that?"

"What are you—are you drunk?" she asks. The annoyance in her eyes goes with each blink, softening.

"Be happy with me, Dave." It's a plea. Broken and shattered, but she doesn't know that. Probably doesn't care.

Sutton uncurls my fingers from her ankle. "Cooper, stop. You're saying things you don't mean. You're drunk."

"I'm not." I pull my hand away before embarrassment hits me.

"Really?"

She stands from my bed when I don't answer her. Tugs at the hem of her periwinkle dress. "I'm going, and you should sleep this off."

I fall back against my headboard. I let the tears consume me. Ignited by the fear and unknown of my future, the feelings of being adrift, and the reminder of who I'm supposed to be. They consume me till I'm a blazing bonfire.

NINETEEN

SUTTON

THE ROOM ECHOES WITH A WHIMPER. A hammer made of his tears chips away at my heart. Any anger that I walked in here with has melted away, a puddle on his floor, and if I don't leave now, I'll slip. Tumble further into the confusing mess that is us like a knot in your favorite necklace that every time you try to untangle, it miraculously makes it worse.

Quickly, before I make a stupid decision, I leave. Tug the door closed behind me, then let my back sink into it.

Breathing hurts. Each inhale is a spike, puncturing my heart. Each exhale, a reminder that once upon a dream, I *was* happy because of Cooper.

It doesn't stop when I get home, or as I take off my make up. A scolding shower relieves absolutely nothing. Who decided that showers were the best place to think? Is that a universal thing? Even thoughts you've successfully dodged for years manage to weasel their way inside the sacred space.

"I give up." I toss my book on the floor. Reading isn't even a distraction, a movie either.

Finally, I find solace at four a.m., restlessly tossing and turning till then.

Stretching out this morning, my joints are tight, and my knee is achy. I rub at my eyes before climbing out of bed, slipping my feet into fuzzy purple smiley face slippers.

A yawn rips out of me. I decide to make a cup of tea before I look in the mirror at my probably disheveled and sleep-deprived face. Not to mention my hair that I didn't take care of before tucking myself in.

I find Elliot in the kitchen.

"You look tired," she comments. "Zach?" Her eyebrows do the worm.

"I wish." The words are sour, tasting like a lie. Do I? Yeah. Yeah, I do-don't know.

"Oh?" Expression losing its excitement with caution and tension. She hands me a mug with an English tea bag steeping in it and my ice roller. Great, face must be puffy too. We sit on the couch, and I tell her about my date, and that's it. Nothing about Cooper. Her curiosity has me forcing the spotlight on me to her.

"What did you do last night?"

A door opens, and heavy footsteps make their way to us. Elliot's rosy bottom lip is between her teeth, bringing her black coffee slowly up to her mouth. "That."

The quarterback of the football team leans over the couch, brushing his lips against Elliot's temple.

"Morning, E."

"Hey, QB. There's a pot of decaf in the kitchen. Mugs are in their usual spot." I drag my cup away from my mouth. Elliot shrugs, smirking.

"Do you two want breakfast?" he offers. "I've been meaning to show you my breakfast sandwich. Sutton, are you a vegetarian?"

"Omnivore! I prefer turkey bacon," I holler. He laughs a nod, turning his back on us to rummage through the fridge. "There should be some in the middle right drawer. Thanks!"

He waves the package in the air like a flag when he locates it. We don't move from the couch as he cooks in our kitchen. QB—I think his name is Kendall—is comfortable in our kitchen, not asking for locations of olive oil spray or pans, as if he's been here making breakfast before.

I smack Elliot's knee. "Have you been holding out on me?"

"No!" The secret-keeping traitor gasps.

"You're such a liar. Tell me everything."

"I don't kiss and tell."

"Bullshit."

"There's nothing to tell." My brows raise, silently calling her out again. Her voice goes up an octave as she says, "I mean it!" Then returns to normal. "I have an extremely casual friends with benefit agreement with the QB of the football team"—her words per minute gradually increase—"that's been going on since freshman year."

"Freshman year!? We've been living together this entire time, and I've never known?"

She pretends to zip her lips.

"Babe—"

Babe? I mouth to Elliot, fanning myself.

Kendall—I remember that is his name, and when they met. They hit it off, finding it hilarious their names are typically used for the opposite sex—is fan worthy. If they sold calendars on campus, he'd easily get July.

Zach would be May.

Cooper is absolutely December.

I'd give April to Jaxon, and Chase March. Beckett is October through and through—he is the definition of an autumn. Dawson is February.

My best friend is nonchalant. Legs tucked up under her, a glowy aura about her.

"How do you want your eggs?" Kendall leans over the counter.

"Anyway you'll give it to me. Thank you." She winks at him.

I pretend to gag.

"That's my girl."

It's like I woke up and was dropped into a scene in a romance book. I burst out in fit of giggles, but I'm also the lightest shade of jealous.

There's a knock on the door.

"I'll get it." Elliot bounces off the couch, flashing me her toned, round butt. She's in what must be his shirt, and I pray at least a G-string. "Cooper."

He's behind Elliot, who is tilting her head, eyebrows up asking the same question rolling around in my head: what is he doing here?

Cooper is carrying a tray of to-go cups, and from the way his shoulders sag and the dark bags under his brown eyes, he didn't get any more sleep than I did last night.

I already know he's having issues sleeping, and I hate thinking I had anything to do with that last night. Drinking included.

Cooper and Kendall do that strange boy hand-clap-hug-thing. Whenever guys do this, I question why they get weird about girls going to the bathroom together. Especially knowing, at max, they're just acquaintances.

The tray sits on our counter while Cooper helps Kendall finish making the over-medium eggs. He sighs when he accidentally drops one on the ground. Bumped out of the way, he's placed on bread duty. Plating the toasted bagels lathered with butter, Cooper gets out of the way for Kendall to construct his pride and joy.

Elliot smacks my good knee, giving me the exact attitude I gave her merely ten minutes ago. We both watch in awe as the guys chit-chat about their respective sports. Sipping on our drinks. Heads tilt and track their movements.

There's a buzz in the air that shocks me whenever he looks my way. Sneaking peeks over his shoulder or from behind the fridge door.

He's smiling, but his eyes are sad.

It's fleeting, but for a moment, I think he might be sad about us. Apologetic at the least.

"Breakfast is ready," Kendall calls out. He has two plates in his hands, carrying them to us. Cooper is behind him with another two.

Cooper cleans up everyone's dishes, collecting them as we finish. Elliot and Kendall disappeared into her room. Thankfully returning less than five minutes later fully dressed, and not a hair out of place or lip gloss stained skin.

"Don't study too hard." Elliot plops a kiss on the top of my head before floating out of the apartment, Kendall right behind her.

The door closing echoes against running water as I pad into kitchen to retrieve my second caffeinated beverage of the morning. I brush past Cooper, the smell of him overtaking the kitchen and me.

Wordlessly he does the dishes. Doesn't even flinch or laugh when I tease him about not using the dishwasher. His chin is tilted down, focus strictly on the suds and vigorous, circular scrubbing he's doing.

I return to the living room, tug the blanket hanging over the chaise. It dawns on me I'm not wearing pants. The worn shirt falls to an inch or two above my knees. One sock slouched to my ankles, the other pressing down the short hairs needing shaved. I adjust the fleece rectangle, turning to catch him watching me.

The tension between us is palpable. Cuttable by a knife, but not how it typically is. Lately, it's like I'm in a fun house with him. Stuck in one of the halls of mirrors, that's a never-ending maze. I turn a corner, gaining a new vantage point. Seeing him, myself, and us in a different light.

The grudge and frustration I've held onto seem more and more pointless the more time we spend together. Blaming him for my injury. Hating him...

Maybe I got it wrong.

Maybe I let us slip through my fingers.

Maybe it wasn't him who decided to throw us away.

Maybe I should have pushed for more answers. I could now.

I've had years to, but I chicken out, scared to be wrong. Petrified to be right.

I lean forward, grab my laptop from the console table, and open it up to my paper. Distractions. Anything to shift my focus from him.

He doesn't leave. He dries his large hands on a towel, hanging it on the oven handle. He picks up his coffee and joins me on the couch. Sits opposite of me, tucking a sweatpant clad leg up underneath him.

"I should learn how to make these," I tell him, hating the silence but not knowing what to say. I chest laugh, shaking my dirty chai. Awkward and uncomfortable. "It would save me, and you, money."

"Worse things to spend my money on."

"Are you going to work at the marina again this summer?"

Cooper's worked the last two summers at the marina on Lake Bensen teaching sailing and water sports. "Only way to be your sugar daddy. What's your summer plan?"

"If my cocky sugar daddy keeps up his participation, hopefully an internship."

I applied to a handful on a whim. Manifesting that the University would approve my independent study. If I get one interview, I'll be stoked. If I get zero, it'll suck, but I get it. My resume doesn't have the buzz words they are quickly scanning for.

"You'll get one." Hollow brown eyes finally meet mine. There's a pause before he asks, "How was your date?"

My fingers freeze, tighten over the keyboard. It takes everything in me to close the device and set it aside instead of hitting him upside the head with it.

Was he so drunk last night he forgot what happened after?

"How was my date?" I shake my head, flutter my eyes so he can't see the record setting eye roll I do. A similar irritation from last night rises my blood pressure. Standing, I snatch my latte before starting to head to my room. If that's all he has to say, I have no response.

The couch exhales from his weight, but I'm inhaling sharply as he catches my wrist, calluses digging into my skin, spinning me into him.

Our height difference isn't much, maybe four or five inches. He's staring down at me, free hand running along the hem of the old T-shirt I'm wearing as a sleep shirt.

"I hate that you still have this. Hate that you're wearing it."

Cooper lets me go when I step away from him. Again shaking my head.

We share a mutual hate that I still have this shirt. It's my high school boyfriend's shirt and I probably should have dumped it when he unexpectedly dumped me, but it's so comfy. Conformed to body. Holes in the armpits from overwear. There's zero emotional attachment to it. Cooper and Dylan didn't like each other, but after our breakup, that was pushed to the extreme.

It was confusing. This is confusing. Cooper is confusing.

I rub my palms into my eyes. "You are so obtuse," I spew.

Opening my eyes, I can tell Cooper's trying his best not to laugh. "Obtuse?"

"Yes, obtuse. You come here this morning with coffee, kindly clean up the breakfast dishes, and instead of leaving you sit on my couch and ask how my date was—"

"Which you didn't answer," he cuts in.

"Then follow me and tell me you hate my T-shirt. You are confusing and obtuse, Carmichael."

"I do hate the shirt. Would love to burn it off you."

"You've got to be kidding me," I groan. "Seriously? Are you trying to annoy me?"

"No." Cooper slumps. "I came here to apologize about last night." I cross my arms over my chest, waiting. "I'm sorry, Dave. I'm sorry for what I said to you and if I ruined everything."

"There was nothing for you to ruin." And for a quick second, I believe my own words.

The reason my date wasn't great is standing in front of me running a hand through his mop of hair.

Ruining every assumption I have about us. I'm one subtle breeze away from falling off the tightrope I'm balancing on.

"You mean that?"

"The date was good. A plus, professor." I smile tightly, answering his previous question.

"Good." His tongue runs along his bottom teeth. "Great. Well, I can go then. I'm sorry again, Sutton."

Sutton. How can I hate and love how he says my name?

It's the sun after a storm. A breeze on a scorching day. Perfect, and possessive. As if he's the only one that should be using it.

"Why'd you get drunk last night?"

"Because I don't want things to change between us." He reaches for my hand, and I let him. "I don't want to lose you again."

"Nothings changing," I falsely promise.

"Good." Cooper squeezes my hand. "I'm gonna use the bathroom, then will go."

"Wait. Are you busy right now?" I ask, suddenly attached to his presence and not wanting it gone. "I have a test coming up. I could...um...wanna help me study?"

"Only if you change." He smirks, and I allow it. Rolling my eyes and striding into my bedroom.

———

TWO HOURS LATER, we've gone through an endless amount of flash cards. The confidence I have for my test I wish bled into how I felt about Cooper.

He left so I could get ready to go to the movies with Elliot. Folded on my dresser is a Bears Men's Hockey T-shirt. There's a note on top of it.

Stop wearing his shirt. Wear or don't wear mine.
But please, for me, get rid of his.

I stare at the chair in my reading corner, my ex's T-shirt is slung across the arm from where I tossed it.

There's a small push from my brain to toss it. The encouragement has my two feet carrying me to the chair. I ball it up and shoot it into the metal trash can next to my desk. Shuffling back to my dresser, I pick up Cooper's shirt. Run the cotton between my fingers.

He was wearing a crewneck earlier, and didn't have a bag with him. No pocket on the front of the sweatshirt to have stuffed an extra shirt. And there's no way this would have fit in his pants pockets...

It clicks.

The fabric still warm from his body. I bring it up to my nose and inhale. Woven threads doused in his smell that's the same since we were kids. Sandalwood and a breeze off the lake. Rich, earthy, and comforting as if the sun is setting and we're coming in for dinner from spending all day outdoors.

Elliot pops her head into my room. "What's that?"

Caught, I drop the shirt from my grasp. "Nothing," I respond too quickly.

"Ready to go?"

"Gimme five minutes."

"Only five. I want to pick up candy from the store before we go and one of those boxed wines."

I pick up Cooper's shirt and stuff the shirt into a drawer alongside these recycled feelings churning within me.

TWENTY

COOPER

I STARE at it all night.

Sutton sent me a photo of her in bed. A book and her readers on one side, and a sleepy tea on the nightstand. My shirt—the one I left on her dresser earlier today—is on her body. Lakeland Men's Hockey stitched across the chest.

The image starts at her mouth. A simple, devastatingly beautiful smile spreads across her lips. The bottom is heavier than the top, so it hangs out a bit. The feeling of it already haunts me. I feel them now on my lips like a ghost of a memory.

There is nothing overtly sexy about the photo—I doubt she's even trying—but it's the hottest thing anyone has ever sent me.

I save it instantly, but wait to respond...after typing out several responses and deleting them.

I want to tell her how good she looks and offer the rest of my closet to her. I also want to ask her if she tossed Dylan's shirt.

Who keeps their ex's shirt? After how their breakup went down, I'm surprised she'd have it all these years later.

You could tell her, the voice inside me that I hate creeps out of its dark recess. Holding what I did, what I saw, over my head instead of encouraging me to tell her. The guilt I do feel is held hostage.

My phone buzzes again, it's a group chat, but it has me going back to my conversation with Sutton.

> Knew you'd look good in my clothes.

SUTTON

> How many other girls have you fed that line to?

> Let me count...

> Zero

SUTTON

> I'm honored. Do I get a badge or something?

Or something. Like the truth.

God, why did I tell her I didn't want things to change? I want things to change. Desperately. And in stolen moments, ones like this, I think they are.

Again, I'm typing and retyping a message before deciding to call her. Sutton answers on the third ring, her voice hazy with sleep.

"If this is to ask for a different type of picture, good luck."

"It's not." I chuckle lightly. "But if you were to offer..."

"Not happening."

"How was the movie?"

"You know I've never been a fan of thrillers. Accidentally punctured my Styrofoam cup, then moved on to squeezing Elliot's hand to the point of bruising." There's a rustling of sheets across the line. "Is this phone call my something?"

"Sort of." I get quiet, and roll over on my side, staring at the bracelet on my nightstand. I rarely take it off, wearing it except when I sleep or shower. It's been through countless practices and games.

A long stretch of silence passes between us.

"Are you still there?" Sutton yawns.

"Yeah, sorry."

There's another wrestling of sheets and a creak of a headboard as if she's sitting up. "Can I ask you something?" Maybe she's finally being bold enough for the both of us. I thought I was, calling her to finally tell her, but the sound of her voice had me chickening out. I wanted to protect her then, and I still want to protect her now.

Without a response, she asks, "You didn't start the rumor, did you?"

One word. One word that has me hanging off the edge of a cliff.

You'd think with the years I've had to ruminate on my decision that I'd have the words to tell her. Rehearsed and memorized. But I don't.

"No."

"W-why?" Sutton breaks around the words. "You lied?"

"I lied when I said I started it."

"Why?" she asks again.

"Because I wanted to protect you. I never meant to hurt you."

"Protect me?" Her voice cracks. "Telling me you started it is what broke me. Not what people said."

I hate her tone. Hate the images in my head of her in bed, eyes probably welling up, pulling at her curls or arms wrapped protectively around herself like I wish I could.

"I know...but I need you to believe that telling you I did was to protect you."

"Why should I believe you?"

"Because you know me better than anyone else, and I think we can both agree deep down you never thought I did it."

"Will you tell me who started it then? I assume you know."

I wish I didn't. "Dave, if I tell you, what's that going to change? What is that going to do for you now?"

Isn't it good enough knowing it's not me? I would ask that, but it sounds too desperate in my head.

She sighs. "Nothing, I suppose. It was years ago, and I've mov

—" Sutton stops mid-word, but I know exactly the lie she was about to say absentmindedly.

"Were you really about to say you've moved on?"

"I'd like to think I have recently." Her tone lightens, a playful edge to it. "Wouldn't you agree?"

"I would. Can I ask you something now?"

"Sure."

"Can we officially be best *friends* again?" Friends. Because if one thing should change, then it has to be this.

She laughs and if it isn't the best sound, I don't know what is. I haven't traveled much, but I bet Sutton has the best laugh in the world.

"No." She's teasing me. "But I'll think about it. Might have to see if I have any open slots."

"Fine. Just know that I might not be your best friend, but you've always been my best friend." I swear I can hear her eyeroll. "And I'm going to prove it to you."

"Give it your best shot, Carmichael."

"Dave?"

"Yeah?"

"What are you wearing under my shirt?"

Her laughter floats through the phone, filling my eardrum and bedroom. I press the phone closer to my ear as if I could lock the sound inside my head.

"Goodnight, Carmichael."

She hangs up, and I fall asleep with a smile on my face.

TWENTY-ONE
SUTTON

I SWEAR HAVING a crush is like being stuck on a rollercoaster of emotions. Highs and lows. Belly dropping and heart pounding emotions we are too young to be experiencing or trying to understand. At least that's what society convinces you.

You can't possibly love someone at such an immature age. Its fleeting, childish, more infatuation. If it were to work, it most certainly won't last.

How could you truly know who or what you want when you aren't even legal?

I'm not afraid to admit that I had a crush on Cooper when I was a kid. I even told him I loved him when I was ten.

But that was just infatuation, displaced feelings because we spent all our time together.

Sophomore year of high school, when Izzy rushed to the cafeteria table, giddy to tell me that Dylan Martin had a crush on me, I gravitated toward the high of knowing someone liked me. He was cute. Curly blond hair with a crooked smile. Recently got his braces off, had an ear pierced, and into snowboarding.

We started dating a week later.

It lasted all of seven months—but that was a record among my friends. No one else had surpassed the five-month mark.

Maybe that's why we ended, Dylan always thought he was hotter shit than he was. The school bell hadn't even rung the morning he strolled up to my locker and announced *I'm dumping you* way too casually.

When I asked for an explanation, he laughed and sauntered away back to his friends, who were all laughing. The hallway went silent, and all eyes were on me. I was devastated. Colossally embarrassed. I could never show my face in school again.

Spinning on my heels, ready to ditch school, he caught me. Arms on each of my shoulders.

"Hey. Hey, Dave. It's okay," he consoled me.

"I'm fine." I wasn't. Lips wobbling, tears ready to spill, shoulders curled in. I tugged on a curl, till Cooper took my hand.

I clung to him, and he let me for days. It wasn't out of the ordinary for us to be glued together. But this was different. Our dynamic had shifted, and that's when the questioning started: did Cooper finally feel the same way about me?

Spoiler alert: he didn't, and I learned the hard way.

He hurt me. Shattered my heart, and ruined our friendship along with it.

Through it, I still loved him because I couldn't figure out how to get off that damn rollercoaster. If I couldn't get off, then I might as well channel those emotions into something else.

What's the opposite of love? Hate.

Love to hate, and friends to rivals.

Everything after became a competition. We were already competitive people at our core, but this was different. Cooper would find every single opportunity to spite me. Academics, athletics, extracurriculars, college, friends, and even chores. I couldn't go anywhere or do anything without him being right there.

It annoyed me.

Cooper became a festering wound.

If I could go back, I wouldn't. A part of me hates myself for succumbing to all of it so easily...but that reflection can be saved for another rainy day to dissect.

I'm still trying to dissect the fact that he didn't start the rumor. If he didn't, who did? And why would he lie about it?

Dr. Manning flips around a tablet with an article about burnout pulled up. "I thought this would be more beneficial for you to read this week. The other reading is outdated in my opinion."

I change the brightness and tug the tablet into my lap. "Thank you," I say, diving into the article. When a sentence rings with a new idea to try with Cooper, I pause, hurrying to grab my notebook and pen. I take frivolous notes, layering the page with sticky notes.

It takes me another thirty minutes to work through the article. When I come up for air, Dr. Manning is grinning at me. Soft and gentle.

"Have I ever told you that you remind me of myself when I was your age?" she asks, arms folded on her desk.

"No?" I ask, lit up like a Christmas tree. "Really?"

Deep auburn hair, almost brown, that frames her face and shoulders in loose waves moves when she nods. Dr. Manning relaxes into her desk chair. "I, too, was an eager learner. A sponge for any and all bits of information."

"My mom calls me that. La mia spugnetta."

"In Italian?"

"Yeah?" I tilt my head. "You know Italian?"

"Spanish and French, too. Moved around a lot as a kid. Does your mom?"

"No." I muster a reminiscent laugh. "But one summer we were on a family trip to Lake Como, and I packed an entire backpack of books. Mom unpacked them, only to find I snuck them into a different suitcase and my sister's bag." The memory pulls at me. It was a trip to celebrate our first adoption anniversary and Dad winning the Stanley Cup. Before I started playing hockey.

"Most of my memories from that trip are reading by the lake, reading on a boat, reading in bed. Pretty much reading."

"Chapter books?" Dr. Manning doesn't appear to mind my tangent.

"Only one. They were educational children's books—I was eight. That's why mom calls me a sponge in Italian."

"I see."

"Sorry, you didn't need to hear all that."

"That's okay. I enjoy getting to see another side of you, Sutton." She leans forward on her desk.

"Do you have time to review the edits on my paper? I still have a few more components to work through with Cooper, but I'd love your feedback right now."

"Hand it here." Dr. Manning puts her glasses on, pushing them up her nose when they fall. Eyes shift left to right as she makes her way through my messy first-ish draft.

The original, completed except for a few *insert data points here*, found a new home in the trash can.

It was a rash decision, I'll admit that. Following Cooper's practice I watched, I did two things: called my physical therapist to determine what I needed to do to get cleared to skate (again) and reconfigure my case study.

Operation help Cooper fall back in love with hockey.

It's why I took him to play MOOSE. Help remind him why he's playing, of the fun we used to have skating on the ice together. We've also tried other forms of movement, and discovering other hobbies for him to channel time and energy into.

I slip my phone out of my bag while I wait for her to finish. It shouldn't take her long. My research paper has a minimum twenty-page requirement, but it's only ten so far. Butterflies flutter around my stomach at the notifications on my screen.

ZACH

Do you have plans tomorrow night?

COOPER

Coffee after you're done?

It's eenie, meenie, miney, moe to pick who to text first. I opt for Zach, something telling me that's who I *should* be choosing.

I'm going to my sister's art show.

I swipe out of our messages and go to Cooper's.

I don't drink coffee. A friend would know that.

COOPER

Technically speaking…a dirty chai latte is coffee. It has espresso in it.

I've already had caffeine today.

COOPER

Didn't realize there was a law about how much caffeine you can have.

Have some more so you can tolerate hanging out with me.

Who said we're hanging out?

COOPER

Pretty sure you did.

Must've been a different Sutton.

COOPER

Interesting…there's only one in my life.

I'll be outside the building.

This is the second time in the past two hours that I've lifted my head and found Dr. Manning smiling at me.

"Someone special?" she asks teasingly.

I swallow. Yeah, someone.

"Just a friend."

"Same friend as the one in this?" She spins my laptop around, tapping the corner of the screen. "This is...wonderful, Sutton. Some of your best work. You speak through experience and compassion. There's a sincerity that I haven't seen in this line of work in years. If you read between the lines"—a knowing look pulls on her face—"you can see how much you care for your patient."

"I'm not supposed to care about him." It comes out of me with a bite. Defensive as if she can see through the weakening walls I erected as a fortress when it comes to Cooper.

"Is that so?" she challenges.

"Unbiased. I should be unbiased and neutral as a psychologist."

"Why?" Why? That's not the response I expected.

"I-I-I." I lick my lips, a dryness coating my throat. I don't know if we are talking about school and my future career anymore. "I can't...I can't care for him."

"Caring is at the core of who we are. Caring is different from being unbiased. We work on being non-judgmental and strive for objectivity, but that doesn't mean we can't care. Is wanting the best for someone not caring about them?"

"I guess."

"Do you think having compassion for the athletes you'll work with is a weakness?"

"No." It comes out as a whisper.

She asks me several more questions. Each one expanding the guardrails I've put up. Not around what I'm doing, but who I'm doing this with.

"Mr. Carmichael is lucky to have you on his team," she says. "I'm excited to see how this wraps up."

After we talk through the second half of my case study, I exit her office. Tense. Excited. Relieved. Confused—contradicting emotions mix inside of me.

Spring air rushes my exposed skin when I push open the door.

My chin tips up and warm rays of sun heat my cheeks. I close my eyes and take a languid inhale, relishing in my favorite time of year.

I open my eyes, and Cooper is standing there. Plastic cups in each hand.

"Hi, Dave."

I exhale all of the feelings worming their way through me. Exhale the nerves and hurt I've held on to.

"Hi, Carmichael."

"Ooooh. She's last naming me." He smiles, and it's like an eraser. Erasing the years I've kept him at arm's length. Erasing the animosity.

"Seems fitting."

"Yeah?"

"*Coffee* if I'm putting up with you, remember?" I turn my hand over and wiggle my fingers in a gimme movement. He hands me the cup, and I take a sip quickly.

So good.

"What else would you like me to call you?"

He shrugs. I poke his stomach.

The hard muscle must be quicksand because I can't pull my finger away, instead it sinks further into the fabric covering him.

"What?" I ask, gaze grazing up from his abdomen to his face through my lashes.

"Nothing." I tilt my head. "I'll tell you another time," Cooper follows up with. "Let's go. I have a game tonight."

"Where are we going?" His pace is quick, and I chase after him.

"I don't know. Just wanted to spend time with you." I take a sip of my drink, eyeing him over the hood of his car. "Is that okay?" he adds.

Sirens go off in my head, warning me that this is also a mistake. My heart shuts it off, tries to unplug the alarm and toss it out.

"Yeah, it is."

TWENTY-TWO

COOPER

DO I have any clue where we are going? No. All I know is that I wanted to spend time with her, especially before tonight.

We're playing Ohio State tonight, Dad's alma mater.

They were supposed to come, but Mom has the stomach flu. She apologized twice over the phone, and I could hear Dad's inner turmoil of staying home to take care of her or coming to the game. He'll still watch, always finding a way to stream our games.

I shouldn't be happy that he won't be in the crowd.

There's always an added layer of pressure around this game. Ohio State's coach is the same one who coached Dad and didn't recruit me. He's cordial. Friendly because he has to be.

I don't only want to impress him, I want to prove to him what he missed out on.

My teeth clench. Always having to prove myself.

I open the door to my Jeep for Sutton. She's the only person I don't feel the need to be something I'm not. Over the past month, I've cut myself open for her to see everything. If I didn't know better, I'd think she was a doctor. Removing the dying parts of me, fixing me, and sewing me back together.

She slips her tote bag off her shoulder.

"Want me to put that in the back?"

She takes her phone out before passing it to me. Her hands adjust her skirt when she sits down, pulling it over the scar on her thigh. Closing her door, and putting our bags in the back, I round the car and climb in the driver's seat.

Sutton is texting. I wonder who? Zach?

Probably. Her cheeks lift, a hint of pink to them.

Maybe I should just take her home.

My car roars to life, and I pull out of the campus parking lot. The playlist Jaxon and I were listening to earlier pours out of the speakers.

"Hannah Montana, really?" She snickers at me in surprise. I go to change it, but her hand stops mine. "Leave it."

Sutton and I drive around for twenty minutes, landing ourselves back at my house. We don't speak except for her reading Elliot's text that she's at my place.

Inside, I head upstairs to start my pre-game prep, and she follows me to my room. Echoes of my roommates' voices trail behind us from the living room.

"You didn't have to come up here with me," I admit.

"You have my bag." She points at the canvas tote printed with fruit.

One of my shoulders is being dragged down. "Sorry. Here."

I hand it to her. She takes it but doesn't leave. Sutton walks further into my room, claiming my desk chair as a bag hook.

"Can I stay?" she asks over her shoulder, eyes wandering over my bulletin board. Pictures taped to it.

"Please." *Don't sound desperate, Cooper.*

"When do you have to leave for your game?" Sutton turns around, laptop and notebook in her hands.

"An hour."

"Okay. That's enough time to—"

I shake my head no, and she pauses. Mouth hanging open, and I want to kiss it again. Perfectly pink, recently glossed. Unabashedly, my gaze dips to them, and I know she catches me because she closes them and swallows slowly.

That only makes me want to kiss down her neck, following the motion. Press my mouth in the hollow of her collarbone, over each freckle. Whisper sonnets over the parts of her I'm desperate to love on, the invisible parts of her that make her beautiful and that I cling to.

Her mouth curls into a smirk. "No more practice kisses."

"What about good luck kisses?"

"Nice try." She rights her shoulders. "I'm not like the other girls you've been with. I'm not going to beg for it."

Sutton doesn't know what she's talking about. There aren't other girls, not since she's been single.

And if anyone is going to beg for it, it'll be me.

Maybe not.

Forty-five minutes later, when I exit my bathroom in my game day suit, her eyes are locked on me. Pupils widen, irises morphing into an electric shade of blue-green. Her telltale color of anticipation, excitement, and desire.

Maybe if I'm good enough, she'll beg for me.

"Are you coming to my game?" I ask, leaning against the doorframe, taking in the way she's stretched out on her stomach on my bed.

"Do you want me to?" Her question is more of a challenge, like I'm daring her.

Of course I want her there, but I think I want her to want to be there more.

"Yes," I answer simply.

"We'll see, Superstar."

———

SUPERSTAR.

The nickname rings in my head with each touch of the puck during warm-ups, and I'm grinning as Coach wraps up his pregame speech.

Our game against Ohio State is under thirty minutes away from puck drop.

We're tied in our conference standings. The last time we met, we lost in overtime, but that was at the beginning of the season. We're better now. More in sync. Stronger and faster. Our team is young after eight seniors graduated last year.

I skate out onto the ice to stretch.

An Ohio State player skates by me, purposely slow, a cruel curl to his mouth. "No daddy tonight? Couldn't stand to watch his disappointment in person?"

Another Ohio State player joins them, this one I don't recognize right away. They go back and forth with other insults as my hearing starts to ring, chest tightening. Dammit, this can't be happening right now.

Jaxon skates up next to me, glowering at the other player. "Fuck off, Gentry. And Shrivner? Your shooting average is that of a dog trying to get its ball from under the couch."

They skate off when their coach yells at them.

I want to ask him if they are right, but no words come out; my brain is too focused on slowing my breathing.

"Sutton's here."

"She is?" The words fumble out of me, part like a little boy, part because the constriction of my lungs is finally relinquishing.

I know I asked her to come, but I didn't think she would. Jaxon spins me in her direction and points. Elliot sees us first. Sipping on a fountain drink, she waves. Big and bold.

My eyes zoom in on Sutton...and Zach.

We skate over to where they are sitting.

"Are you wearing jerseys?" Jaxon yells at them.

Elliot nods. Twisting her upper body to show off the name on her back. She picks up the shoulders of the jersey, showing off Jones printed on the back.

Sutton is lost in conversation with Zach. Someone's better with small talk now. Or is there more to their relationship than I know? Is this why she said no more practice kissing?

Finally, she spins forward and sees us. Her lips are pressed in a line. A red-brown brow arches, mouthing *gonna score tonight?*

Looks like you will I mouth back, both our eyes flicking to Zach.

Jaxon teases Elliot on her choice. "Greene looks better."

"What's yours?" I ask Sutton.

"Not yours."

"It would look good on you."

"Davis would have looked better on you."

Would have, but her number looks pretty good too.

TWENTY-THREE

SUTTON

THE BOYS LOST BY ONE. Four to three.

All three periods were intense. From the first puck drop, it was fast and physical. Jaxon might be goofy off the ice, but on the ice, he is a bruiser. Ohio State players were getting chippy with Cooper, and he was there pushing them around, protecting his teammate and best friend.

Still, Cooper had two goals and one assist.

Zach left immediately when the game ended, needing to catch back up with his teammates. We'd bumped into each other at concessions, and Elliot invited him to come sit with us—which involved flirting with the person next to us and convincing them to sit much higher up.

After the game, Elliot and I hung around, waiting for the guys. They shuffled their way in pairs out into the lobby. Chase and Dawson. Jaxon and Beck.

No Cooper in sight.

No one knew if he was coming.

I tried calling him, but it went directly to voicemail.

An hour later, I'm in bed reading when my phone buzzes, a text from him coming through.

COOPER

Is my therapist on call?

I'm not your therapist.

COOPER

Still on call? I need to talk to someone.

Please.

Give me five and I'll call you.

COOPER

I'm at your door.

I hastily tug on a pair of sleep shorts. Throw my curls haphazardly into a claw clip and rush to the door. I open it, and he's breathing heavily. A large hand pressed to the center of his chest.

"Did you run here?" Cooper nods, barely. I sigh. "Are you stupid? You played thirty minutes tonight and took a nasty hit."

"I'm fine." I shut the door, then follow him into my living room. "You live seven minutes away."

There's a layer of glistening moisture on his skin. His chocolate brown hair is disheveled, the ends of it sticking out in different directions, as if he was tugging on it after he took his helmet off.

Cooper is in a matching sweatsuit with our school's logo, a growling grizzly bear, in the center of his chest. This is what he wears after the game—a bit of me wishes he came in his suit. He leans down, unbalanced, to untie his sneakers.

"Your socks are inside out."

He appears dazed. Confused. Not entirely here. Broad shoulders are hunched over, making him smaller than the larger-than-life boy he is.

I take a step closer to him, and that's when I see it. The small tremors in his hand. Tight, quick breaths—I don't think his chest is heaving from running, he's too in shape for that—and small hiccups. Dark lashes fall across the tops of his cheeks when he shuts his eyes.

Instinctively—I think, but I'm not too sure anymore—there are a lot of things with Cooper now that I feel called to do, maybe want to do, that I'd run away from before. I shove them aside and say something bratty to compensate as my hand reaches for his. As soon as my fingers graze the bare skin of his wrist, his head jerks away. Then it's back on me, eyes open, and he reaches for my hand.

"Come. Sit." I gesture to the couch.

Cooper doesn't budge. "No." The word cracks. He coughs, clearing his throat. "Can we lie in your bed?"

"Oh. Um." Say no, Sutton. Say no. That rings between my ears. I have a million reasons why that's not a good idea, and number one is that we kissed. Even if it was for practice, I think about it. Sometimes I want to do it again.

Sometimes? Okay, a lot of times.

And earlier, when he was staring at my mouth, it took all of my willpower not to ask him to kiss me again. The first time was for practice. Good, but maybe a fluke?

Cooper might be the bad kisser, not me.

Plus, it's intimate. My room, my space.

"Yeah, sure," I say despite myself and the common sense I pride myself on having.

He follows me down the hall to my bedroom. Elliot and I's bedrooms are next to each other. Our headboards are against the shared wall, making it quite interesting when she has a "friend" over. She has an en suite, while my bathroom is across the hall from my room.

Like the rest of our apartment, it is a hodge-podge of thrifted and Facebook Marketplace decor. Nothing but everything goes together. Picture frames—round, square, gold, chipped neon paint, seashells, and zoo animals—litter the large wall in the hallway containing photos of our friends.

I open my door, once again pulling him with me. Inside, we disconnect. The tight grip on my hand is gone.

Cooper lies on my bed. Back against the queen-sized mattress, staring up at the ceiling fan. I turn on the light.

"Turn it off," he croaks. "P-pl-please."

The room is dunked into darkness, only the thinnest beams of light coming in from the cracks in my blinds. They're like spot-lights on him. On the boy who broke me, but I think broke himself too.

The carpet is soft against the soles of my feet. Sitting down next to him, the bed dips and shifts as I scoot back and lie down too.

"I like the dark. I think it understands me the best," he admits to me, or maybe he's admitting it to the darkness. Bonding them even deeper together. "None of me feels real in the dark. I don't have to prove anything in the dark."

"What do you mean?"

"I can just be me in the dark."

"You are real, Cooper." I let my fingers dance across my bedding, finding his, softly brushing against them, a silent request to touch him, to hold him. He curls his pinky around mine. "You are real to me; and there's nothing you need to prove to me...or anyone else. The only person you owe anything to is yourself. What you think about yourself, how you view yourself isn't deter-mined by what others expect. It never has been, and it never will be."

We lie there for a bit longer. His breathing slows, allowing us to breathe together. My head rolls to the side, cheek pressing into the bed.

"I tried calling you after the game."

"I know, but you were with Zach."

I swallow. Cooper can't see me or my frown. "It wasn't on purpose. Elliot invited him to sit with us."

"You don't have to make up an excuse."

"It's the truth." I push at his hair with my free hand, clearing his forehead. "I called to check on you."

He sighs and tells me everything. About the players before the game, and how he feels the pressure to win, especially this game. Mentions his parents not being there in which I remind him his mom is sick, and otherwise they would be. Besides that, I listen and only speak when he asks a question. Cooper rattles off every 'mistake' he made in the game, and his last few words stun me: "And...and you were there with him."

Cooper sits up, cursing at himself.

"I already told you, it wasn't on purpose."

"But—"

"I'm sorry." I don't let him finish.

He runs his hands through his hair, interlacing them behind his neck. "Things with Zach are going well? Yeah, you're happy?"

We've been through this before. "Cooper..."

"Can I take a shower or bath?" he asks, taking this conversation in a one-eighty, letting a third mention of Zach tonight fall away.

"Um. Yeah, sure." I had assumed from his dishelved appearance when he showed up that he'd rushed to get dressed and get here...but I'm confused. Getting whiplash from him helping me date Zach, then upset about seeing us together. Drunkenly telling me he wants to be happy together and giving me his shirt to wear. I can barely keep up with my changing emotions, I can't keep up with him, but for whatever reason, right now none of it matters. I leave my bedroom to grab him a clean towel from the linen closet. "Here."

In the bathroom, he's already stripped off his shirt and sweatpants. He's in his boxer briefs. Black. Tight. Revealing.

Cooper's XXL shirt suddenly feels like the size of an American Girl Doll shirt. Constricting around my neck, I tug at it and suck in an inhale. Then again. Digging my teeth into my bottom lip.

Stop looking, Sutton.

We don't like him.

But wow. Wowowowow.

Cooper turns, dropping his clothes on top of the sink.

It takes everything in me not to groan.

"Twist the knob to the left twice for hot water," I say, jamming my eyes closed.

I start to exit, my back to Cooper, but I stop. Turn around, and close the door. The darkness might be how he hides, but I can hide with him. Stay with him. Pretend that the world doesn't exist, and inside these four walls there's only us.

He sits on the toilet, folding in on himself. Elbows digging into his knees.

I start the water, letting the rush from the spout tune out his heavy breathing. From a container next to the bath, I spoon in a few tablespoons of lavender epsom salt to help him relax. I dip a finger in the tub once full.

"It's ready."

He stands, silent. Climbs in and sits down. He's still in his boxers. I mentioned that he forgot to take them off, but he shook his head left and right. Is it bad I would have been okay if he did take them off?

The tub is too small for his frame. Knees bent, the tops stick out of the water. His head falls back against the tile where he's leaning back.

Whatever halted me from leaving, comes over me again. I don't question it. I don't know what it is, but I let it happen. "Let me." I take the washcloth from his hand. Squeeze soap onto it.

Cooper sits up. On my knees, leaning over the tub, I wash his back and chest, careful of the bruise from his game. His breathing shudders under my touch. When my fingers dip into the curve of his muscles, they tighten.

I wash his hair. Using my fingers as a comb to work the shampoo and conditioner into the strands. He's going to smell like me, but I don't think that's a problem. I don't mind having him in that way.

He's quiet the entire time. Eyes closing occasionally, grip tight on the tub edge.

Finishing up, I start to stand, but Cooper tugs on my arm, and I fall into the tub. Water splashes over the edge, soaking me and the bathmat.

His hand still wrapped around my wrist, he tugs again. I fall forward onto him and into a kiss.

Cooper drops his hold on my wrist. Relocating his hands to the back of my head. Gripping it possessively. Fingers weaving into my curls, my clip broken and lost in the tub somewhere.

"I'm sorry, I shouldn't have done that." He pulls back.

"It's okay," I say against his lips before pressing my mouth back to his.

"I'm not kissing you because—" Cooper pulls away, but I lean into him, not wanting to lose this moment or connection. A desperate version of me claws her way to the surface. I need him. I want him.

"I know. I'm not either."

We kiss again, I don't know who initiates it. Mouths gliding over each other, his tongue slipping past my parted lips. The kiss is messy, unyielding, a desperation that makes me think I'm his breath of air.

The water around us goes cold, but I barely register it. All I can sense is him.

I brace my hands on his shoulders. The sound that vibrates through him when my hands move over the tense muscle pulses through me, an invitation to keep touching him. I move a hand up into the hair at his nape and tug. Our kiss deepening.

The doorknob turns, and I'm grateful I locked it. Elliot's voice floats through the crack.

"Sutton, you in there? I'm home."

I pull back from Cooper. "Yeah, taking a bath."

"Want a glass of wine? Or your book? I saw it on your bed."

"Oh, um. No, that's okay!"

"Okay." There's a pause. "Can you ask Cooper not to leave his shoes in the middle of the living room?"

Our eyes flare wide.

"Oops," Cooper jokes and I feel like I've won a carnival prize with the brightness that's returned to his features.

We can hear her walk away.

My focus is back on him. "Wanna get out? You are getting a little pruney."

Cooper shakes his head no. Eyes flooded with emotions, I don't think either of us cares to admit. "I'll have to go if we get out."

"I didn't say that."

"No, but I should."

"Cooper—"

"Dave, you want to date someone else."

"I—" I don't know if that's true anymore. I don't think I know what I want anymore.

"Take the towel. I'll get another one."

"No, wait—you're soaked. You'll get water everywhere." I hand him the towel. "Take this, mine is on the hook."

I pull my towel from the door, but am spun around, and drop it. Cooper holds my waist in one hand, pinning my hands above my head with the other, and pushes me up against the bathroom door. He kisses me hard. Commanding, overtaking, and it feels like a claim. I've never felt so alive within a kiss itself.

"What was that?" I push my head against the door, touch my fingers to my lips.

"Don't bring him to my games. Don't bring anyone else." Cooper licks his lips. "I'd ask you to lose him, but we both know I'm competitive."

"Are you telling me you're—"

"An option? Yeah, I am, Sutton. I'm making myself an option."

Cooper picks up the towel. Dries off his torso, then runs it up and down his muscular legs. I watch the entire thing. He gives me a casual, quick smirk when he stands up. Ruffles his hair with the towel.

Water droplets hit my forehead.

"Here. Let me," he says when I go to dry it off.

Cooper takes the corner of the aqua terry cloth towel in my hand and dries my forehead.

My eyelids flutter, the tips brushing against his skin.

I want to kiss him again.

I think I want to do a lot more than kiss him.

Cooper must sense it. He kisses me again, squeezing my chin, dragging my mouth up to him so that I'm on my tiptoes.

Then he stops. Drops my chin. I hit the ground and reality.

"And that?" I pant.

"I'm greedy."

TWENTY-FOUR

COOPER

ELLIOT IS LEANING over the counter, eating ice cream out of the container, when I waltz into the kitchen giddy. I'm fully clothed now, but when the cotton-polyester shifts against my skin, it's Sutton's fingertips I feel. Nails scratching into me, explorative and selfish.

Elliot's mouth makes a popping noise when she drags the silver spoon out of it. She lets it dangle between her pointer finger and thumb.

"Nothing to say?"

"I don't know what you are talking about," she replies smugly.

"Hey, Elliot. Do you have any moisturizer? I'm out," Sutton calls from her bathroom.

"Top drawer in my bathroom."

"Thanks!" Sutton's feet slap against the floor in a scurry to Elliot's room. I'm frozen in the archway, steadied by the sound of her voice.

"You like her, don't you?" Elliot spoons another bite of vanilla.

"Since the day I met her." Something settles in my chest.

Different from the dread that's been there. Different than when I showed up here earlier. It's smothered by…by…no, that's just quietness. Peace. "Have a good night, Elliot."

"Yeah, you too, Coop." Her mouth moves to the side in way as if she's calculating tonight and the years prior.

———

"COOPER!" Madeline, Beck's little sister, bounces off the couch to me. "I kept asking Beck where you were."

"I was visiting a friend, but I would have been home sooner if I knew you were going to be here." I drop to my haunches to put us at eye level and let her lanky arms wrap around my neck.

She's nine, but petite for her age. Arms secure, I scoop her up in a hug and spin her around in a circle. Madeline laughs, and I see it rejuvenate her brother.

There's very little that makes him smile. I honestly don't remember the last time I saw a smile break through his steel of a face. Not even when we won our conference last year, or when he was named conference MVP.

Madeline makes him smile, though. Not a fake one. Real. Big enough that it makes all his other facial features relax and brighten.

When I set her down, I ask, "What have you and your brother been up to?"

"He made homemade chicken nuggets. Then I painted his nails. And—" She pauses, contemplating something. "He was going to let me paint *your* nails while we watched a movie."

"Is that so?" I let out a ha, flick my brows up at him over my shoulder.

Luckily, the remainder of my roommates walk through the door.

"Are you sure you have time for my appointment?" I ask, pointing at the guys over my shoulder.

"*Wow*. Madeline's salon is going to be busy." She giggles. A dangerous glint to her cobalt eyes.

One after another, we take turns getting our nails painted in various shades of the rainbow. My fingers are an alternating shade of orange and green. The colors are horrific, but her work is pretty clean for a third grader.

"You are good at this, Mads," Dawson tells her, checking out my nails. His are sparkly red.

"I know." Her head bobs, eyelashes fluttering like a little princess.

"Mads." Her brother pokes his head in from the kitchen. "What do we say when someone compliments us?"

"Thank you," she groans. Then turns in the direction of Dawson. "Thank you, Dawson."

"Anytime, Mads."

"You're supposed to say you're welcome." In the kitchen, you can hear her brother relent a sigh. "It was career day at school this week. When it was my turn to present, I said I want to work in a salon when I grow up. Or be a singer."

"You can be both," I encourage. Maddie smiles, finishing my topcoat.

An hour later, the five of us are learning a dance routine to "I'll Make a Man Out of You" from *Mulan*.

I love these nights.

I love these guys.

Kissing Sutton was a reset. At least that's what I keep telling myself. Coming home, participating in this isn't a struggle, but it was before. Finding the energy. Finding a reason to laugh.

"No." Madeline grabs Dawson's hand, dragging him to the front of the group. "You are supposed to do it like this." She demonstrates a dance move that feels more advanced than what a third grader should be doing. Maybe she should add dancer to her career list.

Beck is next to me, hands on his hips, uncoordinatedly gyrating. I bark out a laugh.

"Watch it, Carmichael. You're not much better."

"Watch this." I circle my hips, take a crack at a move I saw on Jaxon's social media.

Jaxon is the best dancer out of all of us. He doesn't know that we've seen his secret social media account where he dances and lip-syncs to trending songs. Shirtless, in the campus parking garage, when the rink is empty. He has thousands of followers and the comments on his posts are probably why his ego is always inflated.

"No wonder you haven't won Sutton over yet," Beck jokes.

"All that matters are my moves in bed," I tease, but change the subject. "Have you thought about putting her into dance classes?"

"Yeah, but Mads wants to try soccer next."

We were finally dismissed from dance class when Madeline yawned. It was already past her bedtime. Beck carried her up the stairs to his room—she sleeps over enough that he has a trundle bed for her.

Dawson and Chase are in the kitchen making a second dinner. Jax flops onto the couch next to me. "Where did you go after the game?" he implores.

I shake my head, declining the beer he hands me.

"Nowhere."

"I tracked your location. You were at Elliot and Sutton's."

"Then why'd you ask?"

He's a sad puppy, has been since he got home. I could see through the mask he slipped on when he walked through the door and noticed Madeline. "Wanted to see if you'd tell me the truth. I don't get what's going on, Cooper. Why won't you tell me why you went there?"

"Oh, it was nothing, Mom had sent me something I was supposed to give them," I lie.

"What was it?" His tone is stern, inquisitive.

"What is this? Twenty questions?"

"No, because you won't even answer more than five questions, and when you do, I know you're lying."

"Fine, but promise me this stays between us."

Jaxon raises his pinky to me. I loop mine with his and then I tell him everything.

TWENTY-FIVE
SUTTON

IT'S as if the universe is Team Cooper. I go to start my car the next morning, and the engine sputters. Now, I may know nothing about cars, but from the noises and smell drifting from my hood, I can surmise that I am not driving my car today. Probably a week at best.

Meave's art show is tonight in Chicago. I wanted to be early to surprise her, but instead, the surprise will be her little sister and biggest fan no-showing.

"This can't be happening," I mutter to myself, dropping my forehead to the steering wheel. Disappointment tugging my patchwork jacket tighter around me.

I run through the list of options in my head.

Elliot, no.

Jordan, no.

Beck is probably busy as always. Jaxon doesn't have a car. Dawson—who, like me, loves a color-coordinated calendar and shared his with me—was leaving after practice to go meet his boyfriend's parents. Chase, probably with Elliot.

Cooper...

He mentioned he was planning on going to the show last

week, but I never heard more from him on it. Maybe he's still planning on going.

He isn't my last resort. Truthfully, he's who I thought of first, but then I started replaying last night and...was it too soon to need him?

I unplug my phone from the charging cord and text him.

> Are you still planning to go to Meave's art show?

COOPER

Wouldn't miss it.

His response is unexpectedly immediate. Simple words that would have annoyed me in the past, possibly mocking, now have me grinning at my phone. Cooper's words from last night echo in my mind. *I'm making myself an option.*

He's trying. He's been trying for longer than I care to admit.

I hate admitting it, but Cooper is nice, considerate and complimentary. So friendly that it comes off as flirty, but that's not how he'd treat me. He'd tease and taunt me—eventually it was mutual because I'd throw it right back. Everything was made into a competition—which I thought was a need to be better than me.

But the past couple of months...this is different. I think?

At first, I chopped it up to our arrangement. Teaching me. He was making me comfortable with flirting. However, now, I think he was flirting with me. Intentionally.

And the craziest part? I liked it. I've enjoyed it, craved more of it. Might have unintentionally started flirting back.

COOPER

Do you want to ride together?

> Are you sure this isn't your way to kidnap me and murder me?

COOPER

If I were kidnapping you, it wouldn't be to murder you.

Be ready at 2.

We talked the entire car ride. Bickering over music, our hands accidentally brushing when we both lunged for the aux cord.

When it happened a second time, he curled his fingers around mine, guiding my hand to my lap. Without ever taking his eyes off the road, he finagled my hand, flipping it over and resting it on my thigh. His palm swallowed mine, callouses brushing my skin. Long fingers intertwined with mine.

My gaze wanders up to his face from where we're connected. It looks like he's holding his breath, waiting for me to pull away, but I don't, I relax into the seat and the feeling. Cooper notices, and the corners of his mouth hook up.

I raise his *I'm making myself an option* with I want him to be an option.

In the parking garage connected to the art gallery, he houses a ham and cheese sandwich he packed. My sister is vegan and picked a restaurant that has an exclusively vegan menu to celebrate her show afterward. Meave promised we wouldn't even know the food didn't include meat.

I walk in before Cooper—we planned this in the car. He swore it wouldn't matter that we showed up together or walked in side-by-side, but it does. Tonight is for Meave, not the announcement that Cooper and I are...well whatever we are.

He's two steps behind me, and I know he can see Meave over my shoulder.

Her fluffy brows are ticked up, mouth pursed with a slight glint in one corner.

We speak silently—a secret, unique language we developed years ago. Blinks and brows and smiles are an entire language to us.

She's asking me why he's smirking and why my cheeks are painted the same color as his.

I blink back. *Don't ask questions.*

Her brows dip, a sassy, subtle head movement, and I know this conversation, while over now, is going to be revisited later.

I throw my arms around her, pulling my sister into a suffocating hug.

"Congrats!" I squeal.

"Thank you! I'm so happy you made it." She squeezes me back, just as tight.

"Wouldn't miss it. Even though I was at your first unofficial show."

"Computer paper and finger paints." We release each other. "However, the playdough sculptures never did get the admiration they deserved."

Since the day I met Meave, she's always been an artist. Pictures lining our shared room moved to dotting the fridge and Dad's office. In frames lining the entryway. A full mural at Mom's shop.

Painting—watercolors is her specialty, but she loves all mediums. Photography, ceramics, oil pastels—and she doesn't consider it art, but I do—needlepoint and sewing.

The dress she's wearing, I know, is one of her creations. It's long with a fitted bodice, and scooping silk from the waist down, a dark amethyst. She's the most exquisite piece of art in here tonight. Deep brown hair in big loose waves, one side pinned back with jeweled clip. Blush perfectly placed on her warm olive skin, and an ombre of cool toned eyeshadow.

I quickly peruse the front room with only my eyes. Bright pieces of artwork line the walls. Stationed in the room are cocktail tables with black tablecloths. A handful of servers walk around carrying small bites and wine.

"This. Is. So. Cool."

"I know." Meave beams. Giddy, her feet can't stay still. "Can you imagine if I had accepted that job at the big gallery in London? This probably wouldn't have ever happened."

"It would have," I reassure her, but quietly I'm agreeing. I'm so happy she's a drive away instead of a trans-Atlantic flight.

Cooper's cousin's best friend, Emerson, lives in London. She's an editorial and travel photographer. Meave spent a summer there a few years ago, learning from her and staying in her husband's hotels. Emerson connected Meave with a gallery there which turned into a job offer after graduation.

"Are there more rooms?"

"Two more rooms." Meave can barely contain her excitement. "They gave me the *entire* space."

"As deserved."

She pulls me in the direction of a black and white painting. Cooper waves bye, pocketing his hands into his jeans.

Meave walks me around the gallery, giving me a private tour and explanation about each piece. She politely ignores the people trying to pull at her.

This entire night is about her, but here she is, arm looped into mine, hand grasping my bicep, squeezing when she gets specifically delighted about a piece. Voice octave jumping up with passion. In between pieces, she gossips with me like we are back in middle school and sneaking across the hallway into each other's bedroom to have a sleepover. We'd hide under the comforter with a flashlight and books, talking and giggling till mom and dad cracked open the door, reminding us that it's bedtime. They gave up eventually.

"When were you going to tell me about *that*?" Meave pinches my side, not bothering to lower her voice in the crowd of people that's beginning to form.

"There is no *that*." I laugh. The kind you do when you are hiding something. I'm not hiding anything from her, maybe myself.

"Uh-huh. That's why he's been ten steps behind us, following you like a lost puppy all night."

"No, he hasn't." I throw my chin over my shoulder, looking for Cooper.

"I was joking, but damnnnn."

"We're friends again." No one notices my misstep, my body physically tripping on my verbal admittance.

"Friends or more than friends."

I stumble over my words this time, a road bump in my throat. "Uh—"

Meave whirls in front of me. "You kissed." She points a finger at me.

"Shhh." I relocate her finger to pressing into her mouth, silencing her. Her two-word freakout drew attention to us. "People are watching."

"I don't care!" However, Meave tugs us into the offices in the back. I spot her desk immediately. Cluttered and organized chaos. She pulls out her desk chair, pushing it in my direction. Then moves papers and books around before sitting on her desk.

"Tell me everything. I want allllll the details."

"Meave." I roll my eyes, taking a seat. "He's like a brother to you."

She snickers. "Apparently not to you." When she can tell I'm not going to relinquish any juicy details, she sighs. "You've gotta give me something. At least tell me how it was. One to ten?"

"Mind seizing, body trembling, foot popping." Again, I feel the ghost of his lips on mine. I lean forward, resting my head in her lap. She runs a hand through my curls like she used to. "He told me he didn't start the rumor."

There's a pause, and I hear her take a sharp inhale. I've refused this topic for years. "Do you believe him?"

"I'm not sure. I think so, but I don't understand why he'd lie, or all these years later not come clean. What do you think?"

"Honestly?"

"Yeah." It comes out more like an exhale. Meave taps my shoulder, and I sit up.

"You were quick to believe that he started it...and...never gave him a chance to explain. You kept him at an arm's distance until what? A month or so ago?"

"Okay, but—"

"You needed time and so did he, but that's up."

Is it hot in here? Did they turn off the AC? I'm hot. I take off my jacket, draping it in my lap.

"Sutton." Meave places her hand on mine.

"Meave, I don't know what to do. I've had it all wrong. Blamed him for things that aren't his fault. Built up this hatred for him an-and now I feel stupid." I place my free hand over my eyes willing myself not to cry. I'm already crashing out on her biggest night of the year. "But he won't tell me anymore details. Won't say who did start it. Won't talk about it. Do you think he's protecting them or me?"

"Have you asked?"

"Not exactly. I got scared."

Meave leans forward, swiping at something moist on my cheek. Of course a tear, or ten, slips out. "Scared?"

What I say next comes rushing out of me. The dormant volcano inside of me erupts, memories and emotions are rivers of lava. "I don't want to lose Cooper again, or one day he eventually decides I'm not good enough."

"Sutton."

"I know. I know. Those are irrational thoughts."

"They are. You've always been enough," she reassures me, "for me, Mom and Dad, Elliot, and Cooper. Always Cooper. And you never lost him because that pathetically obsessed boy never let go of you."

That's where I'm caught up. Replaying memories, before and after that day in high school, and trying to see them clearly. I feel like I need glasses or something to see them clearer.

Meave swipes at another tear.

"Shit, Meave, I'm sorry. I ruined my friendship with him and now I'm ruining your night."

"You are not ruining my night, Sutton." She jumps from the desk, smoothing her silky dress before helping me stand.

I grab a tissue from her desk and blot under my eyes, forever grateful for waterproof mascara. "Promise?"

"Pinky. I should probably get back out there though. You're gonna be okay. Give Cooper and yourself grace. And don't navigate this alone. I think he'd be okay if you leaned on him...or at least fucked it out of your system."

"Meave!" I push at my sister's shoulder.

"Oh come on. If the kiss was that good...just imagine it." She wiggles her eyebrows at me.

Trust me, I have. Last night to be precise. Twice.

I jump ship to a new topic. "When do you leave for filming?"

"Not till May," Meave plays it off casually, "but I met someone last week." Lucky girl syndrome, I swear. "So I think I'm gonna bail."

"Bail? After knowing him for a week?"

"Wait till you meet him."

"What?! He's here?" I squeak.

"Well, duh. He's obsessed with me." Meave walks us out of the office and in the direction of someone who looks like they could own half of the Chicago skyline.

———

MEAVE WAS SURPRISINGLY RIGHT. Her new crush is obsessed with her, and dinner was incredible. Cooper enjoyed it so much, he finished off my Buddha bowl.

"Sutton, do you want me to drive you back to campus? We can have a sleepover?" Meave asks me, tucking her to-go boxes into a brown paper bag.

Cooper glances at us across the table. Sly and inconspicuously. He's trying to be a snoop without getting caught.

He is, but it's not his fault.

He isn't to blame for becoming a magnet. Drawing me to him whenever he's in the room. I hate that this is how my current reality is. I keep waiting to wake up, but I'm not sleeping.

After Meave and I's conversation at the art gallery, I'm coming to terms with the reality. Minorly. Searching for the words to tell Cooper, and to make sense of the emotions dwelling within me.

Standing across the room, I don't know if I want to run for the hills or run to him.

"Can we plan a sister night for another weekend? Spring break? Cooper is going to drive me back."

TWENTY-SIX

SUTTON

WE IGNORE the first crackle of thunder. Ignorant of the harsh line in the sky and gray, endless clouds chasing behind us. Above us, through the open top of Cooper's Jeep, is a cotton candy sky. The day fading into warm oranges and pinks, watercolors blending as if the sky is one of Meave's pieces of art.

"Turn it up?" he asks as ODESZA's "Line of Sight" comes on.

I reach to turn up the radio, my fingers twisting the knob, making sure it is on an increment of five for him. I lift my hands when the song hits its peak, stretching up through the roof.

Wind on my fingertips and billowing in my curls. Contentment on my face.

I tip my head up and take a slow inhale of air and the lyrics.

Is he taking them in, too? Can he hear the way I sing the lyrics as a plea to him? A single rain drop hits the tip of my nose, and as I open my eyes, I debate telling Cooper we should put the top back on. We checked the weather before programming the directions to campus. There was a ten percent chance, but the radar only showed a minuscule speck of green.

I turn my attention to him and decide not to.

From his passenger seat, I stare over at him.

Wind in his hair.

Smile on his face.

He's the Cooper I remember. The Cooper I know he's fighting to get back to.

Without another warning, thunder shakes the car. Lightning painting over the sunset by gray clouds. The heavens open up, droplets beating down on us.

Cooper curses. "It wasn't supposed to rain." He urgently turns on the wiper blades.

Definitely should have suggested putting the top up.

"Do you want me to put the cover on?" I ask, tugging my hair into whatever messy ponytail it'll manage. We *were* having a good hair day. And by we, I meant my curls decided to behave, but we are one raindrop away from it becoming a chaotic mane again.

When I reach to unbuckle myself, I plan to climb into the back to attempt to pull the soft top back on, Cooper's hand drops on top of mine.

"Don't." His gaze jumps to me before returning to the road ahead as the rain starts coming down aggressively. "People drive like shit in the rain. I'll pull over at the next exit."

"You sure? I don't mind." Cooper won't remove his hand from mine. "I'll be quick. Nothing will happen."

"Right. Yeah, I'm not letting you do that. I'm not putting you in a position to get hurt, Dave."

"Okay," I say, licking my bottom lip.

Cooper releases my hand, and I search on my phone, shielding it from the rain, for a place we can stop. I reprogram the maps. The stretch of road ahead of us doesn't have many exits but plenty of farmland. That's the middle of the Midwest for you.

We get a reprieve from the rain ten minutes later, but that doesn't last long. The rain kicks up again as we hit the three-mile mark to our stop.

Cooper puts on "Unwritten" and laughs out, "It says to feel the rain on your skin."

Soaking, we finally pull into the parking lot of a strip mall.

Next to it, a neon sign flashes. One of the letters is missing. So, instead of The Cork Stop, it reads The Cok Stop.

Cooper reads it aloud. "There or McDonald's? I have a change of clothes in the back."

"We have to go to The Cok Stop."

"Thank god," he groans jokingly, pulling into the half-packed parking lot. His sleeves are pushed up, exposing veined forearms. I suck in a short pull of air, silently, watching them flex as he turns the wheel.

We get out of the car and immediately pull the soft top back into place. In his trunk, luckily covered and dry, we find a towel and try to dry off the front seats.

I grab his duffle from the back, and we sprint to the front doors.

Under the covering, we laugh, taking in our drowned rat appearances. His shirt is glued to his body, dipping into the carvings of muscles. The light fabric is entirely see-through. His trousers are heavy and cling to his quads. Brown hair is flat. He runs a hand through the front strands, pushing only half off his forehead.

I probably don't look any better.

Our eyes meet, and something passes between us. I can't put a finger on it, what it is, or why it feels important, but it lingers. My body is buzzing from the inside out. I'm forced to swallow, but it's slow, and my throat is dry.

"You good?" he checks in.

"Great." I nod, deciding tonight I'm running to him instead of away. And maybe listen to Meave's suggestion.

Cooper holds the door open for me, taking the bag from my shoulder. We ask a bartender to point us in the direction of the bathroom.

"Over there." She hands us a wooden stick covered in stickers with a key attached to the end. "Only one bathroom."

We head in the direction she points.

I'm not sure what I expected of The Cork Stop. The exterior

screams dive bar with stale cigarette air and cheap beer. However, the interior is moody and cozy. Wine bottles line the wall behind the bar, and there are barrels as standing tables. Cracked linoleum booths line two walls under decor that is all wine puns and dated to whenever this place opened. My personal favorite being the painting of two glasses, with one glass saying nice legs to the other.

If I were in my early thirties, I think this would be my dream spot. A wine dive bar.

Single file, we head down a short hallway that leads to the bathroom. I use the key to unlock the door and walk in. Cooper follows me inside, locking it behind us.

"What are you doing?"

"Changing," he says casually.

"After me?"

"Sure. I don't care."

"Then why are you in here?"

"I'm not going to leave you in a strange place by yourself." He drops the duffle on the sink, unzipping it. Tossing me a pair of his sweats and a sweatshirt.

He turns around, letting me change. I shiver when my checkered maxi skirt pools on the floor, skin lightly damp. I tug the graphic T-shirt I was wearing and sports bra over my head in one sweep. Only in my underwear, I bend down to pull on his sweats. His sweatshirt floods me—size, warmth, smell, emotions a part of me screams we shouldn't be okay with.

When I spin back around, I realize he was facing the mirror. My reflection is unobstructed. Arms crossed over his chest, tongue pushing into his bottom lip, he's pretending to stare up at the ceiling.

Our positions flip, backs to each other. I take paper towels to squeeze the water out of my curls, finger-combing it afterward. In the mirror, I catch a glimpse of Cooper, it's only fair.

He's unbuttoning the collared shirt he wore. One button at a time, slowly. My eyes linger on the sculpted muscles, narrowing into a trim waist. I'm disappointed when he puts on a shirt.

Cooper turns around. The corners of my mouth tug up sloppily. My cheeks are hot. He steps up behind me, an arm reaching around me to brush a strand of hair off my forehead. I watch him intently through the mirror as he pulls off a green hair tie from his wrist. Running his hands through my hair, he pulls it off the nape of my neck, splitting it into three strands. Meticulously, he braids it down my back before tying it off with my hair tie.

"Thank you," I say, it comes out as a whisper.

The energy in the room is pulsing.

Whatever has been passing between us is back.

He turns me around, hands on my waist.

My butt is pressed into the sink—which is surprisingly clean. The whole bathroom is. His legs straddle mine. Arms bracketing me in, but it's his stare that has me anchored. Has me one second from leaning forward and kissing him.

The crush I had on him at eleven, and again at fifteen is resurging. Stronger, and with a vengeance as if it never left.

His stomach growls.

I shake my head. "Always hungry."

"Growing boy."

"I don't know if your body could handle any more growing or muscles."

Cooper's eyes have the tiniest reaction. His throat bobs slowly around a swallow, the tip of his tongue peeking out of his mouth moistening his bottom lip. "Liked what you saw?"

"I could ask the same."

"I always like what I see." A hand reaches for my braid, and he tugs on it, tipping my chin. "Gonna answer me, Dave?"

Our mouths are close.

My eyes drag from his lips and into his brown gaze, and back again.

"No." Yes.

He smirks and releases a throaty laugh that scratches my insides like a match. "Liar. Such a shame. I'm awfully hungry, baby. And not for food."

"Good thing the special of the day is apricot whipped burrata."

"Good thing." Cooper's voice sends a shiver down my spine. "We'd better go order before they run out."

***

The bartender is one of two employees in the establishment. When we sat down in a worn-out booth, she slipped from behind the bar to take our orders.

I've been spinning the straw of my Diet Coke since she left. Cooper is silent, drinking his wine.

We luck out, getting the last order of burrata. We also order a sandwich, in which I joke again about his hunger. Cooper pinches my side playfully, but his eyes are roaring louder with hunger than his stomach.

The bartender returns with our sandwich on separate plates. I take the pickles off my half and hand them to him—I've never liked them, but he does.

Between bites, we talk. Laughing like we used to do when life felt simpler. Easier. There was a bliss about being a teenager—the world at your fingertips without any idea of the responsibilities and pressures that came with it.

Cooper thumbs at the corner of his mouth. "You have a little something," he tells me.

I wipe my napkin over my mouth, but it comes back clean.

Cooper shakes his head. "Here." He leans forward, without a napkin, and brushes his thumb against the corner of my mouth toward the center.

I don't know what comes over me, but my tongue darts out, licking the pad of his thumb clean. His pupils flare when he applies pressure, pushing on my tongue.

Speakers buzz to life, shaking us out of the moment, when someone puts change into the old jukebox.

Cooper pushes his plate to the center with mine and extends a hand to me.

"Dance with me?"

"You don't dance."

"Madeline would disagree. I'll show you."

I don't know what he's supposed to be showing me. We move uncoordinatedly. For as graceful as we both are on the ice, the same cannot be said about right now. Our hips bump, shoulders collide. I think I step on his feet more than I make contact with the planked floor. Despite it all, we're laughing. Continuously. Contagiously.

I can't stop.

My head tips back as I burst out in another fit of laughs.

"I don't think I've had this much fun since—" I attempt to find a time, but I can't. High school, maybe? Definitely not college.

Cooper finishes my thought, "Me either," then adds, "MOOSE and our date if anything."

"That was fake. Practice." We spin and his hold on me tightens, drawing me closer and closer to his chest. "But tonight?"

"Not practice. I told you, Dave, I want you."

TWENTY-SEVEN

COOPER

MY FINGERS FIND the end of one of her curls framing her face. Running the springy auburn strands between the pads, I let it go. Drag my hand slowly to her cheek. Tilt her face up in my direction.

"Give me one night. Give me till midnight, that you're mine."

"Cooper—" Her tone feels like a pot of water on the precipice of boiling.

"One night, Sutton."

She gulps. Head swaying to the right, trying to pull away from me.

"You called me Sutton." The blush on her cheeks spreads, down her neck into the top of my sweatshirt. It's the same color as her hair, this deep red that only happens when I say her name.

Sutton used to get embarrassed by the way she full-body blushed, self-conscious about how red she'd become, but I love it. Loved making her blush, then and now.

"Look at me." I assist in bringing her gaze back to me.

"What does that mean?"

"It's your name."

"No, Cooper. What does it mean to be yours?"

Oh.

It means that you're the only girl I've ever loved or wanted. It means that you are the first and last thing I think about when I go to bed—fuck, with her, she also consumes every other waking thought. I don't know where one ends and the next one starts. It means you are the one who grounds me, but also makes me feel alive. It means you are my home, my family. It means that I'd do anything for you, to make you happy, to have you.

I'd give up hockey if it meant having Sutton.

"It means this."

I cup her cheeks and pull her lips to meet mine. Sutton is on her toes to reach me. Her hands curl around my biceps to stabilize herself.

Her lips part, and I seize the opportunity to slip my tongue into her mouth.

My hands slide up her cheeks, palms resting high on her cheekbones. Fingers sliding into the roots of her auburn curls.

Sutton's kisses sting. A shock to my cold and dying heart. Reviving me with bursts of color and life. The waves of doubt and societal pressures recede, drawn back by her. She coats me in a layer of stillness, peace, of comfort.

We keep kissing. Our tongues and lips are now dancing. You'd think we'd been doing this for years with the way we are in sync.

She lets out the littlest, most delectable whimper when I drag her bottom lip between my teeth.

I don't know how I'm ever going to return from this. Kissing her again. Tasting the way she's sweet, slightly innocent, but there's a creature in her that's clawing its way to the surface.

I always knew she was the start of my world, but I think she's going to be the end of it too.

Sutton grabs my hand.

Her eyes never leave mine, her head turned over her shoulder, as she leads us blindly to the bathroom, snatching the key off the bar counter where we set it earlier.

The hand not in mine pushes open the bathroom door.

Sutton steps away from me, spinning on her heels. Irises flaring, the hazel shifting to a blue-green with each sharp inhale.

Giving her space, physically and mentally, I push my back into the door, flipping the lock behind me.

I want her. I want her so bad, but I'm going to let her take the lead here.

She's always held the leash to my heart. A collar wrapped around it, a dog tag hanging from it that says: *If lost, return to Sutton Davis.*

"I—" Her bottom lip disappears between her teeth. Hands flexing at her sides. Eyelids rapidly blinking. She's thinking this through.

My little genius. My little overthinker.

I'll accept whatever outcome this is, but there is one I'd prefer, and I sense it brewing in her.

"Do it," I encourage.

"Do what?"

"Whatever is spinning in that beautiful mind of yours."

"You mean it?"

"Yeah, Sutton, I fucking mean it."

"But—"

"You can do it." Sutton swallows slowly. "Say it, Sutton baby." She drags her bottom lip between her teeth, again, nibbling on it. "Admit you're mine tonight. Tell me you want me too."

"Yes."

"That's not what I said. And what have I told you? I need your words."

Sutton sways forward and backward, barely noticeable, and I watch the way her chest hitches with a sharp inhale. Eyes closed, she starts to say, "I'm—"

"Eyes on me while you tell me the three words I've been desperate for years to hear."

Eyes now a bright, mossy green lock onto mine, destroying all of my walls, beckoning me to her. My heart seizes with anticipation. "I'm yours, Cooper." Sutton pauses. "I want you—" She pauses again, then attaches two words that I hate hearing. "For tonight, and I want you to make me feel good."

For tonight. For forever. We'll see which one wins.

"You've always been such a good listener. Haven't you, baby?"

As if she needs permission, she asks, "Can I kiss you again?"

"Never have to stop."

Mouths colliding and hands in a frenzy all happen within a blink.

There's barely any space between us, but I need her closer. My free hand tugs at the fabric of *my* sweatshirt she's in. The movement pushes my knee between her legs. Sutton accidentally bites my lip with a small gasp at the friction.

"Sorry," she whispers. I kiss the apology away.

Unlike our initial kiss, which, for the record, was out of this world, this is as if we are both starved. Have been stranded in the desert, and this is the first drink of water we've had in years.

I can't get enough, so I take more. I grip her hair, twist the braid around my fist, exposing her neck as I bite and kiss over it. Push at the collar of the crewneck to get to more of her soft, silky skin.

Sutton grinds herself on my thigh. Working herself back and forth. She mewls, and my grip on her tightens, my knee inches higher, and she moans.

"Cooper. Cooper, what is—"

Sutton is soaked. I can feel it through both pairs of sweats separating us.

I begrudgingly pull away from her neck, a mark already forming. But that internal annoyance is lost when I see her. A hand pushed into my hair, the other braced on the wall. Head tilted slightly back and mouth falling open. Eyelashes ricocheting off her cheeks, but her gaze locked on me.

She's close, I know it.

But she's hesitating. Stalling her movements, and I can sense that she's unsure. A rush of previous comments she's made about her exes come to me.

"Let go, Sutton," I start to talk her through it. Let her know that what she's feeling is good and nothing to be scared of or embarrassed by.

"But…"

"It's okay." I kiss her temple, then correct myself, "More than okay."

"I-I don't—help me." Gladly.

My hands find her waist. The left gripping her tightly, guiding her. The right finding her clit through the cotton and pressing down with my thumb.

Sutton curses, moving faster.

"You're always beautiful, but fuck, I wish you could see…" The words die on my tongue when I spot our reflection from the corner of me eye. "Turn your head. Look at yourself in the mirror." Our cheeks are pressed together, as we watch, and I describe what I see. "Radiant. Truly alluring and pulchritudinous."

Giggles sneak out between whimpers, and I come a little from the sound. Could she be any more perfect?

Junior year of high school, I studied for three weeks straight to beat her in our county's regional spelling bee. She lost while trying to spell pulchritudinous.

I apply more pressure to her as her movements become unco-ordinated. Quick and short till my name is rung out of her like a plea.

If I weren't already bewitched by her, I utterly am now.

"You good?" I ask, touching our foreheads together, stroking the side of her cheek.

"Better than good." Sutton tilts her chin up, steady kisses but more frenzied hands.

Her hand reaches for me, and if I never make it to Team USA I should at least earn a gold medal for this because I stop her. Circling her wrist, I drag and pin it behind her back, taking the other one with me.

It's been me, my hand, and fantasies of Sutton for almost

two years. Call it wishful thinking or manifestation or stupidity. I'd combust if she touched me, I'm barely hanging on as it is now.

"I want to make you feel good too."

"Trust me." An eyebrow flicks up, and I stifle a cocky response. "You have." Her cheeks and ears tip pink. "Later," I tell her, peppering her neck with kisses. Later as in tomorrow and every day after.

"You promise?"

"Yeah, baby, I promise, but I'm not done with *you* yet."

In one fluid motion, our positions are flipped. Her back flush with the wall.

I sink to my knees in front of her, keeping eye contact the entire time. "Is this okay?" Sutton nods. "Thank fuck, because I'm starving."

"Still?" Sutton blushes.

"I'm never not starving for you." She blushes harder.

I push up her top, exposing the waistband of my sweatpants rolled three times, and the drawstring is pulled tight around her waist. I have to use my teeth to get the knot undone.

"Geez, Dave. Didn't want anyone in your pants, did ya?"

"You know, when I was putting them on, it did cross my mind that my best friend of almost fifteen years was going to take them off of me."

I smirk up at her. "Best friend?"

Sutton doesn't have any makeup on, her lashes naked from the dark mascara she typically wears. Her eyelashes are thick and long, and a light shade of red. She's peering down at me with such desire in her eyes. It grows by the minute.

Sutton shrugs a shoulder and rolls her eyes at me. "Don't let it go to your head."

"It's going somewhere else." I wink as her pants fall to the floor, flooding her ankles in gray.

I suck in a hot breath. Grinding my jaw.

Her baby pink underwear is a soft material with a dainty lace trim. In the center, like she's something to unwrap, is a small white bow.

I kiss the center of the fabric.

Snaking my pointer fingers into the band, I pull them down her legs. Sutton shifts to help me get them over the curve of her ass and muscular thighs.

I kiss a triangle of freckles on the inside of a thigh just above her knee. "I've always loved these."

"That triangle?" she questions between a weighted laugh.

I've never laughed this much while with someone, but it doesn't surprise me. In the thick of it, the room pulsing with tension, everything about this is right.

"All of them."

"What? They make me hotter or something?" She's joking, I'm not.

I nip at one on her hip bone. "So." Another nip. "Fucking." Nip. "Hot."

As I kiss up her other leg, my mouth pauses before touching the scarred skin.

"That's not so beautiful." Sutton's tone is meek, the opposite of her. Broken and reeks of a sad memory.

"I don't agree. I think it is." I peer up at Sutton from my position below her. "Can I touch it?"

She nods her head, hesitantly. I run my thumb over the white scar, feeling it's raised edges. The skin around it tight, its texture marred from the stitches. "So beautiful," I tell her.

"Wait. Cooper, I need to say this." I pause, starring up at her. "I'm sorry I blamed you for my injury and having to quit hockey."

"You don't need to apologize."

"I do, and I'm so sorry." I nod. "I know it wasn't your fault, but...you were the closest to me and easiest to blame. I was already so mad at you Cooper, but I know better. I know it's my fault."

I whisper in my kisses, tell her it's not her fault. My fingers trail up and down her inner thighs. Sutton lets out a hiss when I kiss the scar.

I immediately pull away. "Are you okay? Did that hurt?"

"Good kind of pain. I promise."

My mouth returns to her freckled skin. Kissing the scar again, then finally making my way to her center.

Sutton grabs my chin between two fingers, pulling me away and looking up at her. She rubs her thumb over my bottom lip, rubbing her into me.

"Be gentle with me. I'm not...I don't—"

"I know what you need." I blow lightly on her. "I'll take care of you." There's a subtle nod. A subtle yet excited smirk. "Tap my shoulder if it's too much."

"Okay."

The word barely leaves her lips before I'm on her. Giving her what she needs, taking what I want. Which is her. There's no one or anything else.

Sutton's back arches when I push a finger into her. My other hand has to hold on to her waist to keep her from withering and knocking us both over.

Dragging her between my teeth, her legs close in on my head.

"Shit. I didn't—"

"Squeeze harder next time."

Maybe I should have let her finish her comment, but I don't want to hear about her with anyone else. I already had to see her on a date, already know she wants someone else.

But tonight, she's mine.

And I'm hopelessly hers.

My heart beats, crashing into my chest in Morse code. I listen and realize my earlier thought was wrong. I don't just want her to be mine. I want to be hers, maybe even more than the opposite.

"Cooper." My name on her lips like this is something I'll never be able to unhear. Not that I'd try to anyway.

Sutton tightens, I can feel it on my mouth and underneath my hand. Her abs go taut.

She curses and says my name again. And again. It drips down

my spine, furrowing low in my stomach, before the next thing I know, I'm teetering over the edge with her.

I keep going till I can hear her breathing settle. Pull my mouth away from her, and stand up. I try to discreetly adjust myself, but my light gray sweats do a shit job at hiding the mess I made.

"Oh," Sutton says. "You—"

"Came from getting you off. Sounds about right." I sigh-laugh.

"Has that...uh...has that happened before?"

"Never."

That appears to make her happy. I lean in and kiss her, addicted to the feel and taste. Sutton smiles against me.

I grab some paper towels and wet them, turning back to Sutton. Once she's cleaned up and dressed, we head out, grabbing the duffle stuffed with our rain-soaked clothes and head to my car. I leave two twenties on the table.

"The rain stopped. Wanna put the top down?"

"Yeah, why not.

———

"WANT TO COME UPSTAIRS?" Sutton asks me as I pull into the guest parking spot at her apartment, cutting the ignition.

It's past midnight. My night of her being mine technically over, but I don't argue. I open the door for her and scoop her into a piggyback ride when she wobbles.

I end up staying the night unintentionally.

We stay up late into the morning on the couch talking. A movie plays in the background, but it's nothing more than white noise, neither of us able to pull our attention off of each other.

We talk for hours. Recounting stories from our shared child-hood, moments in college we missed or were on opposite sides of the room to avoid each other. Every few minutes, Sutton has to shush me, sometimes pushing a finger into my lips, then gesturing with her head, curls moving with her in the direction of Elliot's room. I kiss her whenever I feel like it.

Sitting crisscross and turned toward each other, our knees bump. Our hands are occupied with a serious and never-ending game of thumb wrestling.

It's almost four when she yawns the first time. When the movie ends, I carry a dozing Sutton to her bed.

"Stay," she breathes out. Eyes shut peacefully, chest rising and falling after she drifts off.

I know I should leave, but I don't. I selfishly walk around her bed and pull back the comforter. Her bed is comfortable, but it's being next to her that has me falling asleep quickly and having the best three hours of sleep I've had in months.

I don't expect anyone to be up when I get home, but walking into the kitchen, I find Jaxon and Dawson sitting over bowls of cereal—some new protein cereal that tastes like stale Cheerios, but Captain Nutrition approved us to eat.

"Well, well, well. Where have you been, young man?" Dawson asks jokingly.

Jax laughs around a big bite, a strawberry falling from the spoon.

I pull a bowl from the cabinet and grab the yogurt from the fridge instead. Layering it with berries and peanut butter while they stare at me.

"Don't worry," Jaxon finally breaks their silence. "I tracked his location. He was at Sutton and Elliot's, and we both know it wasn't for Elliot."

"Did you and Red have a sleepover?"

"Or was she trapping you there against your will? Roasting you to an inch of your life."

"We watched a movie, and I fell asleep."

"Uh-huh." They make eyes at each other and leave it at that.

TWENTY-EIGHT

COOPER

REFRAINING FROM TOUCHING Sutton might be the death of me, especially when she's two feet away from me and chewing on the end of a pen. Neither of us set rules. Neither of us defined what happened the other night. Neither of us have tried to make another move.

Sunday, we crashed girls' night. We tried to fall back into our normal dynamic in front of everyone, but we fooled no one. Jordan flicked me in the ear when she caught my gaze lingering on Sutton for too long.

Monday she observed practice again, and afterward all I wanted to do was drag her into the penalty box, wrap her legs around my head and show her why it's also called the sin bin. Instead, she met with Coach, and I ran errands with her—successfully checking off all of her grocery list this time.

I'm supposed to be working through a survey for the psych department about my experience thus far. Besides my name at the top, a doodle of her name in a heart, the S drawn like Superman, and one question answered, the rest is blank.

I can't stop looking at her.

I can't stop thinking about her. I can't stop thinking about us over the weekend.

I can't stop hearing the little noises she made when she came on my tongue, and I swear I can still taste her.

I need another taste. I'll savor it this time. The first time I was greedy, a little kid let loose in the candy store. Took for granted the opportunity. One more go, and I swear not a second will be wasted. On my knees, I'll worship every part of her. Take my time as if I have eternity with her.

But only if she wants it, and with how her gaze finds mine periodically, heated and wild, I think she does.

As if instructed, flicking to me quickly, our eyes lock. I smirk, and she drops her gaze before it flicks back to me. The tip of Sutton's tongue peeks out of her mouth, running along her bottom lip.

My leg bounces under the tight grip I have on it. Arousal pools in my stomach as she pulls her hair into one hand, twisting it and moving it onto one shoulder, exposing the other. Her oversized knit rainbow sweater is loose, hanging off her. A dainty, lace strap from a camisole sits delicately over her shoulder. And make up covering the mark I left at the base of her neck.

Sutton might be sunshine incarnate and delicate, but her body isn't. She's strong. Sculpted, athletic curves yet soft in all the right places. Powerful and lithe—that's how she was out on the ice playing hockey.

Her brain is just as intoxicating as her body. She's smart. Analytical. A sponge. She played that way, too. She's playing me now—Sutton knows exactly what she's doing. Moving her hair, chewing on the pen, wearing a short skirt.

I could give in, but I'm enjoying the way she shifts in her seat. Not as discreetly as she thinks. Two can play this game.

This continues for another ten minutes. I'm no further into the questions than I was forty minutes ago.

She sighs frustratedly, pulling the pen from her mouth, scratching out line after line on her notebook. Her laptop is off to the side, the screen dark. Sutton's always loved taking notes by hand. A method to the madness, a secret color-coding system that I've never been able to decipher.

I reach into my backpack. "I got you something," I say, unzipping an interior pocket.

Her head tips to me with amusement, maybe a bit of leeriness.

"It's your birthday soon, not mine." I like that she remembers.

"And?"

"I didn't get you anything." Sutton frowns, shoulders slumping.

"I can think of something you could give me." She crumples a sticky note and throws it at me. "I was talking about a hug."

"Yeah, whatever," Sutton says as a threat. Barely.

I laugh. Tauntingly. Knowingly.

"Stop chewing on your pen and giving me those eyes then."

"What eyes?"

"Come on, baby." I lean in across the table. "The 'I want you' eyes."

"I am not giving you those eyes. I'm simply annoyed that you aren't—" She stops, teeth grinding, then stutters over nonsensical words.

"Aren't what?" I run a finger up her forearm, pushing up her sweater, completely forgetting the dual highlighter and pens I got her. She shudders, goosebumps pebble her skin. "Not touching you? Not kissing you?"

"No." It's flat, but not good enough to cover the flick of her hazels to my mouth.

"All you need to do is ask."

I pull her chair toward me with my feet. She's close enough that my hand under the table slips to her bare knee.

Outside is a misleading spring day. Warm and refreshing, a reprieve from our dreary and snowy winter. Campus was alive this morning on Sutton's run. I found her a half mile in and completed the rest of the four miles with her, stealing a headphone to learn that she listens to podcasts while running. This one an interview with a former student athlete on burnout and falling out of love with swimming after competing at an Olympic level.

Whatever seeds were planted in me and have been watered, blossomed.

Sutton tried to change it to music, which she did once the episode ended, but I wanted to listen another episode. Asked if she had another, which she did. I've felt alone in my struggle with hockey, misunderstood, but hearing how the Olympian spoke, I was validated.

Outside my house, Sutton leveled me with a look. Told me to stop running with her. I said no. We bickered back and forth till we compromised. Not on the days I have games—overtraining, or whatever. The swimmer said doing other sports and/or movements helped her. I've always love boating and swimming, was on the summer swim team as a kid. We agreed to go swimming later this week.

My thumb rubs circles on the inside of her knee.

"All you need to do is ask," she parrots my words back, shoulder and mouth set.

"Is that so?" I run my hand up her thigh as far as I can.

Sutton does a shit job at trying to act like this isn't affecting her.

"What's my gift?"

"You can't stop thinking about it, can you?" I ignore her question.

"It wasn't even that good."

"Liar."

"I've had better."

"Promise you haven't."

"You don't know what I did in my free time—"

"Yeah, I do."

"We aren't friends. I still hate you."

"Pretty sure you called me your best friend the other night, while my mouth was between your legs. Need a reminder?" I squeeze her thigh, assertive but gentle. "Or want a reminder? Maybe both."

She stares at me, taking a slow, languid inhale.

I don't know if it's seconds or minutes that pass in our standstill, but the room is a crackle of electricity when she curses under her breath, "Fuck it."

Quickly, I push our computers out of the way. Papers, pens, and whatever else on the table become debris on the floor. Our limbs are a tornado as we latch onto each other.

Her back is pressed against the table. My body over top of hers. Lips crashing.

There's a franticness to us that might come from the fact that the door is unlocked and anyone could walk into the study room. Sutton drew the blinds closed when we entered earlier. Privacy for this or me?

The denim skirt she's wearing is pushed up around her waist.

I skim my hand along her underwear, damp already.

"If it wasn't that good, why are you already so wet?" I whisper in her ear, then bite it.

"Thinking about someone else."

A kernel of anxiety festers, wanting to pop. There is someone else. There's always someone else that I'm not.

I'm losing hockey to it. I don't want to lose her to it either.

When will Cooper Carmichael ever be just enough?

Sutton must see it in my eyes, and changes her response, admitting the truth, "It's for you, Cooper. I think about you."

"When?"

She kisses me hard as I slip her underwear aside, pushing a finger inside her. "Always." There's a sneaky glint to her facial features, and I make a note to ask her about it later.

I kiss down her torso, pushing up her sweater to press my mouth to her stomach. She arches into me.

I climb off the table, hands on her waist, dragging her to the edge. I work her underwear down her legs, up and over her chunky sneakers, and pocket them.

We only have the room reserved for another ten minutes when I check my watch. They are strict about these rooms and being out immediately once your slot is over.

It doesn't matter, I have her coming undone with half that time. My name on her tongue and hands in my hair.

I clean her up with my tongue, savoring everything.

Sutton sits up. I push up on the table, lean into her, and kiss her. Her tongue pushes into my mouth, explorative, and she sighs when she tastes herself on me.

A phone buzzes, one minute warning. I press a final kiss on her mouth, helping her off the table and adjusting her clothing back into place.

"It happened again." Sutton nods at my crotch. "Must like doing that with girls."

Yes, I've always enjoyed going down on a girl, but with her, I love it.

"Girl," I correct. "And I love it."

She rolls her eyes at me. We move around the room, cleaning up our school stuff before heading out of the room.

"Here." I smile at her, fully knowing she is still glistening on my lips.

I hand Sutton the pack of light pastel dual highlighter-pens I got her. My sister, Jordan, and I were hanging out Sunday afternoon in downtown Bensen. Mom's birthday is a handful of days after mine, and we wanted to get her a present. While in the paper store, I saw these and thought of Sutton.

"One side is tipped like a pen. Might make it easier to write or outline the titles on your notes."

"It will. This is really sweet, Coop. Thank you." Her flushed skin blushes. She opens the package and tucks them into her pen carrier. "Can I have my underwear back now?"

I shake my head no, flick my brows up. "*My* birthday present."

TWENTY-NINE

COOPER

A SATISFIED EASE washes over me as I button up my dress shirt for our game tonight. My pre-game ritual is being checked off, and this morning in the study room might be the newest addition.

The person staring back at me in my reflection is lighter, freer, and unapologetically happy. I finished the evaluation for her when I got home; it's sitting on my desk. Carefully, I went through each question, knowing how important this is to her. Seeing how what she's doing is working. I know my participation is part of this, but it's her that's helping me fall back in love with the sport.

She's showed me how to separate who they want me to be with who I am. Reminded me how fun skating can be.

My playing is better. It's still there in the back of my mind—I know I'm creeping up on Dad's record. I know other NHL teams are watching my every move. I know this could be our year to bring home the trophy again—but I'm working to keep it there. Use it as a different type of fuel. Navigating how to want it for myself and not others.

I want to break Dad's record.

I want to play in the NHL.

I want to win the Frozen Four.

The affirmations, the goals, are on a note card in her handwriting taped to my bathroom mirror.

Jaxon knocks on my door. It's a light tap followed by three more, each increasing in sound and pressure. He never waits for an answer to come in but at least he knocked. It's caused some issues in the past, but that's why we have locks—so he says.

"Can I catch a ride to the bus?" he asks. Jaxon doesn't like to drive. "Chase and Dawson already left, and I don't know where Beck is."

"He has to pick up his sister early from school. She has a fever."

"Is everything okay?" Jaxon is as worried as I was when he texted me an hour ago asking me to let Coach know he'll be fifteen minutes late.

"A bug is going around her school. Elliot's going to watch her here since his mom's busy." I tighten my tie. "I'll be ready in ten."

Before heading downstairs, I walk to my nightstand and grab my lucky bracelet.

Our game today is only an hour away against Wisconsin. Everyone is overconfident that we'll crush them. They haven't won a game in the past month, but that means they're hungry.

Our winning streak is expanding. We've won the past eight games.

In the car, Jaxon goes through his pre-game rituals. Which means he's snagged the aux and put on his playlist. He rolls down the windows and is singing at the top of his lungs.

"Is Sutton coming to the game?"

"No, she has a study group tonight." I didn't ask her to come, didn't want to pressure her to be there. I know she has other obligations besides me, other classes and schoolwork.

"Did you ask her to come?"

"No."

"Why didn't you? You could have. Maybe she'd like to know that you want her there."

I always want her there. "She's busy. I don't want to make her feel bad. Plus, it's not home."

"So?" His fingers fire away on his phone.

"What are you doing?"

"Asking her to come to our game. Suggesting that she bring whatever flash cards or homework she has and does it in the stands." We both know she'll get nothing done. This isn't baseball. Hockey isn't a slow game.

I reach across the car, snatch his phone, hopefully before he's hit send. I toss it in the back of the car.

"Come on, Coop." He unbuckles and worms himself across the console to get his phone off the floorboards. Jaxon laughs maniacally, buckling himself back in. "Nice try, but it sent."

We're passing another rec center on campus. Congregated out front is the baseball team. I immediately spot Zach, his Lakeland baseball hat flipped backwards. He's smiling and talking to Sutton.

My face must fall—the outward expression of my heart and stomach plummeting through the seat, out of the car, and being dragged behind us—because Jaxon comments on it.

"It's nothing, man, I promise." She has her tote bag hanging off one shoulder, books in her arms. "Isn't her apartment down the street from here. She was probably walking home and being nice."

I slow down, turn off the music, and because I want to torture myself, I roll down my window. Her voice is carried by the breeze, a sweet sound that fills my car.

"I'll see you around," Zach tells her.

"Bye, Zach," her voice echoes.

"Stop listening," Jaxon whispers, even though he's leaning closer to me to also eavesdrop.

"Let me know what time works for you on Monday." She nods. "Bye, Sutt."

Jaxon rolls up the windows as I stare in the rearview mirror. Sutton is walking away from Zach, both becoming smaller the further I drive. I try to focus. What's Monday? Since when has he called her Sutt? The parking lot to the arena is the next left, but I take a second, third, fourth peek at them.

"Coop." Jaxon jostles my right shoulder. "Cap. Dude, don't worry about him. He's not the one wearing her number."

I turn, drive my shoulder into the seat. "How do you know about that?"

"I'm not as oblivious as people think. I know you combined your jersey number with hers after freshman year."

No one knows about that. I made up a lie that my number was needed for an incoming freshman as part of a recruiting deal. Not even Coach questioned me when I showed up at his office asking—more like begging—to change my number. I'd been twenty my entire hockey career. Since peewee skating and swimming in polyester.

She'd been sixteen since I can remember.

When Mom called to tell me that Sutton was officially done playing, potentially needing another surgery, I dropped what I was doing to sprint to Coach's office. I didn't even think twice about my decision. I'd play for both of us.

Maybe that's why I want her to come to my games, wear my jersey. Maybe she'll realize I changed my number. Maybe she'd realize it's for her, that it's always been her for me.

"It doesn't matter."

"Doesn't matter?" I try to get out of the car, but he pierces me to the seat with a look. His steel eyes threatening me to move. "All of it matters, Cooper. You've been obsessed with her for years. You've never let yourself date, barely hook up with anyone because of Sutton. Both of you act oblivious, but we all see it." He taps on his phone, changing the song. "At least I do."

"She's choosing him! That's why I agreed to help her," I snap, not at him, but in half. My heart, the remaining parts she doesn't have tucked in her back pocket, fissure in half.

"No she's not! Get your head out of your ass and see that—"

I get out of the car, not wanting to hear what he has to say.

THIRTY

SUTTON

"SUTTON!" Elliot calls for me from her bedroom. "Sutton, come here!" I rush into her bedroom, frantic as she barrels out of her closet. "You have to come. Whatever you have going on, reschedule it."

Elliot tugs up a pair of teal blue leggings, matching cap-sleeved top. Grabs a brush from her vanity and immediately starts brushing blonde strands into a high ponytail.

"Come to what?"

"I completely forgot," she groan-screams. "How did I forget about the biggest interview of my life?"

"Hey, hey. Stop moving." Her hands freeze after finishing bubbling a section of her ponytail. "Deep breaths." I motion for her to inhale and exhale. "Start from the top. What interview?"

Elliot takes another calming breath. "After my initial interview with that spin company Momentum they asked me to do a live ride with a full class. Some of their team are going to virtually take it."

"And it's scheduled for today?"

"Unfortunately. I swore I wrote it down."

"What can I do to help? Is there a studio available?" She nods.

"Okay, text your sorority and see if any of them can come." I pause. "Here, toss me your phone, I'll do it."

I type in her passcode and pull up her pledge class group text. I put out a call for any volunteers. There's an immediate response, phone pinging with ten that can come.

"We've got ten."

She's pacing, finishing grabbing her stuff to teach, and heads to the kitchen. I follow after.

"You'll come, right?" Elliot asks, filling a water bottle up.

"Of course, I wouldn't miss it."

I tap my phone that's plugged in on the counter. I was sending Cooper another text before running to Elliot's room.

He's barely responded to me lately. Dropped off his mid-term evaluation, and I had hoped he'd stay, but he left with the guys. The season is wrapping up soon, and they are a few games from clinching the first seed in conference play.

He's busy, that's what I tell myself, but I can't help thinking that I did something wrong.

I've been a ten-sided die with Cooper, rolled daily to determine my feelings. Anger, annoyance, confusion, insecurity, resentment, jealousy, disappointment, bitterness, loneliness, and longing. Most of the time, it was him rolling the dice.

But he's never wavered from me. I've been coming to the conclusion and it's overwhelming. Cooper has always found a way to choose me, care for me, maybe even love me, in big and small ways. I've been too blind, ignorant, to see it.

"Remind me what time?" I ask.

"Noon."

My face falls. *Shit.*

Elliot notices and pauses applying the extra deodorant we keep in our junk drawer. "Everything okay?"

"I'm supposed to be meeting Cooper at 12:30. But—" An idea crosses my mind.

"What's that look for?"

"What look?"

A manicured finger—one layer of funny bunny and two layers of bubble bath—swirls around my face. "That one. You are up to something, Sutton Elizabeth. Now, I want in."

"How many spots are available in the class?"

She counts on her fingers. "The room holds forty. Minus you. Minus the girls. Twenty-nine."

"Save them." I sit up, check the calendar on my phone. "I've gotta go. See you in an hour!"

I'm about to fold in on myself when I make it to the arena. My shoes were already ridiculous for this outfit, even more so for running. I look down at the loafers, the only shoes by the door that I hastily slipped on before taking off, paired with my leggings and oversized crewneck. At least my hair is pulled back with a thick headband.

The team is scheduled for lifting this morning. In—I check my phone—fifteen minutes.

The air conditioning that's blasting in the building is a nice reprieve. That's until my pace picks up, ankles aching with the start of blisters, sprinting down the hallway when I see Coach Mathieson dip into the locker room.

I pause in front of the door, music drifting out from the bottom. Am I really about to walk into the men's locker room?

Apparently.

Gripping the metal handles, I tug the door open. Celine Dion and a scented plug-in that probably needs replaced hits me. There's a small hallway decorated with posters of players before the main part of the locker room.

As I'm about to turn the corner, I stop and lean against the wall.

We can turn around and go to Coach's office. We can...no we can't. Elliot needs this, and you aren't letting her down. You aren't giving her a reason to—I let the irrational thoughts go.

If their coach is in here, this is the quickest way to speak to him. And see Cooper, my traitorous heart beats.

Again, apparently we are doing this. I start to turn the corner, and have to slap a hand over my mouth to stop myself from hysteria.

On a bench are a shirtless Jaxon and Dawson, swaying. Two hip pops to the right before doing the same on the left. It must be Jaxon's solo because he's singing into a deodorant microphone. Their shoulders start to mirror their hips.

I creep a step forward, hug the wall. No one has spotted me yet, and luckily, I've only spotted shirtless versions of them.

I inch another step inward as Jaxon belts the verse of Celine Dion's "Alive" perfectly. With a wave of the deodorant in his hand, the remainder of the room joins in for the chorus. Some singing into their lockers. Some dancing while pulling on shirts, others waving them above their head.

From where my feet are glued to the floor, I can see two-thirds of the locker room. I weave my gaze around players till I land on him in the corner. Leaning back with his hood up, eyes closed, legs stretched on the bench.

Dawson takes over the bridge. Jaxon mouthing along.

I go to slip my phone from my leggings pocket, Elliot and Jordan have to see this, but it's snatched before I can take a discreet video.

"What are you doing here, Dave?" Cooper asks, one brow arched and the smile I've come to expect, the one I think he only reserves for me nowhere to be found. Replaced with a scowl and tight shoulders, I don't recognize the frustration he's greeting me with. "You can't just walk into the locker room. You shouldn't be here. You aren't allowed to be here."

I ignore his acidic tone. "Are they singing 'Alive'?"

"Didn't miss that I see." Again, I try to ignore how he's speaking to me, bitter and condescending, but it hurts and confuses me.

"What's next?" I ask in the lightest way possible. "'That's the Way It Is'?"

"Yup. Jaxon's day to pick music."

"Why doesn't that surprise me?" I reach for my phone, and he holds it out of my reach, above his head. "When is yours? What do you pick?"

"I don't."

"Oh, come on." I go for my phone again.

"I don't." He takes a step into my space. "Why are you here?"

Unintentionally, I lean toward him. Is that...why does he... no...that's weird. My nose must be playing ticks on me. Mind too, overran by the extremely boyish atmosphere.

I take a deep inhale. No...that's my detergent and lingering hints of cherry body wash.

Cooper's wearing the sweatshirt I returned weeks ago. The one from the night of our practice kiss, when he picked me up and pulled it from the backseat when I shivered. I washed it, and maybe wore it once or twice, before giving it back to him.

"I need to speak to Coach," I respond shakily, even more confused and stunned.

"He's not in here." Well he was. "Is it about me?"

"Yes. No. Well, sort of."

"Which is it?"

Chase leans around the corner. "Hey, Sutton, what's up?" he greets me loud enough that we gain attention. "Female in the house. Cover up!" he hollers.

There is a series of curses behind him. Cooper slips my phone into my leggings pocket, then covers my eyes.

"I've seen a penis before, Cooper."

"Don't remind me." Whoever this moody Cooper is, their facade drops, and their response is pained, maybe even jealous.

"Oh, come on. Uncover my eyes."

"No," he growls. "We're turning around and going to Coach's."

Somehow, he maneuvers me, keeping one hand suctioned over my eyes and another spinning me around. His body is flush against me.

I try to swallow, but it comes out as a choked cough.

He takes a step closer to me—how is that even possible?

When I inhale, his chest moves with me. The hand over my eyes falls, outlining my face.

"Walk," he commands. His husky voice barely over a whisper, but demanding.

"Why were you sulking in the locker room? Is everything okay?"

Our steps are in sync, and I hate it. I hate that they are so in tune we've become one. It's like my brain is a radio, and after our night together, its frequency is locked on him. I can't stop thinking about Cooper. I can't get out of my head the way he called me Sutton baby, dropped in between pants and groans. The feel of his mouth on me is a ghost haunting my skin. Whenever a breeze dances across me, and I have to check that it's not him.

At night, I find myself wound up with no luck at a release. My body knows—and craves and desires and wants to indulge—and he might know too.

Cooper stops us. A strong hand splays across my hip. The cotton of my sweatshirt slips between his fingers as he bunches it.

He releases me, but his eyes betray him, telling me he doesn't want to.

Jaw clenches and shifts, teeth grinding together. "Are you enjoying yourself?"

Enjoying myself? "What are you talking about?"

"Having the attention of two guys? Does he know what you were doing that morning before you were with him?"

With him? Who is him? I haven't been with anyone except Cooper...

Cooper scoff-laughs. "I saw you with him!"

I run through the Rolodex in my head. Him has to be Zach. "It wasn—"

"Don't lie, Dave."

I'm not sure how to feel right now. Angry? Confused? Hurt? The implications gut me. Even on my worst days, when hating Cooper was easier than breathing, I'd never do this to him. I'd never play him, especially now. Especially when—there it is again.

It's like a stone or some sort of speed bump that keeps me from admitting the truth to myself.

"Have you been thinking about us?" Cooper asks, hand forming a fist then uncurling and flexing.

The lie rolls off my tongue smoother than freshly Zambonied ice. "No."

Cooper shakes his head while running a hand through his hair, pulling at the grown-out strands. A muffled, unrecognizable sound escapes him.

Another part of my heart breaks off as I watch something in him shatter...or maybe harden. Am I being tucked away in the box he keeps hidden in his head? The one that weighs more than it should.

Standing here, the physical distance between us is barely two tiles, but the emotional distance has never been farther. But I push him away. My heart is screaming at me, rapidly beating, threatening to stop.

He lets out a singular saccharine laugh. "Then, no, I'm not okay. I'll never be okay because I know I'll never really be yours. Not in the way I want." Cooper spins me to face him. "Tell me, how should I be okay?"

My eyes flare. My thighs tighten, squeeze together. My bad knee locks—and for a split second, I think it's going to buckle on me. Give out. Give up on me, same as my traitorous heart, and shoulders pulled together like someone is tying a bow. There aren't tile floors beneath me, but fresh cement keeps me in place.

How should he be okay?

How am I supposed to be okay?

Cooper scrunches his eyes together. Dark, midnight dipped eyelashes meet his cheeks. His chest rises and falls, pecs pressed against his tight, spandex shirt.

"Boundaries. You told me I needed them."

Boundaries. That word rings in my head and snaps mine back into place. Every single one that I put in place over the years. I'm reminded that he pushed them. He never cared for mine, so why should I?

Because you care for him, my heart beats.

"And I'm a boundary." My voice is monotone. Doesn't shake, doesn't waver.

"You have to be Sutton. It's killing me. You're killing me. I can't help you fall in love with someone else when I I—"

"Don't say it. Don't tell me." If he does, then it's real, and I don't know if there's an AED or doctor out there that could restart my heart. I want to tell him, but I don't.

I feel something wet on my cheek. Quickly, I wipe it away.

The battle waging inside of me feels like I'm on a Tilt-A-Whirl.

"I'll find someone new for my study."

Cooper shakes his head no. "We are almost to the end. I'll finish it with you, but besides that..." He trails off, digs his teeth into his bottom lip as if he's trying to stop himself from saying what he ultimately ends up saying. "I'm done."

"Okay." I swallow our reality.

We stare at each other. He blows out a breath, chews on the inside of his cheek.

He spins on his heels, leaving me to my quest for his coach's office.

I watch him walk away. A part of me is hopeful he'll glance back at me, but he doesn't. Which is good—it has to be good.

THIRTY-ONE

SUTTON

THEIR COACH'S office is the next hallway over. Coach Mathieson's lights are on, the door already cracked open. I knock twice.

"Come in," his deep voice calls out.

Everyone on the women's team swoons over him. Deep, husky voice—the kind that has you squirming when listening to an audiobook and it gets spicy. Bright, brown eyes that I swear are magnets. Most fall for his smile, but I was always drawn to his eyes.

A thought starts to form, but I stop it before I find myself running back down these halls to another pair of bright, brown eyes.

"Sutton," he greets me before I have the door fully open. "Have a seat."

"How are you, Coach? Playoffs are looking good."

"Best season we've had in years. Carmichael is at the top of his game. I'm assuming you are to thank for that."

I shake my head no. I could never take credit for his ability. Cooper is talented, truly. "That's all him."

"His head is clearer. He's skating like the kid I saw and recruited in high school." He gives me a knowing head tilt, complete with a brow raise and sly grin. "He's back to being the player he was born to be."

"Can I ask you a question?" Coach's mouth ticks up on one side, I think he knows what I'm about to ask. "How'd you know he'd be a good fit for this?"

"He reminded me of someone I knew."

"You." I'm stunned, struck with clarity. From the little knowledge I have about him, it makes sense.

"Me. Carmichael had too much potential to let it go." My nose scrunches with curiosity, questions I want to ask when there's more time. "However, that is not why you bravely entered my locker room or are stalling practice right now. Is it?"

"I'd like to do something with the whole team. How do you feel about cycling?"

———

THE TEAM IS MORE receptive and enthusiastic about skipping their lifting session to come with me to Elliot's cycling audition than I anticipated.

I did, however, leave out that it is musical themed.

After Coach Mathieson agreed to let me steal them away for the hour, he walked me back to the locker room to inform them. The deal was that afterwards they had to do something as a team, whether it was dinner or playing video games or reading a book together, he didn't care as long as it wasn't hockey.

A sophomore left winger commented, "There is this cowboy romance I've been seeing all over social media, I've been wanting to read."

"I'll read it with you. Send me the link," Jaxon replied. A couple of others chirped up, and I think they are starting a book club. "Girls love that shit. Even you could learn a position or two." He patted Cooper's chest.

I coughed, and everyone's eyes turned on me—mine were

only on Cooper—before grabbing their bags to follow me to the rec center.

Elliot almost peed herself when she saw us roll up.

I set myself up on a bike between Chase and Dawson. Cooper finds a bike in a different row despite the guys calling him over to us. The studio is set up in a blocky U pattern with Elliot in the middle on a square stage. Each of the three sides have rows. My favorite spot is on her right side, in the third row against the wall. Today, I'm in middle of the second row. He's in the first row on Elliot's left.

Elliot starts the camera setup in two corners of the room, then climbs onto her bike. The sound of her shoes clipping in is faint as she turns up the music and dims the lights.

She adjusts the laptop stand to her left and pulls on her mic. "Everyone ready?"

There's a cheer from seventy percent of the room. The other thirty percent is a mixture of groans and mumblings of *what are we getting ourselves into.*

Chase turns and gives me a high five. A giddy smile on his face, cheeks pink, and we haven't even started cycling yet.

"That's the kind of energy I like to see. Thank you for being here today! If you haven't taken a ride with me before, I'm Elliot. This is our power cycling class. During the next forty-five minutes, we'll focus on intensity, combining watts and resistance with RPM. We will ride in and out of the saddle, as well as incorporate upper body movements.

"When you're ready, reach down to the blue dial in the center of the bike and do a full spin to the right. This will control the resistance. I'll provide a range that you can see on the left. The right will be your cadence. Ride at what's comfortable but challenging. This ride is about you...and musical tunes."

She reaches for the volume button, turning up the volume even louder, simultaneously increasing the energy.

We're halfway through the ride and out of the saddle, working up a hill. My resistance is set to sixty-five. This is a record for me.

I feel good. Sweaty as if my body is sweating and riding out my feelings for Cooper...I shake my head, shut my mind back off.

That's what this is supposed to be for the team. A break from hockey. An opportunity to move their body in a new way that's fun and exciting. They're all under pressure to clinch their spot in the playoffs. Every pass, shot, block—every game matters.

They're first in their conference and nation right now. A twelve-game winning streak after a rough start post-winter break.

Dawson towels off, then joins the rest of the room, spinning it above their heads. Elliot's hair is whipping back and forth as the beat drops in a remix of songs from *The Greatest Showman*.

I sit back down and turn the dial to the left. Grab my water and take a sip while I find an easier RPM to maintain. Elliot catches me and gives me a subtle thumbs up to check in with me. I nod and mouth *You're doing great*.

She's glowing. In her groove.

If she doesn't get this position, I'll find the headquarters and throw a pedal at them. I silently chuckle at myself because I could never do anything like that. Not from chickening out, but I can barely kill a spider. I'd rather stand as far away as I can, leaning forward to scoop it up with paper or something to take it outside. I used to sob when my parents would flush my goldfish from the fair down the toilet.

RIP, Cruella and Maleficent.

Elliot will get this, I know it.

"Are all of her classes like this?" Chase leans in my direction.

"Yeah," I huff, speeding up my legs to match the newly called out cadence.

"No wonder I can never get into one."

"You try?"

"Every week." His eyes flick down before finding her again. "Well, when we don't have games or practices."

"Why don't you text her? That's what I do, and I always get in." He shrugs, almost embarrassed. "I try to go every Tuesday morning if you want to come with me next week."

"I'd like that." Chase chews on his cheek, then turns back to me. "You think she'd like that?"

"Having her best friend in class? Just maybe," I manage to get out before becoming out of breath from peddling so fast.

The ride finishes ten minutes later. Once again, I'm a sweaty mess, and Elliot looks like she's ready to be featured on the front of *Sports Illustrated*.

Her sorority sisters and a couple of regulars who were able to make it leave. The team congregates in the back corner. Laughing at each other, snapping their shirts on their abs.

"Oooh. Abs." Elliot winks. "If I knew this would be my reward after a class, I'd beg your coach to let you come every day."

"Yours are better," a freshman says. Chase smacks him in the head with Dawson's shirt that he ripped from his grip. A few others pipe up with the same sentiment.

Elliot does have better abs than a majority of them; and that's saying something because Cooper's abs are layered on top of each other like a six-tiered cake.

I worm my way through the bikes and the team. "Cooper," I call out. He's heading to the door, his shirt hanging around his neck. "Cooper—"

I see his muscles tighten with each syllable.

Someone circles my wrist, pulling me back gently. I glance down and spot Elliot's nails. "Let him brood. You didn't do anything wrong."

But I did.

THIRTY-TWO

COOPER

THE DRIVE HOME is under four hours. At dawn, before everyone is awake, leaving the road scarce, it's shorter.

I pull into my childhood home, as the orange-coppery sky that reminds me of her hair fades into a cloudless blue. Everything is the same, down to the drawn curtains on the first floor. A soft light emanating through the window and Dad's figure walking in to sit down with a coffee and his phone. He's probably playing the NYT word games him and Jordan are competitive over. They do them first thing in the morning over a cup of coffee.

Before I cut the ignition, I call my mom. She answers right away, voice comforting and the reason I came here.

"Mom. Are you home?"

"No, but I can be. Did you need something? I'm at the shop, but you know that's only ten minutes away. Twenty tops and I—"

"That's okay. Have you had breakfast yet?"

She hesitantly responds, "No. Are you...are you home?"

"Be there soon, Mom."

I arrive at the flower shop thirty minutes later. Parked in the back, I still have a spare key on my ring. The back room is over-flowing and disorganized as it always has been. I have to wiggle around tables stacked with buckets and layered in PVC pipe, boxes toppled over with center pieces and who knows what.

Mom went to school for event planning and hospitality, she's an event planner. Sutton's mom is the florist. Together they opened a floral and events business. They operate as your regular run of the mill florist, but also do just about every event type under the sun. You could come to them with the strangest idea and they'd make it happen.

Mom is at one of the work benches putting together what I assume are center pieces. I set the bag of breakfast and tray of drinks I brought for us down before wrapping my arms around her.

"One of my favorite hugs in the world. Hi, honey."

"Hi, Mom." I lean my head on top of hers, closing the large gap between us. "I brought breakfast burritos and coffee. Grabbed avocado toast for Mrs. Davis. I didn't know if she'd be here."

"She isn't, but that's sweet of you. They're out of town for their anniversary." I completely forgot that was this weekend. My mind drifts to Sutton, not like it wasn't occupied by her the entire drive here.

Mom finishes filling the square vase, her fingers showcasing a few cuts—clipping the stems still isn't her strong suit. Turning to face me, she sits on the table.

"Burrito me." I toss her a foiled wrapped burrito. Both of us sighing after the first bite. Mom laughs after taking another bite, a piece of bacon falls to the shop floor. "I tried to recreate these last month. There is a reason I'm a florist." I arch one brow. "Okay an event planner, and not a chef. They were pitiful."

"It's because these are magic. I swear they put something in them that makes them superior." I take another large bite, regretting it instantly because these were the last two and I need to savor it. "Or to make them un-recreateable," I say around a mouthful.

Mom washes down a bite with tea. "But these aren't why you're home."

Shoulders slump, I sink into myself. "No, it's not. Su—there's this girl." I refrain from using Sutton's name, knowing the slippery slope it would become. Derailing today, and me, completely. "I-I've had a crush on her, but she likes someone else."

"I see." Mom hums.

"We were paired on a class project and sort of...we kissed." Heat climbs up my spine like a ladder, landing in my cheeks. Great. Here I am blushing in front of my mother thinking about everything else Sutton and I have also done. "And I thought that maybe she might have started to reciprocate the feelings, but then I saw her with another guy and I...I don't know. Was mad at her. Disappointed in her. Assumed that she was playing me and ended up saying things I shouldn't have."

This dumbed down version of Sutton and I sounds ridiculous. I sound ridiculous. But it doesn't change that I'm mad. I'm mad at her and myself. Disappointment lodged between.

I shouldn't of spoken to her that way. I shouldn't have told her I was done, but I can't keep continuing like this. Wanting her. Needing her. Loving her. It hurts too much.

Before I could handle it. I was comfortable existing around her, but now I want to exist with her.

"Does she know how you feel about her?" It's an easy question. Then why is the answer so complicated.

"I think..." Does Sutton? How could she not? "I told her once but—"

"You show it?" Mom guesses correctly. "Come here." She pats the table next to her. I change positions, sliding in next to her. Her hand takes mine lovingly. "I want to let you in on a little secret. How many times did I pile your shoes by the stairs to try and get you to take them upstairs after I asked? Tons. Weekly. You never did, but when I told you again, you did it. Sometimes you just need to say it again. Words, big or small, are powerful. Use them."

"But what if I did and they hurt her?" I lean my head on her shoulder.

"Apologize. Even if your heart or mind isn't there, apologize." Rough hands rub at my cheek.

"And if she doesn't accept it? Or rejects me?" I don't want our history to repeat itself.

I feel Mom's laugh against my cheek. "Well, you and your sisters were never supposed to date or marry until you were forty. However..." Mom grumbles about Jordan's current boyfriend. "Then she does, and you have to accept it."

The entrance door opens. Mom jumps from the table, and I follow behind her to the front of the store. She starts to greet a customer, but it's Dad. "Cooper, this is a surprise."

————

MOM CONVINCES me to stay for the day for an early birthday celebration. Dad and I help her finish building center pieces and delivering them to a wedding across town. The bride was in tears, ruining her makeup, when we showed up. Apparently, her florist cancelled two days ago, and Mom was her last resort.

After they wanted to take me to dinner, but I requested a home-cooked meal. Mom says she's a terrible cook, but she's not half bad. Still, it's Dad who makes spaghetti with his special sauce and fresh meatballs.

I'm clearing the dishes, ignoring my phone that's blowing up.

SUTTON

Jordan said you drove home. When will you be back?

Can we talk? Please, Cooper.

LOML JAXON

What happened with Sutton? She's had two milkshakes tonight.

Did you know your sister dyed her hair blue?

She could do our bleached tips!

SUTTON

At least talk to your dad…please

"I recorded the game. Wanna watch?" Dad asks, boxing up leftovers.

I check the time. It's almost seven thirty and I should drive back tonight. We have practice tomorrow and I have an unofficial-official pop quiz that'll be an automatic zero if I miss. The professor is a hard-ass that allows no make-ups or extra credit. It's the only class I find myself consistently studying for whilst feeling behind.

Sutton's last text flashes in my head. "A period or two. Let me finish these and pack up." Mom's sending me back with boxes that Jordan requested. "Twenty minutes?"

Mom puts the vase of tulips I requested on the counter before kissing my forehead goodnight. She points in Dad's general vicinity, then at me, and makes a talking hand. I silently sigh, her intuition can be annoying. "Night, Mom. Thank you for this morning."

We'd talked more throughout the day. My frustration with Sutton slipping through my fingers like sand—not that I've ever been able to stay upset with her for long.

I'm disappointed in my reaction. The words I used were unnecessary and not true.

I grab another snack from the kitchen before joining Dad. He's in his mom-approved accent chair, feet kicked up on the gray-striped ottoman.

"One of my buddies just texted," he says, hitting play on the remote. "Got wind that Chicago is putting together a major trade."

Chicago is one of my favorite teams, besides Winnipeg and Minnesota. They're who I've always dreamt of playing for, and maybe someday will…if they'd ever want me. I was drafted last year by Carolina.

"Did they say who or what they were trading for?"

"He didn't say who they were trading, but Carolina needs a goalie desperately." Dad scrolls, pulling his reading glasses down from the top of his head. "Did mention Chicago were trying to get two defenseman I don't recognize the names of, then a draft contract."

I laugh, partially hesitant, partially sarcastic. "When was the last time someone traded a drafted, unsigned player."

"Recently, I believe." Dad puts his phone face down, turning to face me. "You can always become a free agent when your contract is up with Carolina. If it wasn't for their low draft spot, they'd have picked you." I know he's talking about Chicago.

"Would they?"

"Of course. *Would they?*" he quotes me. "What's that supposed to mean?"

I try to swallow, but every criticism, every comparison crawls its way up my throat. Again, Sutton's text flashes in my head.

"I don't think I'll ever be as good as you, but that's what people want. They don't want Cooper Carmichael. They expect Ryn Carmichael's son on the ice, in interviews, and on the street. Teams want—crave. Demand—another you."

Dad's quiet for a moment. Body moving ever so slightly as if he's processing what I've said. "Is that what you want? To be me?"

It's small, but I shake my head no.

"Good, because I've never wanted you to be me. Coop, all I've ever wanted, or expected, is for you to be yourself."

I run a hand through my hair. "I hear you, but..." The critic's words are like a broken stereo. You can't turn them down or off. I do my best to explain what it's been like. The exhausting pressure and daunting, unrealistic expectations. Dad's calm and patient, but from how his knuckles turn white around the remote, and glasses squeeze his temples, he's an array of emotions. But I don't hold back.

"I never realized you felt this way. I'm sorry I've been blinded to it for all these years," he says when I finish.

"That's not your fault, I didn't want you to."

"Still. You're my son. I wish I would have known. About reporters, that's their job. Analyze players. Create clickbait articles and viral clips. A third of them are probably jealous of you. They're always going to be a part of your career, but they don't get to define it. Only you do."

"I'm learning that. Coach, um, signed me up to work with a sports psychology student." He tilts his head knowingly. "It's Sutton. She's been helping with my burnout and overtraining."

"Her parents mentioned her study. I'm happy to hear you have her, and that it's helping."

"Yeah...yeah, me too."

"Is there anything different I can do to support you? How can I help?"

"Um—" I'm not sure, I haven't thought about this. "Can I get back to you on that?"

"Whenever. Nothing they've said about you has ever determined how I see or love you. You constantly make me proud, and I'm forever grateful to be your father."

"I'm proud to be your son, too. What time does open skate end?" Our neighborhood ice rink usually stays open late on the weekends.

He checks the time. "Couple hours, probably."

"Wanna go skate? Play a pick-up game?"

"I'd love nothing more."

THIRTY-THREE

SUTTON

I SLIDE into the plush chair across from Jordan and Elliot the morning after Elliot's class, tucking my sore legs up underneath me. Elliot rises, going to order another coffee and breakfast. Jordan, Cooper's little sister, nudges a glass of water in my direction.

"*Hey*," she says gently.

"Your hair." I ignore her tone or what it implies. Jordan is close with Cooper, they're Irish twins. It wouldn't surprise me if he had already told her about yesterday.

Jordan runs a hand through the long strands. Unlike her siblings, who have wavy hair when grown out, hers is straight. All three of them had deep, chestnut-brown hair until now. Her hair is blue—a midnight shade with hints of indigo in it.

"It's blue," we say in unison. "I love it," I follow up with.

It fits the olive undertones of her skin and makes her gray eyes lean midnight blue.

"When did you dye it?"

"Three days ago." Jordan leans back in her chair, relaxed but shoulders and back stiff—she's always so serious. "Meant to give myself highlights, messed up, and decided to dye it all." She braids a section of it, eyes flickering with various emotions.

"What gave you the idea for blue?"

"Just because." She shrugs nonchalantly, dropping her hair to sip on water.

Jordan is bold. Extremely confident and blunt, but fun-loving or easy-going wouldn't be in my top five characteristics for her.

Dying your hair blue on a whim? That's random, fun, and easy-going.

She wouldn't *just* do this on a whim.

Elliot shows back up before I try to get her to elaborate. "Chai for you." A steaming mug is dropped in front of me. "Decaf for me. And an iced banana bread latte with macadamia nut milk for you." Plopping into the chair beside me, Elliot excitedly asks, "Did you see Jordan's hair? Dontcha love it? Makes me want to dye mine pink!"

I reach for her coffee and smell it, checking that it is decaf.

She pokes my side, snatching the bowl-like mug away from me.

"Would suggest a hair salon if you do."

"Want to, but I'd never. My mom calls me a unicorn because I've never dyed my hair."

"You're a natural blonde?" Jordan is shocked.

"Born and raised. I wrote an essay on it for speech class in high school," Elliot announces proudly.

"Makes so much sense."

I toss a napkin at Jordan. "Don't be mean."

"She's not." Elliot waves off her comment. "Did Cooper answer any of your calls this morning?"

Yup, that's right. Calls. Capital freaking S.

Texts too.

I'm pissed at him, but I'm more confused than anything. After he bailed at the end of the cycle class, I stopped by his house, but his car wasn't there. The guys didn't know where he was either; his location turned off.

I shake my head no behind the mug, pressing into my mouth.

"He drove home this morning. Asked if I wanted to tag along, but I was still asleep," Jordan admits. "Did something happen between you two?"

I catch Jordan up—Elliot filling in the non-existent blanks—she's a better, more extravagant storyteller. When I finish, the confusion she's wearing makes me realize that Cooper didn't tell her about being my dating coach. Or about anything.

The dynamic between the three of us is different, more interconnected, than our other siblings because Jordan and I played hockey together. After Cooper and I's friendship exploded, it put Jordan in more of a precarious position.

We don't talk about her brother, that's the agreement. Made it easier to be teammates and friends. However, I truly assumed he'd tell her.

"Don't forget to tell her about the study room—"

"Elliot!" I smack her shoulder. "I told you that in confidence. Did you tell the rest of the guys, too?"

"Chase and Jaxon guessed!"

Ugh. I let out a groan, a blush rising to my cheeks.

"Was it good? I've been meaning to ask."

I let out another groan and tip my chin in Jordan's direction.

"Sister in the room." I put my hands over Jordan's ears momentarily. "Yes. I can't stop thinking about it, or wanting it to happen again."

Elliot claps joyfully. "I am loving this."

"I am not," Jordan and I both say.

"So what happened between that morning and yesterday?" Jordan searches for the same clarification I've been racking my brain for.

"I don't know, but should I be surprised? Cooper and I were never going to work. I like someone else, he's just helping me out."

"And who is it that you like?"

"Cooper." It comes out abruptly. I'm slapping a hand against my mouth once my brain processes, dropping my attention to my lap.

Cooper? *What?*

No, I don't like Cooper. I can't like-like Cooper.

I don't even like Cooper as a friend.

Yes, you do, my treacherous heart sings. *You even called him your best friend,* my brain teams up with my heart.

Great. Just great.

I tip my chin up and find Elliot's mouth about to break from smiling so big, and Jordan's brows are one with her blue hairline.

"That's not what I meant," I try to backtrack. "I thought you asked something else."

"No, you didn't."

"Sutton, it's okay to have feelings for my brother." When I open my mouth, she hastily adds, "That's not hatred."

"But—"

I don't know why I'm fighting myself internally. I know I like-like Cooper. These rediscovered, renewed feelings for Cooper have already stuck themselves in the driver's seat.

And maybe I wanted to deny it? Never admit it aloud. I'd rather let them burn out again than anyone know the truth.

Jordan hands me her phone, her brother on the line. *Tell him* she mouths.

"What? Right now?" I whisper-yell despite tapping mute.

She points to her hair. "Be spontaneous."

I roll my eyes.

"Jord, you okay? I'm with mom. Jord?"

I unmute myself and hold the phone up to my ear. "Cooper—"

The line goes dead.

———

MY FAVORITE PLACE on campus is empty, but that's probably because no one knows about it. An old, wood dock hidden in a canopy of overgrown emergent plants. The path out here is discreet and if you don't know where it is, you'll more than likely never find it.

I've been coming out here since freshman year, and rarely see another soul, except Chase. We've bumped into each other twice. From the dock, tucked in a small alcove, you'll find fishermen along the distant shoreline, boats from the marina, or our rowing team out practicing. Sometimes, students are brave enough to swim, or skinny dip, in the water.

I come here in the mornings or to catch the sunset. Mainly on my runs. A pit stop for my knee and brain. It's peaceful.

My feet dangle off the edge, gaze out on the water where I tossed a pebble.

I had a missed call from Cooper last night. When I called him back, he didn't answer. He drove back late, and was studying this morning for a quiz.

A part of me thought he'd show up to walk me to class or be outside with a coffee, but I haven't seen him all day.

I understand why he's angry with me. If the roles were reversed, I'd be too.

I saw you with him.

Cooper must've seen or heard me and Zach. When and where, I don't know. What I do know is that it had to be out of context. Outside our class together or bumping into each other in the psych building, Zach and I haven't hung out. I like someone else, and we both know it. I told Zach that when he asked me on a second date.

Our last interaction was on my walk home from campus last week. Zach asked to borrow my notes for the lectures he was going to miss. Asked if I could bring them by on Monday when he got back, which I did before this run.

Maybe I'm stalling. Maybe I'm letting him stew in his assumptions.

Either way he's about to leave practice. Either way, I plan to go over there tonight to tell him how I feel.

Elliot's in the living room putting on shoes when I get back. "Those were left for you."

On the counter is a vase of my favorite flowers, Tulips. They're from Cooper, I have no doubt. Tulip season starts mid-April around here, but mid-March or sometimes earlier in warmer climates. Mom sent me a picture of a shipment on orange and pink ones that came in late last week.

"The guys and I are going to catch a movie." Elliot walks to the kitchen island, leans across it to steady my hand playing with the orange petals. "Wanna come?"

"I need to shower, and midterms are coming up," I list off miscellaneous items on an imaginary to-do list looking for a reason not to go.

"Cooper's not going if that's what you want to know."

"Oh." I turn away from her and pace the kitchen.

Elliot pops up behind me. "I can drop you off there. I'm picking them up."

"Why'd I have you do that?"

"Oh for the love of my sanity. I know you're going to end up there."

"Am not—"

"Whatever. Take your shower and shave and moisturize. I left my container in there since you still haven't bought more." Elliot's walking toward the door. "Wear cute pajamas, and at least text me if you aren't coming home tonight."

I ignore her, repositioning the vase next to the sink, but she's right.

I take a shower and rehearse what I'm going to say to him for the millionth time before leaving.

THIRTY-FOUR

COOPER

MY ROOMMATES TOOK off to catch a new action movie with Elliot. I stayed back when Chase innocently told me *she* wasn't going.

She's not going because it's Monday and Sutton has another date with Zach.

I tried to catch her before she left, fully intending to tell her not to go. No one was home when I stopped by, so I left the vase outside their door.

That was three hours ago.

If anyone peeked in through the kitchen window, they'd think I'm tunneling myself into the laminate with my pacing. I can't stop. I tried sitting on the couch, but my knee wouldn't stop bouncing. Even making a bowl of popcorn and turning on a movie was a complete fail. Sweet and salty pieces litter the carpet.

It's been this way since everyone left.

The doorbell rings, louder than her favorite movie I'm punishing myself with playing low in the background. I ignore it.

I hear a key in the lock, and rush to the front window to see who it is—Jaxon moved the hook-up-key this morning, texting our group chat with Elliot and Sutton the new location. Elliot is with them now, and Sutton is *occupied*...

Peeling back the blinds, I can't see anyone from this angle. The darkness masking both of us.

In desperate need for some WD-40, the door creaks open.

"Cooper?"

I'm frozen.

She closes the door. "Cooper, are you here?"

I'm still frozen. *Move, Cooper.*

Sutton scoff-laughs in amusement at the TV, rotating her body around the room. She doesn't see me, and heads to the kitchen.

"Carmichael, I know you're here."

Sutton.

My Sutton. My brain doesn't even correct me, reminding me that she's never been mine—not like that.

"I guess I'll go lie in your bed naked or raid your underwear drawer. I know that's where you keep your diary."

Finally, my feet move. I stand in front of her, keeping my distance, barely. Barefoot, and a pair of Levi's that need retired, they hang loose on my hips. No shirt, I discarded that after my sixty-third lap in the kitchen.

Itching to touch her, I shove my hands in my pockets. "Hi."

"Hi."

"What are you doing here?"

Sutton's eyes do all the talking, that's how I know—just in time—to pull my hands from my jeans. Soft hands are thrown around my neck as she throws herself into my arms. Mouth sealed to mine. I catch her with one hand around her back, the other under her thighs hauling her closer, flush against me.

I walk us up against a wall, move a hand to cradle her head as we hit it. Run my fingers through her curls, kissing her deeper. Sutton's explorative. Frantic, desperate hands in my hair, clawing at my back, grasping my biceps, slipped into my back pockets as I kiss her back just as needy.

I keep her pinned to the wall, leaning back to look at her. Thumbs rub over her cheeks, pressing into them as if I can feel and count each freckle. Twenty-seven on her left check, and I lost count on the other.

"Sutton." I breathe, maybe pant, a sigh of disbelief. "What are you doing here?" Breathe, again. "Zach? Your date?"

"Date?" Her hazel eyes shimmer green. "We traded notes for a classes he missed Friday and today because of a pre-season games. If you would have answered my calls, or let me explain, you would have known that." I open my mouth to speak, but the words die on my tongue. "You would have also known I told him that we can only be friends. There's someone else that I like leaving me flowers, knowing all my secrets, making me laugh."

I press a light kiss to her lips. "Who is that?"

Sutton leans further into my touch. "You." She says it as if she's relinquishing power, giving me the keys her heart.

It doesn't take much for a smile to work its way onto my face, pressing my dimple in. Or for the remaining disappointment and doubt around Sutton and I to fade away.

"Sutton Elizabeth Davis. You *like* me," I tease, emphasizing the words playfully. "Tell me."

"I have a speech of things I want to—"

"They can wait. Tell me this."

Sutton rolls her eyes at me—her signature one just for me. "Why? So your ego suffocates both of us?"

I shake my head no, giving her a quick peck. "Haven't I already told you, I need to hear you say it."

"Your words of affirmation love language is going to be insufferable, isn't it?" I shrug playfully, scraping my teeth alongside her jaw and whisper in her ear before pulling back. "Don't make me say it."

"Now, I *really* want you to."

"Fine. I *like* you, Cooper Carmichael."

"Was that too hard?"

Sutton looks annoyed. She exhales through her nose, all dragon-like. "No," she relents. "But you could say something back besides taunting me. I was trying to be all cute and romantic showing up here."

I reach forward to tuck a strand of auburn hair behind her ear. "Very romantic, but you aren't cute. You're beautiful, Sutton. Always have been, and always will be to me. I like you, too, by the way." My hand trails down her jaw. "Have for a really long time," I say quietly, not sure if she heard me. Not sure if I want her to have heard me. "And I should have told you sooner."

"I'm here now." She steals a kiss. "Guess I have some catching up to do."

"No you don't." This is the part in her books where the boy tells her he's loved her enough for the both of them, and maybe I have. I could tell her that, but I don't want her feeling like she's behind with us, because she isn't. We are exactly where we are supposed to be, and I tell her so. "Buuuuuttttt...I can think of some other ways we can make up for it."

THIRTY-FIVE

COOPER

SUTTON HAS no willpower when it comes to a 2000s rom-com. Thus, our makeup plans were quickly confiscated when I laid her on the couch and she finally noticed the movie playing in the background.

When she yawned, I carried her upstairs—Sutton tried to tell me she'd drive home, but I wasn't letting her go again—and tucked her into my bed after helping her change into one of my shirts per her request.

She's lying on her side, facing me.

I can't stop touching her. We can't stop touching each other.

Her long legs are pretzeled with mine. One of my hands is holding hers, the other playing with a loose curl from the top bun she pulled her hair into.

"I'm happy I'm here," she murmurs.

"I'm happy you chose me," I admit.

The corners of her mouth pull upward. "Did I even have a choice?"

"You always do." Truthful, but... "But I was going to make it hard not to pick me."

"Didn't take you as a pick-me boy when it came to girls."

"Girl."

"Why do you keep saying girl?" She yawns. The alarm clock on my bedside table reads after midnight.

Sutton's eyes flutter closed when I say, "Because there's only ever been you."

I kiss her temple. Let my forehead rest there and fall asleep right behind her.

———

BEFORE THIS, I didn't do sleepovers. I barely even let my roommates or girls into my room. For the past year or so, the four walls of my dorm and bedroom were a battleground.

I stopped bringing people back to my place, too consumed and worried with what they'd see when they entered. Girls expect the Cooper Carmichael that's out on the ice or in their classroom. The one who is a stained glass window, letting light reflect through me to reflect the painting of who I'm supposed to be.

But what would they see? I can't fake that here.

Would they see a coward, or think I'm ungrateful for the life paved for me? Selfish to be considering anything other than going professional? Would they see the pole balancing on my shoulders? One side loaded with comparison, the other with obligation.

Even with Sutton, at the start, I was worried. Before that day years ago, I wouldn't have thought twice, but then she hated me. I became another version of myself, yearning for her but hiding it by becoming the villain in her story. Clinging to tossed hazel daggers across rooms, competing with her in class, teasing and taunts, a nickname she outwardly hated, but I saw inwardly how much she loved it. Wearing her favorite bracelet and combining our jersey numbers.

Now, she sees through me. I think if I let her, she would have earlier.

Maybe I should have apologized, or told her the truth, all those years ago. Maybe I wouldn't have ended up as big of a mess as I am now.

Maybe, maybe, maybe.

Sutton shifts, hogging more comforter. She fell asleep in my arms, but I quickly learned she doesn't cuddle. I don't even think I'm a sleeping cuddler. My arm awkwardly positioned under her, my bicep fell asleep, and it took twenty minutes to stop the tingling.

I roll over, dragging the sleeping beauty into me.

"Mmmm."

"Morning, baby," I mumble into the fabric by her ear.

"*Baby.*"

"Do you want me to call you something else?"

"No. I like baby."

"Okay, baby."

"Sutton and Dave are still good, too."

"They'll be on rotation. Mine somewhere in the mix, too." I can feel her smile. "How'd you sleep?"

"Good. You?" She turns over, faces me.

"Me too."

She wiggles further into me. Kisses my nose. "I like waking up with you."

"I could get used to it."

"Our roommates might get sick of us."

"As if they aren't already." I kiss her lips. "What are your plans today?"

"I was going to go on a run. I'm up to five miles now," she says proudly. "Or skating."

"Want to go after breakfast?"

"Cooper, no. You have a game later. Aren't you late for morning skate, already? What time is it?"

"The game is at eight." The girls are playing before us, which is why Coach cancelled our morning skate. The Pond is open from eleven to twelve if we want to go. "We have the morning off, and you don't have morning classes today, which means"—I undo her confines, push myself over top of her—"I have all morning to spend with you." I drop my weight onto her. Bring my mouth to hers and murmur, "Thinking I could spend time here." Roll my hips against hers. Sutton swallows a moan. "Then some real breakfast. Then we can go on the run. Maybe some lunch." I roll my hips against her again, this time, I capture her light, airy moan. "You could study or whatever in my bed. Your bed or couch, I don't care. You drive me to my game, and then afterward I could go home with you."

I roll my hips a third time. Sutton circles her legs around my hips, holding me to her.

"I'd like that." Her hips move over mine. "A lot, but there's one problem with your plans."

She leans to her right, flipping us over. Her thighs on either side of mine. She rolls her hips and leans down to kiss me.

"What's that?" I ask breathily, extremely turned on.

"It's finally later."

She starts kissing along my jaw, down my bare chest. Her tongue traces the divots of my abdomen. Leaving a sizzling trail of heat behind.

Dainty fingers curl in the waistband of my boxer briefs. Her nails tickle the sensitive skin as she drags them down my legs.

Sutton sits up. Her nipples hard and pointed, their outline visible through my white shirt. The same color as her underwear with the smallest pink bow in the center, which was the center of most of my dreams last night.

I don't think she realizes how her eyes are tracking over my body. Her lower body shifts, rubbing against my thigh as she tracks lower and lower. Sutton's tongue peeks out, licking her lips demurely.

"You're so...Wow. I...um...well..."

She falters for a minute. It shows in the way her eyes widen, pupils flare. Hesitation. Unhabituated. Her eyes flick left and right. "So like, I've only—"

"You don't need to do this." I swipe a knuckle down her cheek.

"I want to. Just—"

"You're going to make it so good, baby." I let out a gentle, hopefully soothing, more pathetic than anything, laugh. "Look at me. One touch, any touch, of yours and I'm already barely hanging on." I run a curl through my fingers.

With a slight wiggle, I move my body up the bed, push my shoulders into a crunch against the headboard so I can comfortably see her.

She's beautiful.

Positioned above me. Heated and desire-soaked hazels, and cheeks dipped cherry red. I pull a scrunchie off my wrist, lean forward an inch to gather her hair curtaining her face. I tie it off for her.

"Is that mine?"

"You left it here a couple of weeks ago." She arches a brow. "Finders keepers, losers weepers."

She sticks her tongue out at me teasingly. "You'll teach me though? Tell me what you like."

When I nod, Sutton lowers her mouth onto me. All. The. Way. The hesitation from minutes ago dissipating. Holy fuck. My groan works through my body. Rolling its way from where she is through my abs and chest, and up my throat.

Sutton works up and down, once. Her mouth makes a popping noise when she pulls herself off me and sits up. I whimper at the loss of contact.

Her hand wraps around me, and she pulls a slow, hesitant stroke. Then repeats it again and again. "Is this okay?"

"M-mor-more than okay," I can barely get out. "So good."

"So you like it?"

"Sutton. Baby, please. Keep going."

Sutton leans forward, returns her mouth to me.

I'm a goner for this girl, always have been. But now? I'm rocketed out of this world. Her touch is the flames that carry me straight through the atmosphere.

I've never seen stars before, not like this.

My chest rises and falls, picking up as she drags her mouth

down and up in a god-sent pace. I can't hold myself back much longer.

Sutton takes her hand, finds my free one, placing it on her head. My fucking girl. She wants direction, not that she needs it. Always hungry to learn.

I twist her messy ponytail around my fist, push down on the back of her head. There's a quiet choking noise. "You're so good. That's perfect."

It happens again, but she doesn't let up.

I don't conceal the noises coming out of me. My hips thrusting up. It hits me out of nowhere, without warning. My body stills with exhilaration and a new intoxicating high that I think I'm already addicted to.

She works around my twitching, taking everything.

Sutton sits up, licks her lips, and smiles down at me.

———

THIRTY MINUTES LATER, Sutton pulls my shirt over her head. It drowns her, but that's okay, she drowns out a lot of things in my life.

Her hair is tied back in a much neater ponytail now.

I'm tugging on sweatpants, but can't stop looking or smiling at her. She's the same way.

I hold the door open for her. Sutton slips under my arm, bending down to taunt me about my height.

"I'm tall," I say, catching her at the top of the stairs.

"Yeah, for an average guy."

She jogs down a few stairs. I go after her. Scoop her up with my arms around her waist. "We both know there's nothing average about me."

"I mean..."

I nip at her ear, and she starts laughing. Shaking her head to avoid my teeth. I push my fingers in her side like I'm playing an instrument. Tickling her without dropping her as we make our way down the stairs.

She's laughing around her meaningless *stops*.

I put her on the ground, move my hands to her shoulders, and help guide her to the kitchen—

"Whoa, there, Cap."

The entire room is filled with my team. Twenty-six sets of eyes are on us.

Dawson stands up, hand extended in the direction of one of the senior wingers. "You owe me twenty. Told you he was upstairs with a girl."

"You owe me ten of that," our backup goalie pipes in.

"Why?" he scoffs like a girl.

"I bet it was someone we know."

"You know who Sutton is?"

"Yeah? Who doesn't?" the goalie questions back.

There's an exchange of cash among several of my teammates, roommates, and best friends included. Some clap. Some shovel food into their mouths, pretending not to notice us.

We take a seat together in the kitchen.

"What's going on?" she asks into my shoulder.

"Team breakfast."

"Since when did you do team breakfast?"

"Since early February." Jaxon hands us two plates. "Cooper had the idea after some project he's working on."

Sutton eyes me knowingly. She steps out of my embrace to take the plate. "What's for breakfast?"

"Becky made pancakes. But you've gotta catch 'em—only way to eat. Whoever catches the most gets to pick the music on the bus for our next away game."

"What's the record this morning?"

"Six," Beckett grunts.

"Alright, hit me, Chef."

Beckett turns and gets in position. Even he's enjoying these breakfasts, might not speak much during them, grunt and elbow people out of the way to clean up after, but he cracks a smile here and there.

Sutton catches the first two. "What happens if I miss one?"

"Your turn is over." I saddle up next to her. Try to step in front of her to block the next pancake.

"Oh no way, Superstar." It slips from her lips so casually. "Ha." She catches the next two despite my attempts at distraction. Then catches another two, and the entire room leans in with anticipation.

When the seventh pancake falls onto her plate, the room erupts.

"What are you going to pick? Taylor Swift," Tristan, the sophomore I spent all last year training one-on-one under Coach's request, speaks up. The disappointed tone leads me to believe he was the one who caught six.

"Pick 1989, please. That's my favorite album," Jaxon adds. Of course it is.

Sutton laughs. "I'll let your captain pick."

Tristan eyes her up and down. "Fine. At least he has good taste."

I chuck a pancake at him.

The guys make room for us at one of the folding tables set up. There are four of them that run from our kitchen into the living room.

I inhale my breakfast, one arm tossed around the back of her chair.

For the first time in what feels like forever, I feel completely light. Present and engaged. Like the guy I want to be, who I really am.

Our front door opens, and a leggy blonde flounces in.

"Good morning, hockey boys." Elliot coos. "Ooo, pancakes."

"Who invited you?" Chase asks.

"Did I need to be invited? I'm Elliot Jones."

THIRTY-SIX

SUTTON

"YOU ARE GOING to have to tell Mom." Meave bumps my shoulder as we peruse a new romance-only bookstore in Chicago. We've already been to two art stores, and are going to her favorite thrift store after this. "She's been planning your wedding to Cooper for years."

"We aren't even dating, Meave."

"Does he know that?"

She pulls a book from the shelf and adds it to her pile. I run my finger along another shelf, reading titles to distract from answering her question.

"Sutton..."

"No, I suppose he doesn't. We aren't *not* together. I like how things are going. There's no pressure. No..." It's barely two weeks, ten days to be exact, but each day feels like a year. In the best way possible.

"Do you love him?"

"Don't ask stupid questions, Meave."

"So that's a yes." She rests her chin on my shoulder and leans her head into mine. "And now I can finally admit, while you are good at a lot of things, sis, you are a terrible doodler. The doodles you did of you and Cooper are hideous."

"How does that have anything to do with this?"

"I've just needed to get that off my chest for about fifteen years."

"I was six!" I interject.

We head to the checkout desk, arms stacked with books. "But this is it for you two, yeah?"

There are still unspoken truths that sit between me and Cooper. High school lingering like the ghost of Christmas past. As good as things have been between us, there are moments it's as if there is another person in the relationship, a hurdle we haven't jumped yet.

"I hope."

We stop to have lunch after thrifting and before returning to her loft apartment. Meave has a commission to finish and locks herself away in her makeshift studio with promises of takeout and a movie later.

I decided to go on a long walk, explore the Chicago more.

Making my way back, from a block over, I spot a familiar profile throwing pebbles at a window. I sneak closer.

Cooper throws another, hitting the rectangle in the center. He's been in the city volunteering with his cousin's charity. Dawson and Jaxon, too, but they left.

"That's her neighbor's window," I announce.

Cooper spins on his heels, a smile on his face. "Oops."

"You're lucky they aren't here this week." I peep the duffle bag resting at his feet. "Going somewhere?"

"Was hoping for a sleepover on Meave's pull-out couch."

Speak of the devil, she waves from her window—next door to the one that he was throwing rocks at—a paintbrush in one hand.

"I think I can squeeze."

He squeezes me into his side, dropping a kiss to the top of my head. "I missed you."

"It's been three days."

"And?" He picks up his bag, sliding it on the arm not

wrapped around me. We head into Meave's building. "Don't be scared to admit you missed me too."

"Fine." I lift my leg backward and kick his butt. "I missed you too."

———

WE CRASH with Meave for the night, before driving back to campus. Unlike our last drive, we triple checked the weather. No precipitation in the forecast for the next week.

Cloudless blue skies stretches for miles in every direction.

Cooper keeps singing the lyrics wrong. By the seventh song, I know it's on purpose. It's remarkable how quickly someone can learn, or remember, your buttons. What makes me smile or roll my eyes. How to make me laugh or get into my pants. The limit of how hard to push before he annoys me too much.

Maybe it was quick, or maybe it's what happens when you grow up together.

His body is like a puzzle piece I'm fitted to. A hand I grew up holding, picking me up when I fell learning to ride a bike and how to skate. He's a Tempur-Pedic mattress that's memorized my shape and grown around it.

MOM appears on the screen in his car. We turn off the music and answer it. I tap my chest, then bring a finger in front of my mouth, communicating silently a *shh, I'm not here.*

"Hey, Mom. How are you?"

"Cooper, honey." She sounds delighted but surprised that he answered. "Better now. How are you? Midterms go well?"

"B plus in two, A minus in another, and I don't have the results for the others yet. I was a little distracted while studying." He shoots me a taunting look, reminding me that I'm the distraction. The hand firmly placed on my thigh squeezes. A giggle shoots out of me.

"B's get degrees," she singsongs.

"I think it's C's get degrees, Mom."

"Then you'll be graduating summa cum laude," she jokes. "A B plus in statistical mathematics is like a triple A plus compared to what your father took while he was in school."

I prepare myself for him to recoil, but it doesn't come. Cooper chuckles. "What was it again that he studied?"

"Something that sounded made up." His mom makes a handful of jokes about his dad in college, and trying to cheat off of her in the class where they had their meet-cute.

I laugh, managing to pick the moment there's a lull in the conversation.

"Is that my daughter?" Of course she's with my mom. Where there's one, there's usually the other.

"Hi, Mom," I pipe in, leaning back into the seat to stare at Cooper with my eyes wide. How we are going to explain this? Our siblings are the only ones who know about our rekindled *friendship*.

"I didn't realize you were with Cooper. Where are you two going?"

"Back to campus. Cooper was in Chicago volunteering."

"And you went with him?"

"No." I get nervous. "I spent spring break with Meave. Remember?"

"Yes, yes, that's right. Sorry, we've been out for drinks." There's a muffling of laughter from their end.

I glance at Cooper and mouth *Are our moms tipsy?*

Totally he mouths back.

"First the gallery, now this. Have you two been spending a lot of time together?" my mom asks.

Comparative to before? Yes.

Almost every day outside of spring break. Cooper walks me to class in the morning, showing up with a perfect dirty chai latte in hand. Between classes, studying for midterms, therapy, practice, and games, we take any stolen moments we can—last week he found me in the psych building, after getting back from an away game the day before, surprising me from behind with strong arms wrapped around my shoulders. Walked me backward and into a closet that I'm still not sure how he opened because his arms never left my body. A hand was running up my outer thigh, tickling and bringing to life the bare skin as he found his way underneath the skirt part of my overall dress. His other hand tugged my chin, twisting my head up to his and kissing me. My mouth opened to let his tongue in.

"I've never played seven minutes in heaven," I whispered to him.

"I've never been to heaven," he responded against the skin between my jaw and ear. "But I imagine this is what it'll be like."

The hand up my skirt drew circles over my underwear. A finger snapped the waistband, then snaked under it.

"Can I take you to heaven, baby?" I nodded. He stared into my hazel eyes pointedly. "That's not gonna work for me. Can I, Sutton baby?" he said the term of endearment again, and I almost melt. If it weren't for his body holding mine, my legs would have given out, a mess on the floor.

"Cooper," I whimpered.

"Fuck," he whimpered back. "Say my name again."

"Cooper, please."

He pushed a finger inside of me and kissed me again.

Kisses moved down my throat, rotating our positions, my back now against the shelf. The next kiss stung, and I tossed my head back when there was a thud. He pulled his mouth away from me, eyes frantically looking over me, checking me for injuries. "Are you okay?"

"Uh-huh. I think that was a paint can. Keep going."

Cooper started again, continuing his escapade of my body, not that he hadn't already learned all of it. Sometimes I think he's making up for lost time, or savoring me like I'm the final drops of the perfect summer day on the lake.

He pushed the denim up, then my ribbed long sleeve. Kissed the skin along the hem and a soft one to my outer belly button whilst his fingers worked inside of me.

Finally—I acted like that wasn't his destination and that it's been more than two whole agonizing minutes—he's on his knees in front of me, moving a leg over his shoulder and pulling aside my underwear.

My favorite mouth in the world finally on me. Stealing from me the way we've stolen glances at each other the past five years.

I cried out his name, not caring who was in the hallway or could open the door. All I wanted was to be with him. Give in to the cravings that festered inside of me, taking shape as dislike for so long, when I think all I ever wanted to do was love him and be loved by him.

Cooper squeeze my thigh, and I snap my head to his, realizing we aren't in the closet anymore but in his car on the phone with our moms.

"Sorry, what did you say?"

Mom repeats herself.

My jaw drops when Cooper answers, "Actually. We're dating. Sutton's my girlfriend."

"Girlfriend!" his mom, Susan, squeals. "I had a feeling when you asked for tulips."

"Dating? Susan, you knew about this?"

"No. Maybe. Sort of! He didn't say Sutton's name. How long have you two been together?"

"About a month or so."

"A month? Cooper James Carmichael, you have been dating Sutton Elizabeth Davis" Why are we both being full named now? "For a month, and you've failed to mention it once? Not at dinner or a game or—"

A month? I count back days. Is he referring to the night in the bar or our fake date? Counting all of that time?

"Or Sutton, could you have mentioned it when we were planning our summer holiday over family FaceTime. This is huge."

"Monumental."

"We have to call your fathers. They are going to be…" Sutton's mom trails off. "Maybe not right now."

"Why?" Cooper asks.

"I'm going to go out on a limb and assume that you two have been intimate, definitely more than kissing, and—"

Our moms are in an in-sync double Dutch routine. Susan jumps in. "Oh, I beg of you to please use protection."

Cooper throws a second curveball. "We haven't had sex. No worries, no grandkids yet."

That sends them on a second frenzy.

"Grandkids? Oh, Suz, we are going to be grandparents together." I think one of them is crying. "At least another five years, maybe ten."

"Or tomorrow. I kind of want to be a grandma. I'd be such a cool grandma."

"The coolest," my mom backs her.

They've been best friends forever. I've never not known them as being two peas in a pod. Even before I was adopted, they've been inseparable. Through his mom getting pregnant in college, to my mom's miscarriages and unsuccessful rounds of IVF. They're the type of best friend relationship you always dream of having—including your kids dating.

Cooper huffs out a laugh over this conversation. He tells them goodbye with a promise that the six of us can get dinner next time they visit.

The song we were two minutes and thirty-three seconds into starts playing again. He spins the dial to the left, lowers the volume to barely above an echo.

"You okay? You went quiet."

"You never asked."

"Asked what?"

"You never asked me to be your girlfriend. I didn't know that's what I was."

"Of course you are, Dave. I don't want to see anyone but you. You feel the same way, right?"

"Yes, but—"

"But. There shouldn't be a but. We're dating. This is it."

"But you never asked," I repeat. "You still need to ask."

He chuckles. I don't hear it, but see it in the way his chest rises and falls. Shoulders bounce against the seat. "Okay, then. Will you be my girlfriend, Sutton Davis?"

"No."

We're pulling into his driveway. His roommates' cars are parked in their Tetris configuration to work for their busy schedules. Cooper cuts the ignition. Jerking the gear shift into park first.

"No?" He's taken aback.

"Try again." His mouth starts to split. "Not right now. You've waited how long for this?" I unbuckle myself and open the door. Lean across the console and kiss him. "Goodbye, Carmichael."

He's smirking, shaking his head at me. Gotta keep him on his toes somehow.

"Goodbye, Davis."

I tilt my head over my shoulder, run my tongue along my top teeth. Give him an eye roll and close the door behind me.

Not that I'm going very far. I walk inside, find Elliot and Jordan on the couch. We leave two minutes later.

Leaning against his car, Cooper has his arms crossed in front of his chest. Sunglasses pushed up into his thick hair.

We lock eyes, stare at each other my entire walk to Elliot's small SUV.

"What's wrong with my brother?" Jordan asks.

"Nothing," Cooper and I say in unison.

THIRTY-SEVEN

COOPER

"SO, how is this supposed to work?" Chase holds up a face mask. Head tilted and a brow arched. "Why is it wet? What are the flaps for? Am I supposed to tuck that into my mouth?"

"No." Elliot laughs, scooting closer to him on the couch. "Here. Let me help you." Chase hands her the charcoal mask, cheeks tickled pink. "You want to place the top at your hairline right here, then work down the rest of the mask. This goes over the bridge of your nose. And the flaps..." She snickers. "They are to help bend around your chin, jaw line, and mouth. Most definitely *not* to go into your mouth. Pat it down and make sure it won't slip off your face. Now start your timer for fifteen minutes and enjoy your wine."

Chase follows her instructions, leaning back into the couch with an oversized glass of red wine.

"Good boy." Elliot pats his shoulder before moving to help Beckett with his mask.

This isn't the first girls' night we've crashed...or wanted to be a part of. Classes kick back up tomorrow. Coach gave us last Monday after practice through today off. It was a welcome reprieve for everyone with the conference tournament right around the corner. From here on out, everything is about the road to the Frozen Four, hauling the trophy over our head, and bringing it back to Lakeland. Both the women's and men's teams are leading the standings.

However, before departing from the locker room, Coach gave us a stern lecture on behavior over break, which went in and out of the ears of half my teammates.

My cousin, who plays for Chicago, had called a couple of weeks ago to catch up. I opened up after he asked about NHL prospects, and yet another article about my dad and me. I don't know why I hadn't sooner, he understands. He reminded me that people criticize us because they're jealous or have nothing better to do and don't want to face their insecurities. Comparing me to my dad is easy, buzzworthy, and clickbait; they don't care about what it's doing to me. All of which were reiterations of what Sutton and Dad have said to me.

When I asked him about how he stays grounded, he invited me to volunteer with his and his twin sister's charity. A couple of the guys came with me, but the rest of the team was scattered across the US doing who knows what.

It's relaxing the eight of us being back together now.

Sutton's bathroom door opens, and I can hear Jordan and Jaxon heading toward us.

"That hurt," Jaxon groans.

"You wanted to bleach your tips. Bleach hurts."

"You purposely got it in my eyes."

"It didn't get anywhere near your eyes. Stop being a big baby. You wanted this."

"I wanted your hands on me," Jaxon mutters, but unfortunately for him, I hear him from the kitchen.

"That's my little sister you dick. Stop thinking about her like that," I holler.

Jaxon leans over the counter and apologizes when he reaches the eat-in. Jordan is behind him, pulling off the plastic gloves she's wearing and washing her hands. His hair doesn't look as ridiculous as I thought. The blond tips are...interesting to say the least.

He had two ideas for team bonding: frosted tips and mustaches. Thankfully, everyone vetoed the frosted tips. Now we're growing out mustaches for the rest of the season and, crossing-fingers, into the tournament.

I rub a thumb over mine.

Unlike my best friend, I grow facial hair quickly. I'll have a full-fledged mustache by the time the first round happens if we make it. Sutton keeps saying I'm going to jinx us if I keep trimming it.

Topping off Sutton's drink, I rejoin her on the couch. Jaxon is now droning on about his disappointment in Lakeland cancelling our annual sports lip-sync battle. It's a twenty-year tradition that our new Athletic Director deemed unnecessary and a waste of time.

"We had the perfect dance too."

Dawson pats Jaxon's bare thigh, his already short shorts riding up his long legs. "Want Chase and I to film it with you?"

"You'd do that?" He perks up.

"Anything for you babe," Dawson replies as Chase throws popcorn at them and says, "Don't volunteer me. I can't dance."

"Stop talking!" Elliot warns Chase again. "You have three minutes left."

Even with our friends the world falls away when Sutton is around. Words become sounds. People become blurry, out of focus. Except for her. We're a snow globe on a shelf. Our own little world, that we've shaken up and living in the flurries around us.

My fingers are tangled in her hair massaging her scalp, watching her debate which color to paint her toes. When she can't decide, I pick, taking the bottle of polish from the table. Holding the two in one hand, I drag an unpainted foot into my lap.

"Is it weird that I'm bummed I won't get to see you dance?"

"You should be," I tease. "Because your man was looking mighty fine."

"Is that so?"

"Yeah. These hips, baby, you should see the way they move."

"Are you holding out on me?"

I lean in toward her, my chest brushing her bare knees. The polka-dot lounge shorts are adorable. Sutton's also in my sweatshirt, one of the six she has conveniently forgotten to give back. I don't care, I like seeing her in them, or when I spend the night and sneak one to wear in the morning, and they smell like her.

"Whenever you're ready," I remind her.

Sutton and I haven't had sex yet. We've done everything else, and it's good. So. Good. Everything has been better with her, and I know this will be too, and I'd wait forever if that's what she wanted or needed.

She bites her bottom lip, blush rushing her cheeks. "Thank you."

Kissing her cheek, I resume my masterpiece, moving to her other foot.

"Isn't this nice?" Jaxon asks no one in particular. "I thought something was missing, then remembered that Cooper and Sutton are dating now."

"We aren't dating," Sutton chirps.

"Then what the fuck is this?" Beckett gestures in our direction, his larger body shoved against mine.

"You still haven't asked her out?" Jordan sighs, and from over my shoulder she's trading her wine glass for her phone. "I'm texting Dad—" she starts to threaten before, of all people, Elliot snatches her phone.

Good thing. He's coming to our game this week with Sutton's dad, plus who knows what Mom ended up saying to him.

"Let's not ruin the peace before we've gotten to thoroughly enjoy it." Elliot then turns to me, blocking herself from Sutton and mouths *If you don't ask her soon, you're dead. I know where you live.* Her other hand pretends to pull a knife across her neck.

I give her a thumbs up.

They leave us alone, catching Beck in a moment of chattiness gabbing about his sister. I'm almost done with Sutton's toes.

"I like this color." It's a bright blue-green. "Reminds me of your eyes."

"Pay attention." Sutton giggles. "You're getting it on my skin."

"Have you seen your hands?" I hook a finger around her pinky, tickle her palm, and she squeals. "Admit I'm better at this than you, Dave."

She narrows her eyes at me.

"No." Sutton leans forward, snatching the polish. "Gimme your feet, I'll show you."

FRIDAY IS our last game before the conference tournament starts, and Dad's here. I didn't see him or Mr. Davis during warm-ups, but they're there now. The empty seat next to them was empty till right before puck drop. My favorite, steadying redhead, rushing in. Her dad's arm around her shoulder, pulling her into a hug.

I throw one leg over the boards, dig my skate into the ice, and kick the other over. Taking a lap around our half of the ice before stretching for the next period. I skate by them, wink at Sutton, and make a hand heart on the glass, stick in my armpit.

Her dad blows a kiss with his free hand. Mine folds over laughing.

Everyone is having a great game. Beck hasn't given up a single shot. He passes his most recent save to Dawson, who passes it to the freshman defenseman, who is lightning quick and speeds down the ice into offensive territory. Nudging it off before being slammed into the boards by the opposing team, Jaxon scoops it and passes the puck to me behind the net.

I skate, brushing off the defenders on me. Our other winger

comes in for the rescue, and I get him the puck before skating back around the net, getting into position for a backside goal.

That goal puts us up four to zero, and I'm officially three goals out from Dad's record.

Jaxon throws his arms around me in a hug. The rest of my teammates on the ice are joining him.

I skate by Sutton, again, and point my stick at her to claim her.

I hope the guys sitting around her realize she's *mine* and stop looking at her butt every time she jumps to her feet.

She won't be mad to learn the goal wasn't for her, she knows it's because of her. That goal was for me. Even with Dad here, this game is for me, for my team.

After the game, the three of them are waiting for me. Sutton's in her light denim overalls and a ribbed, long-sleeve, navy shirt. Curls pinned half-up with a matching clip with the Bears logo painted on it.

Absentmindedly, and oblivious to our dads standing over her, I walk up to her, cup her cheeks, and kiss her. Hard. Possessively.

There's a cough.

Sutton pulls away with a full-body blush.

"Hi, Mr. Davis."

"Carmichael."

"I—" I'm about to apologize, but for what? "I like your daughter a lot, and she's a good kisser."

My dad sighs into his hands. Sutton gasps. And her dad chuckles, messing up my freshly showered hair.

"Happy that she's kissing you, son." He drops his hand. "Great game tonight."

Dad chimes in next. "That goal—what number is that?" We both know the answer. "Eighty-two. You're going to do it, Cooper." When I take in a slow inhale, he adds, "If there's anyone I want to break my records, it's you. Watching you play and share the love of this sport with you is the highlight of my career, Cooper."

His words fight off the lingering voice in my head.

I was four when I asked if I could skate with Dad. Told my mom I wanted to be like him when I grew up. When Dad came home from that stretch of away games and she told him, he cried. The next day, he took me to get skates, and we spent the entire afternoon skating.

In middle school, I wanted to try other sports. It didn't surprise me that he was at every practice or throwing the baseball with me, calling his brother-in-law for tips.

In the midst of the darkness in my head, drowned out by voices, it was easy to lump him in with everyone else. Believe that what they were saying was also his opinion, but it never was.

I had lost sight of my love for the sport because of my fears of not being good enough. But I also lost sight of getting to do this with him. I love sharing hockey with him.

I smile, a reflection of his. "Then you better get ready to be dethroned. I bet it'll happen before we even make the semifinals."

Dad laughs. "I'm ready. You hungry? Want to get dinner?"

Sutton steps away from our dads, slips her hand in mine. I swear one of her psychology classes is mind reading because of the understanding she portrays. She squeezes my hand and murmurs, "Never kiss me in front of my dad again."

"Tough luck, baby. I'm addicted to those lips."

THIRTY-EIGHT

COOPER

A FEW DAYS later I'm on Pinterest after practice. I've never been on Pinterest before. Heard of it, but have never gone down the rabbit hole of recipes and outfit ideas.

My sisters and mom have used it. Pretty sure Jaxon's found all of our past Halloween costumes on the app too. Plus, this felt easier than having 'How to ask your best friend to be your girl-friend?' in your recent internet searches.

Chase and Jaxon are walking back into the main part of the locker room, towels wrapped around their waists, hair damp from their showers. I was supposed to shower twenty minutes ago, but I'm lost on this stupid app.

"Come here. I need help," I request.

They sit next to me. Chase at least grabs a pair of shorts from his stall behind us, but Jaxon leans into me, not a care about his towel or what's up for show-n-tell.

"Whatcha doing?" Jaxon asks, peering at the screen. He shakes out his hair, droplets scattering everywhere. "Ooo. I've been waiting for you to ask me about this."

Truthfully, I'm surprised he hasn't tried to input himself. He's never been shy to share an idea or what's on his mind. At first I wondered if the distance I've put between us at the start of this season, school year even, was finally starting to affect us. Jaxon's always happy, and I didn't want to drag him down on my bad days, but it's people like him, opening up, that make those bad days good.

I turn to face him, green puppy eyes, and ridiculous frosted tips. He's always reminded me of a golden retriever, even more so now that his light brown hair is tipped in an English cream.

Jaxon, with extreme flexibility and dexterity, reaches around himself to snag his phone. In two swipes, he's opening the app, and taps on a board that is labeled 'How to Get the Girl.'

"Seriously?" He nods, wide-eyed and enthusiastically. "Who are you trying to get?"

Chase snorts.

"You have no room to talk." Jaxon flicks him in the head.

"What am I missing?"

"Nothing," they say hastily in unison.

We go through Jaxon's board. Veto flowers and writing on paper. Overdone. I veto a similar tactic, but with her favorite drink. He suggests I lie naked in her bed, I veto that too. Chase is quick to veto before I can even finish the idea of using a Jumbotron at a game or showing up at her apartment with a boombox. We bounce around getting Dr. Manning involved or her sister, but that idea deflates.

Jaxon keeps scrolling while I take a shower. More and more of the team joins in, and when I return ten minutes later they are all huddled around my locker...with no good ideas.

"You're overthinking this, dude. Just ask her out," one of the freshmen say.

"And that's not boring?"

"This isn't prom or a wedding proposal," someone else chirps.

"But—" I'm about to tell him how I didn't get to ask her to prom.

Jaxon presses a finger to my mouth. "Stop overthinking it. Have you been on a date yet?"

"Our practice one." That didn't feel very practice, nor did I consider it a practice one.

Besides being caught up in Sutton, we've both been caught up in school and hockey. She's prepping for an internship interview and final revisions on her paper. I'm focused on conference play next week. We spend time together, but we haven't been out on a date-date.

"There you go." He claps as if he's solved life's greatest mystery. He does have a point, though.

I'm throwing on a pair of jeans and a Bears sweatshirt. When I reach into my bag to grab my socks and shoes, a bracelet falls out of the pocket I tucked it away in before showering.

Her beaded charm bracelet.

Beck walks over to us, shouldering his bag. "The idiot is right. Just ask the question, that's all Sutton's looking for."

"See! Beck's got it."

I think about it again, and have an idea in my head.

———

"HI. GIMME A MINUTE," her tender voice echoes. I must be on speakerphone.

Setting my phone down, I press the mute button and take a large breath. Slowly inhaling. Then exhaling out my nerves—only for them to return when I take my next breath.

The guys were right, I should take her on a date, and I want to take Sutton on a date. A proper one—pick her up, hold the car door open. Hold her hand. Drag the sensitive skin of her knuckles up to my lips and kiss them. Kiss her.

I want to kiss her. A lot.

Maybe sit on the same side of the booth. Be those people, because I've waited almost a decade to be those people with her.

Nudge the tip of her shoes with mine. Watch as she blushes because even as much as we know each other, turning a new page in our book, she's still Sutton. She's still the girl who asked for help at the beginning of the semester. She's confident in everything but this.

Maybe we'd share a shake—no. That'd be pretty hard. We aren't going anywhere with shakes. We could pick them up though. Yeah, that'll work.

Maybe she'd like Italian instead, or maybe she'd hate both and wants takeout.

"Sorry about that. You still there? Coop?" Her voice stops me from spiraling over our date and replanning the entire thing. "I was cleaning up my lab."

Sutton rambles on about it.

Why is her talking nerdy to me turning me on right now? I've always admired her brain, found it hot in recent years.

"Nerdy?" She laughs.

I must have said that out loud. I roll with it. "Truthfully, any way you talk to me usually does it."

"Even when I'm being mean to you," she challenges my piece of truth.

"You mean bratty. You were never mean." A smirk curls at the corners of my mouth. "But yeah, Dave, even then. You might have tried to be mean, but it never worked."

"What did it do instead? Make you want me more?"

"Yes," I reply pointedly. "I want to take you out on a date."

"Really?" Her voice jumps up an octave.

"Don't sound so surprised. People who like each other do that."

"I also like Jaxon and Beckett. I'm not going on dates with them." There's her teasing, borderline bratty, tone.

"Stop making this difficult. Will you go on a date with me?" I ask this time, and then add, "Please."

Sutton giggles, and I know it's accompanied by a fluttering eye roll. "Yes, I'd love to go on a date with you. When is this date?"

"Tonight. I'll pick you up at seven."

"What if I wasn't free?"

"According to your color-coded fridge calendar, you are."

WHEN I PULL into the parking lot of the apartment complex, I spot someone in the entryway. I park and sprint to the door. Sneak in as they are leaving.

Taking three stairs at a time, I knock on her door.

Music is playing loudly from the other side of the door. I knock again. Harder. Louder.

She swings the door open, and my breath is stolen.

"Wow."

"Is this too much?" She smooths down a little green dress. A slip—I think that's what it's called—dress with dainty spaghetti straps. There's a slit in the right leg.

My jaw hangs open. I shake my head, unable to form words.

Sutton stands there, eyes fixed on me. She raises her brow and bites her bottom lip.

"Do you want to come in? I need to grab shoes."

I follow her in. Follow her to her bedroom at the back of the apartment.

"What are we doing tonight?" she asks, but I can't stop staring at her. I run a hand over my mouth. "Are you okay?"

"You're beautiful." I'm finally able to formulate a sentence. "We're going to the movies."

"This is way too much for the movies."

"It's not."

"I was going to wear those." She points to a pair of heels.

Okay, so maybe those won't exactly be perfect for tonight, but...

Everything I'm thinking is on my face.

Sutton blows out an audible breath. "I'm going to change."

I step into her. "No, I love this dress." I kiss her forehead. Tilt her chin up to me and kiss her softly.

"I'm going to change," she whispers against my lips. Kisses me again.

"Can I watch?"

Sutton slips into her closet, reappearing in a pair of leggings, pink fuzzy socks, and an oversized graphic shirt. Her hair is pulled back into a checkered clip. She spins and does a tada movement with her hand, dragging down her body. "Ready." There's an excited smile on her face. I match it, and she blushes.

On our way out of her apartment, she stops, grabbing her vintage patchwork jacket.

I pick up the pizza I ordered and head back to my house. Sutton is confused the entire time, even commenting on how the theater is in the opposite direction.

The gate to our backyard is open. I pull my Jeep through the back, barely missing the string lights.

"Cooper..."

"The drive-in closed. You never went, did you?"

"No. I always wanted to go."

"What about your grass?"

"I'll reseed it or glue blades back into the ground."

I park. She tries to climb out, but I run around the car, almost parkour over the top. Open her door and help her out. Sutton turns around to grab the pizza.

We walk to the back of my car. I unlatch the trunk door, push up the top window, revealing a palette of pillows and blankets already stacked in the back.

I vacuumed earlier. Made sure any hints of my gear were removed, which is a feat in itself. Found every spare blanket in the house—and Jordan's dorm room—washed them, and lined my car for us to lie on.

The side of our house has a large white sheet stuck to it. A small projector is set up at the perfect distance, plugged into my laptop with an HDMI cable. Two movies are queued up for the evening.

Sutton climbs in first. I climb in after her.

She sits cross-legged, leaning back.

"How did you know that I wanted to go to the drive-in?" she asks me. I hand her a sparkling water.

"Or do you want wine?"

"No, this works." The can cracks open, but Sutton's attention doesn't leave me. "Are you ignoring my question?"

I shake my head no, putting the pizza between us and scooting back next to her. I lean back on my elbow to face Sutton. My legs are straight out in front of me, and I toe off my shoes, kicking them to the yard below.

I hang on to every word you say. There's a special place in my brain that records it, and I can hit play whenever I need to. That's what I could say, but I don't.

"You've mentioned it a couple times, and—"

"And you remember."

"There's not much about you that I don't."

"Hmmm." She scrunches her mouth to one side. "What was the name of the stuffed animal that I lost in Disney World?"

"Mr. Bunny, but he wasn't a bunny. He was a white unicorn with purple hair and a pink metallic horn that fell out in the Winnie-the-Pooh ride. We rode it five more times trying to find it."

"Where's the scar I got when Meave pushed me off my bike?"

"Under your chin." I tap the small scar. "The buckle of your helmet clipped your skin."

"Favorite color..."

"Give me an age, because you change it every year, because you never want one color to feel left out. Seven, sky blue. Twelve, lemon-lime green. Fourteen, that disastrous shade of orange."

"It clashed so badly with my hair."

I laugh with her, but continue getting into the years she probably thought I didn't pay attention. "Eighteen, that was your black clothing era. Last year, yellow. Right now, purple."

"And your favorite color has always been red."

"Red," I say at the same time.

We scoot closer together, careful of the pizza going cold at our feet.

She runs a hand along my jawline demurely, almost as if she's studying me. "I never forgot or stopped caring about you. Not that you exactly let me." Sutton levels me with a look. "What are we watching?"

I wiggle my way out of the back of the car. Extremely uncoordinated, and I hear her laughing at me. I tap the space bar on my computer, the intro to *How To Lose A Guy in 10 Days* starts.

When I climb back into the trunk, Sutton's pulling the pizza into her lap.

We each take a slice and tap it together in a cheers motion. Sutton brings the point of her slice to her lips and slowly parts them to take a bite.

Three-quarters of the movie later, Sutton turns to face me.

"Cooper."

"What's up?" I mirror her position.

"I need to ask you something." Her cheeks go red.

"Ask away."

"Will you be my boyfriend?"

I bolt upright. "No."

"No?!"

"I'm supposed to ask you!"

"Who said so?"

"You."

"Okay, maybe, but you dragged your feet—"

I point a finger at her. "You wanted this."

"Wanted what?" She plays dumb, but from the glint in her eyes, she knows I'm right.

"Brat."

"What are you going to do about it? Say no?" Sutton sits up, crossing her arms.

"No, I'm saying yes. You. Are. My. Girlfriend." I sneak a kiss between the words, moving until she's pinned underneath me. Hair spilled out around her as a red halo.

Sutton laughs manically. "You might have won this round, but just wait," I say as a promise.

We make out till the credits begin to roll.

"I was going to ask you tonight."

"You're just saying that."

I sit up, straddling her thighs, and pull out the bracelets from my back pocket. The first is a friendship bracelet that says *Will you be my girlfriend*. The other is as close to a replica of her other one as I could find. A few charms are different. A *C* for me, a skate, a book, flowers, a paintbrush for Meave, a bike for Elliot, a bear for Lakeland, and a sun.

"Gimme your right hand." She's left-handed and hates wearing jewelry on that hand. I push the first bracelet on her wrist, spin it so she can read it. "Told ya."

"Cute."

"Cute?"

"I'd have said yes."

I roll my eyes at her. "And so enthusiastic about it."

She shrugs, then I put the other bracelet on her. Eyes widen. "Is that...is that my bracelet?"

THIRTY-NINE

SUTTON

"A SIMILAR ONE." Cooper runs the tip of tongue from the right to center of his lips before tugging his heavier—almost like it's been stung by a bee or freshly kissed—bottom lip between his teeth. "I—"

Without skipping a beat, three words roll off my tongue. "I love it." I do, even though it makes me miss the original one. It's been gone for years. Forgotten somewhere in a trash dump by now. "Thank you, *boyfriend*."

Cooper comes alive at that. Eyes sparking to life, clear and brighter than the stars in the sky above us. A relaxed and boyish smile stretches into blushing cheeks. Appreciative and wondrous and one-hundred percent mine.

Mine. Mine. *Mine.*

My heart beats the chant. My brain doesn't let any other thoughts. My lungs breathe in him and this moment. My body... my body needs him.

I crunch my shoulders up, kissing him possessively, running a hand through his hair. Finding, seizing, every opportunity to bring our bodies closer together.

His kiss, his touch, none of it is enough.

When Cooper matches my intensity, my body rejoices.

With how the atmosphere around us is buzzing, pulsing and heating up, you'd think it's mid-summer. There's a desperation that surges between us.

Cooper hits pause to climb out of the car, picking me up like a koala and carrying me to his room through the empty house. Kicking the bedroom door shut behind him, he sits me on his bed. Standing at the end.

I pull my shirt over my head, leaving me in a basic camisole-style bra. He stares at me, running a hand along his stubbled jaw as if he's in disbelief. Heated, transfixed eyes roam over me. "You're so beautiful."

I reach for his shirt. Trying to simultaneously bring him to me and push it up his torso at the same time. "Cooper—"

"You sure?" he asks.

"More than I've ever been."

Cooper pulls his sweater over his head, careful with one sleeve. Pinching the sleeve and folding it. He leans down to take off his socks and stands to unbutton his jeans. I don't think the slow stripping is intentionally a tease, and I'm not trying to be impatient...I just need him. Want him.

He stretches a hand out to me, and I climb off the bed, standing before him as he kneels in front of me. Hands slip into the top of my leggings, his warm mouth presses a kiss to my stomach.

As my pants work down my legs, Cooper appears to be surprised to find nothing underneath. His brown eyes flick up to me through thick lashes.

"No more underwear stealing."

He lets out a husky laugh against my skin, and it shoots a thrill through my body that lands between my legs.

Cooper kisses up my body, then gently—damn, he's stupidly good at this—lays my body down on the bed.

With one swift kiss to my mouth, he's lost between my legs. It doesn't take long for me to dive headfirst into pleasure.

After, he kneels between my legs, reaching into his side table to get a condom. The box is unopened, and he groans impatiently getting the plastic off.

Stupidly, I ask, "Going through so many, you needed a new box for this?"

He freezes. I freeze, too.

"Sutton." Cooper repositions himself to hover over me. The box discarded, tossed to the floor, he sweeps his hand caringly along my jaw. "Just so we are clear, I haven't bought or needed these in years. There hasn't been anyone since March freshman year."

I blink. That's...that's when my last boyfriend and I broke up. "Two years?" I whisper for no reason. "But—"

"There's no one else I've wanted. No one else is Sutton Davis."

Do not cry. I repeat the mantra.

Cooper is a sea softly dousing a beach, and I'm the sand waves dribble into. Our tide, our friendship, our everything harmonious. Working together instead of pushing and pulling.

I lean forward to kiss him. I've never wanted this, or Cooper, more.

He smiles against me in our next kiss. "I." Kiss. "Know," he says as if he's reading my mind. Maybe, scratch that, I feel confident saying he feels the same way.

Cooper reclines, leaning back on his heels. Quads flexed and... my words fall away as my gaze finds him rolling a condom down his lengthy and extremely hard dick.

My eyelids flutter with a bolt of nerves. I have to use my mouth and hand with him, how the hell am I supposed to...

"I'll go slow," Cooper reassures me.

"Wouldn't fast and just shoving it in be better?" Telling myself not to make a stupid retort seconds ago doesn't work this time.

He bursts out laughing, gazing down at me like he doesn't know what to do with me sometimes. "No."

Repositioning himself between my legs, I swallow when the

tip nudges at my entrance. I watch him the entire time, never letting my gaze drop to where he is, just as he said, inching into me slowly. Cooper hisses, jaw taut and eyes fluttering closed. He is forced to take a deep inhale with the next inch.

"You okay?" I check in.

I don't understand what comes out of his mouth. It blends and ends on a hiss, but I take it as a yes. He then asks me the same question.

I can sense how flushed my skin is, feel how full I am. "I want all of it, Superstar."

Cooper curses and bottoms out. Pausing. "Give me a minute," he requests. He curses again. His eyes roam over me and catch on my bra. "Why is that still on? Take it off."

I slip out of it, the wiggling has us both cursing, and I whimper.

"Might have been a bad decision, but dear lord, Sutton. Pretty. So Perfect."

"Your minute is up," I say desperately.

Cooper smiles. Pulls out, then pushes back in. He does this a few times, continuously making sure I'm okay.

I appreciate the sweetness, but I need more. I need him to—I say it instead, "Shut up, and fuck me, Cooper. Like you have in your dreams."

A slow, lazy smirk works its way up his mouth. He picks up his pace, but I can tell he's still being gentle, careful, and I can appreciate that. It doesn't surprise me how good this is, but what catches me off guard is how complimentive Cooper is. Continuously telling me how beautiful I am between other praises.

"Can you come like this?" he asks.

I haven't before. My ex and I only had sex a handful of times, and it was never anything like this. My body has never felt so alive, stimulated, and worked up before. "I want to."

My eyes shut as I try to focus on getting there.

"Eyes on me, baby."

They flutter open, burning into his. "Will you help me?"

"That does something to me, baby. Hearing you ask, wanting my help to come." He thrusts into me hard. Pulling one of my legs up, resting my ankle on his shoulder. "You have no clue the hold you have over me."

"*Cooper.*"

"Say it again."

"Cooper," I repeat. His name is a plea on my tongue.

My insides clench around him, and I know I'm close. This wave he's already talked me through before is on the horizon, working its way through me.

He senses it too. Picking up his pace. Gripping my hips to tilt them where he's the deepest he's been yet, and I'm not sure how I could become even fuller. The position grinds me into him in a spectacular and mind-bending way.

"Sutton," he whimpers. "I need you to—"

My body is the violin he's playing because with that, I let go. Cooper thrusts three more times before his back muscles flex, and he lets go with my name on his tongue. Once we both can breathe normally again and the condom is disposed of, he pulls me into him.

"Stay the night?"

"Only because it's your birthday tomorrow," I joke.

He kisses my temple before climbing out of bed.

I watch his tight butt as he walks to the bathroom, flipping on the light. "Come brush your teeth and wash your face. I don't need you mad at me on your first full day as my girlfriend."

In the bathroom, he pulls out a container of my favorite skin and hair care products. "This is new."

"I wanted you to be comfortable here." I already am. Comfortable, safe, and at home.

I wrap my arms around his waist. "Wow. You are so in love with me."

He close-mouth laughs, but says nothing and instead reaches for his toothbrush to brush his teeth.

FORTY

SUTTON

I SWEAR, whenever I sleepover at Cooper's, there's always something happening in the morning. When we wake up, Jaxon is sitting and smiling brightly at us from the foot of the bed.

I rub my eyes to make sure I'm not dreaming.

"Gooooood morning!"

"Jax, what are you doing in here?" Cooper yawns, pulling the comforter up my body. It slipped when I sat up. "What time is it?"

"Five and it's your birthday," Jaxon responds. "You know what that means." He pauses, waiting for us to respond, but half asleep, neither of us do. "Shots. Shots. Shots."

"Make it stop," I groan, pulling a pillow over my head.

"We don't need to be up till seven...at the earliest." Cooper sighs. "This can wait."

"Wrong. You see, Dawson's boyfriend, Jake, has soccer conditioning at six, and he spent the night here."

The stupid birthday shot rule.

I don't remember who started it, but it originated freshman year. Whenever it's someone's birthday, the boys take a shot first thing in the morning. Before practice, a game, class—whatever comes first, whatever time it may be.

Elliot and I somehow got looped into the festivities.

Luckily, Jaxon, Beckett, and Dawson's birthdays are during the summer. We all still take a shot, but it's not before the sun is up.

"Since when do we include significant others?"

"Since when have any of us dated?" Jaxon combats.

"We didn't include my ex." It comes out muffled because I'm still hiding under the covers. Cooper pinches my side.

"No one liked the loser."

Beckett calls for us from downstairs. Chase opens the door. "You coming?"

"Two minutes. Get dressed." Jaxon walks to the door. He grabs onto the edge, and glances back at us. "Soot, gotta tell ya, you look great in his bed."

Cooper throws something at him, and Jaxon pretends to be scared, shutting the door behind him.

"Did you have to be born today?"

"Unfortunately."

"I don't want to do it." I groan.

"Me neither," Cooper agrees. "But it is my birthday and they won't stop bugging us till we go downstairs. Come on, it'll be quick."

He pulls the covers off me. Eyes bulge at my nakedness.

"I got hot in the middle of the night." I shrug.

"Expect the thermostat to be turned up every night."

Cooper climbs out of bed, pulling on a pair of sweatpants. He doesn't bother with a shirt, instead tossing one to me. I throw it on and tug up leggings from last night up.

Before we go downstairs, I curl into his lap. "Happy birthday, Superstar." I give him a swift kiss on the lips.

He tries to confiscate more, but there is a pounding on his door and a summons from Jaxon. "Your two minutes are up."

Downstairs, all of our friends—Elliot included—plus Jake are standing around the kitchen island. Shot glasses are lined up, and

Dawson pulls a bottle of liquor from the freezer. He pours each of us a friendly-sized shot.

I slink in next to Elliot. "Sleepover with Chase?"

"I've told you before"—she boops my nose—"it's not like that with us. We are just friends."

"Friends who have sleepovers." Another weird tradition that started freshman year. Completely platonic, so they say.

"Pot meet kettle."

"I'm having sleepovers with my boyfriend."

"You little slut."

"That would be you," I joke.

"Whateverrrrr. You happy?"

I glance across the island at Cooper. "That's one way to put it."

She slides an arm over my shoulder, hugging me. Our heads lean into each other.

"I love our little family," she says quietly enough for my ears only as shots are dispersed.

Me too, I exhale.

I remember a time when I didn't think I'd get to have this. Passed over by family after family.

"Happy Birthday" breaks out amongst the group. Out of tune, and definitely out of key, but no one cares. No one truthfully cares about the time either. There might be yawns floating around between lyrics, but there's also smiles and laughter.

I may not have my biological family, but I have these people. I have Meave. I have Mom and Dad. I have the Carmichaels. Heck, I even have Dr. Manning. I have Cooper.

"And a pinch to grow an inch," Jaxon hollers above the clinking of glasses. "Cheers!"

We all toss back the chilled clear liquor, grimaces on everyone's faces.

"Way too early for this," Jake says. "Why do you guys do this?"

"I don't think anyone truly knows." Cooper shakes his head, collecting the glasses and taking them to the sink.

———

COOPER and I went back to his room and slept for another hour. Or I did, he was up reading when I woke again—no Jaxon this time, the door was securely locked when we got back up here.

I roll over, loving the sight in front of me.

Lickable muscles. Bedhead. And all completely mine.

"Good morning, again, birthday boy." I sit up, lean my head on his shoulder. "What are you reading?"

He closes the book, using a finger as his bookmark, to show me the cover. Smart man to not dog ear the page. I recognize it as one from my bookshelf.

"Isn't this your favorite?"

"It is. When did you start it?" He's about sixty percent of the way through the fantasy novel.

"Spring break. I took it from your room after one of our sessions. That okay?"

"Mhmmm."

He keeps reading. I read over his shoulder, picking up where he left off. The next chapter is spicy, and Cooper giggles when he reads it, ears tipped pink.

I take back my earlier statement, cringing when he dog-ears the page, but forgive him instantly when he drags me to the shower to reenact the scene.

Cooper offers to wash my hair since my curls are already wet. The specialty products I use filling one of the plastic tiered shelves. He's thorough, asking and memorizing the steps. Fingers digging into my scalp and temples with meticulous pressure.

We're standing in the water washing off the soap lathered on our skin. Laughing between stolen kisses and touches when his phone rings, Dad's photo popping up on the screen.

"Go," I tell him. Cooper quickly rinses and hops out of the shower, towel loosely hanging on his waist.

I finish rinsing, grabbing the fresh towel on the bathroom counter. Walking back into his bedroom, Cooper's folding a jersey, setting it on his dresser.

"Giving that to someone?"

"Would you want to wear it?"

"Wanna try that again? If you want me to wear your jersey, just tell me."

A dimpled grin emerges. "I'd like my girlfriend to wear my jersey."

They don't have a game tonight, but conference play starts later this week. It won't be the first jersey I've worn...but truthfully I can't wait to wear his. Show off how proud I am of Cooper, how proud I am to finally be his.

However, we are still us, and I'll never turn down a moment to keep him on his toes. "We'll see, boyfriend."

———

LAKELAND'S NCAA conference changed its rules this year. The conference tournament for women's and men's hockey is no longer happening at a neutral site. Whoever is leading the conference is allowed to host.

It's why the guys had a small break over our spring break. The university was preparing the arena for the conference tournament this weekend.

Downtown Bensen has also been preparing. I was supposed to run four miles this morning, but with weaving in and out of people grabbing coffee or shopping in our local stores, I added a half mile to my distance.

When I loop around, I stop at the Mean Bean to grab coffees for Elliot and me.

Classes have continued, no matter the commotion on campus all week.

Luckily for most, professors cancelled evening classes for students to attend tonight's semifinal, single-elimination game. Our boys won the first round in a two-game sweep.

Unlucky for me, my human anatomy lab professor was not one of them. He isn't, and I quote, *a sports guy.* I text Cooper before lab starts.

Good luck, Superstar

COOPER
Thanks, baby. You'll be there after lab?

Wouldn't miss it.

I bail early on lab.

Elliot waited for me before going to the game. By the time I'm back and have scrubbed the smell of formaldehyde off my skin and changed into Cooper's jersey, we make it right as the game starts.

We're sitting across from the benches, along the boards. We both kick our feet up, and Elliot balances a container of popcorn between her knees.

"Isn't this the team Jordan's ex plays for?" she asks, pouring an entire king-sized package of peanut M&Ms into the extra buttered container.

"Unfortunately."

It's a good thing the girls' team is away—they have one more week in their season—otherwise Jordan would be dressed up as her brother, and finding a way to play tonight just to fight the guy.

"Which one is he?"

Both teams are starting to reemerge from the tunnels. University of Minnesota skates a lap, and I keep my eyes peeled for him. He's the last to skate onto the ice.

"There." I point discreetly to number fifty-two.

When he skates by us, Elliot throws popcorn at the glass and boos.

"Elliot, stop." I playfully swat at her, grabbing a handful of popcorn while I'm at it.

Luka glares through his visor over at us. I know he recognizes me when he stops sharply and skates backwards to us.

"Sutton Davis."

"Luka Valentini."

"It's been a few years since I've seen you near the ice. Two, three years?"

"Two. Thanks for the reminder." I force a grin.

"And who are you?" He shifts his attention away from taunting me with information he already knows, a part of my life he was adjacent to by association, to Elliot.

"She's none of your business." Two players in Kelly green skate up on either side of him. Stopping quickly, Chase's stick hits the glass. Cooper is on the other side, close enough to Luka without it being threatening for penalty time.

"Carmichael."

"Valentini." Cooper rolls his shoulders back. His jaw is tight, skin stretched across it. It doesn't matter that Jordan was the one to break up with Luka; Cooper still can't stand him.

The atmosphere between them is at least amicable, neither willing to risk the game, especially Luka. Minnesota has to win to make it to the NCAA tournament. Their season isn't good enough to get an at-large bid.

That is, till Jaxon shows up. Skating by Luka, he nicks his shoulder before turning to stop in front of his face.

"What the fuck are you doing over here? Get back on your side, bellini."

Cooper breaks them up. Dragging Jaxon away by the navy and white striped collar and back to where some of the team is stretching.

"Isn't a bellini a drink?" Elliot leans over, stealing my bag of gummy candies. "He might want to work on his insults."

"Luka is kind of fruity. I like it."

Luka skates away, and Jaxon tracks the movement, keeping a carefully sharp eye on him.

The first line is taking their places. Jaxon in the face-off. Cooper's on our side and moves slowly before getting into position, skating by us again. Against the glass, he makes a heart with his bulky gloves. He does this before every period.

I blow him a kiss. He catches it and drags it over his heart. Cooper skates up to the outskirts of the circle.

The puck drops, and we win the face-off, passing to Cooper. He's fast, zipping up the left side before cutting in toward the goal. He fakes out the defenseman before gently pushing the puck between the guy's skates and passing to our right winger. Two people are on him as he maneuvers behind the net.

Minnesota's goalie blocks their shot.

We dominate the first and second periods, keeping possession of the puck for most of the play. Only one of their fifteen shots on goal sneaks past the goalie. We're up by one.

The third period doesn't turn out much different, except for more chirping and Minnesota starting to play rough. Cooper takes a brutal hit to the boards, and Chase is hit with a high stick.

If fighting were allowed, one would have broken out when Luka charged at Beckett after he blocked a shot. One of our guys snatched the back of Jaxon's jersey before he could throw hands.

The period ends up being scoreless.

But when the clock hits zero, the crowd erupts. Students are jumping from their seats around us. Elliot accidentally elbows me in the gut, and her hair smacks me in the face when she stands and throws her hands in the air. I'm right behind her, standing and screaming for our guys. They dog pile in the center of the ice, moving on to the championship game in two days, and at a minimum clinching a spot in the Frozen Four playoffs.

FORTY-ONE

COOPER

SUTTON TOLD me to go celebrate with the team after our win; she wanted to get ahead of some schoolwork before our parents get in for the conference championship. But being here without her felt wrong. She's the only person I want to celebrate with— big or small wins.

I sneak out, leaving my full beer on the bar, before walking back to my house. We were at one of the campus bars, and it was nice for once not having everyone packed into our place and knowing that in the morning I won't have to clean up after everyone.

The right side of my body is sore from a hit I took in the third period. An angry bruise is already working its way to the surface of my ribs, the skin sensitive and tender.

It took me an extra twenty minutes to strip off my gear. The pull of my jersey over my head frustrated my side with each lengthening of my muscles. Now, convincing my quads to lift and lower my legs, working my way up the stairs to my bedroom, all I can think about is pancaking myself on my bed.

My phone died, and I need to charge it so I can call Sutton to come over. I thought about walking to her place, but I genuinely didn't know if I'd make it.

At the top of the stairs, I contemplate lying down right here. Could roll or army crawl to my door.

You're a big boy, Cooper. Go to your room. Sometimes the nags from the voice in my head are beneficial.

I reach for the doorknob to my room when I hear a soft pattering of feet behind it. Peeling the door open, the pain in my side is reduced to an ache that relocates itself to a different region of my body. I collapse to my knees at the sight of *her* on my bed.

There's no controlling the whimper that works its way out of me.

Wrapped in a jersey like a present, is Sutton. I spy the navy and white underwear she has on underneath.

I fall forward, bracing myself with unsteady palms. My dead phone hits the floor like a brick. The area rug burns against my palms as I'm completely hypnotized by her. Sutton wouldn't say I'm patient, but she doesn't know how long I've waited to see my name on her back, or the fantasies I have of giving it to her one day.

Her chin tilts up. "Hi, Superstar."

"Sutton baby, please." I bring one fist to my mouth, biting on a knuckle. "Tell me that's my name on your back." I caught a glimpse of the number, but I crave confirmation.

She turns around. Knees spread wide, Sutton pushes up on them, pulling her curls across her back. Letter by letter, she reveals my name.

Carmichael.

I force myself in a staring contest with my number. Twenty plus sixteen. Ours combined. *Does she know I changed it? Has she realized the combination? Understand the meaning?*

Sutton turns back around, sitting on her knees. An innocence to her. An answer to my questions. No she hasn't.

"Looks good, right?" I nod robotically, my mouth hanging open. Drool is probably collecting on the floor. "Come here," she beckons.

I crawl across the floor. The scrape of the carpet burns into my knees. She's staring at me like a lioness does her prey. Hungry. Calculating. Unwavering.

When I'm at the edge of the bed, I push up on my knees and circle her ankles. It takes nothing to tug her to the edge of the bed.

"How much do you care about these underwear?"

"Not much. Why?"

I rip them down the front and toss the scraps to the side. Silently curse at the surprised sound that comes out of her. She closes her knees, but I open them back up.

Fingers curl into the bottom of *my* jersey. "Stop." There's no way she's taking that off tonight. "Leave it."

Sutton listens. Leaning forward, I teasingly blow on her center, before planting kisses up her right thigh. I relish in Sutton's soft mews when my grown out facial hair scrapes the inside of her thigh. It's so sweet that I repeat this up her other leg before kissing her where she's trying to drag me by my hair to.

Her hands turn desperate after her release. Standing in front of her, Sutton is undressing me quickly. My jeans and long-sleeve joining the shreds of her underwear.

"Do you trust me?" I lick my barely there mustache, tasting her on me. Sutton watches the movement of my tongue. "Want a taste?" Her nods are quick and fast, slightly disjointed. "Come here."

She pulls herself up to me, the comforter bunches between her legs and she hisses, still swollen and sensitive. When I think she's about to kiss me, she licks my mustache instead, eyelids fluttering.

"More?" I gently take her wrist, guiding her hand down between her legs. Aiding two fingers inside of her, I bring her hand back to her mouth. "Open." She follows each command, always eager to learn.

Her cheeks hollow out, and I need her now.

"Do you trust me?" I ask again, since we got distracted before.

"Yes," she verbalizes.

My heart surges. She might be saying yes in this moment, but

I know she's saying yes in general. She trusts me again. Sutton's trust is a prized possession. I'm going to care for it this time like I didn't before.

"Lie down, back on the bed. Let your head hang off the edge."

Again, she does as she is told. My words landing somewhere between a request and a demand. I'm doing my best to maintain control.

Auburn curls are a waterfall over the side. Long enough that they brush against the ground. I adjust my position. Her eyes sparkle with realization. Giant gemstones gleam with need. Her mouth falls open, tongue darting out and tasting me.

Sutton's cheeks hollow out as she takes me into her mouth. Slowly. Tears brimming in the corner of her eyes from the position.

"Breath," I tell her, giving her a moment. "Relax."

She takes an inhale and releases it all as I touch the back of her throat. Sutton has drool forming at the corners of her mouth, tears now trailing down her cheek, as I move in and out of her. I reach a hand forward, circling her neck just above her collarbones.

"Such a good girl for me, Sutton baby, taking me like this. So so so good."

She whimpers, then sucks hard, and I curse.

I don't last much longer, when she reaches down to play with herself.

After, I'm spent and all I can do is lie down next to her. We both roll on our sides and stare at each other. I trace the outline of her face. So many years of wanting her, wanting this, and I don't think I'll ever get enough.

Eventually, Sutton excuses herself to the bathroom, and I exchange places with her when she exits in sleep shorts and a cami. She climbs in on her side. Curled in my bed, hair wild across the pillows, and reading a new book. I lean against the side and drink her in.

When she notices me, she lights up. I know it then.

I love her.

FORTY-TWO

SUTTON

WEEK NUMBER—I'VE lost track at this point—of the semester, and I'm reminded why Dr. Manning warned me that an independent study isn't for those weak of heart.

You can do this. You have what it takes.

I repeat the affirmation as I rush into the psych building. I'm running behind for my slotted 'class' time with Dr. Manning. Most of my work is self-led; however, we meet twice a week. Even if the two hours are spent with minimal chatting and my nose deep into an article or headphones playing podcasts or TED Talks.

Dr. Manning isn't in her office when I get there, but the door is propped open, so I let myself in. I pull the stain stick out of my tote and attempt to get the red-brown splotch courtesy of Jaxon scaring me this morning while I was making breakfast out of my white shirt. It's one of my favorites. Mom had taken one of Meave's art pieces and digitized it into shirts for us.

Letting out a frustrated sigh, I give up and tuck the shirt back into my overalls. I pull out my laptop to check my student email. The amount of junk I've subscribed to for a student discount is lowkey disgusting and not worth the dollar or two off.

Sorting between junk and moving emails into their color-coordinated folders, I open an email regarding my upcoming, and only, internship interview.

I'm lucky to even have this one.

The independent study wasn't the only undertaking. Finding an internship that would read between my transcript was important. I wasn't a sports psychology major by title till this semester, but when you comb through my coursework, it's all there. I've connected every dot possible.

Transferring would have been easier.

But Lakeland University is home.

I know I have another year left, but I wouldn't change a thing.

Dr. Manning comes in with a stack of paper binder clipped together in one arm. An orchid delicately balanced in the other. "Can you take this?" she huffs out.

She turns the plant in my direction. I rush to stand and configure my hands to take the unexpectedly heavy potted plant from her. I set it on the windowsill next to a dying succulent.

"Should I ask?"

"Maybe when you graduate."

We both sit down, and I let out an awkward laugh. Then another when I notice the title page to the stack of paper.

"Is that my paper?" I sit up straighter, giving myself an ample view of her mahogany desk. "You printed it? And read it already?"

"My older eyes prefer printed paper." Her older eyes are thirty-six. She pushes her red-rim glasses up the bridge of her nose. "Only the first six pages."

"They emailed me about my interview," I nervously tell her.

"Are you ready?"

Am I?

I think so, but that sentiment doesn't make me confident. For most, this interview is probably one in a dozen. For me, it's my only one. As much as I want it, I think I need it more. It's the final percentage of reassurance that I can do this. I can be a sports psychologist.

"You are," she answers for me. Dr. Manning must see something I don't, but I latch onto her faith in me.

We spend the remainder of the two hours practicing interview questions.

Walking outside, it's the time of year when the Midwest comes down with the biggest case of decision fatigue. It never knows which season it wants to be. Some days start winter and end summer. While others, like today, are full-blown spring.

Sixty degrees out, and you'd think it was the middle of July and not mid-March.

The psych building is right off the lawn. From Dr. Manning's office, I could already see clumps of students forming. Studying, reading, sunbathing, throwing a football, or my favorite, people watching. There's barely any green space left. Students overflow onto the brick walkways, cutting paths across what resembles a watering hole.

Leaning against a trash can out front, Cooper is waiting for me with a coffee. His smile fading, brown eyes softening when they land on Zach holding the door for me—which isn't uncommon. We have similar majors with a majority of our classes being in the same building. The plastic cup in Cooper's hand curves in on itself.

"Hey, Carmichael."

"Zach," he grits between his teeth before forcing a smile when I level him with a look and mouth *your jealousy is showing*.

"You're girl"—the semi-sour bite to those words are almost gone, but Cooper still picks up on them—"was only explaining a part of our lecture I didn't understand, promise." I roll my eyes, knowing he's joking. "Good luck tonight, the team is coming after batting practice."

"Cool," Cooper mumbles, body language doesn't loosen. I step away from Zach and slide an arm around his waist.

"See ya, Sutton." Zach walks around us, disappearing into the mass of students changing classes. He's kind, and when we have bumped into each other has been nothing but a friend. Respectful. Earlier this week he told me a girl from our Cognitive Psychology class asked him out. We shared an awkward laugh when I suggested not to take her to the same place we went.

I snatch the decadent liquid from my boyfriend's hand, spinning in front of him and jabbing a finger into his spectacularly hard chest all in one movement.

"What was that?"

"What was what?" He rubs at the spot after removing my finger. Interlacing our hands.

"Zach and I are *friends*."

"He's also the guy you had a crush on for what...the better part of the past year?"

"Okay, and?" I take a sip of my chai latte. It's perfect. I arch a brow at him, awaiting a response. "Who got the girl?" I egg on an answer.

He huffs like a little girl. And I think he even stomps a foot?

"I expected more of a cocky response. Maybe some bragging."

"I'm internally applauding myself." Cooper wraps an arm around my waist and pulls me to him and kisses my temple. "But there was no competition. You were always mine."

Unfortunately, he's right. But I don't tell him that.

Instead, I keep poking the bear.

"If I remember correctly, I believe you were the one pining after me, like a dog on a leash. Wouldn't that make you always mine?"

"Woof," he keeps barking in my ear, walking me to my next class.

———

EVERYONE CAME in for the game this evening.

Mom had an oncoming migraine, so she and Dad went back to the hotel an hour or so ago. Cooper is with his parents, Molly, and Jordan—the women's conference tournament is next week in Columbus.

We all grabbed a late lunch together after Cooper's morning skate and my classes. I don't know why I thought it would be awkward, us holding hands in front of them, or the gentle touches and kisses to my temple.

Meave was the interrogator, asking about his intentions with me. I had half expected Dad to be the one with burning questions, but I think seeing us together was a relief. Sure, he's known Cooper his entire life, but I know his top priority is seeing us healthy and happy.

Cooper makes me happy. So happy.

I don't know how I was ever repulsed by him. *Repulsed. In love. What's the difference?*

Meave and I were lying on my bed gossiping when Elliot got back from teaching, and we started getting ready for the game.

A new playlist—all remixes, definitely dance-worthy songs— she created fills the apartment from the speaker in the living room.

She's standing in front of my mirror putting on mascara, using the brush as a microphone between upstrokes. I'm sitting on the counter with Meave carefully painting my face. From the corner of my eye, I take a quick look at her work, finding the start of a number taking up the majority of my cheek.

"Wait." I stop her with a hand around her wrist. "That should be a two, not a three. Cooper is twenty."

"No, he's not," she says, dumbfounded, puzzled confusion pinching her brow.

Elliot stops, too, turning to face me. "He's thirty-six."

"I know what my boyfriend's hockey number is. He's always been twenty."

They both shake their head.

"Are you positive about that?"

I push off the counter and head across the hall to my bedroom. Laid out on my bed is a pair of light denim, patchwork overalls that Meave made for me.

"See—" My words tumble back down my throat. Rubbing a

thumb over the glittery varsity numbers on the pocket, I see thirty-six, not twenty. "No."

I drop them and storm into my closet, the door smashing into the wall. His practice jersey that he gave me to wear is hang drying.

I flip the hanger around.

"Thirty-six," I whisper to myself. "How have I completely missed this?"

He's always been twenty. Since we were kids.

Recalling memories, I can see it now. The varsity print letters I told myself were twenty are now replaced with thirty-six. Us in his bedroom, how he collapsed on the floor and crawled to me. He traced them on my back before I changed.

I walk back out of the closet to find my sister and roommate sitting on my bed, cross-legged and biting their tongues.

"He changed his jersey number. When? Why thirty-six? What was wrong with twenty?" My words come out slow, as I keep trying to catch up.

They make eye contact.

"Well..." Meave starts.

"You see..." Elliot chimes in.

"You both knew?"

"Knew is an extremely loose term for inferring." Elliot gives me a placating smile, dragging her long bubble braid over her shoulder.

"When you think about it, it's quite romantic—" They talk over and around each other. I don't know who says what.

"But makes a little sense in a weird way. I haven't asked to confirm though."

"Same," Meave agrees.

"Would you two mind clueing me in?" I demand, fisting the damp jersey.

"Sutton. Babe, you are light-years ahead of us when it comes to being book smart, supposedly an obsessively observant athlete. Think. About. It. Do. The. Math."

I stare blankly at them. Was that a backhanded insult?

"Thirty-six minus twenty." Meave circles her hand, encouraging my intellectual skills.

"Sixteen," I answer, then repeat, "Sixteen. Sixteen. Sixtee—you've got to be kidding me. That's my number."

Meave makes an explosive hand motion from one side of her head, complete with a sound effect. Elliot shrugs.

"When did he do it?"

My sister nudges Elliot to tell me. "After you decided to stop playing."

They give me my minute—okay, it might be more like twenty minutes of disbelief before reminding me we need to leave.

Meave finishes painting my face with thirty-six. The last stroke of her brush has my stomach somersaulting.

He changed his number for me.

He changed his number for me when I wasn't able to play.

He's...he's been playing for me. All these years and I...I never noticed.

I change, a stupid, partially naive, smile on my face the entire time. How many other things has Cooper done for me all this time?

The overalls I put on are epic, and for an actual minute, I'm jealous of how talented my sister is. Besides his—or should I be calling it ours?—number stitched into the pocket, there are patches on the legs. An outline of a bear with a star and hockey stick print, Lakeland ironed one in navy blue and silver. My left back pocket has a twenty and a thirty-six. What must be an old shirt is now the other pocket.

Everything about them is perfect.

We meet up with the rest of our families at the rink, but don't sit with them. We aren't even sitting in the student section but adjacent, closer to the plexiglass per Cooper's *request*.

When the Bears take the ice, Cooper is next to last. In front of Beck. The somersault my stomach was doing earlier is nothing compared to the free fall it's actively doing. It's him making his pre-game heart hands that catch my heart, free-falling in love with him.

FORTY-THREE

COOPER

THE PUCK HITS the back of the net. Instantaneously the buzzer goes off. Red light flashing: goal.

We've scored. I scored.

Not just any goal, my eighty-fifth of the season. Before this, the record was eighty-four by Ryn Carmichael, or better known to me as *Dad*.

I did it. I broke his record.

It wasn't an achievement I set out for at the start of the season. Thought it was impossible. A month or two in, I didn't even think scoring this much was on the horizon. We'd been through a rough patch, losing games in the third period by one goal after having the lead most of the first and second.

Things started to change around late November. A minor change up to our lines and we became a new team. It was around then that I started to notice the pace at which I was accumulating goals. I knew Dad's record—there's a plaque in his office and a piece of the net from that game on a shelf with his college jersey.

I know all of his records and stats, proudly and unfortunately.

A week doesn't go by that I'm not reminded of them during an interview or from a stupid article. I've come close to a lot of them. Some I've surpassed, some I'm nowhere near—this is when

I'd like to remind people that I'm not the great Ryn Carmichael, but I don't. Bite my tongue. Plaster the smile they expect, followed by an expected answer. I'm conditioned to it now.

But this record? Not a single NCAA player has come close to it in over a decade.

I ignored the nagging feeling inside of me, convincing me that I had to break it. Wish I could admit that I was strong enough to turn it off, but the strength I find on the ice vanishes as soon as I'm off it.

Then the interview with ESPN happened.

By January, it was another layer on top of all the others I was already wearing.

When I went a week without scoring, I thought I jinxed myself. Burnt myself out like a supernova. I was a mess on and off the ice.

Then I started with Sutton.

Whatever she's doing is working—or maybe it's the shift in our relationship. Either way, I've felt unstoppable. Repurposed. Aligned. I've felt in love with hockey again.

There's been the added pressure, and yeah, I feel it, but for the first time, it's not dragging me down. It's not burying me away.

Sutton squeezed my hand twice, three nights ago, when I told her that I was okay not accomplishing this. I wanted it, but I knew I'd be okay if it didn't happen. I didn't feel defined by the accolades, but have been finding a way to play for myself again.

Did I give it my all? Am I having fun? I wanted to look back and say yes.

Dad texted me before the game.

DAD

> I'm so proud of you, Cooper. The young man and player you've become makes me feel blessed to be a part of your life. Crush my scoring record, there's no one else I'd want to take it away. I love you.

I read it for the seventeenth time during intermission.

I tied his record in the second period.

Going back out on the ice, everyone in the stands was on the edge of their seats. Even our opponents were holding their breath.

Would Cooper Carmichael steal away the record from his father?

I say all this—that I'm okay if I didn't, and whatnot—but man, does it feel good. So fucking good.

My teammates pile on top of me. Every person is on their feet. Those along the boards pounding their fist, shaking the entire place. Our second and third lines jump over the boards and skate to the opposite side of the ice, joining in on the celebration.

The refs finally blow the whistle, ushering us from the start of what I know is going to be a long night of celebrating.

I wave at the crowd. Do a quick spin till I find her.

Sutton is waving at me. Decked out overalls over my jersey. *Our* number painted on her cheek. Auburn curls pulled up into space buns with our team colors as bows.

She cups her hands around her mouth and yells, "Lucky shot, Superstar." Winks. Then blows me a kiss.

I catch it with my glove, place it over my heart. Then, absent-mindedly, and I'd like to blame the rush of euphoria and endorphins for what I do next, I mouth *I love you, Dave.*

Her hazels are like the eyes on a cartoon where they fall out of their faces. Her mouth is on the floor next to them.

That was not the way I thought I'd tell her that for the first time.

Jaxon skates over to me, claps my shoulder. "That shot was a beauty. You're easily making it onto ESPN's top ten plays of the week. Holy moly that was sexy."

I'm still too stunned at my stupidity to respond.

"Your line is off. Come freak out on the bench." He thinks I'm frozen from the goal.

I shake my head, reel myself back into the present moment, slap on a cheeky and cocky smile before throwing a leg over the boards and sitting on the bench.

Coach comes up behind me. His hands on my shoulders giving him away. "Way to go, Carmichael." He squeezes. "I'm proud of you." We're up four to one with two minutes left of regulation play. "You're done for the game. Rest up."

"Thanks, Coach."

I look back out on the ice, find the section she's sitting in, but I notice a gap. Sutton's gone.

FORTY-FOUR

SUTTON

"YOU SAW THAT, RIGHT?" I push my hands into my cheeks as I run to the bathroom. "He mouthed I love you."

Elliot trails behind me. After Cooper's record-breaking goal and spur-of-the-moment admittance to the crowd that he loved me, I took off. Elliot grabbed my hand, trying to convince me to stay for the rest of the game, but my body was—still is—on fire.

I'm surprised I didn't burn her hand. Heat licking up my body, my chest and face are a deep shade of red.

"Slow down," she calls to me. Meave is right behind her. Cooper's sisters stayed, but they saw. How could they not?

I throw open the door and go to the furthest sink. Gripping the porcelain, I drag in a deep inhale. "He said I love you."

"He did." My best friends are smiling, way too exuberant about the situation. "Personally, I loved it. One of the biggest moments in his college career and the first thing he thinks about is you. Oh my gosh. It's almost giving rom-com movie."

Dang it. Elliot has a point.

"But I love you?" I turn on the faucet, all the way to the left, in need of a reprieve. Testing it, I splash my face, careful not to ruin the number painted on my right cheek.

The water does nothing to cool me off.

I splash myself again. Nothing.

When I attempt to do it for the third time, Elliot stops my hands. Turns off the water, then spins me to face her.

"But he...he hated me?"

"Sutton, you are joking right? That boy has never hated you."

"Bu—"

"Ah." She tilts her head sternly. "Whatever you were about to say, save the words. You also never hated him. Rival, shmival. That's also a load of bullshit, let's get that straight right now." Elliot stops me from speaking again. "Tell me I'm right."

I blow out a hot breath into the hand cupping my mouth. "Can you move your hand?" I garble. "Thank you. And fine, you're right. My hatred of Cooper was displaced interest."

"Infatuation," she bickers.

"Any annoyance. A nuisance."

My sister snorts. "A fixated passion."

"Crush," I relent, eyes finding the ceiling.

"Love."

I shake my head no. "I don't...I don't...damnit."

I'm not falling. I've landed. I love Cooper.

"You love him, too." She smiles brightly. "I think if you look back, you'll realize you've loved him for quite some time."

"Yeah, maybe when we were kids and I didn't know the difference between being smitten and love."

"No, Sutton. These years. Come on. Streaming his games when you can, checking the school's athletic website for live updates, keeping his signed playing card, hiding his high school T-shirt in the back of your closet behind your winter gear basket, only to wear it when you're anxious."

I feel exposed. No one was supposed to know about all that. And so what if I've maybe loved him for longer and didn't realize it? I realize it, know it, now.

"H-ho-how'd you know?"

"Blondes are a lot smarter than people think." She sassily tosses her long blonde hair. "Because you're my best friend and I care about you. I know—and notice—more about you than you'd think. You're one of my favorite people ever, so why wouldn't I?"

Elliot's words are a warm hug. A hug that I didn't realize I needed, or have been craving. After what happened in high school and then leaving for college, I lost the people I was closest to. Once again felt cast aside like I didn't matter. Forgotten.

That's when I met Elliot.

"You're my favorite, too."

"Number three to Meave and Cooper, but—"

"They don't count." Meave huffs, arms crossed in front of her chest. "Number one." I give her shoulder a nudge. "And on the terms of friendship, I have to admit that I notice things too."

I snag a paper towel to blot my face. The pink of my cheeks still stained from Cooper. When I'm free of potential makeup stains, I grab both of them in a hug. "I love you both."

"We love you too," Meave responds, "but we should probably go now. I bet he's freaked out that he spooked you."

Elliot leads the way out of the bathroom. We head to the hallway that goes to the locker room. Family, significant others, and friends are gathered there for our guys.

"Hey, Sutton. Hey, Elliot," Jake greets. "I was looking for you after the game ended and people cleared out."

"Minor emergency. Cooper mouthed—" Meave smacks Elliot in the stomach. "Cooper's goal really got to our girl here."

"If that was Dawson, I would have reacted the same." Jake didn't know anything about hockey before they started dating. Not that Dawson knows that much about soccer. "Does he get a medal or trophy for it?"

"No. The school might do something for him, but otherwise it's bragging rights."

"He'd probably love a blow job as his prize," Elliot teases. Jake concurs, nodding his head. My sister pretends to belch.

I roll my eyes. "He'd much rather go down on me as his prize." It rolls off my tongue before I can stop it.

"I knew it!" Elliot squeals after her initial shock that I even responded.

An arm is thrown around my shoulders, and a kiss dropped to the crown of my head. "Knew what?"

"That you were a little munch."

"Well, I'm not little, but yes, I am a munch. And someone"—he drags me into his body—"is my favorite flavor."

"I can't decide if I want to go pout in the corner, gag, or swoon," Meave says.

I spin in Cooper's arms, loop mine around his neck. My fingers tango with the ends of his damp hair. "Earned your nickname tonight."

"Oh, yeah?"

"Two goals, one assist, and one power play kill. New Most Goals In One Season record holder."

"I could get used to this praise thing."

"Oh, yeah?" I parrot his words and tone. Pressing onto my tip toes, I hover my mouth next to his ear. "Need me to tell you how good of a boy you are, Superstar?"

He swallows, lips smack. "Maybe." My hunky superstar blushes. The color fades. "About what I said on the ice—"

"Carmichael!" his coach hollers.

He turns us, arm wound around my shoulders and chest. Cooper's chin rests on the top of my head.

Coach Mathieson is standing with three men—two in suits and one in a pair of worn jeans, a vintage 1996 Atlanta Olympics shirt, a leather jacket, and a hat pulled snug enough to hide his face.

"What's up?"

"I have some people who would like to meet you. Come here." Coach raises a dark brow, then adds, "Please."

"Does he ever say please?" I ask.

"No," Cooper chuckles out. "You good for a minute?"

"Go, Superstar. I'm not going anywhere."

I watch through the crowd, peaking around people's shoulders to see what is happening. Lipreading would be a great skill to have right now. I can't make out anything.

They shake hands, exchange smiles, and what I'm going to assume are congratulations. The men in suits appeared serious, but now that they are talking to him, they've lightened up. Cooper's body language is animated. Whatever is transpiring, he's excited.

Another five minutes pass before he returns. Most of the people in the hallway have left.

Cooper saunters over to me, mouth curled with the faintest of smiles. Eyes twinkling against the fluorescent lights reflecting off the white brick walls.

I tip my chin up.

"That was Chicago." He stops in front of me. Wipes a hand over his forehead, bumps his hat. "The rumor trade...it was me. They traded my draft rights. Chicago has them. Chicago wants me."

I think I know, but I ask, wanting to hear him say it. "What does this mean?"

"I'm playing for Chicago after graduation." His hand is massaging the facial hair on his jaw, brown eyes blinking in disbelief.

I throw my arms around his neck and hug him into me. Tears prickling, working to escape. "You're playing for Chicago," I repeat. His dream team.

"They want me." It's said into my shoulder, a dampness seeping into my clothes.

"Cooper, you are incredible." He finally hugs me, squeezing me senseless, my feet pop off the ground. "I'm so proud of you. You did it."

It's a whisper, as if he thinks the is a dream and doesn't want to wake up. "I did it."

"We have to celebrate." I run my fingers through the damp hair at the nape of his neck. Arms circled around his neck, heart in his back pocket.

"I was thinking about going to get milkshakes and fries with my girlfriend, then taking her back to her place because mine is going to have all of my teammates packed into it and no privacy. Undress her"—he leans forward, takes up most of my breathing space, but I don't care—"with my teeth. Bury my head between her legs, probably twice, a time for each goal, before I show her exactly how good of a boy I can be."

I bite my lip. Mentally buckle myself into the rollercoaster that Cooper just sent me on.

"This already feels like a dream and if it is, that's how I'd like to spend it before waking up and realizing it's not real."

I kiss him. He might not believe it, think it's true, but I do. He's wanted to play for them since we were kids daydreaming about our futures.

There's so much going on, I almost forget that he said I love you. That floats around in the back of my mind, slipping out of the butterfly net I've managed to capture and maintain it in. "I love that plan, but this is real...and your team and family is going to the bar. We should go at least for a little bit."

———

THE BAR IS PACKED. Our families come with us. Even Coach is here with his wife.

Everyone comes up to Cooper to congratulate him. He returns the high fives or fist bumps with one hand, the other never leaves the back pocket of my overalls.

He squeezes my butt. "I'm digging these," he tells me.

My sister pushes her hand into the other pocket, swinging her upper body around the front of us. "Thank you. Only took me ten hours to make them, so please be careful when you are removing them from her."

She pulls her hand away and winks before going to stand on the other side of the table. One of the seniors on the team drags her away to the makeshift dance floor. Tables were pushed to the outskirts of the place to make room for the influx of people. Meave shrugs, then Molly saunters off to join her with another player.

Our moms are crushing our dads in a game of darts.

Chase and Elliot are at the bar getting drinks with Dawson.

Beckett took off an hour ago to celebrate with his sister which coincidentally was when a brown-haired dancer showed up. A vague memory of us drunkenly dancing at a house party earlier this semester flashes. It makes me happy to see her around again.

Jordan is leaning against the table next to us, arms folded and scowling at Jaxon, who is recounting a story to her. "How do you not find that funny, little Carmichael?" We overhear him.

"That was pointless. Stupid."

"You need to lighten up."

"This is light."

"Okay, then you need to learn to have fun." Jaxon does a weird dance move, making a fool of himself. Jordan stares at him, but I think the corner of her mouth moves upward for a split second.

"Wanna get out of here?" Cooper asks, mouth on the shell of my ear.

We walk hand in hand back to my apartment complex after Irish goodbying—a mutual agreement that if we said bye to every person, we'd be stuck all night. I at least text everyone.

The late March sky clear except for stars speckling it.

"How do you feel?" I break the silence.

Cooper tips his head up to the sky. "Good. Happy. Gosh, Sutton, I can't shake this feeling. Everything I've been chasing is mine or on the horizon."

"I think we can both agree you were going to end up in the NHL, but Chicago. Cooper, they want you."

"I know." His shoulders relax. "But that's not the only thing I'm talking about."

There's a squeeze on my hand, a move with precise dexterity, repositioning me in front of him on the sidewalk.

"I meant what I said on the ice. I love you, Sutton. I'm sorry that's how and where it came out, but I'm not sorry that I do."

"I don't want you to be sorry."

"Good because loving you is the best part of my day. I loved scoring that goal. I loved winning the conference. But I love having you by my side every day even more. Whatever this future is? I'm excited for it because I know no matter what I'll get to love you more than I do now. To love you till there are no words to express it, that all I can do is let it bleed out of me—in my choices. In my actions. In everything that I am."

He wraps a loose curl around his finger.

"Like combining our jersey numbers," I tease.

"Exactly." Cooper drops the strand, runs his finger over the number stitched into the denim. "Took you long enough to realize."

"Why?"

"Same reason I couldn't leave you alone. Having you hating me was easier to bare than you feeling nothing for me. You thought I was competing with you, but I was only desperate for any attention from you."

The intensity of his words has me clinging to his hand in mine.

Again and again, he proves in actions and words that he wants me. But I...

That day. We need to talk about it, but does it even matter anymore? Not when we are here now? I don't blame him for my injury anymore. He said it wasn't him who started the rumor, and I believe him...but it's a road bump I have to pass over every day.

"And my project?"

"Selfishly, I wanted an excuse to get close to you again. But I needed it more than you or Coach knew. Today wouldn't have been possible without you."

"It would have."

"On my worst days, when my mind was a rampant war, you were peace. I already found ways to tie parts of me to you, hold myself afloat. Do I think I'm in the clear? No, but you helped me find a way through. Helped me fall in love with hockey again." He tilts his head back up to the sky, then locks eyes with me. "Thank you."

"You're welcome." I lick my lips. "I love you, too, Cooper. I fell in love with you when I didn't want to. When I was refusing to face the truth and pushing you away. It's always been you and me...and this idea that we'll figure it out."

"There's always going to be something to figure out."

"But we'll do it together."

FORTY-FIVE

SUTTON

THE PAST TEN days have been mayhem. Not only did the guys win the conference tournament, but the women's team did too for the first time in program history. Between going to their games and school, I've been prepping for my internship interview with the Big Ten.

It's today.

Elliot came to Chicago with me. We left first thing in the morning, giving us more than enough time to grab breakfast at our favorite cafe in the West Loop. She's shopping now before meeting up with my sister.

Interviews are being held at Northwestern University. I thought Lakeland had an incredible campus, but wow. Their sports facilities and rec center have all been recently updated. Large, angular buildings with large windows that overlook Lake Michigan. It makes the lake our campus is on seem minuscule.

Early-afternoon sunlight reflects off the lake, sparkling through the panes of glass into the booth I'm sitting at in the lobby. It's cool out today, barely sixty degrees with a breeze, but in the sunlight, I'm sweating.

Or maybe that's my nerves.

Most of the students who are interviewing today have been

studying for three years. They've wanted to be a psychologist probably since it was career day in third grade. No one probably took a nasty hit and a skate to the thigh on their path to getting here.

I shift against the purple vinyl, a bead of sweat dripping down my back. I shuffle the flash cards, start at the top again with my talking points and potential answers to questions.

A trio of girls walks past me, all wearing loose fighting trousers and blouses. They're chatting about the other internships they applied for and graduate programs they started applications for.

For a split second, I find myself too far out of my league—and highly underdressed. I'm in a tan tartan skirt with a pressed white button-down shirt tucked into it. Slipped over top with the collar sticking out is a navy knit sweater. Elliot tried to convince me to wear navy tights and borrow her navy knee-high leather boots, but I opted for a pair of white ruffled mid-calf socks and a heeled loafer. My hair is pulled back with a navy clip.

I let Elliot do my makeup in the car. Simple, clean, and as she says, understated.

I smooth out my skirt. Take a deep breath.

You've got this, Sutton.

I haven't had these types of butterflies in years—it's kind of nice that they are still there. Rusty, a few in need of a warm-up or an extra stretch of their wings. They move around my stomach and work their way up my spine—not since my last game. I used to get them before every game, no matter what.

Just like then, I pull out a pair of headphones and slip on the same playlist I've listened to since high school. The volume is low enough that if my name is called, I'm ready—we already did a group interview, now it's individual.

The trio passes by me again. The brunette—with a familiar bow pulling half her hair up—stays back. Tells the other two she'll catch up with them in a bit.

"Sutton?" Izzy, my former high school friend, asks. "Oh my gosh! It is you." Her tone doesn't match her body language.

"Hi, Izzy." I pull out a headphone from my ear, confused why she's here.

"Is this seat taken? Can I sit?" She's already sliding into the booth before I can answer.

I haven't seen Izzy Adams since the summer going into my senior year of high school. Her mom accepted a Cardiothoracic Surgeon position in California, and they moved at the end of our junior year.

We had a falling out shortly after. It was slow at first. Less communication—she was busy making new friends; I was busy with injury recovery. Then over the summer, Izzy was visiting our hometown, which I didn't know till I saw her out, holding hands with my ex-boyfriend.

I pretended I didn't seem them. Pretended there wasn't this weird buzz within me that something wasn't right about the picture. Pretended to not see her few texts that next year.

Did it hurt losing her as a friend? Naturally. Friendship breakups suck even as a kid. It took me till I became friends with Elliot to realize that I didn't miss Izzy though.

"How have you been?" we both ask at the same time. "You first," I follow-up with.

"Great!" she tells me, more like brags about attending the University of Minnesota—my dream team to have played hockey for—and the sorority she's in.

"And your parents?" Izzy is an only child.

"Divorced. Mom's already remarried to this steamy doctor from the hospital. Dad's back in Minnesota. I was actually visiting the other week, and I heard a *little rumor*."

I internally cringe at the way she says rumor. It transports me back to high school. Back to the name calling, whispers, and stares. Boiling to the surface my insecurities of being wanted and being enough. I tamper them down, and think about the people in my life who do care for me.

"You're dating Cooper Carmichael."

"I am."

"Interesting."

"How's that interesting?"

She shrugs casually. "Just is." Izzy pulls out lip gloss and reapplies. "You know I thought after everything in high school—"

"He didn't start the rumor," I cut her off defensively.

Izzy lets out a dull laugh. "He said that?" I nod demurely. "Of course, he did. And did he say who did?" When I shake my head no, she hmms. "And you're sure he didn't? Seems like another tactic to get what he wants. What other extremes did he go to?" There's another dull laugh. "Always a game with him."

Manicured nails tap on the table as silence stretches between us.

I go tight, whatever nerve she was aiming at, she hit it. My body rigid as I fight off the second-guessing. Would he tell me that just to earn my trust back? Are him and I a game? Why won't he or can't he say who did start the rumor?

"Anyways. What is your time slot for the solo interview?"

I cough, clearing my throat. "Four."

"That's right after me. I thought I was last, but now that I know I'm not, I'm so relieved." Her body visibly shows that relief, slouching into the seat. It's a little dramatic, almost fake. "But don't worry, I bet you'll still do okay. You were always better at studying and finding ways to make people like you." She nods to my notecards, and I try not to take offense to her subtle jab. I think in these years not being friends, my Izzy-colored glasses have been removed.

"I didn't realize you wanted to be a sports psychologist?" Or any interest in sports. When we were friends, she never came to my games. Once even said she hated sports, didn't get them. How do you go from that to wanting to intern with one of the biggest college conferences?

One of Izzy's brows arches. Eye twitches and hands curl into fists. Something in her switches.

Izzy can be mean, but I'd never been at the end of it...at least I think, but now I'm not positive.

I didn't think I was being rude by asking. I was genuinely curious how she decided on majoring in sports psychology.

"People are allowed to change their minds, Sutton. I've worked hard the past year and a half to get here. Did you not change your major and decide to go into psychology, too? Just because Minnesota didn't want you—hockey team and school— and wanted me, doesn't mean I can't pursue the career I want?"

"Izzy...I-I didn't mean it like that. I was only curious."

"Uh-huh. I'm sorry I'm not the washed-up, injured athlete that's going to use that to get an internship." There's a callous bite to her tone, and an odor that smells a lot like jealousy.

"I'd never do that."

"Why not? They aren't going to want you otherwise. Think about it, Sutton. No one ever has just wanted you, there's always a reason." Her eyelids are dropped into slits as she glowers at me.

I...I don't even know what I'm feeling.

No matter what concoction is stirring inside of me, I bite my tongue.

Izzy slides out of the booth. Before leaving, her hands planted on the table, she leans down. "No need to call me when Cooper dumps you. I already know I'm right. Was in high school, am now."

I don't watch her go. My gaze frozen to the vinyl in front of me.

My phone buzzes with a message from Elliot. Mindlessly, I swipe it away.

I try to make sense of what just happened. There's something scratching at the back of my brain. An insistent, maybe left field, thought.

And did he say who?

The *hmm* afterward.

Was it her?

Elliot texts me again and I see the time. I have to focus, but that's next to impossible.

I text Cooper, fully knowing that he should be getting dressed for practice right now; and despite my insecurities telling me she's right about him.

Tell me I can do this.

Please.

My phone rings immediately, his name and picture taking over the entire screen.

"Sutton baby. What's the matter?"

"I'm sorry, I shouldn't have texted you. You need to focus on practice, not me."

He laughs, and it's like smelling your favorite home-cooked meal. There's something so familiar and calming about it. I crave to hear it more, taste it coming from his mouth, but he's over three hours away at his game.

"Have you not realized that I'm always focused on you? Nothing is more important to me than you."

"I love you."

"I love you, too." There's a shuffling of shoes and then a door closing. "What color underwear are you wearing?"

"What?" I gasp.

"Come on. Black or green or purple."

"White..." I play along.

"The ones with the pink bow in the center," he whimpers.

"Yes?"

"Those are my favorite."

"Is that why you ripped my other pair in half? Is that how you treat your favorite things?"

"Well...if you are putting it that way, it was blocking me from a favorite activity, and we just simply couldn't have that."

"What is the point of asking this?" I sigh-laugh, shoulders

relaxed into the booth and slow smile peeling at the corners of my mouth.

"Did I distract you?"

"Yes?" I repeat, same tone and all.

"Good. Stop getting in your head. All you need to do is give it your best, forget about everything else. Okay?"

"Okay."

"Plus, you can tell them all about me." I laugh. "No one can't love me."

"You're so full of it."

"And you'll be full of me later." Heat prickles my cheeks. The blush Elliot blended into my skin probably matches my hair now. "You've got this. I promise, baby. I believe in you."

"Thank you," I whisper.

I can hear Coach Mathieson yell in the background.

"Gotta jump, but text me after. I'll check my phone in the locker room."

Cooper hangs up, and I sink into the seat. I plop my earbud back in to try and drown out Izzy's stupid voice, but all I can do is replay that stretch of high school.

FORTY-SIX

SUTTON

FIVE YEARS AGO

"EXCITED FOR YOUR GAME TONIGHT?" Dad asks me, turning on his turn signal to join the drop-off line in front of my high school.

He's driving me today because Meave is on a college visit with Mom. She drives me right now—she's a senior, I'm a junior—but not for long.

We were supposed to pick up Cooper and Jordan, but their dad decided to take them to breakfast and let them miss first period.

"Mhm." I nod, twisting over in the seat to make sure I brought my bag with me. I won't have time to go home before we have to get on the bus after school. "You're coming, right?"

"Wouldn't miss it."

Dad has never missed a game, even if it means showing up late. He's always there. I know I didn't need to ask, but I like to. I like the reminder that I have people in my corner now.

When we are second from the drop-off area, Dad pulls out his wallet and hands me a fifty.

"Dad." I sigh. "What's this for?"

"Buy lunch, we both know what I packed is probably terrible." It was, but he didn't know I swapped out the containers.

"Then get a smoothie, or whatever, for you and your friends before the bus."

"Fine." I give him a cheesy smile.

He rolls down the windows and turns up the music as we pull into the turnaround.

"Stop." I laugh, trying to roll up my passenger window. He rolls it right back down. "You are going to embarrass me."

"That's the whole point." He starts to sing the ABBA song loudly.

I sink into my seat and use my tote bag to try to hide my face. My freckled skin heats, and I know it's as red as my hair.

Dad puts the car in park for a moment. My best friend, Izzy, pops her head into the car. Arms crossed on the windowsill.

"Hi, Mr. Davis."

"Izzy. How are you? I haven't seen you over at the house in a bit."

"Tell this one to invite me over." She pokes at my cheek.

"I did last week," I remind her.

She pops a shoulder. "I was busy."

Izzy backs up, and I unbuckle and get out of the car. Before Dad drives off, I grab my hockey bag and set it on the curb.

I lean into the window like Izzy did. "Bye, Dad. I love you."

"I love you, too, Firecracker."

I love hearing those three words. Collect and cherish them like people do with rare coins. There were days before he and Mom adopted me that I didn't think I ever would.

"See you tonight."

The teacher working the drop-off whistles at him to move his car. He waves an apology at them and puts his car back into drive. Giving me another *love you* before heading off.

I spin around, and Izzy has my bag resting on her shoulder.

"Geez, Sutt. What do you have in here?"

"Give it here." She passes it to me, dramatically sagging and rubbing her shoulder afterward.

Izzy Adams and I have been friends for the past two years.

We've known each other longer than that, but it wasn't till eighth grade that she invited me to eat lunch with her. Outside of Meave and Cooper, I didn't have many friends. Because of her, I now have a solid group of four. Sammie, Jasmine, and Clara were Izzy's other friends. Cooper calls them her minions.

"Did you get a haircut?" I ask.

She fiddles with the ends of her now shoulder-length brunette hair, which is always tied back with a bow.

"After school, yesterday. Clara and I both went, and then we got our nails done. I would have invited you, but"—I glance down at her nails, painted in the color I told her I was going to get this weekend when we were supposed to go—"you had practice."

"It's fine." I blow it off, only slightly hurt.

Things have been...weird lately.

Izzy's been more withdrawn. Same with the girls.

Hockey is in season, so I know I'm busier, but I've always made time for my friends. I can't get jealous of them hanging out without me when I have a game or practice, but this is different from freshman year. We've been through this before.

A couple of weeks ago, a small rumor about me started: why I was adopted, who my parents are, why they didn't want me. It started as whispers. But our high school isn't big, maybe two hundred kids per class. We are the perfect size to know everyone, and rumors spread like weeds.

My friends said they shut them down but I'm hesitant to believe them.

Then why are they withdrawn? Maybe they think the rumors are true?

Izzy loops her arm in mine as we walk through the front doors of the building, promising me we can still go this weekend.

She asks me about my game and where Meave is touring. I ask if she's ready for our World History quiz, which she freaks out about, realizing she forgot.

At my locker, she abandons me to go cram.

But that's okay, because my boyfriend, Dylan, is there waiting for me.

"Hi." I blush, something I've never been able to control, leaning in for a kiss. He pulls away. My shoulders slump with confusion, feet sinking into my loafers. "Everything okay?"

"I'm breaking up with you," Dylan announces casually and from out of nowhere.

"What? Seriously?"

"Yeah, Sutton." He repeats himself more slowly, "I'm breaking up with you."

"I heard you. Why?"

He checks over his shoulder. It's then that I see how busy the hallway is, and his posse standing by the drinking fountain, snickering.

"Did I do something wrong?"

"Eh. Don't like you anymore." Dylan pushes off the locker and walks away.

"Dylan. Wait!" Trying to get his attention only draws more on me. Other students in the hallway are laughing, whispering to each other, or even pointing at me.

He doesn't pay me any attention. Doesn't care that I'm confused and hurt, or—*do not cry, Sutton.*

I stand there, frozen.

Dylan walks away with his friends. One of them walks backward and makes eye contact with me, and says, "He doesn't want you. Nobody wants you. You should be used to it by now."

I'm a smart girl. I put the pieces together quickly. Dylan is breaking up with me because of the rumor. The rumor is now no longer whispered, but full-fledged.

Before it was easier to know my truth, but not so much now.

I think I forgot just how cruel people can be—even when they know something isn't true and are only doing it for attention.

A tear slips down my cheek. Then another when someone walks by and calls me a name under their breath.

I scan the hallway for Meave, forgetting she isn't here. Then I look for Izzy or any of the girls. The air in my lungs catches when I spot Cooper strolling down the hallway, bookbag slung over one shoulder, his hat still on and backwards.

His smile fades when he sees me.

He picks up his pace, jogging over to me and dragging my trembling body into his arms.

"Sutton, what happened?"

"He broke up with me. And—"

Another person walks by us, brushes shoulders with Cooper, and makes a comment that I can't fully hear, but Cooper does. He lets go of me, grabbing onto the back of the guy's backpack. "What did you say to her?"

The student, I can't remember the name of right now, but I know we have English together, repeats himself.

"That's not funny," I hear Cooper say. "And not true. Get her name out of your mouth."

"If I don't?"

"Good thing I know how to fight."

Cooper shoves him forward and comes back to me, wrapping his arms around me again. Blocking me from the world.

"Want to get out of here?" he asks.

Yes. "I can't, I have a game tonight."

"Right. We'll I'm walking you to class, I've got you."

Cooper walks me to class, then is there when it's over to walk me to my next one. At lunch, he sneaks us into an outdoor corridor. This happens daily for a week.

———

DYLAN and I's breakup does little to help kill the rumor. Instead, it only enhances it. I hate going to school. I hate going to school without my best friend slash bodyguard even more.

Cooper has a dentist appointment today. He's supposed to be at school by lunch, but he hasn't texted me yet.

I'm sitting with my friends. They were all shocked to see me since I've been avoiding anyone who doesn't have the last name Carmichael since I was dumped.

Izzy had called me after she found out Dylan broke up with me, but the other three haven't said anything.

At lunch, so far, they've attempted to get me to bad-mouth him, but I don't. Can't bring myself to, especially since everyone is saying mean things about me all over school. I refuse to stoop to their level.

I tear the crust off my sandwich. Then, tear it into smaller pieces. My appetite non-existent.

"You know who started this rumor," Izzy says, bumping her shoulder into mine to get my attention.

"Who?" Clara pipes up.

"Cooper." His name is an alarm in my head.

"What?" I shake my head, dropping the crumbs in my hands. "No way."

"Why not him?"

"Because he'd never do anything like that."

"Really?" Izzy rests her elbows on the table, leaning my direction. "I think he's always had a crush on you and was jealous of Dylan. What if he started the rumor to get Dylan to dump you?"

I hate that she makes sense. Still...I don't think Cooper would do this to me.

"Wait," Jasmine chimes in, "did he tell you that?"

"You're talking to him?" I ask.

Izzy moves her head from one shoulder to the next. "I mean... we bumped into each other over the weekend, and I asked." She turns to me, placing a hand on my forearm. "I didn't want to say anything then because you've been upset, and Cooper has been hoarding you."

"But Cooper told you that?" I seek out the confirmation.

"Yes," Izzy says plainly.

Clara, Jasmine, and Sammie all eye each other. Sammie bites her lip as if she has something to say. Jasmine shakes her head no at her.

CHAPTER FORTY-SIX

"I don't think Cooper would do this."

There was only a semi-truthful part of the rumor, everything else was a lie. My worries about being enough were, while accurate, twisted. *Desperate. Will do anything to make someone love her. Manipulate boys into being with her.*

"Come on, just give it a thought. Who knows the most about your feelings on being adopted?"

I swallow harshly. Cooper...

Some things I can't tell Meave.

I don't talk about it with Jordan, Cooper's little sister. I don't talk about it with my teammates or the girls that often either, not like I do with him.

Would he really do this?

Could he have been jealous?

We've always been friends, and sure, I've had a crush on him before, but he's never thought or seen me like that.

I think about how he's been this week. Encouraging me not to reach out to Dylan. Helping me avoid everyone...

I think Izzy is right. Cooper started the rumor.

COOPER

Getting dropped off. Is it too late for lunch?

I grab my lunch and thrust it into the overflowing trash can. Storming to the front doors, I push them open. He's walking up the sidewalk.

"Excited to see me?"

When he's in front of me, I shove him. Two hands on his chest.

I might be strong, have an athletic figure, but Cooper is stronger. More solid. He barely budges.

"You did this." I shove him again, and he lets me. "Tell me. Admit that you did it."

"Sutton—"

"Don't Sutton me. Not now, not ever again. Were you that jealous of Dylan that you had to break us up? Could you not share me? Or stand to see me happy with someone that wasn't you?"

He pulls his head back, tips up his chin, but still doesn't say anything.

I push at him again, tears welling up in my eyes.

"Admit it," I demand. "Did you start the rumor?"

Cooper swallows harshly, gaze tipping to mine. "Yes."

"I knew it." Tears stream down my face, and I can feel the fissure going through my heart. "I told you how I felt in confidence. How could you do that to me?"

"I'm sorry—"

I could handle the rumor. I could handle the breakup, but knowing that Cooper betrayed me...it's taking me down.

"You're sorry?" I take a step away from him. My face becoming a maze of moisture. "Screw you." I take a deep inhale, and the words come out of my mouth quicker than my opponents blade sliced through my skin that night. "I hate you."

FORTY-SEVEN

SUTTON

I RELEASE A LOW, annoyed groan. I can't focus when all I want to do is refresh my phone.

"Everything good over there?" Cooper asks from across his room.

We've both been busy, but we manage to do our best to squeeze in time together where we can—studying, even if in silence, is better than going a day without him.

He's sitting at his desk, broad shoulders hunched over his math homework. Forearm flexing when he grabs his calculator. Straightening, Cooper turns in my direction, a pencil tucked into his backwards hat. Yesterday, he shaved his scruff, leaving only the mustache he's been growing out for the playoffs. I kind of hate how much I like it, but pigs will fly before I ever admit that to him. I also sort of hate how hot it is watching him do math.

I'm sprawled out on his bed. On my stomach with all of my textbooks and notebooks spread out around me in a half circle. Dotted with Post-its and highlighters, my pen is half chewed on and hanging out of my mouth.

I roll over on my back, paper crunches under me.

"Thinking about the internship. I should have applied to

more. Gotten at least one other interview. I would have heard back by now if they selected me. Right?"

"It's been a week—"

"They said they were making a decision quickly. A week, two tops. What am I supposed to do if I don't get it?"

"Stop thinking about it. You are stressing yourself out," he presses.

"Because—"

"Nope," he cuts me off. "I'm not letting you talk negatively about yourself. There's nothing about you that should, *or deserves*, to be spoken about like that."

I roll into a seated position, knees tucked up into me. I pull his sweatshirt over them and play with the drawstrings. Cooper dotes on me, and because he knows me as he does, each positive affirmation feels like a kiss on my skin, an invisible tattoo, and is the exact opposite of what I was about to say about myself.

"You understand?" he asks after he finishes what could be a new encyclopedia.

"Yes." I roll my eyes. Lovingly, of course. "Thank you."

"You're welcome. I never want you to question how I see you, Sutton."

Cooper rubs the back of his left shoulder. A wince creeps out every so many touches.

"You okay over there?"

"Just sore." My eyes must be communicating with him, because he adds, "I'm not overtraining again, I promise. Coach is pushing us hard in practice. The teams we are going up against are some of the most physical ones. He wants us prepared for the pressure and hits we can expect."

"Weren't you supposed to go to the trainers after practice"

"Yes," he hisses. "They we're busy."

"That's not a good enough excuse." I pat the bed. "Come here."

Having been around enough athletic training rooms and gone through my fair share of therapy, I've picked up a few tricks.

Cooper stands, stalking intentionally to the bed. I should be clearing my things, but my attention keeps getting dragged to him.

I don't think he's purposely moving like a snail. The distance between his king-sized bed and the desk is maybe seven steps. Four for his long stride.

Long fingers, decorated with calluses where they meet his palm, curl into the hem of his self-cropped team shirt. The hem rolling up, teasing the tanned muscles underneath. Arms criss-crossed, biceps bulge against the sleeves—have they gotten bigger? —as he tugs it upward.

It's as if I'm cutting a cake and slowly pulling the slice back, revealing the layers of deliciousness underneath. Each layer of abs is displayed as the shirt works its way up his abdomen. Over his pecs.

I tug my bottom lip between my teeth. It doesn't matter how many times I see it, I can't believe his left nipple is pierced. A dare between his housemates that resulted in Jaxon and Cooper with the bling.

Once his shirt is flipped inside out, face hidden, I let my gaze wander. Map out his torso, even though I have it memorized.

The bruises from his most recent games are still visible. One rimmed in yellow, the other still purple and blue.

I grind my teeth, cringing at the sight. Can't say I miss those. The scar on my thigh is already bad enough.

Brown, shaggy hair pops through the neck of the shirt. A Cheshire cat-worthy smile on his face. Cooper tilts his head up to make eye contact with me.

I pat his bed again.

He closes the remaining inches. Cleans up my belongings. Tucking bookmarks into my textbook and stacking everything neatly on the ground. Gives me a quick kiss.

On his stomach, I straddle his back and start pushing into his knotted muscles.

"A little lower," he requests, voice muffled in the comforter.

I shift my hands lower down his trapezius, digging more into his rhomboid minor and major. "Here?" I press in using the heel of my hand.

Cooper whimpers. Twice.

It drips down my spine like honey.

I press in again, then repeat on the other side. The yellowing bruise is there, wrapping around his ribcage. I'm careful not to touch it, but I do lean down to softly kiss the skin around it. I notice a new one forming almost under it.

"New?" I rub a gentle finger around it. "What's this one from?"

"I don't know. Must have been a slow burn." He laughs, cheek on the comforter, eyes flicking to me in his peripheral vision.

"Oh yeah? It didn't kiss your skin till seventy-five percent through?"

"At least it didn't take fifteen years."

"Funny." I pinch his unbruised side above his Levi's.

"I think it's from the hit in our game against Minnesota. That side is achy and tender, but I figured it's my other bruise. Popped up this morning."

I lean forward and press a kiss next to it. "Now it's better."

"Mhmm."

I keep massaging his back. Eventually, he takes off his jeans and I move to his legs. Little noises slip out of him while we talk about everything and nothing at the same time.

I stop when my phone buzzes. An email notification pops up. I glance over at it and read up to where the subject line cuts off. I pick up my phone, fingers moving quicker than my racing heart.

Tapping and swiping open the notification, I curse under my breath as the screen goes white before loading.

I scurry to the end of the bed and swing my legs over. The brightness on my phone is low, but enough to highlight the tear wetting my cheek like you do a slip and slide before everyone takes their turns.

A couple more tears sneak out, and I use the back of my hand to wipe them away.

I reread the email again. And again.

The bed dips next to me. Cooper sidles up next to me.

"Everything okay?" He peers over at my phone. "What is that?"

"I didn't get the internship."

It was a long shot, I know that. By the time the psych department approved my study, I was already late to the game, applying for internships or fellowship programs. This one didn't have as strict requirements as the others.

It was my only shot. And I think I put a lot more weight on it than I intended. I wanted this, needed this, and didn't get it.

His arm slips around my shoulders, fingers digging into my shoulder like he's playing the piano.

"I-I can't believe it." Well, I can. I'm never the one picked. The one that's wanted. "This was my only option." My voice cracks, barely above a mumble.

Cooper pulls me into his chest and holds me. "*We'll* figure it out."

———

A HANDFUL OF DAYS LATER, I'm trying to enjoy the rare quietness of campus. Slowly strolling through the lawn, sipping on chai, and catching up on social media.

My favorite author announced a new book. Antonio's is trying a pickle pizza. And...I scroll up and back down, making sure my suggested for you post isn't fake.

It's Izzy in Chicago. She got the internship.

I unfollowed her last year, but can't lie and say I didn't look her up after the interview. Now here she is.

I try to be excited for her, think about texting her congrats as I walk up the stairs to Dr. Manning's office.

Leaning against the wall next to her door, I find the photo for a third time, and accidentally like it. Immediately I tap my phone to remove the red heart and shove my phone into my bag.

Good for Izzy. I'm happy for Izzy—*valiant effort at sounding convincing, Sutton.* I roll my eyes at myself. All I can convince myself about right now is that she's right.

"You wanted to see me?" Dr. Manning's office door opens, light pouring into her office, coating everything in a warmth, as she calls me in.

After I didn't get into the internship, I've been avoiding her. I know I still have a full year left at school, but it doesn't negate the fact that I feel like I wasted her time. I failed her. It won't be worth it to work with me again next year.

The self-doubt and insecurities I used to know well are back. Printed on my body as if they are a temporary tattoo that won't rub off. The more I try, the more irritated I become.

"Sutton. How are you today?" She smiles at me brightly, her fresh bobbed hair brushing her high cheekbones as she spins in her oversized leather chair.

"I'm okay." I gulp, swallow a shard of another ruined dream. "Busy," I add.

"Well, I'm about to make that okay, great."

Impossible, but okay.

I shift awkwardly in the chair across from her, my shoulders straight and legs crossed at the ankles.

"I met with the Dean of Students and the department chair this morning." My throat goes dry. Any optimism is wrung out of me. "They are impressed with you. The whole package—paper, dedication to the study, application of real-life experience. They've accepted the addition. Sports psychology is officially a minor at Lakeland."

My stomach does a somersault. "What?"

"That's not all. They are adding additional resources for student-athletes in the Student Health Center. Bringing on specific therapists to work with the teams. At the start of every season, there will be a seminar on mental health."

"Wait, I'm confused. How is this all happening?"

"Coach Mathieson and Mr. Carmichael spoke to the University and attended the meeting this morning."

That's where he snuck off early this morning and wouldn't tell me. I'm in disbelief. Half of me wants to be excited, but the other half of me knows that it still wasn't enough.

"I didn't get the internship," I blurt.

"Yes, I know."

"You do?"

"Avoiding me? I'm older and wiser than you think." She walks around the front of her desk, leaning back on it. "Plus, I know someone in the office. Sutton, there were three hundred students who applied for that internship. Twenty were interviewed."

"Let me guess, I was ranked twenty." Cooper would be scolding me for my self-deprecation.

"No." Dr. Manning shakes her head. "Just because this door is closed, doesn't mean another one isn't opening."

As if on cue, her office door swings open.

"I didn't have an internship the summer after my junior year, and I turned out great."

"Great? How humble of you, Vivi," the newcomer says. Vivi?

Heels click across the hardwood. I turn over my shoulder to find Dr. Zando, a Senior Psychological Service Provider for Team USA.

"Allie." Allie?

My list of idols, people I want to be, isn't long. Meave tops it, then Mom and Dad, followed by Kendall Coyne Schofield, and recently Dr. Zando.

My eyes bug. Holy shit. I smack a hand over my mouth before I say something stupid.

She sits down next to me. Her deep chestnut hair is pulled into a slicked-back bun, exposing her striking facial features. Powerful, intimidating, and—I wonder if my curls could be manhandled enough to do that hairstyle?

"Is this her?" Dr. Zando pretends to discreetly whisper to Dr. Manning behind a cupped hand.

My advisor rolls her eyes. "Yes."

"Hi." I stretch out my hand to her. "I'm Sutton Davis."

"Dr. Zando, but please, call me Allison or Allie." She shakes my hand. "You know, Vivi, she reminds me more of myself than you."

"Is that so?"

"Way cooler." Dr. Zando laughs, then turns back to me. "Your advisor talks non-stop about her psych student protege."

Huh? What? Me?

"Don't let Allison fool you. I only talk about you once a day." She smirks. "And the words protege did leave my mouth once or twice."

"It's a pleasure to meet you, Dr.—Allison. Are you in town visiting? Did you two go to school together?" I have so many questions.

She licks her lips, glancing back at my advisor. "You could say visiting. Vivian and I went to grad school together. I could give you a good story or two about her."

"Please do."

"Maybe later. I'll give you my number." Opening her designer purse, Allison pulls out a business card and hands it to me. I tuck it securely in the back of my phone case. "My email is also on there. Send me your resume and a copy of your transcript."

Wait...what? I wish I could rewind to make sure I heard that correctly.

"While Team USA doesn't have formal internships, they do allow certain doctors to take on interns or allow students to shadow them," Dr. Manning announces. The cadence and enunciation of her words lets me read between them.

Stay calm, Sutton.

"Really?!"

I'm about to burst out of my seat like a jumping bean.

"No promises." Allie passes me a reassuring smile. "However, sometimes it's good to know someone."

Can they hear my heart thumping against my chest? Can they see the stars in my eyes?

"I'd love the opportunity to do that." I turn to Dr. Manning. "Thank you."

"All you, but you're welcome." Dr. Manning stands, grabbing her purse. "I'm starved. Sutton, do you want to join us for lunch?"

FORTY-EIGHT

COOPER

MY PLAYING IS SHIT.

I've dropped at least five passes, spent more minutes in the penalty box in the first two periods than I have in my last ten games, and I can't remember when I haven't had double digits of shots on net by the third.

I've never been superstitious—Jordan tells me I'm just stitious—but maybe I should be. Lots of the guys on the team are.

When was the last time I played without that bracelet?

Where is that bracelet? I curse at myself.

After Coach yells at us, dropping his favorite colorful words several times, I turn to my cubby in the away team locker room.

The space is acceptable, but even our away locker room is nicer than this. Wood is chipped and the metal hook holding up my team bag is missing two of three screws. And it smells like Jaxon came a week early to plant his socks in the air duct—dude has got to learn how to do laundry before we graduate.

My gloves are off. Tossed aside on the metal bench. I grab my bag, shaking the entire hook loose from the wood. Unzipping it quickly and violently, it startles Chase and Dawson, who are on either side of me.

I curse. Curse again and run a hand through my hair. "Where is it?"

I rummage around the main cavity of the bag. Checking each pocket twice and taking out every article of clothing. I shake out my shirt and sweats. Stick my hands into the pockets. Unfold my three extra pairs of socks and underwear.

Nothing. Absolutely nothing.

"What are you looking for?" Chase asks. They lean into my space.

"Nothing," I grunt.

"Are you sure?" Dawson chimes in. "You've checked that pocket four...five times now."

"It has to be in here. Has to be. I couldn't have lost it."

"What does?"

"Her—my bracelet."

They look at each other. Then look at me.

"Like a bracelet Madeline made you? She'll probably make you another. Here, I'll ask Be—"

"No." I clench my jaw and squeeze my eyes shut. "It's Sutton's bracelet."

I toss my bag back into the cubby. Turn around and sink on the bench and fold over. My elbows resting on my knees, forehead cupped in my hands.

"We can help you find it," Chase reassures me. "Did you have it at the start of the game? Maybe you took it off and dropped it in the wrong bag. We all have the exact same one."

"If I had it with me, I wouldn't suck right now. We wouldn't be losing."

"We aren't losing because of you, Cap."

"I suck. I suck. I suck," I repeat the negative affirmation. Quiet enough not to alert my teammates. The dark cavity of the lockers is becoming more enticing. I wonder if I could disappear into it. No one would even notice. Not at least until they needed something.

"Stop." Beckett is hovering over me.

I glare up at him. He glares back at me. Fierce, scary, beady blue eyes saying a thousand words. A voice pops up in my head, another bout of words that I let settle deep in my bones. It's Sutton.

"I don't suck," I tell myself and him. I'm more upset with myself for losing her bracelet than my playing; and I know there isn't anything correlating the two.

He helps pull me up from the bench. Hands me my gloves, leveling me with another look.

"It's just a bracelet."

It's not, and that's the thing.

———

WE WIN IN OVERTIME. Miraculously somehow.

Tied it up in the third quickly with two freshmen scoring their first goals of the season.

But my playing never got better, and I'm pissed at myself because we almost lost when I missed a pass and their team scored. The refs called back the goal because the other team's player kicked the puck.

Where are you?

Any chance you can come over?

I'm not home, but I will be. Hour maybe?"

I need you, Sutton.

SUTTON

What if I say I'm already here?

FORTY-NINE

SUTTON

I WAS ALREADY SEARCHING for the spare key when Cooper texted me. Their game wasn't his finest display of athleticism—honestly, anyone's. The entire team was off tonight.

Somehow, probably my shaking hands and heart, I broke the pot they keep their Barbie pink key in. Lucky for the fake plant, it'll survive.

Hot pink and groovy style flowers, this is the house puck bunny key. They will tell a girl where it is, and after she leaves, they change its spot.

Inside, I grab a sports drink from the kitchen and raid the secret snack stash. A bag of white cheddar Cheetos Puffs and a pack of fun-sized M&Ms—please, can we all finally admit, they are *the elite* candy?

I've never been an emotional snacker. Maybe overindulging in grapes or strawberries, and the occasional milkshake. But I needed something to occupy my hands, my mind.

After lunch with Dr. Manning, I took one of Elliot's classes. She proceeded to drive me here after I fumbled my keys, dropping them twice before she snatched them up.

Cooper's bedroom is clean. Probably because he isn't one for stuff. He keeps a small bookshelf with books next to his desk, and has a gallery wall of hockey memorabilia that his mom put together when he moved in here.

I sink into his king-sized bed, on my side. The right side. I've been staying here enough that there is an additional IKEA metal side table, a phone charger, a book light, and a claw clip clipped onto the ledge. Some mornings—my favorite mornings—it also has a note from Cooper if he has to leave before me. Usually, we wind up here after a long day, wrapping ourselves up in the sheets.

It dawns on me that in the past few months, I've never really explored his bedroom.

I climb off his bed, take my bag of candy with me, and walk around his room as if it's a museum, and it is in ways.

On his desk is a photo of him and his sisters. Meave took it. I remember the day fondly. There's a photo of Meave and me next to it. She's on my back, her lanky limbs sticking out like our tongues. There's another photo, a Polaroid. It's not in a frame, but stuck to the shelf with tape. It's him and I in our hockey sweaters.

Sixteen and twenty.

My cheeks heat, prickles dance up my spine, but freeze as my insecurities spin me into their arms next. I love my brain, but right now I wish it would relinquish the hold it has on me and let go of the ropes it's tugging on. My heart is stumbling over itself trying to maintain its footing.

I keep touring, popping an orange candy into my mouth.

The gallery wall consists of more photos and jerseys in frames. A pendant from school that says *Go Bears!* and the team our dads played for. There used to be a vintage poster of his dad on the wall, but it's backwards. Taped to the back is a piece of notebook paper with his chicken scratch scrolled on it: *You are allowed to be different.*

It's one of the first things that I told him when he was assigned to my independent study. The session after he had his panic attack and confessed everything.

I can't believe he remembered...or that I haven't noticed this...

His area rug is soft under my feet as I make my way back to his bed when my eyes catch on something on his bedside table.

There's a bracelet sitting on it. Bright colors clash with the black metal.

That's...that's my bracelet. The one that's been missing for years.

I ditch my snack, crawling to his side of the bed. Snatching it up quickly, I throw my legs over the side of the bed and sit there.

Stunned.

I run my fingers over the beads. The material is familiar against my skin. I've missed this bracelet. I truly thought I had lost it, or it had broken off.

Why does he have it? Did he...did he steal it? Is this what he's always playing with under his sleeve?

I try not to let myself get angry, but questions are running through me like a pack of wild horses. Stampeding against this current version of us, leaving it in the dust.

I'm not sure how much time passes. Enough that Cooper and his roommates are finally home. I can hear them. Closing cabinet doors, groans and laughter, and stomping around the first floor. Loud, thumping music that decreases at the start-up of a gaming station turns on.

Footsteps echo up the stairs.

Cooper swings his door open. His smile is weak and forced, but brightens when he finds me on his bed.

"I'm so excited to see you. You have no—"

"Why do you have this?" I hold up the bracelet, letting it dangle between my thumb and pointer finger.

COOPER

My mouth hangs open. The words on the tip of my tongue.

When we pulled into the driveway, I didn't see her car, but I knew she was here. Walking into the house, I felt her. The string

—once frayed, that I pinched to keep together—tying us to one another, goes taut, pulling me to her.

I wish I was happy to see that damn bracelet, but I'm not.

"I-I—" The truth fumbles out of me. "I found it." I take a step toward her, coughing to clear my throat. "The day after our fight. When I got to school, it was in the mulch out front."

"And you didn't think to give it back to me?"

"I did."

I take another step forward. My approach is hesitant with the stirring her hazels are doing. Amber and flecks of onyx swirl in them.

My response isn't a lie; I had every intention of returning the bracelet to her. Maybe even be her hero for finding it. Sutton *loved* this bracelet.

Stupidly, I only attempted to give it to her once. A smarter man, or someone who wasn't rounding the corner of puberty, would have tried again.

We were going over to her house for Sunday dinner. Mom and Dad loved to do family dinners, and since the Davises have always been family, we did them together. Rotated weekly which house we went to.

Our dads—attractive professional hockey players that never lost a tooth *and* can whip up a mean potato gratin and roasted chicken—cooked. Even though I believed Mrs. Davis prepped everything.

It was almost a month after our big fight and her injury. Sutton hadn't uttered a word to me in the weeks following, blatantly ignoring me and turning the opposite direction at school, switching assigned seats in class. When we showed up that week to her house, I wasn't supposed to be there, but our team bonding was cancelled. As soon as Sutton saw me, she bolted upstairs as quick as someone on crutches could. Her bedroom door slammed shut. Meave chasing after her. Five minutes later, they were back down the stairs, Meave hot behind her, trying to convince Sutton to stay.

Sutton told her parents she forgot she had a school project that needed a poster board, and left with keys tight in her fist.

Her bracelet was snug in the front pocket of my jeans. I slipped one of my hands in the pocket and played with the beads —a weird tick I still have. Honestly, probably why I'm attached to it the way I am now.

"Really fucked that friendship up," Jordan said, kicking me under the table.

"Jordan. Language," Mom scolded.

Sutton's mom laid her hand over mine. "She knows the injury isn't your fault. That day upset her and...don't worry about it sweetheart, it's only an association. She'll get over whatever happened between you two."

Yeah, I'm afraid not. That's what I wanted to tell her mom then, and little did I know that it would take over five years for her to be remotely over it.

I didn't want to lose or misplace the bracelet. Terrified to accidentally wash it, I started wearing it. It was dainty enough that it fit under long-sleeved shirts and sweatshirts. The only time I took it off was to sleep, shower, or play hockey.

One day, I forgot to take it off and had the best game of my life. When I took off my gloves and gear in the locker room after, I saw it there on my wrist.

I've worn it every game since—except tonight.

When the stress of the game and my future blurred my love for hockey, the bracelet became more than luck. I'd run my fingers over it or slip it off and play with it during a press conference after games, at home on the couch, and reading a new article about my insufficiencies. I clung to it to steady my racing mind.

There's always been a steadying aura with Sutton, even when she wanted nothing to do with me. Finding ways to insert myself into her life might have made her loathe me more, but at least she was feeling something toward me. Gave me pieces of her energy, her mind...of herself along the way. Whether she realized it or not.

These years, I've watched her grow. Experience challenges. Fall in love with new dreams. I hated doing it from the sidelines, but at least I was in her orbit somehow.

Maybe now I realize I've been selfish and should have given it back. I don't know.

My eyes lift to hers, and they're looking at me as if I'm hurting her.

"Dave..."

She shakes her head, puts a hand up. "Do not Dave me. Or Sutton baby."

"Can I explain?"

Sutton laughs. "The same way you explained what happened in high school?"

"You said it didn't matter anymore."

"Izzy was right." She shakes her head, disappointed. What does she have to do with this? From what I know, they haven't spoken in years. "Were you lying the night you told me you love me? Were we only ever some type of game to you?"

"This—we," I correct and emphasize the word, "aren't a game. You aren't some prize that I'm trying to win."

Sutton stands from my bed. "I need a minute to breathe."

FIFTY

COOPER

SHE PACES toward my bathroom before spinning around, grabbing a sweatshirt littered on the floor and her sneakers. Out my bedroom door, I hear her quickly sprinting down the stairs.

"Sutton. Stop." I chase after her blindly, hopping from one foot then the other putting my shoes back on. I miss a step and slide down the last four stairs.

All of my roommates are in the living room. They're all lounging on the couch playing video games. Dawson thumb points at the front door over his shoulder.

I curse under my breath.

Sutton's car wasn't in our driveway or parked on the street when we got back. Peach skies turning gray with an oncoming spring shower. It was sprinkling then, pouring now.

The sidewalk is barely visible through the droplets pounding the pavement.

I turn my head left and right to determine which direction she went. I can't see her, but I trust my gut and run in the direction of her apartment.

Drenched, I pick up my pace, pushing my exhausted body—physically and mentally.

I shouldn't have let her leave.

I shouldn't have kept secrets.

I shouldn't have loved her from afar. This mess would be a lot easier to clean—*or avoidable,* my inner voice is sarcastic today—if I hadn't lied to protect her.

A car drives by, hitting a puddle and spraying me with water.

My sweats are heavy. Head and heart heavier.

I make it to her apartment complex and huddle under the awning of the main doors. Reaching into my pockets, there's nothing. In my haste, I didn't grab my phone, student ID, or keys. Earlier this month Sutton fibbed, said she lost her key fob, and the University made her another, which is now on my key ring.

I pound on the glass. Someone will have to hear me or walk by.

My prayers are answered several minutes later when none other than Elliot walks out of the elevator.

"Cooper?" She opens the door to the lobby.

"Is Sutton upstairs?"

"No. I thought she was at your place..." Her words come out slowly.

I pinch the bridge of my nose, then run a hand through my wet hair. "We got—I messed up, and she left. I figured she'd come back here."

"She didn't. Car keys are up there too."

"She said she needs to breathe. Does she...where does she go when she needs to breathe?"

Elliot thinks, using seconds I don't have.

"Come on, Elliot. Think."

"I'm thin—Oh! There is a hidden dock on the lake she goes to."

"How do I get to it?" I ask frantically.

She shrugs, uncertainty tightening her features. "I've never been, but let me track her."

Elliot locates Sutton, and I take off without a goodbye.

There's a path at the back of her complex connecting to another that loops around the circumference of Lake Bensen. I follow it in the direction of her dot on Elliot's phone. Stretching my memory, I go south.

Keeping my eyes peeled, I'm searching for an opening. Anything not paved or marked. There's nothing in the trees that line this portion of the lake.

Found it.

A small opening, barely the width of a person, is carved into the vegetation. It takes maybe twenty steps before it opens up to a dock that stretches out into the water. Across the water, the sky hasn't been overthrown by the clouds swarming us. At least the rain is letting up.

Sutton's here. Sitting on the edge.

I try to be quiet, but all it takes is one gentle step for the old dock to creak. Sutton turns over her shoulder, gaze a magnet to mine. The hand playing with her hair halts.

"It was Izzy. Wasn't it?"

I meet her at the edge, kneeling to sit beside her. Sutton turns back to peer out at the water before looking at me again. "Yes."

FIFTY-ONE

COOPER

FIVE YEARS AGO

HIGH SCHOOL PARTIES aren't typically my scene. The basement or garage of someone's house—if you're lucky. Sneaking shitty liquor from their parents' cabinet because you're afraid to touch the good stuff.

I've drank before. Dad told me if there was anything I ever wanted to try, he'd rather me do it in a safe environment and have someone there to take care of me. Needless to say, the first time I got wasted, Dad was there. Mom was the one to try weed with me. I hated it.

When I got to Izzy's I knew her parents kept a white drink fridge in the garage. I snuck a beer and headed down to her basement.

I'm late. Most people were already buzzed. A game of spin the bottle is happening on the ground in front of the couch. Couples are making out on the sectional. Some playing on the ping-pong table. Others dancing anywhere they can find space.

I take a lap in search of Sutton. Izzy said she was coming when she invited me at school today.

Sutton's boyfriend, Dylan, is playing pong with one of his friends, Sid. He catches my attention and gives me an arrogant grin. She's not with him, so I keep looking. Making it back to the bottom of the stairs, I don't spot Izzy or her minions either.

I snag a spot on the couch as a few guys from the hockey team start up a game I've never heard of. I finish my beer, but before getting another, I text Sutton.

> Are you at the party?

SUTTON
> What party?

> Izzy's?

SUTTON
> Oh. Yeah. Didn't feel well.

Unless she took a turn in the past two hours, Sutton wasn't sick when I saw her. She's lying, she didn't know about the party. Why would Dylan or Izzy not invite her? It's not like Sutton to forget something.

I run a hand through my hair and decide to head home. There's no point in me being here.

> I'm going to head out. Need anything? Mom's soup?

SUTTON
> You should stay.

> Hang out with your friends.

I end up having a Diet Coke and then decide to head home. Before leaving, I dip into the bathroom.

I'm washing my hands when the door opens.

I could have sworn I locked it.

Through the mirror, I spot Izzy. A tiny bandage dress—honestly it might be a stretched-out tube top—and hair tied back in her signature bow. Her makeup is overdone. Our eyes lock and I can easily tell how glassy hers are.

She steps up beside me. Izzy is about a foot shorter than me. Fingers walking along the porcelain and up my hand white-knuckling the edge.

"Cooper. I've been looking for you." Her fingers creep up my forearm and I hate the sensation. It's as if a spider is crawling over me. "I was happy when I saw you gesture to the bathroom."

Gesture? "Huh?"

She's made her way to my chest, spinning her pointer finger and thumb into the fabric and pulling me to her.

"You wanted me to meet you in here," she slurs her words.

"No. No, I didn't." I try to take a step away from her but am surprised by her strength.

"Yes. Yes, you did."

"Seriously, Iz, I *wouldn't*."

She pulls away from me, disgusted. "Wouldn't? What is that supposed to mean? Because I'm not a curly redhead that wears stupid overalls or skirts and plays hockey, I'm not good enough?"

Izzy sways. She's more than tipsy. In this moment, I hate that it's an involuntary movement to steady her.

"Come on. Let's go upstairs and get you some water." I reach for her hand and she swats mine away.

"No."

"Iz," I warn and plea.

"You know she doesn't even like you, Cooper, but I do. And I'm here with you now. Not her."

"Izzy."

Her gaze flicks over me and I'm having whiplash because she tries to kiss me next. My hands find her waist and I push her away gently.

"Stop."

She's back to being pissed at me. Arms folded across her chest—and is she pushing up her boobs? I want to jab my fingers into my eyes. I will never understand girls.

"I'm sorry if you misunderstood me. If I did something to lead you on. I never meant to." I open the bathroom door to leave, but apologize one more time. I don't think I did anything, but just in case. "I am sorry, Iz."

"Yeah, *she* will be."

———

A MONTH LATER, I'm volunteering in the library shelving returns.

I do this during study hall sometimes. I enjoy the quiet, the mundane of shelving books. Plus, our librarian, Mrs. Knight makes a mean oatmeal chocolate chip cookie.

This week, my study halls have been monopolized by Sutton. Dylan dumped her, and there's a rumor surrounding her being adopted. Specifically why.

It's ranged from hurtful ideas to idiotic reasons. My favorite exaggeration is that her parents are spies for NASA and abducted by aliens. Make that one make sense?

It's trickled into name calling and out-of-line questions.

It's been floating around for a couple weeks now. Thought it would have died out, but someone is still stirring the pot despite my efforts to snuff it out. None of it's true. Sutton doesn't know anything about her birth parents.

We've spent our study halls hiding out, but she told me she was meeting with her hockey coach today, so I opted for the library.

I'm pushing the book cart toward the poetry section. Tucked away in the back corner of the library, dimmer, the only windows are from skylights in the ceiling. Having a poetry book to shelve is rare, this was only my second time ever—and I'll never admit it to anyone, but I'm the one who checked this book out.

I'm leaning over the cart, flipping through the pages to take a picture of my favorite poem. When I turn the corner to the aisle, my phone clatters out of my hand.

Pushed up against one of the shelves is a brunette female, and making out with her, is the last person I'd want to see.

Now what I do next, I'm not entirely proud of. I've never liked to let the aggression and power I have on the ice bleed into other areas of my life.

Before I know it, I'm grabbing the back of his shirt. Turning and shoving Dylan into the shelf next to Izzy.

"What the hell, man," Dylan seethes.

"I should be asking you that. Does Sutton know about this?"

"Cooper. Stop." Izzy grabs at my forearm, fingers pulling at the fabric of my crewneck.

"How long has this been going on?" I glower at him, our faces centimeters away. My breath is that of a dragon, hot and pungent with furry. I whip my gaze to Izzy. "Do you care to answer?"

Her jaw tightens, arms cross in front of her, similar to her posture in the bathroom at her house. Some of her lip gloss is missing.

"We didn't mean to let it happen, it just did." She's lying. Her tone is too casual. You'd assume there would be remorse, but there isn't.

"It was you."

"What was?" she challenges.

"You started the rumor." It burns as I say it.

"You don't know what you're talking about."

I turn to Dylan. "Did you know she started it?"

"Not till Sutton and I had already split."

"Dylan!" Izzy groans, as he reveals the truth.

"Come on, Iz. She was bound to find out."

"Why'd you do it?" I ask even though I think I know the answer.

Dylan backs away, my grasp on him loosening. His hands are in front of his chest. "I am not needed here. Got biology in ten. Gonna go."

Izzy rolls her eyes, and when it's just us, I ask her again.

"Because I'm jealous! Sutton had you, even after I set her up with Dylan. All the boys like her, but she's oblivious to it." Her hands flex into balls at her side. "She's athletic, and smart, and good at anything she does. Gets perfect grades and then goes home to her perfect family."

"And kissing Dylan? That was jealousy?"

"That was an accident. He kissed me first and I didn't know how to stop it. I do feel bad about it." I level her with a look. "Okay, fine. He wanted me and what was I supposed to say? No?"

"Yes. She's your friend!" At least I thought so.

"I feel bad about the kiss." She slumps into a bookshelf.

"Because you were caught. What about the rumor? Do you feel bad about it?" She shrugs. "Izzy—"

"Yes. Okay, Cooper, yes. It was terrible of me, but there's no taking it back now. It'll eventually fizzle out; and Sutton never needs to know. It'll alllll be fine."

"This is not fine. You put an end to the rumor today. Fucking squash it, and then you need to tell her the truth." I don't know if I've ever been more angry than I am now, or had a deeper urge to protect Sutton.

"It'll destroy her."

"Tell her today, or I'll tell her tomorrow. You decide."

"Is that a threat?" A mocha brow arches.

"I guess you'll have to see. I'll be waiting."

I resume pushing the cart to the next section, when Izzy calls out, "You know she'll never love you back."

———

SUTTON PUSHES AT ME AGAIN, tears welling up in her eyes. I had a dentist appointment this morning and it ran long. We were supposed to meet during lunch.

"Admit it," she demands. "Did you start the rumor?"

Izzy. I seethe internally.

She convinced her it was me.

"Yes," I lie.

The word is pungent on my tongue. A poison that I swallow down and will have to live with forever while it slowly kills me.

I swallow harshly, gaze tipping from the sidewalk to hers. The answer to why that came out of my mouth isn't chalked or pressed into the concrete. I don't think there is a valid enough answer or reason for why I said it.

Izzy was right about one thing: no matter what, this was going to hurt her.

Sutton has wanted a group of friends more than anything, people to be her family. I think that's why I do it. I don't want her to be disappointed in Izzy, lose everything she's searched for.

I'd rather her be upset with me. We're young. We've been friends for a decade...she'll forgive me, just give it a couple months.

"I knew it." Tears stream down her face, and I can feel the fissure going through my heart. "I told you how I felt in confidence. How could you do that to me?"

"I'm sorry—" What a loaded two words.

"You're sorry?" She takes a step away from me. "Screw you." She takes a deep breath and then three words I never wanted to hear her say roll off her tongue, smooth, like a puck on fresh ice. "I hate you."

FIFTY-TWO

SUTTON

THE TRUTH WAS ALWAYS THERE. Connecting the dots, the image it revealed compounded, and I couldn't breathe. Couldn't believe how stupid and naive I'd been.

I had to get out of his room. It was suffocating. It was rain after a drought. Surrounded by all the ways Cooper's loved and chosen me, kept me at the forefront of his life. Everything I've ever longed for was always there, hanging in the shadows—the shadows I created.

He sees me and knows me, but I pushed him away. All because I believed someone who was never my friend, never saw me.

There are things I want to ask or say to her; and I almost did. Izzy's contact was a beacon, my thumb hovering over the call button. But who would that benefit? What would any of that bring me?

It might give me resolution but it wouldn't make me feel better about myself. If she wants to still behave as if we are in high school, never grow up or mature, that's on her not me.

Instead, I deleted her texts, then her contact.

That's when Cooper showed up. I'm appreciative he told me

the whole story, but I can't lie...it almost makes me hate myself. Mad at minimum.

It's as if he can sense it. Cooper takes my face, hands cupping the sides, pulling my attention to him. "Don't. Don't hate yourself because of this."

"But—" I close my eyes and take a deep breath. The last of the raindrops press into my skin. "I'm mad at you. Mad at myself."

Cooper nods, but smiles loosely. The dimple carved into his cheek deepens. "Me too. For years."

"You should have told me the truth."

"Trust me, I know. I've lived with that regret every day. I've questioned myself why I never corrected you. Why I let this go on for years. I think I convinced myself that you would've hated me more."

He's probably right, but how are we to know. Before this year, I don't think I was in the space to understand the truth, but now that I do...

I get why he didn't. Wish he hadn't, but I can't change the past.

"I'm sorry I didn't."

"Shouldn't I be the one apologizing? I'm the one who believed her, twice. *God, Cooper.* How much time did I waste pushing you away?"

"You might've tried, but I wasn't going anywhere." He kisses me. The boyish smile on his face makes me smile, brings a light to the grayness around us. "Being in your orbit, Sutton, it's the best form of gravity."

I push my lips to his, helpless from any other thought when he says sweet nothings like that. He's the best form of gravity, too.

Cooper removes his hands, slipping my bracelet off his wrist, running the beads through his fingers. "In high school, you wanted nothing to do with me, but wearing your bracelet was as if I was holding you close. Memories of our childhood contained in each bead—and I think it's my good luck charm on the ice." He winks at me. "When we got to Lakeland, I convinced myself I had to let you go—thought about sneaking your bracelet into one of your boxes—but that worked out horribly because I needed you. And if this was all I had? I'd cling onto it forever."

I sigh, then poke his chest. "Damnit, Carmichael. I can't even be annoyed about you keeping the bracelet. It makes me love you more."

"Good because I'm so in love with you."

My hand splays out on his chest before fisting the fabric, pulling him into me. It's not elegant. It's messy, teeth crashing, but I wouldn't want it any other way. I work my hands through his rain-soaked hair as he lays me down. He kisses me harder, definitely tasting the candy I had earlier.

Years knowing each other. Months of kissing each other, and we're still discovering new things about each other. Touches we like, little noises we make, food combinations I strongly oppose.

I don't ever want to stop getting to know Cooper. I don't ever want to stop falling in love with him. Year after year, one chapter of our life after another. Messy and mistake filled but isn't that part of life? Part of every relationship?

We'll learn and grow—individually and together. We'll fight and communicate—better than we have in the past. We'll be us and that's more than enough for me.

There's a nip at my bottom lip, and I moan.

Cooper is a kiss thief. Could easily kiss me till our bodies become raisins, but stops when I shiver in his arms. He sits us up before helping me stand.

At the other end of the dock, he stops us. Pushes my wet hair out of my face as he promises me, "It's okay, I'll always chase after you. I don't know what Izzy said to you, but it's not true. I only ever want to and will choose you. There's only ever been me about you."

I can't wait to tease him about how down bad he is later because some things between us will never change.

"I love you, Cooper."

"I love you, too." He singularly laughs, then adds, "So much that I'm stupid enough to potentially give myself hypothermia or ammonia."

"You mean pneumonia. Silent p."

He rolls his eyes at me as he slyly maneuvers my bracelet onto my wrist. Cooper intertwines our fingers, leading me back down the secret path. "Can you pencil me in for five years from now?"

"Five years?" I ask, a confused gaze bouncing from him to the bracelet.

"That's your cycle. Took you five years to love me, so I wanted to give you five years to change your mind again."

"Hey now! How do I know you won't change your mind?"

"Baby, it never has."

FIFTY-THREE

COOPER

"THE MUSTACHES ARE MAGIC." Jaxon runs his thumb and pointer finger over his sandy mustache. His facial hair grew in lighter than his honey brown hair.

Maybe so. We did win the Frozen Four.

Plus, someone gave me back my lucky bracelet. The night before the Frozen Four tournament, Sutton snuck into my hotel room. Jaxon made sure to make himself sparse as soon as she knocked on the door.

She wanted to show me another Meave original. Our old jerseys stitched together. Finally, I got to undress her with my teeth like I've wanted to do. Sutton slipped her bracelet on my wrist while I was going down on her.

I tried to give it back to her after, but she told me, "Keep it. Can't let my superstar boyfriend suck at hockey before the Frozen Four."

Now I have to debate if I'm going to keep the mustache. Agreeing with Jaxon right now will only lead to him keeping it forever, and begging me to do the same.

Jaxon refused to let any of us shave them before today. An added week for the women's Frozen Four—with the changes in conference play, the women are playing a week after us this year. Otherwise, these mustaches would have been gone.

I'm ready to shave this off. My upper lip is dying to see the sun and feel the breeze, even though Sutton has admitted to it giving cowboy chic. Halloween, I promised her.

Coach made the team come to support the girls at the championship game.

My roommates were already planning to come; and there's no way I was missing this for Jordan. They drove up this morning with Elliot. Sutton and I have already been here all weekend with my parents.

The women beat Cornell three to two in the National Semifinals and are about to start the third period of the National Championship against Boston University. They're tied one to one.

They're taking the ice, and when Jordan skates out behind her roommate, Xanie, we all pound on the glass. Jaxon stands up, wearing her jersey, holding a giant picture of her face with a mustache taped over it.

Jordan skates by and shakes her head at him.

I do too, but at least I'm wearing a larger-than-life smile on my face—at least that's what I'm assuming it looks like.

The first two periods were fast and physical, but they don't compare to the third. Doesn't help that the officials are either missing calls or calling the stupidest stuff.

Our game wasn't even this brutal. I thought I wouldn't want Jordan to play with us, but I think I'd rather not play with the girls.

"If you wanted to watch the game, you could have done it at home!" Elliot yells, throwing a handful of popcorn at the plexiglass after one of our players was definitely being held by their jersey.

"Nice costumes but Halloween isn't till October!" Dawson surprises all of us by shouting after Boston scores on a missed call.

"Your ex-wife has better calls than you," Jaxon shouts.

The next play, Jordan gets called for tripping and sent to the penalty box with a minor when the Boston player clearly tripped over herself.

As soon as she's out of the box, she's roughed up. Despite her show of strength, she's double-teamed and laid out on the ice. I jump to my feet, Sutton grabbing my hand. A mirror to Mom and Dad behind us.

Jordan gets up, and skates to the bench. She gives me a thumbs up to let me know she's okay.

Her roommate, Xanie, scores an equalizer a minute later.

No more goals are scored during regulation.

They end up winning in a shoot out.

My Carmichael smile is back, and there's no denying it. The way my cheeks pinch, the corners of my mouth starting to strain from how they are ticked up.

It's the same joy I felt after my first time skating, first game, first goal.

The same way my heart beats when I look at Sutton.

She's squeezing Elliot into a hug, jumping up and down as the women's team throw their arms around each other.

"Let's fucking goooooooooo." Jaxon is pumping the big cardboard head of my sister in the air.

Dawson and Chase have their shirts off, whipping them around in the air above them. Beck has his little sister on his shoulders. Mads is waving her blue, green, and silver pom-poms.

"See! Hot and lucky? We should have grown them sooner. I'm not shaving this, going to get a head start for next season," Jaxon shouts at us. There it is.

I loop an arm around him and tug my best friend into me.

"Manifesting baby. Back-to-back Frozen Four," he keeps talking.

"I like the sound of that." Chase keeps spinning his shirt. "Party at our place tonight? I'll text the team."

"Dibs on aux!" Elliot beats Jaxon to it. "I have a new playlist."

We stick around and watch the girls accept the trophy, then file out to the lobby and wait around for them.

My parents are standing against a pillar with my other sister, Molly.

I walk over to them with Jaxon hot on my heels. "Hopefully the sun will help my tips stay fresh this summer. Do you think if I try lemon juice when we're at the lake house it'll work?" he asks.

"Dude, you're asking the wrong person. Ask Molly."

He does. She laughs, and before she can answer, Jordan shows up.

"You're coming to the lake house with us?"

"What little Carmichael, scared of having fun?"

Mom steps around him, hugging Jordan. "Congratulations, honey."

Dad ruffles her blue hair as a reporter I recognize from the ESPN special rushes to us.

"Ryn, any comments on your kids? How do you feel about the legacy and impact you've made on them with your career? What have you done to get them here this championship season?"

"I'm proud of Cooper and Jordan"—he turns over his shoulder to Molly and mouths *you too*—"but their success has nothing to do with my career. Now, if you'll excuse us, she has a bus to catch."

Jordan sticks her tongue out at the guy, and I shrug, wearing the Carmichael smile proudly.

FIFTY-FOUR

COOPER

THREE WEEKS LATER

"SUTTON! SLOW DOWN," I yell between sharp inhales at Sutton.

She spins, her curls pulled into a ponytail, whipping her in the face, and runs backward. "Aren't you the captain of the Frozen Four champions? Shouldn't you be faster?" Her hands come out to her sides, palms up, and she shrugs.

I roll my eyes at her and speed up, pushing my sluggish legs to their breaking point to catch up with her. It helps that she slowed down. I may be taking our break a little too seriously. I've been to the gym, but have been giving my body a break. Focusing on finals, my friends, and Sutton.

Our semester ended last week. We both are staying on campus this summer, as of right now at least. Sutton hasn't heard back yet about her interview with Team USA. She keeps trying to tell me she's okay, but I still find her refreshing her email in the middle of the night or checking to make sure her ringer is on.

A step behind her now, I snatch her up in my arms.

"Cooper!" She squeal-laughs.

"Don't test me, woman."

"But it's one of my favorite hobbies." I set her down, and we start running again, side by side. "Want to go to the dock?"

It's another mile before we get to the dock. We were sitting, looking out over the water, trading secrets and talking about nonsense, when I couldn't get over how beautiful she looked. The sun came out from behind a cloud and painted her in this golden glow, and my hands were on her.

Fingers pulling at her scrunchie to release her wild curls. Mouth kissing up and down her neck, lingering and marking her collarbone—which I won't be apologizing for.

Finding our feet, Sutton pulls off her tank top, leaving her in a sports bra that's the prettiest shade of purple and complements her freckles, pushing her breasts together and up.

"Fuck, Sutton." It comes out a growl as she reaches for my shorts. "Here?"

She nods. "No one comes out here except for Ch—"

"Let another man's name come out of your mouth right now and see what happens."

"Ohhh. He's jealous," she teases.

"Jealous? That doesn't even skim the surface of what I've been. I watched my best friends interact and have a relationship with you. Then I volunteered to help you fall in love when I was pathetically in love with you, Sutton. You're mine, and my name is the only one I want you saying forever."

"If you'd let me finish, I was going to say Cooper."

"You weren't."

"It does feel better on the tongue."

"You know what else will?"

We both go in for the kiss at the same time, our noses bumping. I roam her body, her hands roam only one part of me.

Her cell phone buzzes, and we both pause. It's my least—and probably only one I'll allow—favorite ice bucket that freezes whatever we are doing.

Sutton removes her hands from my shorts and pats the drawstring. "I'll make up for it later." She hikes one shoulder up, biting her lip apologetically.

"Check it." I nod toward her running belt.

Time passes slowly, or maybe she's just scared, as Sutton unzips the black pouch clipped around her waist.

Tomorrow is the deadline her professor's friend, who works for Team USA, said that they'd follow up with her. Either way, acceptance or rejection, she'd be hearing from them.

"It's from them." Sutton flips her phone around so that I can see the notification.

Sutton, thank you for taking the time and
dedication...

I start to read the preview when she shoves the phone into my chest. "You read it. I can't do it."

"You need to let go if you want me to read it." She's gripping her phone to the point that her knuckles are white. I help peel her fingers off the device. "Good, Sutton baby."

She takes a step backward. Then turns around.

"What are you doing?" I laugh out.

"Can't look at you. Can't watch. Just push me in the water and leave me to my misery after you read that I didn't get it."

I tap in her code: 0131

The day we met.

It's been set to this since she got her first cell phone. And she tries to say she hated me for five years. Yeah, if hate were a synonym for love.

The email opens, and it takes everything in me not to tackle her into the water with excitement. I can't have her believing she didn't get it, because she did.

Welcome to Team USA.

"Oh my gosh. They are giving reasons why I didn't get it. Dang it, Cooper, I knew we should have added in—"

"You got it," I cut her off. "Sutton, you got it. You are part of Team USA."

Tears well in her eyes, and she quickly swipes at them.

Sutton shakes her head. "No," she whispers.

"Yes," I whisper back. "You did it. You made it to Team USA."

"It's an internship."

"Stop. It doesn't matter. I'm so proud of you, baby."

She scrunches her nose again. Eyes closing as she laughs fully and lets out an excited scream.

I throw my arms around her, swinging her into a hug.

"Do you want to read the full email?"

"Not yet. I want to enjoy the moment a little bit longer."

The sun reflecting off Lake Bensen catches my eye. I run us off the dock, jumping into the lake. It's cold as we plunge under the surface. The water won't become much warmer than it is now. Come late July, it'll still be refreshing with a side of pin pricks when you first get in.

I relinquish my hold on Sutton while we are underwater. We kick our feet and swim to the top, cresting the surface at the same time.

She flicks her hand, sending a miniature wave at me. I tuck my head into my shoulder to avoid the splash, but she strikes again.

My fingers skim the waistband of her biker shorts. I tug on it, bringing her flush with me. Sutton wraps her legs around my waist.

"You're incredible, you know that?"

"Yeah, I know," she says confidently. "I love you," she says to me, raking a hand through my wet hair.

"I love you more."

"Can *that* not be a competition between us?"

"I love you the same. Is that better?"

Sutton nods. "I love you the same," she repeats, then kisses me. "Just to make this clear, everything else is still a competition."

"Is that so?" I pull back to look at her.

Her legs unknot from behind my back, and her hazels twinkle with mischievousness.

"Yeah. Race you to the dock." Sutton pushes me under and takes off swimming.

CHAPTER FIFTY-FOUR

Soaked, we lie out on the dock. There's nowhere for us to be except right here. The sun is slowly drying us out. Her auburn curls will take hours, though.

Sutton put on one of Elliot's playlists. Her phone is somewhere above our heads, as our feet dangle off the edge of the dock. The music is soft, blending with the sound of birds chirping and water sloshing up against the muddy beach next to us. A few students are out on the water kayaking and paddleboarding, but they never get close enough to spot us.

"Do you remember when we were nine and sitting in your tree house?" Sutton asks me, staring up at the drifting clouds.

"Of course." There's nothing I've forgotten about her or us. Most warm days were spent in that tree house with her and my sisters, but I know specifically what day she is asking about.

Dad had built an addition that wasn't covered. Someone at school raved about being able to see the Northern Lights over the weekend. Sutton and I stayed up, dragging pillows and blankets up the ladder into the tree house, sneaking cookies that were supposed to be for Molly's theater bake sale. There were zero colors in the sky that night, but there were plenty of stars. Constellation after constellation.

"We made a pact that we'd reach our dreams together."

"And would you look at that, our dreams are coming true." I turn my head to look at Sutton. She's staring at me with tenderness and appreciation and something I can't quite put my finger on.

"Yeah. I guess dreams do come true."

I push a strand of hair behind her ear. Part of the curl gets stuck in the back of her earring, and I have to finagle it loose. It's not smooth or cute, but Sutton's smile grows, and a tiny giggle slips out.

There are unspoken words that pass between us. I lean forward and press my lips gently against hers.

"You're my greatest dream, too." I've never had a dream or life goal that she hasn't been a part of. College, hockey, and my future family. The years before her are fuzzy, fundamental childhood memories I should probably remember, but I don't. I was blind before Sutton. She was and still is the clarity, the start of me. "Before hockey, before all of it, it was you. It's always been me about you, Sutton."

EPILOGUE
SUTTON

THE PLASTIC TEST in my hand is cold but electric. The potential it holds pulses, my heart thumping in rhythm. My wrist twitches, shaking like I'm in one of Elliot's cycling classes. I close my eyes and take a deep breath, trying not to watch the timer on my phone count down.

Twenty...Nineteen...Eighteen...

The numbers trickle down slowly. I swear, as they decrease, the time between them increases, or maybe that's my anticipation.

What is Cooper going to think? This was not part of our plan—well, it was always a dream, but not for another three to five years.

What about school? I have one year left of my PhD program, and a full-time contract with Team USA. Our wedding is in two months...

What about my dress?

A year ago, Cooper proposed. Twenty-five, and the summer after he won his first Stanley Cup. We were in our apartment. I came out of our bedroom in my favorite shirt of his. Ironically, the one I'm in right now. My hair was thrown into a lopsided bun balanced delicately on the crown of my head.

He was in the kitchen pulling out plates for the pizzas we ordered for dinner. His hands had a slight tremor to them.

"Are you okay?" I asked him, trekking through my memory to make sure he took his anxiety medicine this morning.

He clocked his hands. "Sore from my workout. My biceps are destroyed." Cooper smiled. He's just as handsome as he was in college, maybe even more. Aging like fine wine, I remember being excited for the days when he goes salt and pepper. "Top one is yours if you want to dig in. Want a Diet Coke?"

"Yes, please." I slid into the chair at our waterfall counter. I had to stretch to reach the corner of the pizza boxes.

Cooper spun around, setting a fountain Diet Coke in front of me before pushing the boxes into reach. He stood on the opposite side of the counter, staring at me.

"What?" My eyes flicked around the room, then up as if I could see my hair. "Is it my hair? I blame *you*."

"You're beautiful," he responded, the smile on his face unwavering.

I bite the side of my lip. Any compliment or praise has me gushing. My insides become playdough instantly.

Opening the lid, my mouth fell open, and I fell silent. On the cheese pizza, spelled out in M&Ms, was *Will you marry me?*

Cooper stole the idea from my favorite movie, *The Princess Diaries*, but I didn't care. I loved every second of it and felt seen. The chocolate candies transporting me back to our fake date, which he finally told me that following Fall, he considered a real date.

My gaze kept moving from the pizza to Cooper. He moved quickly around the counter. Next to me, he spun my chair to face him and helped me stand up. Holding my hands, he got down on one knee and proposed.

Cooper stood and pulled a ring box out of his pocket. He

must have slipped it in there while I was in the bathroom. He opened it, and again my jaw was on the ground.

My dream ring was there, reflecting the light from the pendants above the island.

Three...Two...One...

My timer goes off, dragging me out of one of my most beloved memories.

I open my eyes.

Two pink lines.

I'm pregnant. We're pregnant.

This is not how I expected to start my bachelorette party.

Debatable.

My period is two weeks late, and for the past week, I have thrown up every morning. I thought it was our takeout from over the weekend—I told Cooper the chicken tasted funky.

There's a knock on the door.

"Sutton, you in here?" It's Elliot. "You okay?"

"Yeah." My voice cracks like a middle schooler hitting puberty.

Elliot tries the doorknob. "Wanna unlock the door?"

I unlock and open it for her before tugging her into the space and relocking the door. She stumbles. Balancing herself, Elliot spins to face me. If there's anyone who'll know what to do right now, it's her. I found her in a bathroom crying over a pregnancy test spring of our senior year.

Her gaze falls to the plastic test in my hand, then up to my face. A hand covers her mouth. "Oh, Sutton. You're pregnant." Elliot drops her hand, throwing her arms around me in a hug. "These are happy tears, right?"

I don't answer, too stunned to speak.

Are these happy tears?

I think so. Cooper and I are having a baby. I'm ecstatic to be a mom and see him become a dad. But that was years down the road...

Or are these sad tears?

Impossible.

My brain fights with itself.

"Both." Elliot reads my mind.

I nod.

"How did Coop take it?" My eyes flare. "He doesn't know?"

I shake my head no. "I picked up a test on the way here from the airport. I had a suspicion."

"Do you have another?"

"This is the fourth one I've taken." It's then she spots the other tests on the bathroom counter.

"He's going to be thrilled," she reassures me. "Do you remember how he was when he found out about Juniper? Do you remember how he took care of me? That man will be over the moon and then put you in Bubble Wrap."

That gets a quiet laugh out of me.

Worries wash away.

"I hope it's a boy," I admit quietly. "I hope it's a boy and has Coop's eyes. Maybe not his size...I don't want to push out an NHL player's baby."

Elliot gives me a knowing smirk.

She helps clean up my running makeup from the happy tears —that's what we determined them to be after Elliot talked me off the ledge of our wedding being ruined.

We exit the bathroom, joining the rest of my bachelorette party. We're at the beach, and our relaxing bachelorette weekend has just become even more special.

Jordan walked over to me with a mimosa in her hand. Elliot quickly sweeps it from her, tossing it back in one drink. "Thanks, I was parched."

"You're welcome?" Jordan eyes Elliot.

I don't want to tell everyone here, especially before even telling Cooper, but having another person who knows and can help make sure no one funnels me drinks or doesn't question if I get sick, would be nice.

Elliot slips her arm out of mine, and I pull Jordan into the room where we are staying.

"I'm pregnant," I tell her as soon as the door closes. "You can't tell your brother. I just found out."

She squeals, hugging me tightly. "Sorry." Jordan drops her arms. "I shouldn't squeeze the baby too tightly." Her long brown hair, streaked with blue, hangs over one shoulder. "Oh my god, I'm going to be an aunt. When are you going to tell Cooper?"

"When we get back, I suppose."

"Do you want to go back now?" She spins on her heels and heads to the closet where our suitcases are.

"No. We're staying. It'll give me the weekend to wrap my mind around this."

"Okay...if you change your mind, I'll book you on the first flight out of here!"

———

MID-MONDAY, I get back to our apartment. I'm exhausted. I leave my suitcase in the entryway, fully anticipating Cooper to take care of it when he returns from his workout.

When my head hits my pillow, I'm out cold.

Two hours later, the bed dips, and I roll over. Instantly, I can smell the minty gum he's always chewed.

"Hi, Dave."

"Hi, Superstar."

"My beautiful girl, sleepy still?" Sleepy is one way to describe this all-consuming exhaustion. I nod against the pillow, eyes fluttering open to find his nose brushing against mine. "I missed you this weekend."

"I missed you, too."

I scoot my head forward to kiss him. We've shared countless kisses, and I know we have an infinity to go, but I swear each one is enchanted. With each one, I fall even more in love with him.

"You sleep. I'll make dinner, and then I want you to tell me about your weekend."

We didn't speak much over the weekend. Honestly, we aren't big texters. Communicators, yes, but if you go through our messages, there are probably days without a message to each other—especially since he's in the off-season. Cooper and I call each other if we need to talk.

This weekend, I sent him a few photos—a couple of beach bikini selfies, a few nudes at his request. That was the extent of our messages. If Jordan and Elliot sent him any, I don't know about them.

"Thank you." I move my mouth against his.

An hour later, I walk into the kitchen. It's decked in the aroma of grilled salmon and veggies.

"Mmmm. Smells good," I fib, gritting my teeth at a wave of nausea.

"You smell good." Cooper buries his nose in the crook of my neck. He places an open-mouth kiss on my sensitive skin before nipping at it. I let out a whimper. His hands are on my waist, guiding me to the counter. They slip under my thighs, picking me up and setting me on the counter near where he's whipping up homemade protein mac and cheese. Cooper is on the add protein to everything kick. We have this dish at least three times a week during the off-season, but I don't care.

I recount my bachelorette trip to him. His sister and Iris, one of our college friends, only danced on two tables, a new record low for them. Elliot forgot to put sunscreen on one part of her thighs and has the weirdest burn. Molly mothered us all. Meave surprised me on day two—she wasn't going to be able to attend because of an art show, but she flew out right after. Jake, Dawson's now husband, came and made the best beach cocktails—at least that's what I was told! My mocktail was great, though.

In the middle of my stories, Cooper plates dinner, and we move to the table to eat. He catches me up on his weekend. Chase was recently traded to his team, and they spent the weekend playing video games and touring apartments.

After dinner—the only thing I was able to touch was the pasta and a minor bite of salmon—we find ourselves back in a position that got us pregnant in the first place. Cooper's naked body crawls over mine on the couch. He hovers over me, his elbows digging into the cushions next to me.

"You have new freckles."

I giggle. "How can you tell?"

He gives me a cocky smirk. "Superpowers." I roll my eyes at him, and his smirk grows. "They're one of my favorite parts of you, so I just know." He plants a kiss on my lips, then another. Cooper starts trailing kisses down my jaw, to my neck, and then chest. Leaning on his right arm, he uses the left to trail a finger down my stomach.

It lingers there.

"Sooooooo."

"So," I parrot.

"When were you going to tell me you're pregnant?"

My mouth falls open. Silently, I'm cursing Jordan and Elliot.

Cooper tugs something out from underneath the couch. It's the toddler-sized jersey I custom ordered. Thirty-six printed on the back with DADDY in place of his last name. I didn't expect expedited shipping to be this fast. Two days? With production, too?

"When did that come in?" A tear that I tried to blink away sneaks out.

"While you were asleep."

"It's for—"

He cuts me off not buying my bullshit. "Are we pregnant?"

"Yes," I whisper, "we are."

"Seriously?" I can't tell if he's excited or upset or—

"I found out at my bachelorette party."

"That means you're"—his eyes find the ceiling as he counts backward—"seven or eight weeks?"

"Aren't you supposed to be good at math? I'm five, maybe six, weeks." I take the jersey from his hands, run the tips of my fingers over the letters and numbers before placing it on the back of the couch. "Are you upset?"

"Upset?" He looks caught off guard by the question. "Why would I be upset?"

"This wasn't part of our plan." Another tear sneaks out and kiss wipes it away with the pad of his thumb.

"Having a family with you, Sutton, was always part of my plan."

"I meant right now. With the wedding and grad school and the season."

"And we'll figure it out." Elliot was right. I'm probably going to be wearing a custom Bubble Wrap outfit by the end of the week with the onslaught of questions he's asking.

"I'm feeling okay. No morning sickness since last week...but the salmon..." I cringe, and Cooper lets out a guilty laugh. He was trying to get me to cave. "We need to schedule a doctor's appointment."

Cooper grabs his phone, leaving a voicemail with my OBGYN, then adding them to his favorites. I ask him to grab my phone and show him the video of me taking the first test.

He swipes quickly at a tear on each of his cheeks. I press on a fresh one falling into my skin, wanting to commit this to memory forever. When two more race down my cheek, he kisses them away. Kisses me before gazing into my eyes with an intensity of love I didn't think I'd ever have. I found a version of it in Meave. Another when Mom and Dad adopted me. Again with our friends at Lakeland.

But the love I see in his brown eyes...it's all could ever dream for or need.

"I love you, Dave, and I'm going to love this baby." Cooper kisses me again, then kisses my stomach. Mouth moves against my skin as he tells our baby he loves them.

"I love you both with my whole heart."
Our intertwined hands rub my stomach, and in this moment,
I know my whole world is going to be me about them.

ACKNOWLEDGMENTS

Thank YOU for reading Me About You! I'm forever grateful to every reader who decides to pick up or download my books. You are the backbone of this community. Each review, post, or recommendation makes a difference.

To the baseball player who did get the girl, Casey—thanks for watching countless hockey games with me and let me pick your brain about Midwestern colleges. Most of all, thank you for your endless support, love, and dreaming together.

Thank you to my beta readers for your impactful comments on the earlier versions of Cooper and Sutton. And to Hannah, my editor, I can't express enough gratitude for what you did for this story and me as an author. Thank you!

Jay, you brought these characters to life so beautifully and snippets of their story in polaroid photos. Thank you for taking my brain dump and making magic with the cover art.

Thank you to Brenna, who did the typography for the cover and gave me the spine of my dreams.

I remember the summer going into my senior year of college and realizing that the dream I had for myself, the one conjured up as a child, was no longer what I wanted. Years of hyping myself up, going as some version of a doctor for Halloween (hello third-grade me, when I thought putting powdered sugar from those bagged donuts on my face to be a zombie doctor for our class party was smart), raising money to go on volunteer medical trips, and countless hours studying and memorizing medical terms all down the drain.

What was worse was trying to figure out what's next. Or being asked, "So what are you going to do now?" Truthfully, I had no freaking clue, and there are still days now that I ask myself that question. However, I'm grateful for the plans and dreams that have evolved over the years. Thank you for shaking me up and pushing me outside my comfort zone.

Anyway, all these words to say that I'm happy where I'm at. Writing and daydreaming about fictional characters.

I hope that if you get anything out of this story, it's that your dreams are worth chasing. Big or small. What you thought they were planned to be or ones that changed. Go after them. I believe in you, and so does Cooper Carmichael.

Thank you again for reading Me About You and I'll see you next semester for book 2!

ALSO BY HANNAH HAMRICK

Close To You Series

Summertime Friends

We Can't Be Friends

The Lakeland Bears Series

Me About You

ABOUT THE AUTHOR

Hannah Hamrick is a self-published romance author. When not spending time writing about book boyfriends, she's reading and obsessing over another one usually with a Diet Coke or coffee in hand and her dogs cuddled next to her.